BRAC
12/2021

D1590602

Windfall

SHAWNA BARNETT

This is a work of fiction. Names, characters, places, and incidents either are the product of the author's imagination or are used fictitiously. Any resemblance to actual persons, living or dead, events, or locales is entirely coincidental.

WINDFALL. Copyright 2021 © Shawna Barnett. All rights reserved. No part of this book may be used or reproduced in any manner whatsoever without written permission except in the case of brief quotations embodied in critical articles and reviews. For more information visit www.hansenhousebooks.com.

Cover design by Elizabeth Jeannel

ISBN 978-1-7353239-4-7 (hardcover)

ISBN 978-1-7353239-3-0 (paperback)

ISBN 978-1-7353239-2-3 (eBook)

First Edition

First Edition: August 2021

This eBook edition first published in 2021

Published by Hansen House

www.hansenhousebooks.com

Hansen House

This book is dedicated in loving memory to Gloria, matriarch among a group of women who taught me that true strength is in family, love and faith.

1944-2020

Acknowledgements

My deepest gratitude goes to so many people who helped to make this ship sail. In addition to the beta readers, teachers, friends, colleagues and mentors who otherwise helped me with this journey, I'd like to thank:

My mom Shelly, who sparked my love of literature. Thank you for reading to me, thank you for reading with me. You gave me a lifelong gift and I will always be grateful.

My dad Blaine, who I am very much like in more ways than I can count. Thank you for aggressively supporting me when I needed it most.

My sister Marisa, for being with me in the thick of things, always and without hesitation, no matter where we are in life. I know you always have my back.

My Tia Teri, for being my first person in the world to finish reading Windfall, in its earliest form. For making me realize that there was a great story there. And for letting me talk through plot points before they were written. You gave me confidence to speak my dream aloud.

My grandpa Sammie, for sharing his passion for politics and leadership with me. You taught me how to look at the world in a critical, thoughtful way.

The BLBG Writer's Group. Thank you for being there at the conception of this book and bolstering my confidence through to its publication.

I'd also specifically like to thank the Hansen House Team.

Ellie, for taking a chance on me and my pirate-princess book. For making it the best that it could be. Thank you for cherishing my dream.

Cate, for being at my side during this publishing journey. I'm so glad that fate allowed us to walk this road together. More than that, I'm excited to see where it takes us.

Kae, for strengthening the voice of this story with your enthusiasm and small tweaks.

Brandon, thank you for your undying patience and support for so many years.

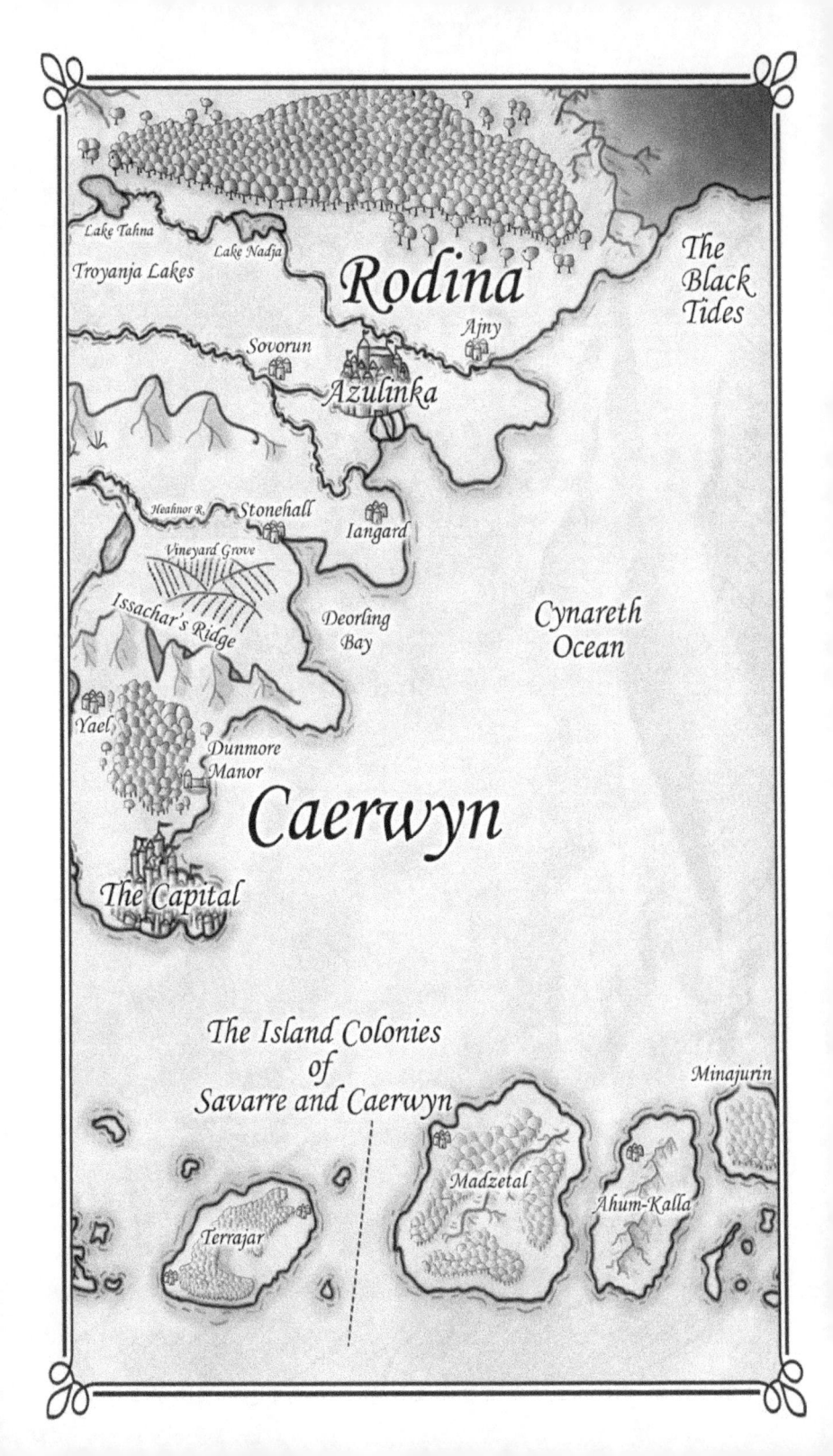

PART ONE

The most Favored of Kings please not themselves, but
their People.

A worthy King is not served. He lives to serve and is
hospitable, for the Kingdom is his Home.

He feeds his People. He offers the Poor and the
Crippled from the same plate as his own Family. He gives Love
to his Friends and Mercy to his Enemies.

— Scroll of Evanderus the King,
The Book of the Divine

Chapter 1

To Go on the Account
6th of Lengnath, 1715
The Capital of Caerwyn

A shadow crept around a stone archway, unseen by a passing pair of guards on patrol. The woman who cast it pulled down her hood and peered about. Her thick, unkempt black hair fell over her shoulders. A long cloak covered her curves, but she had flung it back to rest a hand on her hip, revealing a sword in its sheath. Her fingers, ruddy and coarse with use, pinched her bottom lip. She strained her ears to hear over the soft slaps of water in the harbor, the creaking of the ships' hulls as they swayed, and the occasional caw of laughter from the nearby row of pubs.

Just as she began to wring her hands under the cloak, another duo approached. They weren't dressed in soldiers' uniforms, but sailors' garb. She took a step forward and allowed her silhouette to be revealed. "There you are. What took you so long?"

"I'm sorry, Captain," her quartermaster, Ameen Almasi, said, stopping at her side and turning on his heel to face his companion. "Our young friend was... distracted."

The youth in question tucked his chin and smiled guiltily at his captain.

"Damn it, Squiddy," she scolded. "Learn to keep up."

Her expression softened to amusement as he scowled. His real name was Sava, but she'd settled on calling him "Squiddy." Not much would be able to change her mind.

Ameen chuckled, deep and quiet. Sava looked much like a young Ameen—slight, lanky, and youthfully energetic. Ameen towered over him. He held his posture, straight and sure, lean with muscle gained by nautical labor. The boy still had some way to go before he would be able to carry himself so confidently. Tonight, he would have a chance to prove himself. She beckoned them to follow her.

The Capital of Caerwyn rose before them in layers, on a crest overlooking the sea. The docks formed its base, spanning out south, east, and west like the fingers of an outstretched hand. The rest of the city stacked upon the palm; rows upon rows of buildings, each one smaller than the width of the one below it. The Royal Palace stood at the zenith of this view, like a crooked mountain range, sporting banners of blue and silver. The ocean-side of the palace stretched out like the hand's thumb, wide and thick.

"Liana," Ameen breathed her name rather than her title. His voice plucked her from the high towers of the palace and steadily anchored her back to the alley behind the harbormaster's office.

She looked about the alley to make sure they hadn't been noticed creeping about. "This is it?" Sava's voice cracked.

"Yes. Do you remember what you have to do?"

He nodded. Even in the dark, she could see him shake. Placing a firm hold on his arm, she looked into his face. His eyebrow twitched.

Liana breathed in deeply, nodding to invite him to mimic her. "You can do this."

"I'm ready," he said as he twisted a lockpick between his fingers.

The building had suffered some damage since the last storm season and was under renovation, therefore it had an outer shell of scaffolding that looked sturdy enough to climb. Ameen knelt to give Sava a lift, and he was off, scaling the walls as easily as strolling the streets. They watched as he reached the third story, settled himself on a beam, and picked open the window. He scrambled through it and disappeared.

Liana saw Ameen lift his hand to his chest, where a Circle of the Divine hung on a chain under his linen shirt.

"He'll be alright," she assured him.

His eyes grazed over her face, then downward. "You weren't supposed to bring that."

She followed his line of sight to the cutlass at her side. "It's for protection, if we're caught."

"If we *are* caught, we agreed you would distract them while Sava and I get away. Soldiers won't harm an unarmed Caerwyn woman." He looked straight back at her expectantly with an extended hand, wagging his fingers. After a meaningful silence, she begrudgingly loosened her belt. He was right, after all. It *was* the reason she was wearing her Mass dress.

"Insubordination is what I call *that*, Almasi," she spat. Her tone could cut as deeply as the blade she handed over. But Ameen knew her well enough not to be offended. He grinned, obviously pleased with himself. His amber eyes lit up as he caught her looking for a moment too long. Liana began to pace, her shoulder purposefully knocking against his side as a final jab. She didn't need to look back to know he was still smiling.

The lighthearted energy between them evaporated as they heard a whistling call in the distance—a warning. Sava's head emerged from the window. Liana waved for him to come down. In return, he made an exaggerated shrugging gesture and went back in.

"That stupid little—" She rushed to the base of the scaffold and gathered her skirts. "Lift me up, I'm going to get him."

"You're in a dress."

"And whose *brilliant* idea was that?!"

Deep voices and the light of a lantern cut through the darkness. Despite the cool breeze, she began to sweat. She could hear the patrolmen at the front of the building now. They must have taken a shorter route than usual.

An object landed at Liana's feet with a flutter and thud. She snatched up the book and flipped it open. The ledger was unreadable in the pale moonlight, but she knew it was exactly what they had come for. "Blimey, Squiddy! You've done it."

"Who's back there?" came a gruff voice from the front, cutting their victory short. The sound of the ledger's landing had alerted the patrol.

Liana whirled around and shoved the ledger into Ameen's hands. She unfastened her cloak and threw that at him as well. "Wait for him but go as quickly as you can."

He tucked it under his arm with her sword. "Be careful, Captain."

As she lifted her skirts and sprinted off, Sava was already halfway to the ground.

But, by the Divine, this dress!

She hadn't gone to Mass in years and had outgrown the gown. Ameen had insisted on this particular one—the rest she owned were plain, albeit comfortable. She'd been a fool to think she could have climbed after Sava. Between the binding bodice around her torso and carrying the weight of the layers of the skirt, she was out of breath within seconds. Still, it made her distress all the more convincing as she collided into the chest of the soldier before her.

The man grunted in surprise and took a step back to steady himself. She clung to his dark blue long-skirted coat. His jaw unhinged.

"It's a woman!" his friend declared.

"Thank the Divine you're here!" she gasped out. "Th-these men had me cornered and robbed me!"

She gave a doe-eyed shrug, feigning helplessness. The soldier settled his hands on her shoulders. It made her feel uncomfortably small. The other one, a fair young man, threw himself in the direction she had come.

"It's alright, ye're safe now," the soldier who stayed with her said, beginning to stroke her upper back. He had a slight Northern accent, and his features were darker than the other soldier. She arched away.

The fair soldier returned at a slower pace this time. "Whoever attacked you, miss, they've gone now. Likely pirates who've come to port for the season."

"Thank you." She spoke as demurely as her pride would allow. "I'll be on my way, now."

"Shall we escort you home——?"

"No!" She realized too late she had interrupted him. "No... Thank you."

He took in her loose disheveled locks of hair that curled about her face, her dress that was slightly too small for her, her boot heels that scuffed the cobblestones as she began to quietly shuffle away. He gave his Northern companion a glance. Looking over her shoulder, she saw the other soldier's frame blocked her way out.

"What's the hurry, miss?"

She bolted, aiming for the space between the archway and the swarthy soldier's arm. He caught her and dragged her down. As she hit the ground, pain exploded along her cheek and jaw. The Northman pressed her hard against the cold stone.

"Let me go! I've done nothing wrong!"

"Why are you running, then? We can see as clear as day what you're up to back here!"

She turned her head as best as she could, glaring up at him. "Just what crime do you think I'm committing?"

"Kelvin, I believe the lass is trying to get out of the Harlot's Tax."

"You think I'm a bloody prostitute?!"

"No wrong in it, luv, but it *is* a crime."

"We have no room in the cells to imprison a woman, so ye must pay the tax."

"I told you, I was robbed!" she snarled. She supposed it was safer for them to think of her as a troublesome whore than a budding pirate. She was wrong.

"The tax isn't paid with coin, luv."

Liana wriggled and bucked, but to no avail. Her heart beat as hard as a drum in her throat. Even through the panic, she thought perhaps Sava and Ameen hadn't gotten far. She let out a note of a scream before it was killed by a rough, clammy palm. Another hand started to rustle around her skirts. Harsh, moist breath in her ear made her senses prickle.

Quick footsteps approached, and she was freed of the weight that pinned her to the ground. The hand over her mouth disappeared. She twisted about and kicked up hard. Out of pure luck, her foot collided with the Northman's groin. He had been too busy gaping like a hooked fish at his deposed friend to protect himself.

Ameen stood with his shoulders square over the now lifeless corpse. He gripped a bloody sword, baring his teeth to the surviving soldier. Her limbs wobbled; she felt like a foolish damsel as she struggled to stand. He rushed to her. She leaned back against him, and his arms circled her waist to keep her on her feet.

"Gallagher? Kelvin? Is that you?" Another soldier with short, honey-colored hair that reflected his lantern's radiance rounded the corner. He lifted a pistol, pressed the hammer down, and aimed it for Ameen. "Unhand the lady!"

"Whyte! He killed Kelvin! Shoot him!" the dark soldier, apparently Gallagher, ordered as he writhed on the ground, still holding his groin.

Liana began to shout, but it was too late. The gun fired. Reflexively, she ducked at the blast. Ameen folded in half and fell, taking her down with him. Another two shots fired from the other end of the alley. She looked up to see five men racing toward them, and she knew them all. Sava led them, shouting and pointing. Their shots had missed, but they rushed the two soldiers.

She turned over to Ameen, who lay curled on his side, facing her with a pained grimace. He breathed in shallow gulps of air with his eyes shut tightly. His dark complexion shone with sweat in the moonlight. The ball had buried itself in his left shoulder.

"Are ya alright, lass?" A weathered face, tense with worry, crossed into her sights. *Marin.* She thanked the Divine he was here. He would know what to do.

She croaked wordlessly. Her throat was as dry as a bag of flour, and her heart had made its way back up to her jugular. Tears began to fill her eyes, and she tried again. "He's..."

"We'll tend to him," Marin promised. "He'll make it. I give ye my word. But we must go. Others will have heard the shots."

A pair of matching hands moved over Ameen. Twin orphans, Jamil and Kahil, gently got him to his feet. Ameen's head bowed in pain as he let out a groan that made Liana clutch her chest.

"What'll we do with these filthy codpieces?" Lucky, an experienced seaman with an array of nautical tattoos covering his arms and chest to prove it, stood behind Gallagher. Both soldiers knelt before her now. The man who had moments ago attacked her now sniveled at her feet.

The honey-haired man surrendered gallantly. His hands poised up, and he looked directly at her face. Sava stood behind him and looked at her expectantly, albeit nervously. He held the pistol out to her. She took it, feeling the grit of the powder on the handle. It was still warm.

"We haven't much time," Marin reminded her.

Liana blinked until her eyes were bone dry and hardened her features.

"You," she said, looking down her nose at Gallagher. "How many others?"

Gallagher sealed his lips tight. He hissed when Lucky dug his fingers into his shoulder sharply. "Answer the captain."

"How many other women?"

Whyte turned to Gallagher in confusion. Gallagher bowed forward, refusing to answer. Liana grimly nodded to Lucky. He took the cue and fisted the tail of Gallagher's hair, pulling his head back to give himself an easier target. Out of the corner of her eye, she saw Marin blanch and look away. Lucky cut the soldier deep enough that the blood pooled under the wound. After one gargling breath, the soldier went limp. Lucky dropped him, giving Liana a look of high esteem.

"And this one?" He nodded over at the last soldier. She bent and looked into Whyte's sickly pale face. He bravely stared back into her eyes, accepting whatever justice she felt right to deliver. She turned the pistol, swung it back, and cracked him across the skull. His eyes rolled back, and he crumpled.

"I'm the bloody captain, here," Liana said, clenching her fist with the utmost authority. "And I will *not* be leaving this deck!"

Kahil raised his hands up in surrender. "Aye, Captain. Not another word."

The truth was she wanted nothing more than to curl up in a hammock below, but knew she wouldn't be able to rest. After being nearly raped, witnessing her dearest friend being shot, and narrowly escaping the Capital, Liana felt like she could vomit on the spot. But that they were on the ship, and her duties as captain had barely begun.

"I'm sorry, Captain Foley," said Jamil meekly. "We meant no disrespect."

"Too right," she muttered. As they left, she leaned over the bow, looking ahead at the open water, dark and mysterious in the early morning hours. She had gotten out of the dress and changed into a pair of trousers. Turning away from the sea, she donned her tricorn and surveyed the ship.

My ship. Unable to let it go unnamed before the first voyage, Marin had pressed her for a title for the vessel. She had chosen *Windfall*—a strike of fortune. But thinking of Ameen's injury, she felt anything but fortunate. If she was going to go through with this, she would need an iron stomach, a more lenient conscience, and definitely a hired surgeon.

Liana straightened up, adjusted her hat, and crossed the deck.

"Well, my girl, ya made a believer out of me!" a cheerfully paternal voice said. Marin beamed at her, despite the bloodstains on his shirt and the sweat on his brow. "Ye've done it!"

"We've done nothing yet, Marin." She sighed. "We've barely begun, and we almost lost everything. We almost lost Ameen."

"Och, the boy is sturdy enough." He shrugged. "We were never close tah losin' him."

"He'll be alright, you think?"

"I always keep my word. Ye know that."

"I do." She smiled and handed Marin the ledger. She trusted no one more. Ameen was perhaps a close second.

He tilted his head to the side, his sandy brown and gray hair falling into his eyes. "I must say I think it honorable that ya didna kill the last soldier."

"I wanted him to remember who we are and what we're capable of. Besides, I felt as though I owed him," she told him. "As stupid as he was, he thought he was rescuing me."

He seemed satisfied with that. "Oh, and one more thing," he added, as he turned to leave. "He's asking for ya."

She balked. "He's still conscious?"

Marin nodded, round face rising in a smile. "Won't let himself rest until he sees ye're alright."

"The most stubborn sailor I've *ever*..." she growled, shook her head, and stomped away, cursing under her breath.

As she parted ways with Marin, she thought she heard him chuckle.

Her cabin didn't have much more to it than the berth and a long table—both nailed securely to the floorboards. Paned glass held together by heavy timber made up the back bulkhead. Through it, she could see the orange glow of sunrise spreading like marmalade over the horizon behind the ship. She removed her hat once more and set it on the table.

Upon her entrance, Ameen tried to sit up, but cursed at the attempted movement.

"Serves you right," she jibed, dragging a chair from the table to sit at his bedside. As she settled in the seat, she checked the bandages wrapped around his arm and chest. No signs of bleeding, thankfully. "You should be sleeping. Now, what do you want?"

His eyes tight with pain, he adjusted to look at her. The lantern flickered, making the lines of his face waver. When he spoke, his voice was grated and as quiet as a whisper. "Did they hurt you?"

"No," she told him, softening when she saw his sincere concern. "Thanks to you."

"I'm sorry..." he said, even quieter than before. She thought she might not have heard him right.

"What did you say?"

"It was my fault," he said, a little louder now, but she could tell it took effort. "I put you in danger and left you no way to protect yourself."

"That's what you think?"

"It's what happened," he said, breathless. He jerked when she pressed her palm against his forehead. "What in the name of the Guardians are you doing?"

"Checking for fever," she said cheerfully. "Seems like you were babbling, so I had to see if you were going into a fit."

He removed her hand, allowing himself a ghost of a smile.

"It wasn't your fault," she insisted. "You should be proud. We got the ledger. We know where the ships are and what they'll be carrying. This was your plan, and because of you, we all made it out alive."

"Barely."

"Be grateful," she huffed. "I certainly am. You saved me."

"I know." He still did not sound satisfied. With an idea as to why, she patted his hand.

"You feel guilty," she surmised, "for killing them..."

As she trailed off, he shook his head. "They deserved to die. It was worth it, to keep you safe."

It could've been the pitch and roll of the ship, but she found herself leaning closer. She admired the way his dark lashes framed his warm amber eyes—charcoal around a burning fire. It wasn't the first time she had been taken by such strong feelings. Like moths to the flame, they had always been drawn to each other, fluttering in a careful dance around their attraction. But now, in the wake of nearly losing each other, they closed the gap.

She took him by surprise, but the kiss was certainly not unwanted. Her nose brushed his cheek first, before she felt his lips part under hers. It was gentle and quick, so as not to jostle him in his fragile state. When she moved away, his eyes were still closed.

"Liana, I've…" he started. He opened his eyes, realizing that she was standing up.

"Get some sleep," she said, turning the lantern low before taking up her tricorn once more. The rising sun's bright rays streaked through the thick glass of the bulkhead.

"After that?" He watched her as she stopped at the doorway.

She smiled crookedly and looked back at him, tipping the brim of the tricorn forward in farewell. "Heal up, sailor. Your captain needs you at your best."

Chapter 2

No Prey, No Pay
17th of Baelfest, 1723
Quemala Ocean, North of Silili

Swirling smoke filled the salty air in the aftermath of cannon fire. The crew of the *Windfall* rushed through it with ease, howling like mad dogs. A black flag whipped above their heads on the mizzenmast, rousing fear in the crew of the captured ship as they boarded.

Captain Liana Foley's voice carried over the smoke and shouts, disembodied to those out of her close proximity. It cut through the chaos, resounding deep, throaty, and as dangerous as the call of a siren. She waved her sword arm as her men subdued the merchant crew. The swirls dissipated around her swift movements, fleeing like the shadows of dying wraiths.

It was an easy surrender. If given the choice between their lives and some cargo, most in their right minds would choose the former.

Liana went below deck as she called out, "What do we have?"

Jewels spilled out onto the lower deck. Perfectly cut rubies, sapphires, and emeralds glimmered a reflection in her eyes. A smile quirked her lips as Ameen appeared at her side and let out an appreciative whistle. "That'll do."

"That'll do, indeed," she echoed. After giving some direction, she went above to oversee the rest of the men taking formation around the imprisoned crew. There was no sense in taking them all to the brig. They wouldn't be aboard for long. A young man with springy black curls, the last to emerge from below, stood to attention.

"That'll be all of them, Captain."

"You're sure?"

"We've covered every step of the ship," Sava said. He gave her a confident nod before she dismissed him to step back into line.

She looked about. "Which of you lot is the captain?"

Many of the sailors edged toward a silent silver-haired man to Liana's left. Presuming this coward was indeed in charge, she turned to give her usual spiel—the promise of safety in return for compliance. Before she could get any words in, a grating voice spat at her.

"Bitch!"

Liana kept her demeanor calm, even as some of her men reached for their weapons. The man who had insulted her looked at her with a vile hatred that drew deep lines in his forehead and around his thin mouth. An outburst like this wasn't typical. Sailors on merchant vessels would be paid their salary, no matter what happened to the cargo. She wasn't stealing anything from him directly.

"I will only address my equal," she said, keeping her eyes on the captain. He was begging the man to stop with a sharp shake of his head, but Liana demanded further action. "Captain, you will keep your men in line, or I will—"

"Equal?" the man shouted now, his voice cracking against the strain of his hostility. "Thieving whore! May the Divine take you and your Creatures to Hell!"

Murmurs rumbled from the prisoners. Some were in agreement, while others whispered in fear.

"Another word out of your man, Captain, and he'll be keelhauled," Liana warned, bending to the captain's level. Ameen, in an effort to move things along, directed the cargo across the boards onto the *Windfall*. He exchanged glances with Liana, and she gave him a nod to go on. But he hesitated as a volley of insults were thrown at her—crude and vicious vulgarities even her crew of pirates would never dare to speak in her presence. Sava made a move to pounce on the offender, but Ameen caught his arm and held him back.

"Pritchard!" the captain hissed, finally speaking up. "You fool! You'll get us all killed!"

Liana already had enough. "Samara! Reed!"

Maiz Samara stepped out of formation. He tried to restrain Pritchard, who squirmed away like an eel. Samara already had his hands on him again by the time Everett Reed came hastily to his aid.

A shiv materialized from Pritchard's boot. He swiped at Samara, who managed to tear himself away just in time. Pritchard drew back again before careening forward with all his might at Samara. Reed was too far away to protect him, but Liana wasn't. She sank her cutlass into Pritchard's back and through the other side. He was dead before he hit the deck. For the first time since they had boarded, complete silence fell. It only lasted a moment.

"Th-thank you, Captain," Samara said.

"Take the body below," was her only response. Fury coursed through her as she looked at Reed, who wiped sweat off his brow. "Help him. The rest of you, follow Almasi's orders to move the cargo. I want to weigh anchor as soon as possible."

Everett Reed had the sense to remove his hat when he entered the captain's cabin. Ameen shut the door behind him and leaned against the bulkhead, crossing his arms. Reed swallowed, his gaze settling on the irate captain before him. If looks could kill, he would have been dust in the wind.

"Empty your pockets, Reed." Liana snapped.

He hesitated.

"Now."

He exhaled sharply through his nose and dug into his coat, procuring two fistfuls of rubies. They scattered on her desk, scuttling like shimmering beetles. Behind Reed, Ameen scoffed and shifted against the bulkhead.

With the proof to confirm her suspicions, she removed her tricorn and hung her head, pressing her hands on a clear space on the desk. "Do you have anything to say for yourself?"

"I couldn't help it, Captain," he said, ashamed. "I have a wife, children…"

"Isn't your share enough to feed them, clothe them, keep their comforts?" She lifted up and scowled at him. His silence gave way to a pause. "Your crewmate was nearly gutted because you were stuffing your pockets, you selfish ass!"

Reed shifted his shoulders, his face burning red. "With all due respect, Captain, my share is a fraction of yours. So please forgive me for not having the same restraint as—"

Liana's palm cracked across Reed's face. It was something of a spectacle, seeing a man of such brawn subdued so quickly; though for Reed's sake, she was glad the crew was not there to witness it. She had meant to make a fist, but at the last moment granted him the mercy of a stinging mark over a black eye. He cradled his cheek, eyes bulging and glassy with humiliation. Ameen took a step off the bulkhead, ready in case Reed tried to strike her back. He didn't.

"You may have heard," she said when Reed finally looked up, "That I take three shares."

She held up her index finger and continued. "One, for the upkeep of this ship. Without the *Windfall* you'd still be scraping together enough money to house your family in a single room, like you did in Riven.

"Two," she said, lifting another finger. "For The Black Barricade, where you and your family came when you were starving and without a home.

"And three, for myself. I am personally paid the same as you. But you know not all of our seasons are as good to us as this one. No prey, no pay. I will supplement the *Windfall* and the Barricade when necessary because the people need us, just like you needed us. So, don't you dare accuse me of taking more than I deserve after what you did. After you disobeyed your captain and put your fellow crewmate in danger."

The mortification was clear in the inverted curve of his shoulders and the way the lump in his throat trembled.

"When we make landfall, you will never take a step on the *Windfall* again," she said with finality. "I can't have you put anyone else at risk."

"Captain, please…"

"You have two choices. You can resume your duties with grace until we return to the Capital. Or, if you insist on being defiant, then you can spend the rest of the voyage in the brig."

He rubbed above his beard where she had struck him. "I won't argue."

"Good. I'll give you a moment to pull yourself together." Liana stepped around the desk and gathered the rubies together. Ameen gave her an empty pouch. "Take these, as well. Consider them your severance pay."

Reed took what she offered before backing out of the cabin. Once he was gone, Liana flung her tricorn aside and sniffed, swiping at her eyes.

Ameen took her by the hand. "You did what you had to do."

"I shouldn't have hit him."

"You showed more control than I expected."

"We'll make sure he finds a job," she said, thinking of Reed's wife. "It wouldn't be fair to Adela."

"You've already been more than fair, Captain Foley."

When they stepped outside, the wind tugged her hair off her shoulders. The *Windfall* sailed low, burdened with treasure. Despite the punishment she just delivered, she found the joyful mood of the crew to be infectious.

Marin, exhilarated and breathless, came to her with a skip in his step. He danced his way to the upper deck, sliding a hand along the bannister. "Quite a haul we have, Captain! The best in years!"

Liana allowed a triumphant laugh to bubble past her lips. "Have we lost the vessel yet, Marin?"

"A speck on the horizon, last I looked."

"Good. Keep our heading northeast."

"To the Capital it is, then?"

"Yes." She nodded. "It's time to go home."

Chapter 3

Groundswell
5th of Regnsfall, 1723
The Capital of Caerwyn

As Ameen entered The Black Barricade tavern and sealed out the late autumn night, warmth saturated his bones. The single but spacious dining room glimmered gold in the iron chandelier's light. It contained several wooden tables full of men, a good mixture of Caerwyn, Savarran, Rodinian, and a variety of Islanders, laughing and drinking in merriment together.

"Camila, these go to the far corner table!"

Behind the bar, a beautiful Rodinian woman directed the staff, her quick movements as fluid as the liquid in the pewter cups. The candlelight glowed against her porcelain skin, making her look impossibly flawless to the drunken patrons.

"Bess, luv! Another round when ya get a chance!"

No one noticed Ameen come in through the door, except for Bess. He caught her eye and gave a short wave of greeting. He added an inquisitive air to it by twisting his wrist and shrugging. *Where is she?*

Bess pointed at a figure making their way from a back table.

A few familiar patrons raised their glasses with respect as the captain passed. She responded with a broad smile and light wave of her hand. Ameen followed in her wake. When he finally made it to her, her head was thrown back in loud laughter at something Lucky had said.

"Bess, Bess—you have to hear this one!"

"Look who's back," Bess told Liana as Ameen approached.

A grin immediately spread across Liana's face when she saw him, making him feel significantly lighter.

"The buyers were true to their word," he reported, leaning in.

"Oh, good, we can finish the numbers tonight, then." Liana kept her hand beneath his while she picked up her glass of dark ale.

Bess rolled her eyes. "I'll do them in the morning. You two have earned yourself a break. We'll start preparing for distribution tomorrow. *Relax*, just for one evening."

Liana gave a short and thoughtful "hmm" and took a long drink, eyeing him sidelong to gauge his reaction. He hoped she would agree and tried to convey that in a singular look.

"Go on," Bess told them before being called away by another order. "I've got everything handled here."

They needed no further encouragement. After draining her glass, Liana slipped around the bar, but not before snatching a bottle of wine. He followed her upstairs, taking up a candelabra from one of the empty tables.

Ameen soon found himself in their room, standing by the closed door. All of the essentials were there—a bed, a trunk, a wardrobe, and a writing desk. A scarlet duvet covered the bed with a canopy of matching curtains. Maps, both local and regional, covered the walls. A cluster of them depicted foreign lands, such as Rodina, Savarre, and even the Islands to the south. Loose parchment and notes in Liana's scrawled writing covered the desk. A few books lay here and there about the space, all open to the page she had left off.

The room held some accents of luxury and decorative tokens from their travels, like the rug from Zan Monre or the nightstand and mirror from Caluz. They had been to so many places together, and every single one had felt like home, because he had been with her.

He placed the candelabra on the nightstand as she stepped in front of the mirror. With a resounding *thunk* she set the bottle down. She removed the pin that loosely kept her hair up. Like ink on paper, it spilled over her white linen shirt. She raked through it with her fingers.

"We're taking a long holiday," she declared.

He closed the curtains, hoping it would keep the cold out. "Somewhere warm, I hope."

She pressed her thumbs to the cork and it popped free. After kissing the lips of the bottle and taking a pull, she handed it to him. "Any suggestions?"

"On the continent—so we don't have to sail," he said before sipping the wine. The bittersweet taste of Island berries lingered on his tongue.

"I thought you wanted to go back to Terrajar," she said, picking through the armoire, likely for something comfortable to wear.

"I do," he admitted. He wanted to see what his home island was like since it had been freed of the Savarran empire. "But if we sail, we'd use the *Windfall*. It wouldn't be a holiday."

"Right. No sailing. But that leaves out anywhere warm this time of year."

"Savarre is a desert. It's always warm."

"Except at night."

"Hmm, you're right. Let's just stay here, then. We can just… *be*."

A smile crossed her face. "Sounds nice."

"Doesn't it?"

It didn't take long for Liana to change into a warm nightgown and crawl to her corner of the bed with the bottle. Some time went by as they shared it, spent talking about what they would do with their shares of the jewel profits, the Charity Day coming up next week, and some of the more humorous moments during the last voyage.

"Poor Marin," she snorted. She sat between his outstretched legs, leaning her head back into his shoulder. "He's never going to be able to tell the twins apart, is he?"

"Jamil says he's going to cut his hair so it'll be easier," he said with a lilt of hope. She accepted his offer of the last drink. "He may actually do it."

The empty bottle slipped from her fingers as he took it and reached down to place it on the floor. He pinched out the candles, something Liana always hated to see him do.

"Don't burn yourself," she sleepily chastised, making him smile. As he did, she turned over against his chest. They rested in peaceful silence. Even the sounds of the Barricade below had quieted. Ameen could hear Bess and Camila closing up downstairs.

Feeling an uncomfortable prickling in his arm, he adjusted himself, and Liana rolled away, already asleep. After wriggling the blood back into his fingers, he leaned over her.

Liana Foley was everything his father had warned against—a rough spun, irreligious woman with a sharp tongue and dreams that spanned the map of Vioria and beyond. *Find a good wife dedicated to the Divine to keep your home. You will not regret it.* They often joked with each other about his father's advice to him on women. She knew what she was. He loved her for it.

His hand wandered to hers and she stirred, curling her fingers around his before settling back into well-deserved slumber. He closed his eyes and allowed sleep to take him along with her with his mind made up.

Before even opening her eyes the following morning, Liana knew she wasn't alone. The familiar presence of Ameen's warm body beside hers was not what she felt. No, he had already gone. Someone else was there.

Another quiet shuffle prickled her senses. She kept her breath even. Her arm hung over the side of her bed. She only had to flex her fingers to touch the knife she kept underneath. Her hand curled around the base, and she readied herself. Tightening her grip on the blade, she launched herself to the end of the bed.

Two screams made her freeze before she could stab.

"Bess!" Liana cried and dropped the knife onto the floor. The two children continued to wail as they sped out of the room. She teetered her way to the door. "I told you to keep them out of my room!"

Violently, she slammed the door and struck her elbow against it before turning away to dress herself.

Liana overheard Bess and Ameen's Rodinian lessons as she descended the stairs shortly after.

"Say it once more. You must speak the word with *feeling*."

The innkeeper had already broken her fast with porridge. At her right hand sat the accounting books. Ameen looked to have already eaten something much more filling, for his plate was both large and empty except for a single bread roll.

Ameen had a talent for languages. He had been raised in the Island colonies, like Liana had. But she grew up in Madzetal, an island still under Caerwyn's rule. Terrajar had been on the Savarran side of the imperial divide. His parents had taught him the native language. During his youth, he had worked on a Savarran trade vessel with his father and easily learned the language of the crew. Somewhere along the way to adulthood, he also picked up Caerwyn. Now he sought to add Rodinian to his collection.

The children were there, too. When they saw Liana, they hid behind their mother.

"Did you forget to lock your door last night?" Bess asked.

"No." Liana made a sour face towards Ameen, who suddenly decided the ceiling was very interesting. "Someone forgot to lock it on his way out this morning."

Bess' daughter, Beatrix, peeked around her mother's chair. She was the older sibling, with the same glossy black hair, pointed nose, and pale complexion as her mother. She was eleven and very, very curious. "Mama says only married ladies should sleep in the same room as a man."

Liana turned her pinched face to the girl, who stared back at her unabashedly. Sebastian, Bess' youngest, peered out from behind his mother's skirts. He was three years younger than his sister, as well as three steps behind her every move. Most likely, Beatrix had convinced him to sneak into Liana's room that morning.

"Well, you can tell your Mama," Liana's eyes glided to Bess, who was trying to contain her laughter, "That I don't give a f—"

Bess abruptly slammed her fist down onto the table, nearly knocking over her porridge bowl. "Liana! For the Divine's sake! Must you be so vulgar?"

Liana snorted with laughter, only encouraged by Ameen's clear efforts to keep a straight face.

Bess rubbed the space between her brows as if nursing a headache and shooed the children away. Just then, the front door opened, and Marin walked through. He greeted them by reaching out his enclosed fists. They squealed in delight as he dropped two sweets in each of their palms.

"Good mornin'." Marin strode cheerfully to the table and sat between Liana and Bess. He neatly set his envelopes on the surface of the table and lit his pipe.

Ameen leaned forward. "Marin, we'll need a few of the men to help Bess with the purchases this week."

"How many should I round up?" Marin asked, waving his match to extinguish it.

Bess wrinkled her nose in thought. "Five, maybe six?"

He paused and looked at them all but settled on Liana. "How much do ya plan tah buy?"

She took the Barricade's ledger and slid it over to him. "We're able to help more recipients with larger families now."

"That's wonderful, isn't it?" Bess beamed.

"Not for our pockets." Liana rolled her eyes. Ameen nudged her with his foot for her joke.

Bess suddenly stood with a yelp and dashed around the table. They all turned to see a guilty Sebastian standing on one of the tables.

As Bess scolded him, Liana turned back to the conversation. "Don't worry, Marin, our loot will cover it all."

Marin reviewed their recent income. "Aye, I can see that. But ye must see that we will not be able to sustain it for long."

"Three months," Liana answered the unasked question. "We'll need to set sail again in three months. We can afford to wait through the season, but no more."

"Oh, good," he replied. "That'll give me time tah have a short visit with Nellie."

He leaned back in his chair to look over the day's letters and bills. Despite having just received some mail from his daughter the day before, he hoped for another, especially one that would bring news of a grandchild on the way. Nellie Foley, now Dunmore, had been married to a wealthy man who bred horses for years now. They lived in a manor north of the Capital.

Liana's grumbling stomach distracted her from the thought of her foster sister. Ameen didn't protest when she reached over to his plate and took his remaining bread roll. In fact, Liana thought she saw a hint of an endearing smile.

"Marin, when you have the time, I need to speak with you privately," he said.

"What about?" Liana said after she swallowed.

"*Privately*," he repeated and shifted his attention back to Marin, who hadn't looked up from the mail. "Marin?"

He started. "Huh? Oh, yes, we can speak later."

"Is something wrong?"

The concern in Marin's expression made Liana lean over. He handed her the parchment he had been reading. She skimmed it. Her eyes flicked up to Ameen, before she reread the letter aloud

Madam,

I embrace this first opportunity of writing a few words to you. I have regretted not having the occasion, until now. It is my understanding your work

takes you considerable distances, while mine limits my association with those of your profession. I am in good fortune, for I have finally found a means of contact that will not have dire consequences for either of us. I write so that you would consider giving me the honor of seeing you again, for it has been some time since we last met. It would be prudent to meet alone, with none of your employees present. It is my hope to see you at midnight at the abandoned Temple of the Divine, in the western district of the Capital proper.

My best wishes and hopes of kept secrets.

"Who the hell wrote this?" Liana examined the blank envelope.

"I was hoping ye could answer that," Marin replied, smoke wafting out of his mouth as he spoke.

"It sounds like *someone* admires you," Ameen said lightly, though he leaned over to read the letter one more time to himself.

"It sounds like *someone* is threatening me." Liana chewed her bottom lip. *Kept secrets? They can't possibly mean...*

Marin took a few more puffs, blinking at her as though the answer was obvious. "He wants tah meet alone at the old temple."

"There's nothing there. Just some relics of the old regime."

"It could be yer brother, lass," Marin suggested in a serious tone.

"I doubt it. Ivan is the last person who would ever call me 'madam.' Besides, he hasn't contacted me in almost a decade. Why would he try now?"

"He's always had a flair of the dramatic, that boy. And who else would ask ya tah meet them at the old temple?"

"None of this makes sense. Why would Ivan want to meet her there?" Ameen interrupted, though he didn't look up from the letter. Marin tilted his head at Liana, who gave him the barest of head shakes. Ameen continued, too absorbed in the mystery to notice. "Are you sure the postman gave you this letter, Marin?"

"Come tah think..." Marin waved his pipe. "A man bumped into me in the market. It may have fallen in the pile I picked up."

"Or dropped purposefully."

"Where were you when you dropped the letters?" asked Liana.

"I was about to step into the sweets shop."

"Do you remember what he looked like?"

"Nah, he was gone by the time I looked up."

Liana puffed out a frustrated sigh before she looked over to Bess, who adorned a fashionable straw hat weaved with small pink roses. Her children, having been properly disciplined, awaited her permission to leave.

A thought seemed to strike Ameen as he followed Liana's gaze. "Bess, why don't you and Liana go to the market, and Marin and I will stay with the children?"

All faces, young and old, turned to him in surprise. Sebastian and Beatrix looked jubilant at the idea—anything to get out of errands. Marin shrugged and grinned behind his pipe.

"Are you sure?" Bess asked him.

"Yes." Ameen crouched down, allowing an ecstatic Sebastian to rush him and climb onto his back. "Go on. We'll be fine. While you're gone you can see if there's anything suspicious where Marin dropped those letters. By the sweets shop you said, Marin?"

Liana clicked her tongue with annoyance, unable to find an excuse to argue. Perhaps it was best to let Ameen have this one. It seemed important to him that he spoke with Marin about *something*. As she left the Barricade with Bess, she could have sworn she saw Ameen wear a soft smile of satisfaction.

Chapter 4

Bonny Lass, Old Salt

Liana hadn't realized how late she slept in until she looked up at the sky over the market. The day was cool but bright, which was typical for late autumn in southern Caerwyn. Squinting against the sunlight, she pulled her deep-brown tricorn hat onto her head and continued walking alongside Bess.

What *is* that man up to?" she mumbled, smoothing out the front of her hair from under the hat's brim.

"Oh, I'm sure it's harmless, whatever it is," Bess drawled in her fading Rodinian accent. Every now and again she would richly roll her tongue on a specific word. Her voice had more depth than the average Caerwyn woman.

"Where to first?"

"Butcher Davies. We need to make a large order."

Liana wondered if she needed to remind Bess, they had a budget to keep to.

"It won't be too expensive, I promise," added Bess, as if reading Liana's thoughts.

They weaved through the thickening mass of people, walking at a steady pace to the butcher. Despite Liana's quick and purposeful strides, Bess kept up with her graceful long-legged steps, the wicker basket bouncing off her hip as she walked. In the throng, the women blended easily.

"Blessed Circles and Magicked Baubles!" A middle-aged woman who sold trinkets crossed their path. Her threadbare dress smelled strongly of some spiced herb. "A Wish Box? Grants anything you desire!"

A necklace with a spherical charm swung forward far enough to nearly touch Liana's nose. She jerked back before pressing Bess along. They turned a corner, rounding a familiar street to approach the butcher's shop.

"Ah! Captain Foley! Mistress Yanova! Aren't the two of you as lovely as the morning?"

The butcher's wife, Mistress Davies, swept out of the open door with a frayed broom. Despite the compliment directed at both of them, Liana was sure it was mostly meant for Bess, who was a vision in her pastel blue, white, and pale pink dress. It perfectly matched the blush cloth roses in her straw hat. A few attractive strands of black hair framed her round face. Liana, on the other hand, let her half-tied hair lie limply under her brown tricorn and down her shoulders. She wore a smoke-colored shirt tucked into a leather belt and striped skirt.

"Good morning, Mistress Davies," Bess greeted the elderly woman. "And please, call me Bess. We are far too familiar for such formalities."

Elizaveta was her real name. Elizaveta Seliverstov. She never used it. It was a mouthful, for one.

"Now, what was all that about a letter earlier?" Bess asked after they had placed the orders with the butcher.

"Oh, right." Liana proceeded to fill her in. They stopped in a shady spot between the jeweler and the florist's cart, and Liana untucked the letter from her belt so Bess could read it. "Marin seems to think it could be my brother, but..."

She trailed off, realizing Bess had gone paler than usual, ashen even. The Rodinian clutched the letter in one hand and laid the other on the hollow of her throat. "Bess?"

"It's him," she gasped, eyes glassy with panic. "He's found me, he's—"

"Bess, you need to breathe! Here." Liana took Bess by the hand and guided her to sit at the fountain in the center of the market plaza. When they sat, Liana meant to take her hand away, but Bess held on so tightly her knuckles were white.

Liana stood and moved between Bess and the shoppers in the market to block their curious gazes. Using her free hand, she took the handkerchief from the wicker basket still hanging at the crook of Bess' elbow and blotted her face.

"If your husband wants a go at me, then let him try," she said, trying to find a dry side to the cloth to dab at her tears.

"No!" Bess dropped her voice to an urgent whisper. "You don't *know* him, Liana. He's *dangerous.*"

"More dangerous than cannon fire?" Liana quirked a smile and tilted her head. "Besides, you've got more strength in you than you think! Remember that night Lucky was harassing the new dash-girl?"

They had just hired a young woman to go around the tables and put dashes of ale in the men's glasses when they needed filling. Lucky, a roguishly attractive man in his late-forties, was quite used to receiving female attention. Despite his efforts, the dash-girl wasn't interested.

"I had never seen you so upset!" Liana laughed. "You called him a... What was it again?"

"A lecherous cretin," Bess blushed and started to giggle. "I felt so terrible afterwards, when he brought me that bouquet of flowers as an apology."

"He cares about you, Bess," Liana insisted as she took the letter back from Bess, folded it up, and tucked it away again. "We all do. We'll always protect you and your children, no matter what happens."

Bess nodded and gave her a watery smile. "Thank you."

"Nothing to it. Now come on, we've got orders to make."

If you're not back in an hour, I'm going out there to get you," Ameen said as Liana fastened her cloak. He sat at the desk, hunched over with his elbows on his knees.

"Fine," Liana said, before twisting her hair up and pinning it high. "I suppose that's ample enough time for something to go horribly wrong."

Ameen didn't look amused.

"I'll be fine." She smoothed out the worry lines on his face. He caught her hand and kept it outstretched before reaching to his side and placing his pistol in her palm. It was the same one that had given him the scar on his shoulder. After his recovery, she had given it to him. He had found the gift ironic and lovely, for it was a fine weapon. It was no soldier's issue; the design was too intricate. It had seen much use over the last several years, but one would hardly be able to tell, since he took such great care of it. She clenched her fingers around the grip. "Well, that's just poor manners. Use up a gift, before returning it..."

"I expect this back. Please, be careful."

"Oh, don't you worry, I'll return it to you safe and sound." She slunk towards the door, dragging her fingers along his shoulders as she passed by him.

She descended to the quiet taproom. Business was slow. The next day was Mass, and even the drunkards were religious in this city. There were only a few for Bess to serve. She acknowledged Liana with a smile as she passed by to attend to Sava, Jamil, and Kahil. They hardly noticed Liana, for they were deep in conversation.

"Up to no good, you three?" she suspected aloud, slipping into one of the chairs for a brief chat.

"Just talking about what we'll be spending our shares on, Captain," said Jamil, the more practical one of the twins. "Kahil and I have never had this much to our names."

"Can't really decide," Kahil added. "Maybe a few rounds of rum, to start."

"What about you, Squiddy?" she looked at the youth. He had grown up well in the last several years, strong and clever under Liana and Ameen's tutelage. Since outgrowing his awkward, gangly frame, he began to catch the eyes of many young men and women alike.

"Rum doesn't sound too bad," he admitted, leaning back in his seat. "But one of those fine bottles that Bess keeps in the back... That's what I'd like."

"Don't go wasting all of your share, now," she warned, catching herself sounding like a hovering mother hen. She stood to allow the boys the rest of the night to themselves. After all, they were off duty. But Sava straightened up, eyeing the lantern she carried.

"Where are you going so late, Captain?"

"Some business to take care of. Why? Worried for my safety?"

He saluted to her. "No, ma'am. That's Almasi's job."

Liana waved and looked to the door. To her surprise, Marin stood, waiting for her.

"A word?" he asked in a tone that gave her a rush of nostalgia. It reminded her of the guilty feeling she would get when he caught her doing something mischievous as a child.

They stepped out together into the keen night air. The sharp bite of winter's imminent arrival caught in her breath as she exhaled a small cloud of visible air. As Marin lit his pipe, she watched the warm flicker of the herb as he breathed in.

"When do ya plan on telling Ameen about yer parents?"

Liana was rendered speechless for a beat before she could gather herself.

"Marin," she said in a harsh whisper, looking around to see if there could be anyone listening, "You're the one who told me and Ivan never to tell anyone who we were. You told us to move on and live a simple life."

"And that's what this is, is it?" Marin gestured to The Black Barricade's iron-rodded sign. "A simple life?"

"Well, whatever it is," she crossed her arms, "You're a part of it."

"Not for much longer." He shook his head. "I mean tah be living with Nellie in a year's time."

"Oh, I'm sure her husband will be happy with that arrangement."

"He'll warm tah the idea, after he knows about it."

Her throat thickened as what he told her sunk in. "You're serious... But why?"

He wiggled the pipe between his teeth before removing it from his mouth. "I'm gettin' older, Liana. I'm at an age when I must see my children settled. Ivan... Well, I canna do much about yer brother. It pained me to see him go and pains me still to wonder where he is. He is the only son I will ever have the pleasure tah raise, though it was only partly. Nellie has a man to take care of 'er, but I can sense when I read her letters that she needs me. She needs *family*. They're doin' their best to start one, but there is somethin' missin' for her, still..."

"And you, my girl," he said. "Ye've always struggled, since ye've been small, to find yer place in this world. And that struggle has made ya stronger than a bottle of aged whiskey."

She choked out a short laugh.

"I thank the Divine every day that ya finally found where you belong," he said, pride twinkling in his eyes. "And ya found someone who understands ya more than I could ever hope to try."

"You've told him already, haven't you?" she asked. "That's why he was so secretive this morning."

He shrugged. "He's sharp as a damned cutlass, that one. And he'd do anythin' for ya. That's why ya need tah tell him who ye really are."

"I can't. I don't even know how to begin to explain..."

"But ye must," he insisted. "Whether ya see it that way or not, ye're makin' a life with him, here. The way ya are with him... It

37

reminds me of my own marriage. But I never had any secrets with my Leda, ya know that."

She did. Liana remembered Leda clearly—a dark and serene Island beauty who cherished her family. Marin had been broken when she had passed, and part of him had never been restored. He had gotten on with his life and took care of Nellie, Liana, and Ivan the best he could. But without Leda, Marin could never be whole.

"And ya also know the two of ye are just one priest short of a marriage," he added with a sly grin.

"Marin, you know how much I enjoy living as a heathen," Liana scoffed and quickly changed the subject. "What time is it?"

"Divine!" he hissed, having a look down at his pocket watch. "Ye'll be late. Ya must leave now. Are ya sure you dinna want me tah come with ye?"

"I'm sure," Liana started to retreat backwards down the road.

"Be careful," he warned, shaking his finger as she left. "And if ye're not back in—"

"I know, I know!" she called, halfway down the block, already rounding the corner.

Chapter 5

A Shot Across the Bow

A hazy mist gathered in the graveyard. Liana padded lightly through, respectfully watching her step and keeping to the marked trail. Moisture soaked the hem of her cloak. The slick grass, tall and overgrown around the stones, crunched under her soles as she walked into the courtyard.

She approached the domed stone building ahead, keeping Ameen's pistol in her right hand and the lantern in her left. The abandoned Temple of the Divine reminded her of her brother. It would stir his memory of the days when their parents had been alive—a time she had been too young to recall.

She stopped before a wooden door with a point at the top. Above it, a crest carved in the stone guarded the entrance. The phoenix was the heraldic creature of the Romenels, an ancient family of royal blood. But it had been decades since anyone of that line sat upon the throne.

Pressing a hand onto the curve of one of the flames etched in the stone, Liana found herself hoping she could absorb its fiery strength. But she could only feel her own resolve. The double doors opened with a loud creak that made her cringe.

Keeping her feet at the threshold, she took in the sight of the decrepit building. Through the foyer, she could see scarlet bug-eaten tapestries hung on the walls. Some of the pews remained whole, but most were half-rotted. The altar, split down the middle, stood above the rest at the other end of the long room. Though dust clouds the stained-glass windows, moonlight still casts itself inside.

Stepping into the Temple, she saw a table of votive candles. Some looked usable. Feeling sentimental, she took the tinderbox and lit one.

Liana had never been the religious type. Marin and Leda didn't raise her that way. They would go to Temple Mass out of obligation on special holidays. Their prayers at meals were usually mumbled, memorized lines. The tradition had died with Leda. But Liana knew that votive candles offered prayers to the Divine, so He may bless loved ones.

She lit one for Ameen. The thin beeswax pooled under the small flame and smelled faintly of honey. She thought he would appreciate it. In the time she had known him, he had never attended Mass. He worshiped in his own private way. Liana could hardly think of a man more worthy of the Divine's favor.

"You came."

Liana whirled around, holding the pistol up to the figure at the entrance. The hooded man's unfamiliar voice confirmed he was not her brother. He approached her, hands rising up peacefully. When he removed his hood, she could see he wasn't Lord Seliverstov, either. Bess had described her husband as in his fifties, but the man before her now couldn't have been much older than thirty.

"Who are you? Stop right there! I *will* shoot you!" She pulled back the hammer of the pistol. He had already halved the distance between them, and he was too close for comfort when he finally did stop.

"I knew you wouldn't remember me as well as I remember you," he said, eyeing the weapon in her hand. His face slackened with surprise. "That's my gun."

"The hell it is," she snarled. "Now tell me who you are."

"Dillon Whyte," he said calmly. "Second son of the late Earl Bayard Whyte and, as of a month ago, the new King's Guard Commander." When Liana did not respond, he continued, "I believe you'll find my family's crest at the bottom of the handle. It was a gift from my father, and I would like it back, so if you please—"

"No, I would not please," she snapped. So, the decision to spare the soldier in the alley all those years ago had come back to bite her in the ass. "And this weapon has a new owner. I have an obligation to return it to him. You may remember him. He's the one you shot."

Whyte blinked at her like a confused horned owl.

"But you didn't ask me here to return the damned gun, so what do you want from me?"

He squared his shoulders as though that would intimidate her. "I want you to stop sailing. End the piracy."

"Doesn't the King's Guard... well, guard the bloody king? Your predecessor had no interest in what happened at sea. Never even saw the man once."

"You steal taxable goods that belong to the kingdom. You attack navy ships and civilians."

"Just a little," she said loftily. "And we always let them go after we've cleaned up their cargo. What's a few ships a year when compared to the rest of the riches the king has? There's enough for a few scum raiders like me to take their fill."

"My predecessor didn't take the time to do his research." Whyte started to move forward again. She raised the barrel at him as a last warning. "You see, I know the danger you pose to this kingdom."

"You flatter me," she replied. "But I'm just a black-hearted brigand, out for myself. I couldn't care less for this Divine-forsaken kingdom."

"No, I know who you really are," he spoke slowly, muscles taut, like a feline ready to spring at a rodent. "Ilyana Romenel."

Liana fired the gun, but Whyte was ready. He made a grab for her wrist and shoved it upwards. The ball discharged into the ceiling, causing a thick cloud of dust and small bits of stone to fall around them.

"Let go!" He coughed, holding firm to her wrist. "I don't want to break your wrist."

"I'll break your kneecaps first!"

Liana kicked, but he caught her ankle. In an effort to regain her balance, she flailed, and the pistol slipped from her hands. It fell on the stone floor. She almost did too, but a powerful yank at her wrist kept her from hitting the ground.

"Oof!" she gasped, colliding into Whyte's chest. He reeled back at the impact.

She seized the moment, sliding her hands around the back of his head. Using his neck as leverage, she drove her knee into his abdomen. He wheezed and doubled over.

In one sweep, she picked up the pistol and made for the door. She left her lantern behind and didn't stop to look back.

Liana tore through the graveyard, taking care not to slip on the grass. Her heart beat frantic and wild in her chest. She gasped for breath, ignoring the stitch in her side. Her fists swung at her sides, the right one squeezing the barrel of the pistol.

Why didn't I just kill him? She berated herself. For a second time, she had let him live. But, she thought, if she had killed him, that would leave too many mysteries unsolved.

How did he know? And who else had he told? What *exactly* did he want from her? If he simply wanted her to "end the piracy," he wouldn't have gone to so much trouble—he would have saved himself the effort and dragged her to the gallows.

What mattered even more than figuring out how Commander Whyte knew was keeping the secret from everyone else at all costs.

Chapter 6

The Grimoire
The Royal Palace

A tall oak clock chimed one o'clock. Princess Rhian rubbed her eyes, desperate for sleep but even more desperate for information. The crushing weight of her predicament felt heavy as she realized she had been in the palace's library for several hours now and still hadn't found an answer. She went back to work, making notes with ink-stained fingers. A wall of books guarded these endeavors. Over the course of the night, it had grown taller, but she always returned to a single tome—Aunt Alcyone's grimoire.

The spell book held an untapped well of scholarship passed down by generations of healers. When Uncle Grigor passed it on to her last year, he had regretfully informed her it was wholly written in the hieroglyphics of the ancient mystics. Now the knowledge was lost, leaving Rhian with a tool she could not use. The hope of Alcyone's legacy rested in Rhian and the grimoire she held.

That hope, however, had been all but snuffed out because of Dillon Whyte.

It was there, in the very library Rhian sat, she had fallen in love with the commander. She spent much of her time here, and it was his duty to oversee the protection of the royal family. They crossed paths often. From afar she found him charming and gallant, like a knight in a fable.

Once, he had approached her when she had been deep in her personal research. After some polite prodding on his part, she showed him her notes. She remembered how he squinted at her record of weather patterns in the Capital's harbor, of which the library windows gave a perfect view. Driven by his clear interest in her studies, she even allowed him to see her volumes of notebooks on various subjects ranging from botany to mechanics to personal reflections on her daily life in the palace.

He had called her a genius.

Rhian let a whisper of a smile pass over her lips, momentarily forgetting the reason why she poured over these books. After carrying on their secret relationship for months, Rhian had found out she was pregnant. Rather than face either the wrath of her brother the king or Dillon's condemnation, she knew she would have to take care of this problem herself. She needed an abortifacient. Quickly, before—

Someone approached the library. Likely a guard, at this hour. Rhian held her breath, waiting for them to pass. But rather than fade away, the steps grew louder and louder until whoever was out there pressed on the door.

Fear flooded her veins, and her thumping heart threatened to burst from her chest. The smell of magic—like the air after rain— filled her nostrils as she began to panic. *No. Not now.* She tried to regain control, scrambling to her feet and squeezing her arms around the grimoire to shut out her powers. Just as the intruder peeked inside, a bright light blinded them, and they staggered back, shielding their eyes. They shouted, but it was drowned out by a crack like thunder rolling over the sky.

When Rhian looked around, she found herself back in her apartments, the scent of wet earth still wafting in the air. She stood in the dark antechamber, facing the open lounge area and the tall marble fireplace. Lifting her shaking hands, she realized they were empty. The grimoire was gone.

"No," she squeaked, grasping at the air as though that would get it back. "No!"

She couldn't go back to the library for it. Not now. Rushing to her bedchamber, she paced, trying to think of what to do. That was when she heard someone burst into her apartments.

"Your Highness?"

She knew that voice. Dillon.

Snatching her nightrobe, she threw it on. She swallowed, thickening her voice to make it sound as though she had been sleeping. "Commander, is that you...?" she called, soft and silver, and swept around the corner.

Dillon, a lifelong soldier possessing the heart of a lion, looked as though he had peered into the eyes of death itself. The blazing fear in his usually gentle hazel eyes struck her hard. But when he saw her, he sagged in relief. He smoothed a hand over his honey blond hair. "Thank the Divine you're safe."

It was him. She smiled serenely past her alarm. "Well, of course I am."

He opened his arms and caught her in an embrace before kissing her deeply.

"Dillon," she scolded with a gentle laugh as he kept her close, though she tried to pull away. She gripped his arms. "Dillon, you're trembling..."

"Don't go to the library," he told her. He interrupted when she tried to speak. "Something... Something happened. Something dangerous. Stay out of the library. Please. Promise me."

"I... I promise... But Dillon, won't you stay again tonight?"

He stepped away, his hands lingering with hers. "I can't. I'm sorry."

She swallowed back the urge to tell him it was her he had seen. The last thing she wanted to do was frighten him even more. "Tomorrow?"

"I hope so."

Rhian didn't sleep. When it was morning, even before the servants rose to begin their duties, she snuck out of her apartments to retrieve the grimoire. All that was left was the crumbled wall of books and a rectangular charred mark on the floor. He had taken it, likely to show the king, who would have no idea of its significance. At best, he would dismiss the commander, but at worst—Rhian didn't want to think about that. She had to get that grimoire back before her uncle found out. He would arrive in the Capital in a matter of days.

In more ways than one, Princess Rhian feared she would soon run out of time.

Chapter 7

Bring a Spring Upon'er
14th of Regnsfall, 1723
The Black Barricade

"I just don't understand why you didn't offer him a bribe."

Liana irritably blew a loose strand of hair out of her face and frowned at Ameen from across the table they were moving. A full week had passed since the meeting gone awry. She had heard nothing from Commander Whyte. With each passing day of silence, she grew more nervous. Ameen's incessant questioning was less than helpful.

"Don't most public officials enjoy bribes?" he continued thoughtfully as he set his end down.

"He's the son of an earl," she replied with unintended bite. "Any amount of money we could afford to give would be nothing to him."

"Right. Forget I said anything."

Feeling a little guilty, she mirrored his movements, and together they lifted another table.

"Sorry," she mumbled, looking down to unroll her cream-colored sleeves when they were done. The long tables were now all lined up in order to fit more people. She rubbed her bloodshot eyes. "I haven't had much sleep."

"I know." Of course, he did. He was the one who felt her toss and turn each night, who was woken when she climbed over him to get out of bed and splash water on her face, who had opened his eyes that morning to find her hunched over the windowpane, looking tensely out at the distant view of the palace.

Ameen offered his hand. She took it, and he pulled her into an embrace. Closing her eyes tightly, she hugged him around the waist and inhaled his familiar heady scent. She ran her hands along his lean back, hard with muscle. For a moment, the sounds around them—bells ringing, calling citizens to Mass, Bess' volunteers working in the kitchen, Marin's gruff voice above, footsteps on the stairs—quieted. But they returned in full as Bess burst into the dining room. The poor woman had been up since before dawn to get everything ready.

On two Mass Days every month, The Black Barricade became a soup kitchen. The Barricade also had a fund for those in dire need—sudden loss of income, death in the family, or an immigrant trying to establish themselves after fleeing their home country. That had been how Liana met Bess. Therefore, Charity Days held a special place in Bess' heart, and now she took pride in organizing them.

Despite the help they gave, a silent agreement amongst their community promised to keep the praises quiet. Everyone knew it was illegal. Under the Vitalis regime, welfare and charity outside the Temple of the Divine was banned. According to the court officials, handouts only encouraged vagrancy. But for Liana, it was an important task to uphold. Besides, what was another line to add to her list of crimes?

"Ah! Perfect!" Bess exclaimed, her hands clasped together, pleased at how they had arranged the dining room. "Now, for the tablecloths."

Liana forced a smile in an attempt to mirror her enthusiasm. Of course, Bess saw through it.

"Liana, what's the matter? You love Charity Days."

"I think she may need some air," Ameen said, placing an arm around Liana's shoulders.

Liana stepped over a puddle, careful not to get any muck on her cloak or her skirt. It had rained during the night, making the road slick. Her arm locked with Ameen's as they walked together toward the docks. She breathed in the salty ocean air, already beginning to relax.

Going the opposite way, Maiz Samara and his wife passed them with their four children. They all went along in a neat line, dressed suitably for Mass. Samara tipped his hat in greeting as they went along. "Captain Foley."

Liana returned the gesture with a smile. She knew they would be seeing them later at the Barricade, despite the large share that Samara had just received from their most recent plunder. Charity Days meant hot meals were served to all. It was a good day for it, too. The probability of rain was imminent, the sky dense with clouds. She leaned into Ameen as a cold breeze lifted off the sea.

"I've been thinking about our holiday," he said.

"Hmm?"

"What if we go to see Nellie, with Marin?"

She made a sound of dissatisfaction, and he laughed.

"Why not?"

"It might snow there soon."

"Oh… Well, never mind then." He shuddered.

"I've never seen snow, though," she teased.

"I will *never* understand how it can be cold enough for ice to float down from the sky, nor do I have any interest in witnessing it."

He stopped walking. She looked around and realized where he had taken her. They stood near the dock that led to the *Windfall*.

"Why are we here? The ship is under repair."

"It's Mass Day. No one will be working," he replied, gently tugging her down the dock.

She only resisted a little, easily swayed by that vulpine glint in his eyes. As they boarded, the scent of freshly dried lacquer swept over her. The repairmen had taken care to repaint the deck before the rain. She ran her hand over the rail, wiping away beaded rainwater gathered on it.

Ameen looked over the repairs with mild approval, and she caught his glance. For the first time, she noticed how deep his smile lines had become. It was a wonder how much they both had changed since they had met.

Liana had found a kindred spirit in Ameen, more than she ever could have hoped for. Her brother, Ivan, had made fast friends with Ameen back when he was a dockworker. It had been lonely since the Foleys had moved back to the Capital of Caerwyn from the Island colonies. One night, Ameen came to share a meal in the Foleys' cramped townhouse. He had taken her hand in greeting, firm but not overpowering. Used to people glossing over her to either Nellie's beauty or business with Marin or Ivan, Liana found herself immediately attracted to him. His eyes—as striking as the sunrise over a sparkling horizon—had made her knees weak.

After that first meeting, their shared love of the sea had brought them closer. She had grown up hearing Marin's tales of his privateering days. She had begged to hear about Ameen's own seafaring stories. He told her about sailing with his father, seeing every port in Savarre and the Islands.

"My father always said," she remembered him saying after dinner one night, "Your heart is a compass— a good sailor always follows it."

Liana meandered to the stern, lost in memory. Everything had been so different back then. Now things were changing again. The subject of fathers lingered on her mind. "Ameen?"

"Hmm?"

"How long have you known about Marin?"

"Ah, he told you?" Squinting one eye, he considered his answer. "Almost... a year?"

"*A year?*"

"Almost! It was more like several months, actually. He went halfway up the steps to the upper deck, eyes begging for forgiveness. "I'm sorry. Marin didn't want you to know. He wanted to wait until the right time to tell you."

"I suppose that was why you were acting so secretive last week."

He gave a small shrug. That crafty smile returned once he saw she wasn't upset.

"Sneaky buggers," she chuckled, and he responded by giving her a sly wink. "I'm not sure I like the two of you conspiring behind my back."

"You'll miss him."

"Of course, I will. He's the only parent I've got left."

"I know."

Liana leaned against the railing to look out at the harbor. She could feel his eyes on her as she chewed on her bottom lip. It was now or bloody never, she supposed.

"What... exactly *have* I told you about my parents?" she asked, testing the waters. "Remind me."

"Only that they were killed."

"Did Ivan ever tell you how?"

"No." His natural thirst for knowledge had never impeded their relationship. He had a great length of patience with her.

"It's not something I like to talk about," she blurted, succumbing to the crushing fear of his potential reaction. "I was young. I don't think you'd believe me, if I told you..."

Cursing herself a coward, she started back down the steps, swallowing back the truth. She couldn't even summon the words to explain.

"If you can't tell me, then who can you tell?"

"It doesn't matter now." She turned back. "They're gone."

"It *does* matter. They're a part of who you are. It's the same with my mother."

It had taken some years for Ameen to be able to speak to her openly about her. Nahveena Almasi had left her family with no explanation to her son. Her absence left his father, Anise, to raise Ameen on his own.

"The Divine tests us," he continued. "He gives us opportunities to prove that we are worthy of His favor."

Liana wasn't sure if she believed in the Divine at all. She remained quiet, though, finding herself soothed by his words. It wasn't entirely about what he was saying, but how. Whenever he spoke of the Divine, his voice would settle back into a melodic Island lilt, so pleasant and tranquil.

"You have great purpose. You do so much for the people," he said. "If we hadn't had our own trials, we'd have gone down different paths."

Much different, she agreed inwardly. She tilted her gaze, spotting the palace's spires, dark against the gray sky. Closing her eyes, she tried to recall a time that was nearly lost to her—a time when she had once resided in the palace.

"I remember lightning," she said, almost in a whisper. "On the night my parents died."

Crackling. Heat. Anger.

"There was a storm?" he asked, just as soft, intrigued but afraid she would stop.

"No. I was running and... There was a flash of lightning, coming for us."

When she opened her eyes, she found him watching her intensely. He held his breath, absorbing the words she spoke. She didn't like it. It made her feel fragile.

"I'm sorry." She withdrew, rubbing a hand down her face. "I don't remember anything else. And Ivan... He never liked to talk about that night. I was three, maybe four years old. I don't even know if that memory is real."

"Thank you," he said, "For telling me."

"Do you believe me?"

"Of course, I do." Ameen kissed the corner of her mouth, making it turn upwards.

"I love you."

"I love you, too."

Liana had always tried to match his devotion to her. He was her protector, and she was his, each always trying to shield the other from distress, disappointment, and, more times than a few, death. She wouldn't know how to even exist without him. Somehow, he had reached into her, filling her very soul, pouring himself into an emptiness she hadn't even realized was there. He was always so willing to give but reluctant to take, loving her with no inhibitions, celebrating her flaws with passion, cradling her weaknesses with care.

And yet, he didn't even know her real name.

"There's something you should—"

"Liana, I want to—"

They both stopped and shared a laugh. He took her hand and swept his thumb over her knuckles. His skin was unnaturally warm, especially given the cold weather. He put his other hand in his coat pocket and cleared his throat.

"Please, just let me say this, or I may not get it out," he said. She fell silent, wondering why he had gone so serious. His lips parted to form a first word, but he couldn't speak. She gently squeezed his fingers. That helped. "Do you remember the first time we came aboard the *Windfall?* You had just spent every last bit of money you had on this old rig. There was so much work that needed to be done."

Liana cracked a lopsided smile. It had been the proudest moment in her life.

"And you stood there—" He pointed behind her at the helm. She turned to see. "You had this look on your face, as though you were daring the world to meet you with any challenge. Since then, I've only wanted to be by your side, facing those challenges together."

When she looked back, he held a ring between his thumb and first two fingers. The gold band, set with three white pearls, gleamed despite the lack of sunlight. The pearls reflected a rainbow sheen, absorbing the colors around them to make up for their own lack of pigment. Delicate swirling gold kept the pearls in place, lifting them up as though in worship.

"Blimey! Is that Leda's ring?" she asked stupidly, knowing well that it was. His hand was the only thing holding her steady as she trembled. Blood rushed to her face. A light drizzle began to fall, and it felt as though steam rose off her skin.

"You want to marry me?"

"Yes," he laughed, then paused, making that guilty squint with his eye again. "Wait, I think we did that the wrong—"

"Are you sure?" she asked, the pitch of her voice heightened now. "I'm not... I don't exactly have the qualities of a good wife, Ameen! I'm a pirate!"

"So am I. Listen, it's colder than your bloody heart out here. Will you give me your answer? Or do I have to shove this ring on your damned finger?"

"So long as you're well aware that you're the one who would be damned," she encouraged with a wicked grin. "Get on with it."

He slid the ring over her knuckle. It fit a little looser than she expected. She pulled her hand back and straightened it, so the pearls showed in the middle.

"Your fate is sealed, sailor."

A euphoric grin lifted his face. Tiny spheres of water ran down the threads of his coat. He caressed her hair, brushing away excess moisture from the now damp locks. He kissed her deeply before pulling away, too soon.

"Ameen," she murmured, eyes half-lidded. "Let's stay out a little longer. Bess won't mind..."

"I don't think so."

"Hmph. You'd defy your captain?"

"You can give me my punishment later. You see, they're waiting on us."

She blinked, snapping out of her elation. "They? Who are *they*?"

Chapter 8

Three Sheets to the Wind

The light drizzle of the morning turned into an afternoon downpour. They returned out of breath and drenched. In the rush, Liana's pins had fallen out, leaving her hair dripping down her shoulders in wet snarls. Ameen, saturated to the bone, attempted to shield both of them with his coat.

When they stepped into The Black Barricade, applause began. Chairs scraped against the floor as people stood to cheer their entrance. A sea of faces greeted them. She recognized them all—crew members and friends, old and new.

"Did you do this?" Liana muttered to Ameen.

"I... didn't think there would be so many—"

"Ye're finally here!" Marin gleefully pushed his way to them. Despite their waterlogged appearance, the old sailor rushed in and pulled them into an embrace.

"Marin!" Liana gasped, ribs creaking as he balanced his beer with one hand and squeezed her tight with the other. "Please tell me you did not cancel Charity Day to give us an engagement party!"

"Of course not! It's a combination! Now, come along and let's get ya dry and celebrate! Everyone is here!"

The near-impossible challenge to find a seat began. Even the stairs were occupied. People leaned against the wall and sat on the steps with their food and drink. By the door, Liana saw the twins dining on upturned buckets. They shouted and waved cheerfully while they passed through. Lucky hopped up, knocking his empty bowl over, to greet them.

"Almasi, you finally got the stones to ask her!"

Lucky dragged Ameen to him, clapping him hard on the back. Ameen grinned wildly over Lucky's shoulder. Lucky turned to Liana and bowed, exaggeratedly waving his tricorn.

"Felicitations and good tidings, Captain," he said, flashing his teeth at her. "I'll play a song tonight, in your honor."

"Thank you, Lucky. I'm looking forward to it."

He tipped his hat once more and returned to his conversation with the pretty young lady with whom he had been sharing a step.

Bess motioned them over to the last stool available, which she had saved for them. Ameen pulled it out, and Liana sat upon it while he leaned against the bar. Bess sent Beatrix to fetch clean towels and presented them with two scalding bowls of a thick meat stew. Before they were allowed to eat, Bess demanded to see the ring.

"Absolutely beautiful!" she said, bringing Liana's fingers closer to candlelight. "Marin, wherever did you find such a treasure?"

"Bess," Liana interrupted. "You knew about all this, too?"

"Why did you think I let you two leave this morning when there was more work to be done?" Bess let go of her hand and leaned back, hands on her wide hips.

Liana mumbled something about how she was, in fact, Bess' employer, not the other way around.

The couple took bites of their stew here and there, while many more congratulations were offered. Fortunately, the bowls had come steaming hot, for it must have taken them nearly an hour to finish them. By that time, the crowd dwindled. The families attending for Charity Day began to head home, while Bess and the other staff unsealed the casks.

"Squiddy!" Liana greeted the young man with a beaming smile as he bounded towards them, splitting the crowd.

"Congratulations, Captain," he said, revealing a globular bottle from behind his back. The black glass hid its liquid contents.

"Is that...?" She felt Ameen lean over her shoulder to see.

A depiction of the *Windfall* decorated the front. Liana took the bottle graciously and looked closely. The rendition displayed her ship at full sail, braving choppy waters. The impossibility of the detail mesmerized her. She knew Sava had artistic talent. She had come upon him countless times while sketching during his leisure time on the ship. But she had no idea he could create something so beautiful.

"Yes, ma'am," Sava answered with pride. "I got that bottle I talked about. Painted it myself. For you, Captain."

"Oh." Liana blinked. The emotions of the day were getting the better of her. She stood and embraced Sava, planting a hard kiss on the cheek. "Squiddy, it's lovely. Thank you."

Though he tried to hide it, a deep blush crept over his tawny cheeks. "I expect that bottle to be empty before the night's over. Though I doubt your husband-to-be will be much help with that."

"What's that?" Ameen looked up with a furrowed brow. Liana snickered. The boy had a way of riling up the usually calm quartermaster.

"Word 'round the crew is that the captain can outdrink you." Sava gave him a playful smile. "Don't worry though, sir, I defended you. I even told the twins you'd be my partner in a game of Down the Hatch."

Down the Hatch, a drinking game Ameen and the *Windfall's* crew invented, had many rules. Liana never joined in, wanting to save face as the captain. From what she understood, beer and rum were involved. The participants usually ended up roaring drunk.

Ameen sighed, "In case you didn't realize, I've just gotten *engaged*—"

She elbowed him. "I'm not going anywhere."

Sava bobbed, animatedly, while Ameen considered the proposition.

"Well... alright," he accepted, making Sava hop with joy. "But if we lose because you can't keep your ale in, I'll throw you in another cart of squids, like I did when you tried to pickpocket me."

The two men left, and Liana settled back on the stool with her bottle. She took a deep swig of rum, surprisingly smooth down her throat. Island sugar and other baking spices lingered behind her teeth.

Marin, appearing behind the bar, set down two stout glasses. "Don't ya know that'll turn yer brain tah mush?"

"And you're a grand example of it, aren't you?" she countered, pouring the rum.

"Fair enough," he agreed. They clinked their glasses together and drank. Afterwards, Marin eyed the remainder of its contents, delightfully surprised. "Laddie knows how tah choose a bottle."

"He learned from the best."

"Same as ya did, lass."

They enjoyed drink after drink, but a thought continued to nag at her.

"Marin," she began, drumming her fingers on the bar and watching how the candlelight played upon the pearls. "Does Nellie know I have Leda's ring now?"

"Well, I havena sent a letter, since ye've only just gotten engaged today."

"Marin."

He tugged his beard nervously and scratched under his chin.

"No. She doesna know I let Ameen have it tah give to ya," he admitted. He hastily added, "I always meant tah save it for ya when the time came for ye to marry."

She pulled off the ring, shaking her head. "She is going to hate me even more than she already does. I can't take it."

His warm, heavy hand, knotted with age, laid itself on hers. "She doesna hate—"

"This is her mother's ring. It's only right she has it."

"No. Leda wanted ye tah have it."

The memory of her foster mother shot a pang of grief through her.

"This ring was always meant for ya, lass," he continued, leaning closer so she could hear him over the shouts and whoops of Down the Hatch. "To Leda and I, ye're as much of a daughter as Nellie."

The thin, sharp scrape of a fiddle made them look towards the stairs. Lucky, back at the steps, held his beloved instrument. With a charming smile, he beckoned at Bess for her to join him.

"Get up here, lassie," Lucky said, over the end of his fiddle. "Let's show this lot what we're made of."

Liana grinned as she watched from afar. As much as the two butted heads, she often noted their common characteristics—musical aptitude; knowledge of ales and spirits; a pliable moral code, but a robust sense of loyalty.

Bess started to shy away, her porcelain cheeks a soft pink. Thiago Venegas, the ship's surgeon, stood behind her. A swarthy, angular Savarran man in his late fifties, Thiago was usually silent. His Caerwyn skills lacked, but he seemed to get on fine.

Bess backed into the poor fellow and bumped his shoulder. She twisted around, sputtering an apology. Thiago shined a toothy smile from beneath his black and silver mustache and offered her his untouched glass of clear Savarran liquor, made from desert cacti. Bess visibly swallowed as she took it, then knocked the drink back with ferocity. The entire pub cheered loudly as she rushed to Lucky. Together, the two broke out into a joyful duet, aided by Lucky's fiddle.

Haul the anchor away
Fill the sails with wind
My course will never sway
Love, keep your eyes skinned
Upon that golden horizon
I'll be back home
Yes, the sun will light my way

Liana leaned back in her stool, sipping on her gifted rum with ease. She enjoyed the music, talking, and laughter around her.

Every now and again, people would come over to her to share a drink and offer congratulations.

"Now, when can we expect little ones?" Mistress Davies pressed with a joyful smile to mask the prying nature of her question.

Liana took another swig of rum as Marin gave her a sly look. She swallowed, and the liquid scorched her throat. "Be a bit hard to raise children with this wild lot around, wouldn't it?"

"Bess certainly manages."

"Darling, they've just become engaged today," her husband chastised. "Leave her be."

In the distraction of the music, Ameen broke away from Down the Hatch and sauntered back to Liana. He pulled her to her feet, away from the conversation with Marin and the Davies, toward whom he gave a polite wave. Happy to get away, she stood on her toes to speak in his ear.

"Did you win?"

"No," he said, nudging his cheek to hers. She felt his warm, ale-laden breath on her jaw. "Dance with me."

Over his shoulder, she could see couples, both married and courting, clearing a space in the middle of the dining area.

"Almasi! Get your ass back here!"

Back at the game he had abandoned, Sava, Jamil, and Kahil gestured to a tall glass of beer that Ameen was expected to suck down. Fueled by a mischievous thrill, Liana pulled her husband-to-be away. He pointed at her and shrugged halfheartedly at the players, as if to say *sorry, Captain's orders*. Despite the disappointed shouts and rude gestures, the young men spotted Thiago peering at their game with intrigue and decided to let him replace their lost comrade.

"Don't step on me, you bloody tree," Liana warned Ameen as he raised her hand. In lieu of an answer, he spun her about, drawing them into the fray of dancers.

Their intoxication made the steps easier, somehow. Perhaps they stomped all over each other, but they didn't notice or care. People watched them, she was sure, as they stumbled and twirled. Once his laughter reached her ears, nothing else mattered. She could scarcely catch her breath. It felt wonderful. *He* was wonderful. After a few songs, she tripped over her own feet—or perhaps they were his. She was too drunk to tell. Her knees turned to water. Leaning into him, she fought to keep herself right. Her insides leapt as she hiccoughed. Ameen veered her out of the way of a passing couple.

To make room for the dancers, those not participating gathered around both the front and back doors as well as the stairs, leaving them with no way to their room. Feeling close to meeting the floor, she let Ameen maneuvered her. Together, they slipped away through a door behind the bar. He turned and shut it, fumbling a bit to make sure that it would close.

Liana felt like an intruder in the kitchen, Bess' proud domain. However, it made for the perfect escape, since no more food would be served that evening. She stepped carefully, groping her way to the fireplace. Above and around the brick hearth hung rows of pots and pans organized by size. A pitcher sat on one of the small end tables. Seeing it was filled with clear water, Ameen poured some into a pewter cup and handed it to her. Sipping, she sank down into a chair beside the long preparation table in the center of the kitchen.

"Better?" he asked.

"Much. Thank you."

Against the fire, she felt like a pile of dough, yielding and heavy. Exhausted as she was, she knew it couldn't have been long past twilight.

"Do I have to carry you to bed?" he asked, moving to refill the cup. She reached out to stop him and he flinched, probably supposing she was going to vomit.

"Nooo," she said, blinking heavy eyelids.

"Just as well. We won't make it through the crowd—Er, what... are you doing?"

She continued to unlace her boots, feeling the answer was self-evident. Her fingers fumbled with the laces, and he bent to help her. He peeled her stockings from her feet and, once they came off, playfully ran his finger along her arch.

"Stop it," she giggled, standing to get away. He drew back, chuckling. She lifted herself to sit on the slab of the kitchen table. Tilting her head back, she stretched her legs out, circling her heels close to the fire.

He sidled beside her. Leaning against him, she looked up to peer at his face and was reminded how big he really was. Their height difference was immense, nearly a foot. But after all this time, she hardly noticed.

For a sailor, he was exceptionally well-groomed. But tonight, he reeked of ale and smoke. She guessed one of the men had offered him a congratulatory puff of their pipe. His stench wasn't entirely unpleasant though, and she could hardly complain with the sweet tang of rum on her own breath.

Though they were still, her head continued to spin. Half-formed thoughts drifted in and out like the tide. To keep herself steady, she focused on the Circle around his neck, gently thumbing it.

"Did Mistress Davies' question bother you?" he asked, catching her hand.

She hummed inquisitively.

"About children."

"It's none of her damned business."

"So, it did."

Early in their romantic relationship, she waited until after he recovered from his gunshot injury to try seducing him. He always shied away, though, avoiding any sort of touch that was too intimate. She gave up, thinking she had been wrong about his affection. Once he realized his constant rejections wounded her pride, he admitted he didn't feel sexual attraction.

She had trouble with it at first. She thought there had to be another reason why he didn't want her in the same way she wanted him. Was he intimidated by her because she was his captain? Was there something wrong or repulsive about her that made him avoid the act? It stung.

But he told her that to him, having a place at her side and building a life together was true love, a real companionship. And he loved her, he had said. More than anything. From that moment on, their commitment to each other remained strong.

"No, but it's bothering you," she said, looking into his eyes. The molten copper of his irises contrasted beautifully to his deep brown skin. "And *that* bothers me."

"There are these... expectations—"

"*Fffuck* expectations," she slurred, circling her finger along his breastbone.

"You're especially mouthy when you're drunk."

"I know," she replied. "But listen here, sailor. Don't you remember? We've already raised a kid together."

Confusion crossed his face, then he relaxed into a smile, realizing who she referred to. "Sava."

"Right. And the best part—he already knew how to wipe his own ass by the time we got him."

They dissolved into laughter, and when they recovered, he said, "I just want you to know, if it was something you ever wanted, then we could try."

"Can you imagine me as a mother?" she asked doubtfully.

"If you can command a ship, especially with this lot as your crew," he jabbed his thumb to the door, where sounds of merriment echoed, "Then you can do anything."

She shook her head and waved her hand dismissively. "I'm happy with the way things are."

A creak from the pantry silenced his reply. He straightened and motioned for her to be still. He crept around the table and opened the door. That was when she saw a flash of honey blond hair bolting out of the pantry. A scream caught in her throat. Ameen pounced at the intruder. Crashing resounded in the kitchen as the two men wrestled each other to the ground.

"Oh, *shit*," she swore in a low hiss.

Chapter 9

Them a Wide Berth

Ameen threw the intruder against the pantry door, his rage eclipsing his intoxication. The impact rattled the adjacent cabinet full of dishes. He reached into his holster and pressed his pistol to the man's neck. Nothing about him appeared familiar.

"What the *hell* are you doing here?" As Liana blinked away her intoxication, clarity reached her face. She slid down from the table, closer to where he had the man cornered.

Ameen couldn't keep the surprise out of his voice. "You know him?"

"So, do you," she said. "He's the one who gave you that scar on your shoulder."

"Commander Dillon Whyte, at your service," the man said dryly. Whyte's jaw clenched as Ameen's gaze shot back to him.

"I should kill you." Ameen pressed the pistol into Whyte's jugular. He didn't actually intend on acting on the threat, but he relished the fear that filled Whyte's eyes.

"And Bess would kill *you* for getting blood in her kitchen," Liana scoffed and looked directly at Whyte. She dropped her voice low. "I believe I was clear at the Temple, Commander."

"My business with you is not done. I must speak with you about other matters."

"How much, then?"

"What?"

"How much money will it take for you to leave us alone?"

"I don't want—This is *not* about money." He stiffened under Ameen's grasp, insulted.

"Then we're done here."

Liana and Whyte shared a tense look. Ameen felt out of place— like there was a second conversation happening in a language he couldn't understand.

"What should we do with him?" he cut in.

"Throw him in the alley. If he knows what's good for him, he won't come back," she told him, turning away.

But before she could get too far, Whyte reached out and grabbed her by the elbow. "Please, Ilyana—"

Ameen struck Whyte in the face, good and hard. Whyte stumbled back. His features contorted, blood smearing from the corner of his mouth and over his fingers. Ameen felt a swell of satisfaction at the sight, until—

"Ameen!" Liana shouted. "I have this under control!"

"If he lays a hand on you again," he growled and flexed his now-throbbing knuckles, "I won't care what Bess will have to say about blood in her kitchen."

He moved to holster his gun, feeling the heat of Liana's gaze. He heard her say his name again, before a heavy force plowed into him. His weapon fell. The air audibly escaped his lungs as he was shoved back onto the preparation table and pinned under Whyte's weight. He struggled to push him off but froze when he found himself staring straight at another pistol.

Out of the corner of his eye, Ameen saw Liana snatch his gun off the floor. She lined it up to Whyte's temple. She was so close to him that, even with her poor aim, the likelihood she would miss was slim to none.

"Let him go!"

"I could kill him before you have time to pull the trigger."

A hard rap on the door to the dining room grabbed all of their attention.

"You don't only have to worry about me," she warned, cocking her head to the door. "There are at least thirty men on the other side of that wall who would give their lives for his and mine."

"I don't want to kill anyone," Whyte said. "All I want is for you to listen to what I have to say."

"I will," she promised. Ameen saw the desperate fear in her eyes. Despite his compromised position, he found comfort in that—the knowledge she would always protect him, and he her. When Whyte released him and Ameen finally began to breathe again, the door flew open. Bess, along with Marin and Lucky, rushed in.

"What is going on?" Bess shrieked. She stared at the gun in Liana's tightly clenched hands.

"Well, luv, it looks like a dirty puzzle gone wrong," Lucky commented, lifting his brows.

Liana's sun-browned cheeks flushed scarlet. She straightened up, lengthening her spine to stand as tall as possible, as she usually did when she was about to give orders. "Marin, make sure the commander does not step a toe out of this kitchen. Bess, send everyone home. The party's over."

They dispersed, and Liana came to Ameen, pressing the pistol back into his hands. Her head bobbed, as though she was dizzy and had trouble keeping him in her focus. She spoke to him breathlessly. "Are you alright?"

He managed to nod.

"Good... I'll meet you upstairs. I just... I need..." On that note, she bolted through the back door and vomited in the alley.

"I'm fine," Liana growled. "The rum just caught up to me."

They made it back to their room to sober up. She splashed water on her face and ran her tongue along a clean rag.

"Liana..."

"What?" she snapped, looking back at him through the mirror.

He looked into her commanding eyes, the color of grit and soil and earth. They pierced through the prideful silence between them. His heart hammered, but he thought it was best to say what was on his mind. "Why did he call you by that other name?"

She balked, and he knew Whyte had not made a mistake.

"Because that *is* my name," she said slowly, as though carefully choosing her words. Her hair fell into her face. It had dried into curving waves and tangles. "Ilyana. My mother was Rodinian, remember? I-I've never used it. Ivan never even called me that."

"How does Whyte know that?" *And why didn't I?*

"I don't know," she said brusquely. "That's what I am going to find out."

"I'll go with you."

"No." She turned fully around.

"Why not?"

"I'd have thought you would be satisfied with one bruised eye. Do you want to make it two?"

"Stop avoiding, Liana," he said, a little angrier than he meant to be. As a realization struck him, he said it out loud. "You're hiding something from me."

"No," she shot back. He couldn't tell if it was a lie. "You hit Whyte. You shouldn't be the one interrogating him."

"I was protecting you!"

"I don't need your protection," she told him, pushing her hair back roughly. "It's not for you to fret every time someone looks at me wrong or touches my elbow!"

"Then who, if not me?" His temper began to slip, though he tried desperately to get control of it. The name. He needed to know more about her name, he reminded himself.

"No one! I don't need you to fight for me! You only get in my way!"

She lit the fuse, already worn by the night's stressful events. He exploded, like a cannon off the broadside. Jumping to his feet, his boots made hard thuds as he stomped to her. She didn't budge and set her jaw, looking him straight in the eye.

"You have no right to say that to me!"

"I have every right to say whatever I damn well please!" she shouted at him, her top lip curling, daring him to contradict her. "I don't need you!"

He flinched as her words cut deep into old wounds. She saw it, and he wished she hadn't, because she reacted in the opposite way, he needed her to. Wringing her hands, she started for the door.

"Liana, don't—"

—*leave*. He couldn't get the last word out. But she turned, wearing a deep, stubborn scowl. She stayed.

"Please," he said. "Just tell me the truth. What does the commander want from you?"

She rubbed her hands down her face.

"I don't know what he wants," she said raggedly. "But I think I know why he's interested in me. And... you deserve to know too. My name... is Ilyana Romenel."

He mouthed the surname under his breath, testing its familiarity as she continued.

"My parents were King Sergus and Queen Valeriya."

The blood drained from his face, leaving him cold. He had no idea what his outward expression looked like, but from her response, it was likely not pleasant. Tears swam in her eyes.

"You're..." he began, but a knock interrupted him.

"Oh, bloody hell, *what?*" Liana threw open the door.

Bess, holding a tray with a pot of hot water and some type of brown powder, made her way inside. She looked apologetic. "Tea?"

"No." Liana turned away, rubbing her eyes.

"It's not for you, it's for him." Bess rolled her eyes, before she looked to Ameen kindly. "Willow tree bark from Thiago, for the swelling and the pain."

"Thank you," he said, forcing himself to be genuine, though she had come at the most inopportune moment. In her usual empathetic way, she looked between them.

"I'll be going."

"It's alright, Bess." Ameen shared a glance with Liana. His head started to hurt. Blood thudded like a drum in his ears and boiled under his eye as hot as the water in the pot. "You should go find out what Whyte wants with us. Get it over with."

She nodded stiffly, looking thankful for an escape. "Then we'll talk."

"Then we'll talk."

Lingering by the door, she softly said, "Get some rest."

After she left with Bess close behind, Ameen went back to the chair and flopped down heavily, trying to process what he had just learned but only succeeded at staring at the space between his feet.

Chapter 10

A Word with the Captain

Liana swept across the kitchen threshold, seething with unbridled rage. Whyte, tied to a chair by thick rigging rope, faced Lucky, who sat in the corner picking his nails with a knife. She stormed straight past Lucky up to Whyte and shoved him in the chest. With a muffled yell and a crash, he fell back, the chair slamming hard on the kitchen floor. He grunted, distressed behind the gag. Lucky stood over him, cackling.

"Thank you, Lucky," said Liana. "You can go now."

The laughter died. "Oh. Are you sure, Captain?"

"Yes. Good night."

As he exited the kitchen, he shot Whyte a pitying look.

Liana towered over the commander like a ship's main mast. She took hold of his gag and jerked it down. "How do you know my name?"

"A bit demeaning to speak from the floor, isn't it?"

She fisted his shirt and yanked him up. "Talk. *Now.*"

"Fine, fine." He closed his eyes, still tied to the chair and likely dizzy. "After our encounter at the docks years ago, I followed your exploits. Like I said, I did my research."

"Why?"

"I wanted to avenge Kelvin and Gallagher's deaths."

"Oh, you mean your friends who tried to ravish a back-alley whore?"

He grimaced. "That's not what I recall."

"Funny. I remember that night quite clearly," she spat. "If my crew hadn't come, your friends would have raped me in that alley."

"I wonder, though, if whatever they did to you warranted their lives."

"And I wonder," she sneered, "How many more rapes we prevented with their deaths."

He fell silent.

"That's what I thought." she scoffed. "Now go on. Before I lose my patience."

"This is you with patience?"

"Yes, and it's wearing dangerously thin."

"Right. Since that night, I rose in the ranks rather quickly. I began to have more resources at my disposal, so I deepened my search. I read sailors' accounts of pirate attacks. There were some with common traits; a crew of all origins, a woman giving orders and little to no casualties.

"And then, I finally found a lead. An account named one of your crew. The sailor had recognized a man by the name of Foley."

Her gut twisted.

"Apparently, this Foley had once been a Caerwyn privateer. So, I looked through the records. It would seem Foley had last sailed on the *Siren*, a ship that had gone out of commission over twenty years ago.

"Foley's last voyage, however, was twenty-*five* years ago. The *Siren* left the Capital for the island port of Madzetal on the morning after King Sergus and Queen Valeriya Romenel were apprehended—the morning after the prince and princess had gone missing."

"That's a stretch. Many ships went out that morning, I'm sure."

"And I remembered you and your face. Has anyone ever told you that you look just like your mother?"

"You... knew my mother?"

"I met her once, briefly, as a child," he said. "Queen Valeriya was... kind. You can imagine that meeting the royal family was an intimidating experience for a boy. I remember Prince Ivan, too. Do you... still have contact with him?"

Liana faltered, reluctantly mournful for a mother she couldn't remember. Stuffing down the feeling, she barked, "This isn't about my brother. Get on with it, Whyte."

"Yes, fine," he said hastily as she lifted her arm, threatening to shove him back again. "The Whytes and the Romenels were once in a close alliance. My father had a portrait of King Sergus and Queen Valeriya. I looked at it nearly every day of my young life. I knew your face, but it took me years to realize why.

"The pieces finally pulled together when I thought to look at passenger records, not commerce, a few months ago. Almost fifteen years after leaving, Marin Foley returned to the Capital with his three children: two daughters and a son. The son and the younger daughter matched the ages of the lost children of the king and queen. I knew that could be no coincidence."

"Wrap it up, Whyte."

"I came to the conclusion that this man, Marin Foley, saved you and your brother and raised you. You could have stayed in the colonies, and no one would have known who you were. But you returned."

"Obviously. Now, what do you mean by seeking me out so persistently?"

"I'll tell you," he said. "But I must ask you a question first."

"And that is?"

"What should I call you?" he asked, shockingly genuine.

"Call me?"

"I could see you were disturbed when I called you by your birth name."

"Because I've never wanted anything to do with my birth. I'm Captain Liana Foley now," she replied. "Liana will do."

"And your betrothed? Does he have no interest in becoming a prince of Caerwyn?" he asked.

"He didn't know," she said, narrowing her eyes. "Not until tonight."

"Oh." He paled. "I hope you could forgive me. But I'm desperate. I need your help."

"Help?"

"Yes. If you help me, then I swear I will leave you and yours be." Whyte wet his lips and looked to the side at his items on the table—a satchel, his cloak, and his gun. "Open the satchel."

She did, eyeing him warily, as she procured a book, its cover burnt black. The pages looked untouched by the flames that had scorched the outside. She leafed through it, confounded by the cryptic markings, drawings, and letters. "What is this?"

"The night we met at the Temple, I was walking in the palace when I heard someone in the library. It was very late, so I went to investigate. When I opened the door, I saw a flash of light and a cracking sound, like... like..."

"Lightning?" As she spoke, she immediately dropped the tome beside his satchel as though it had grown teeth and bitten her. A cloud of dust filled the air when it hit the table.

"Yes, exactly."

"Go on," she urged, shaking her revulsion.

"Whoever was there disappeared, not escaped, but just... vanished," he finished. "They left this book behind. It was covered in this... cold, white flame. When I reached for the book, the flame died out."

Her nostrils flared, and she took another step away from the book.

"There were... rumors about your family," he continued carefully. "People said their power was not limited to the throne— that they used dark magic."

She began to pace. "Magic isn't real. It's not."

"What I saw was real. And I know you have seen this before. I can see it in your eyes."

She squeezed those eyes shut. Could it be the same lightning that killed her parents? A mournful silence hung in the air before she suddenly exclaimed, "The king! It has to be! His father killed them to take the throne for himself."

"King Lyulf was in Yael when your parents died. It couldn't have been him."

"So says *history*..."

"I thought it was you," he admitted. She glanced back his way. "In the palace, with the book. I thought you had come after me, after the Temple."

She snorted. "A pirate and a princess is enough for one woman to be, don't you think? Adding *witch* to that list would be excessive."

"Clearly, I was wrong."

"If it *was* me," she reasoned, "it would have been very stupid to come here alone with only a single gun at your side."

"Someone took my other pistol."

"What about the king? What does he have to say about all this?"

"In short, he… doesn't believe me." He sighed. "He wants evidence."

"What? This wasn't enough?" She gestured to the book.

"Apparently not."

"What if I say no?"

"Don't you want to know the truth about the lightning?"

Yes, of course she did. But would the rewards of letting Dillon Whyte go again outweigh the risks?

"That didn't answer my question," she pressed. "Will you expose me if I refuse?"

"Well," he said frankly. "It wouldn't benefit me at all to say yes while I'm completely at your mercy. I suppose you'll just have to trust me."

Chapter 11

Mapping the Course
15th of Regnsfall, 1723
The Black Barricade

Liana woke the morning after her engagement party cold, alone, and with a splitting headache. Ameen had left the scent of spiced lather in his wake. There was no telling when he would be back. She wasn't sure if she was ready for him to return quite yet, anyway. But she found the wait more agonizing than the band of pain around her head. Rain pounded against the window, and she wondered if he was caught in the downpour. Thoughts washed in and out of her head. She drifted like weightless flotsam in the open sea.

Ameen would be back. They would talk. It was alright that he knew who she was—good, even. Her secret was safe with him. But was *Ameen* safe? What was taking him so long? What if Whyte had betrayed her? What if he'd had Ameen arrested? Would they come for her next?

Thunder tumbled in the distance, rattling her brain. She dragged air into her lungs and shot upright—

No. She wasn't going to go there.

After pathetically crawling out of bed, she dressed herself and went downstairs to persuade a late breakfast from Bess. Seeing Marin alone reading a newspaper, Liana took a seat beside him at their favorite table.

"Thanks," she croaked when Bess brought her a plate of toast and soft eggs.

"Ameen left quite early," said Marin absently.

"He knows," she said before taking a slow bite of toast.

The old sailor put down his paper and looked at her from above the wiry spectacles he used for reading. "Ya told 'im? When?"

"Last night," she mumbled, raising a glass of what she thought was water. Once she got a whiff, she gagged. "Bloody hell, Bess!"

"It's vinegar!" she called from across the taproom while serving another table. "For your stomach. Try sipping it."

After another suspicious sniff, Liana managed a little taste. The burn of vinegar pooled in her stomach and after a moment, it began to settle. She shuddered before turning her attention back to Marin.

"Well? What did he say?" he pressed.

"Nothing. We haven't had the chance to discuss it. But you were right. He deserved to know."

"I'm proud of ya, lass," he said, removing his spectacles.

"I just hope he's alright."

He narrowed his eyes, lengthening his crow's feet. "And why wouldn't he be?"

She shrugged, unwilling to speak her worries for fear they might come true.

"He's likely takin' time tah himself."

Liana lowered her voice. "Marin, the Commander of the King's Guard was here last night."

"And ya let 'im go."

"Exactly. *Again.* Blast it! What was I thinking?" she said, rubbing her eye, where the center of her headache pulsated. "I should have just…"

"Killed him? It's not in yer nature," he said, waving dismissively.

Marin, no matter how well he knew her, would never truly understand. He didn't know about the sleepless nights she spent as a child, convinced someone would come for her. When Leda would try to coax her to sleep, Liana would throw fitful tantrums. She never said it aloud, but it was all for fear that Marin and Leda would be slain in the night, just like her parents. She still worried for Marin sometimes, wondering when the decision to take in two stowaway children would finally catch up to him.

He returned to his paper, leaning back in his chair. "I'm only sayin' that Ameen has a right tah be angry."

"I know that."

Bess returned then, taking a momentary break to join them at the table. "Need anything else?"

"No, thanks." Liana picked up a fork to tuck into her eggs but couldn't stop her hand from trembling. Feeling Bess' eyes on the shaking utensil, she immediately dropped it.

"Why don't you go lie down?" Bess gently suggested.

Liana's chest ached, and she pressed on her heart. She exhaled shakily, smoothing out her skirt. "No. No. I'm going to go look for Ameen—make sure he comes back safely."

Liana stood abruptly. Ignoring her friend's skeptic gaze, she made way for the door, nearly colliding with the tall Islander who entered.

"I have another question."

"Of course."

"How... exactly did you escape the palace?"

Liana sighed heavily. Back to the beginning it was, then. They had already spoken for over an hour. "That's a question for Ivan. I told you, I don't really remember that night."

"I'm sorry, it's just..." Ameen looked at his hands, clasped between his knees as he sat on the bed beside her. "It's just all so..."

"I know."

"And do you really believe Whyte? That he witnessed this— this magic?"

"I do," she told him and went to fetch the satchel. Handing him the tome, she returned to the bed. "The cover is burned, but nothing on the inside is damaged. And he described the same lightning that I saw."

"He might have known about it—it seems he *has* done his research on you."

"He didn't seem like he was lying. I'm not saying he's trustworthy, but... this could be the same person who killed my parents. I should follow through on this."

"You're right. Not to mention, Whyte could expose you if we don't help him," he added. *We.* Despite the dangerous implications of what he said, relief washed over her.

"Exactly."

He didn't look up from the book. In fact, if she didn't know better, she could have sworn he was reading the strange markings. He pressed his lips together, a sign he was deep in thought. As he leaned forward to get a closer look, his Circle of the Divine shimmered in the sunlight through the window. A reflective spark came off of the simple three-lined inscription at the top of the circle.

"I've seen this before." He tapped his finger on one of the pages. "These symbols—they're Savarran."

"What?" She peered over the cover. "But Savarran uses the same alphabet as Caerwyn."

"Not always," he said. "I remember seeing some of these figures in shops and at the docks in Savarre. They use it like shorthand. Let me take the book to Thiago. He would be the most likely to be able to translate it."

"Brilliant," she agreed. She spent the lull of silence watching him run a finger over the spine of the book, likely trying to guess how old it was. "Thank you. I know this isn't easy to come to terms with. I've spent my life hiding this part of myself. It's... a relief to share it with you. I'm sorry I didn't tell you sooner. I—"

"Liana, breathe," he said, and she realized she was indeed winded. He gently closed the book. Something in his slow movements calmed her. She felt the pull to match her temperament with his. If she was a stout glass of rum, then he was the chaser to balance out the burn.

"I think I've always known. Not this, exactly, but... You've always been closed off about your past."

"Can you forgive me?"

"Of course. Liana, you know you are everything to me."

"And you are to me," she murmured in reply. But he shook his head.

"It's not the same."

"Ameen..." she said, a little stung, but he gently raised his hand and placed it on hers.

"When we met, I had nothing. I had just lost my father in that storm... But you, Ivan, and Marin brought me into your family. If I had never met you, I would still be working at the docks, scraping up enough money to live. I would still be alone."

She interrupted. "Without you I wouldn't be alone, but I still wouldn't be where I am. You gave me the confidence to realize my dream of sailing. Remember when I would dress like a boy and go with you to work at the docks so I could learn about the ships?"

He nodded and turned her palm over in his, lamenting, "Your poor hands."

"That's right," she recalled. "They were covered in blisters, always cracked and bleeding from the ropes. You would soak and bandage them, so I could cover them with gloves and hide them from my brother. It's funny... I think I fell in love with you over a bowl of hot saltwater."

"Ours is a love story for the ages."

She laughed.

"We've always worked well together. This—learning about your past—won't change that."

"Do you really mean that?"

"All morning, I thought about how what you told me would change things between us," he said. "But I realized *nothing* had changed. You're still the woman who would give her last coin to a friend in need. You're still the bravest person I've ever known. You're still the woman I love. Nothing will change that."

She threw her arms around him. "I was so worried."

"That I wouldn't want to marry you anymore?"

"Yes, and… I thought something had happened to you," she admitted. "Someone killed my parents. Now Whyte shows up and says someone is using the same power again. I can't rest until I stop them."

And make them pay for what they did.

"I'll help you," he murmured into her hair. "We'll do this together."

PART TWO

A Warrior of the Divine, she had a Dignity most Men would never know. She had faced the Creature and stood with Strength over its defeat. And it was not the first, nor the last Battle she would fight.

Petronella had known defeat in her life, but never did she take Revenge. She was among the most Favored of the Divine and knew His Wrath always would be brought down upon her Enemies.

— Scroll of Petronella the Warrior,
The Book of the Divine

Chapter 12

A Gilded Cage

16th of Regnsfall, 1723
The Royal Palace

Breakfast was Princess Rhian's favorite meal. She liked to slather her toast in the egg yolk, accompanied with butter and a few shakes of pepper. But now, the sight of the yellow spheroid jiggling in the center of the white, half-cooked albumen made her gag.

She composed herself until the maid left her apartments before retching over the—thankfully clean—chamber pot. The efforts only produced acidic bile. Wiping the corners of her mouth, she swallowed thickly and nibbled on the corner of her triangular cut toast without butter.

As difficult as it was, Rhian needed to keep her maids from seeing her vomit every morning. She couldn't be found out. The Divine had blessed Rhian with a voluptuous figure, so her body wouldn't betray her as soon as a thinner woman's would. Still, she had to be careful. If the palace servants had any inkling of her condition, the rumor would spread like a wildfire.

Pressing her plate aside, she rose to greet the day. Her uncle and cousin arrived late last night from Yael to celebrate her birthday. The occasion would be marked by a ball in a week's time, but today began her twenty-first year. When bringing in her breakfast, the maid had informed her the king wished for her to join him in a conference with Commander Whyte in the chantry. Rhian hastily called the maid back through a bell attached to cords strung throughout the grand apartments to help her dress.

Thirty minutes later, Rhian arrived hastily to the oblong hall where her brother's court presided each morning. As a female member of the royal family, she took her designated seat in the balcony to watch the proceedings. When she became old enough to attend a few years ago, she brought an inkwell and notepad to scrawl on. Now, she took everything in with her eyes and ears, soaking in the droning aristocrats that most would find tediously dull. Though no one spoke of it, Rhian's brother, King Lyell, unmarried and childless, didn't have a successor. Rhian took her role as the heir apparent to Caerwyn's throne earnestly. Of course, the expectation that Lyell would eventually have an heir constantly crossed her mind. But still, Rhian hated the thought of being thrust onto the throne unprepared if the occasion were to arise.

Every so often, Rhian peered over the bannister at Commander Whyte, seated at Lyell's right hand, hoping to catch his eye. Ever the soldier, he sat diligently and never looked her way. It wasn't surprising. Their relationship couldn't be revealed. Not yet.

After court, Rhian stood to descend from the balcony using a private staircase, but crossed paths with her cousin, Aliah.

"Your Highness," came his teasing voice. She prodded him playfully before he embraced her. "Happy birthday, dearest."

"I'm so happy you're here," she said, squeezing him back before taking a good look at his slim form. His white-blond hair, neatly pulled back in a blue ribbon, fell between his shoulders. Dressed impeccably in his soldier's uniform, he looked just as glad as she was. Often, she wished Aliah was her real brother and not Lyell. She hated that they lived in Yael and not in the Capital. They joined arms, and he led her to the stairs.

"What shall we do? I absolutely forbid you to hide out in that library on your birthday."

"The library has been closed due to a possible breach in the palace," she mumbled.

"Too wet for the Garden, too... Hmm, which is your favorite salon? We'll drink wine and you can tell me all about... well, whatever little *project* you've got going at the moment." While her Uncle Grigor had fostered her skills and intelligence, Aliah always encouraged her to seek new experiences, even with the limitations of her status.

"The word I believe you're looking for is 'experiment,' Aliah."

He shrugged.

"The king wants me to join him in a conference with the Commander," she said. It took effort to contain her excitement. Perhaps Dillon had finally gathered enough favor from the king to ask for her hand. There was no time to waste about it, she thought, recalling her overturned breakfast.

"About the breach?"

"I doubt it," Rhian said, looking away to cover her deepening blush. "It probably has something to do with the ball."

"When do you meet them?"

"Now."

Aliah escorted her to a meeting room adjacent to the chantry, where they found Dillon waiting alone. He stood and bowed at their entrance.

"Your Highness. I hope you have enjoyed your birthday so far."

Her heart fluttered. "Thank you, Commander."

Aliah stepped forward, clearly irritated by the lack of greeting. "Good to see you too, Whyte."

Dillon chuckled, shaking Aliah's hand. The two men had known each other since before their training days. Both soldiers and sons of earls, their similarities ended at their commissioning oath. While Dillon rose to become the Commander of the King's Guard, Aliah took a post in Yael that would allow him to remain at the castle there. He would eventually inherit Yael Province from his father. His position in the military provided him additional education, but not by much. He hardly took the duty seriously, and no one in command expected much from him. She suspected he only accepted the commission to wear the dashing uniform.

The king entered unceremoniously, sweeping an apathetic gaze over them all. A silver pin on his jacket of an ouroboros, the Vitalis insignia, glinted as he stepped forward. "Let's make this quick, Commander. I have an hour to eat before my meeting with the Tsarina's ambassador."

"Of course, Your Majesty," Dillon stammered as he bowed. Rhian, in turn, curtsied and waited for her brother to take a seat. She caught eyes with Aliah as he slithered out of the room, hardly noticed by the king. "As you know, I have had many concerns about the security of the palace, especially as the ball approaches."

Beneath the table, Rhian clenched her hands, wondering why she had not heard of these concerns before that very moment. After all, the ball would be held in her honor. Her face must have betrayed her emotions, because he glanced at her and visibly swallowed.

"Flickering lights are no security concern, Commander," Lyell huffed.

"The safety of the royal family is my priority, Your Majesty," he continued. "With all due respect, I have an unorthodox proposal."

Her stomach flipped. She knew Dillon had witnessed the flash of her library getaway. But she never expected him to be so persistent.

Lyell's weak chin tucked in, and his pale brows raised. "Unorthodox? Coming from *you*, Commander? I must hear this out."

"I have a contact who could be persuaded to watch over the princess during the ball."

"Don't you and your men already have that covered?"

"My contact is a woman."

"Who?" Rhian interrupted, causing the men's gazes to snap to her.

Lyell's attention passed over her fleetingly. "Indeed. What woman would have the skills that would surpass your soldiers, Commander?"

"Her name is Liana Foley," said Dillon. "She is the captain of a private ship. Her combative skills are impressive, given her sex. She is articulate enough to blend with the guests at the ball. No one who would threaten the princess would look twice at her. And if anything were to happen, I'm confident she would be able to stop it just as well as any soldier."

The king looked more amused than reassured. "She's a commoner?"

Rhian noted the slight hesitation in Dillon's answer. "Yes, Your Majesty."

With a passive shrug and wave of his hand, Lyell stood. So did Rhian and Dillon simultaneously. "I suppose there is no reason not to be too careful. If you trust her, Commander, then so do I. Besides, I'd like to meet this Foley woman. She sounds… fascinating. Is she married?"

"No, b--"

King Lyell laughed, cutting him short. "Commander Whyte, if you simply wanted to court this woman at the ball, then by all means, extend the invitation."

"Your Majesty, I have no such intentions--"

Wiping his eye, the king interrupted again. "Was that all?"

"Yes, Your Majesty."

"Very well." He took his leave, just as abrupt as his entrance. "I look forward to meeting this… Liana Foley."

Silence hung thick in the air after Lyell's departure. Rhian didn't often find herself alone with Dillon in the daylight hours. She held herself high, looking squarely at him. "As do I, Commander."

"Rhian," he began, dropping all sense of formality. "Please, trust me. Something strange is happening in the palace. Something dark and wrong."

It's me, she wanted to tell him. *I'm what's wrong.*

"I thought…" she said, then faltered. "I thought you would have asked him by now. If he trusts you enough to let some *common* woman into the palace, then he should trust you with my hand."

He fell silent. She wanted to scream at him. *Time is running out.* Her pregnancy would begin to show soon. If they were going to marry, it needed to be before then. But he had no idea of the urgency. She hadn't told him. Given his hesitation, she realized it was probably for the best. She would have to take care of this herself, just like everything else.

"Do not come to see me again," she hissed. His hazel eyes bulged, and his posture straightened. He was not expecting this reaction. "I'm finished waiting for you."

"Don't do this, Rhian," he begged as she turned away. "I will marry you. But this *thing*—whatever I saw in the library is a threat. If I could solve it, I would be able to gain enough favor from the king to—"

She restrained her emotions at the risk of choking on her own tears. Keeping her eyes ahead, she threw open the door and crossed the threshold into the chapel, leaving the commander in her wake.

After sweeping through the palace like a storm, she took shelter in her apartments. Gripping her vanity, she finally allowed herself to cry. She wished she had never stayed in the library so late. Now Dillon had the grimoire. She lost it, just like she lost him and her hopes for the future.

In an effort to calm herself down, she fumbled around her drawers for her puzzle-box, a mechanical distraction she made herself. But the moment she became frustrated with a piece, her fury spiked. The smell of rain wafted in the air and the puzzle-box split in her hands, as a bolt surged through her fingertips. She immediately dropped the charred pieces of wood with a yowl of terror. Standing over them, with little surprise but deep disappointment, a single thought persisted.

It's me.

I'm what's wrong.

Chapter 13

By Royal Invitation
22nd of Regnsfall, 1723
The Black Barricade

Liana stopped in front of the door to pluck a stray thread from the front of Ameen's coat when Marin barreled into the Barricade, nearly knocking them over. He clutched an open letter in his right hand and had a rather large but clearly light box tucked under his left arm. He stopped short and looked at her, a wild grin lifting his face.

"I'm going tah be a grandfather!"

"Nellie's pregnant?" Liana gasped, righting herself. "Marin, that's wonderful news."

"Isn't it? First the two of ya are tah be married and now…" His eyes shimmered with pride as he paused to fill his lungs with a joyful breath. "Everything is right."

"Congratulations, Marin," Ameen said. He likely would have shaken his hand had they not been full with the letters and the box. Instead, he gave Marin a beaming smile, and the older man returned it with gusto.

"Thank ya, laddie."

"You have to go to see her," Liana insisted. "How far along is she?"

"Just a few months," he said.

"Will you go see her?"

"I'd like to, but with our *visitor* last Mass Day, I think ye'll need me around."

"Nonsense. Marin, please don't worry about that." She shook her head. "Ameen and I were about to leave to see about the book. We'll have this solved in no time."

"Ah, before ya go," Marin adjusted his arms and handed Liana the box lined in white satin with a matching ribbon to keep it closed. "This came for ye."

She set it on the nearest table to examine it. Indeed, it was meant for her— she ran a finger along the thick, rectangular card attached with her name written in beautiful black calligraphy.

Miss Liana Foley.

She found the Barricade's address below it. Grumbling the word "captain," she flipped the parchment over and saw a semi-familiar logo—a golden lily, the brand of a well-known dressmaker who had a two-story shop near the palace.

"Did ya order a wedding gown already?" Marin asked. Ameen looked up sharply.

"No." Liana raised a brow as she pulled at the ribbon. "And if I had, it would be from Mistress Claycox."

Liana lifted the lid of the box and thought there had been some sort of mistake. The bodice of the dress glimmered as she pulled it out. She felt Ameen step closer behind her.

"Did you send this?" she accused.

"No," Ameen elongated the word, suspiciously eyeing the deep purple gown. He picked up another, larger rectangular parchment that had fallen out of the box when she had taken out the gown. He let out a grunt of disbelief, rolled his eyes, and handed it to her. Marin peered over her shoulder as she read it

His Majesty King Lyell Duarte Vitalis requests the attendance of Miss Liana Foley at the Royal Palace in celebration of the Debut Ball of Her Royal Highness Princess Rhian Ceres Vitalis on the 27th of Regnsfall at Six O'Clock in the Evening

Thiago lived in an old mansion converted into several small townhomes in a quiet corner between the rich districts near the palace and the poor quarters by the docks. A small courtyard boasted a birdbath and garden the tenants shared responsibility over. Thiago's small section was very green, filled with aromatic herbs and spices with dual uses in healing and cooking.

Ameen muttered something under his breath as they approached the gate.

"For the thousandth time," she snapped, "I did not ask for the bloody gown."

"It's not about the gown."

"Well then what is it about? Because all you've done the whole way here is mumble."

He only sighed in response.

"If you're upset about something, then just say it. It won't help either of us if you clam up."

"You're one to talk about clamming up," he said barely audible.

"*Excuse* me?" Liana veered in front of Ameen before he could enter the garden.

"How long has Whyte known about you?"

"I… I don't know. He didn't say, exactly. Is that what's bothering you? That he knew about my past and you didn't?"

He looked away.

"Ameen. I never wanted *anyone* to know."

"Right. Not even me."

She reached out, and he allowed her to take his hand. "If it's any consolation, you're the first person I've ever told—willingly, that is. Granted, it was under considerable pressure, but…"

"It's just…" he began, folding her hand in his and keeping his gaze down at where they touched. "Now that I do know, it feels like there's this other side of you I've never been able to see before. And Whyte, the gown, the ball. I feel… I don't know. It's a lot to take in."

"It is," she agreed, a little hurt. "I can't expect you to accept this all at once. It's not fair. I've had a lifetime to come to terms with this, but you've had three days."

"Thank you for saying that," he said, a bit surprised despite clear efforts for her to think otherwise.

"I just hope you can be patient with me while I deal with this."

"*We*," he corrected, breaking into a warm smile. "We're in this together, remember?"

She followed him through the old creaky gate and over the brick path that led to the Venegas' home. Thiago answered the door and greeted Ameen in Savarran. They spent a moment in quick conversation before Thiago spotted Liana by the garden.

"Captain," Thiago said to her in his heavy Savarran accent as he finally peered around Ameen. He extended his hand to her as Ameen stepped inside.

"Hello, Thiago." Liana smiled, despite the lingering thoughts of the invitation. She shook his hand. "How are the girls?"

"Today, Camila take Lucia to Signora Claycox for fitting." Thiago told Liana. He made his hand flat and raised it high, indicating Lucia had grown again. "She wants me to tell you she is happy for your engagement."

The narrow entranceway of the Venegas' quaint home welcomed them with oil paintings of flowers. One by one, they turned to enter the dining room, where the book laid open. Several papers rested beside it, where Thiago had made some notes.

"Thank you for looking this over," Ameen said as they each took a seat in the cushioned dining chairs. Thiago sat at the head of the table, while Liana and Ameen sat on either side of him. "What do you make of it?"

Liana watched Thiago's expression change from pleasant to worrisome. "This is... troubling."

"Were you able to translate it?" she asked.

Thiago opened the book and made a strained sound of uncertainty, his long deft fingers running over the strange symbols. "Not Savarran. Not exactly. Very old language of the people of the mountains."

"The Highlanders?" Liana questioned, envisioning the map she had in her room at the Barricade.

"The ancients of the Cross Peak. Where life began."

"Until the mountains turned cold, then people spread and made civilization in the lower lands," Ameen finished.

"So, the legends say."

"Legends that might have made sense before the discovery of the Islands," Liana frowned, leaning back in her chair. She moved on when Ameen gave her a tense look, in no mood to debate the Book of the Divine with her. "So why would there be a book full of a dead language in the palace library?"

"A mystery, to be sure," said Thiago. "In Savarre, we use it some."

Liana leaned over to see better as Thiago showed them. He pointed to one symbol with swirling lines. "Water."

His finger stopped at another marking with lines pointing up like a tree. "Life."

Then, he turned to the back of the book, where there were more illustrations of strange creatures. Liana hardly had a chance to look through the tome before she had given it to Ameen, and she was unnerved to see how sinister they looked. Thiago paused on a pictorial of a flying reptilian beast, its wings spread out as it ascended and its tail coiled in a circle.

"Death," said Thiago, showing them a symbol that looked like two jagged lines crossing—like lightning.

"From what he could tell, the book read like instructions. We can only assume it was some type of spell book."

Liana waited for Whyte's reaction as she recounted what they learned. Again, they met at the old Temple of the Divine. This time, Ameen came with her. He stood near the broken altar, a considerable distance away from Whyte.

"Someone has brought something evil into the palace. I'm afraid they mean to do Princess Rhian harm."

"Why her?" asked Ameen from afar.

"Who else?" Whyte twisted so his arm rested on the back of the pew. He chewed his thumbnail nervously. "It's her ball everyone is coming to the Capital for."

"Is that why you sent me the dress and invitation?" Liana cut in.

He paused in his nail biting to give her a small, guilty smile.

"We haven't the time to solve this before the ball," he said, "And the king won't allow me to cancel it. He doesn't believe me about the book."

"He wouldn't even listen?"

"No. This ball is very important, politically," Whyte explained, looking at his hands again. "He wants to find a husband for the princess."

"And so, you want Liana to go to the ball, at the Royal Palace, knowing what you know about her?" Ameen glowered down at him. "You're sending her to her death."

"No one will ever know," he assured him, getting to his own feet. "I swear it."

Again, Liana forced herself between them, physically this time. "You have no idea how dangerous this is for me, Whyte."

"I do, but I wouldn't ask you to do it unless it was necessary."

She crossed her arms, rolling her eyes.

"Think of Princess Rhian."

"Why should I care about her? What is she to me?"

"What if an attack is planned, like the one you survived as a child?"

She looked down at the rubble on the floor, kicking her boot around. Behind her, Ameen sighed. She caught his glance, and he waved his arm.

"As much as I hate to admit this," he said, "He's right."

"You're joking."

"The princess is innocent. We don't let innocent people get hurt."

Liana wanted to tell him she didn't care at all about the princess, but she had to agree with him. Princess Rhian hadn't even been alive when Liana's father was overthrown. Just because she was the daughter of the man who had replaced King Sergus didn't mean she was Liana's enemy.

"The ball is in a week. I'll need to make preparations—get my crew ready in case I need an escape."

"Is that enough time?"

"It should be to gather a skeleton crew." She nodded. "No need to involve more of my men than necessary."

"Good. We shouldn't need to meet again until the ball. I'll have a carriage come to you."

They all walked out together, but Liana paused at the doors, partway into the cold night, allowing the men a step ahead.

"Whyte."

He turned; his face indiscernible in the dark.

"I need your word," she told him. "After this is over, you'll leave me be."

Liana was not surprised to see him hesitate. After all, having a pirate captain and her crew under his thumb could prove very useful to the commander. What did surprise her, however, was the fact that he held out his hand. Watching him, Ameen took a wider stance but remained silent. She allowed Whyte to gently lift her right palm.

"On my honor," he swore gallantly. He delicately turned her hand so her knuckles faced upward. For a moment, she thought he might kiss her fingers, and she nearly recoiled. But he simply bowed his head, a strand of loosely tied honey hair falling over his eye and the bridge of his straight nose. "You have my word."

"We'll believe it when we see it," Ameen said, his mouth curving in disdain as he looked at Whtye. He crossed his arms over his chest. Liana thought perhaps it was to prevent himself from giving the Commander another good wallop to the face.

She tugged her hand back and pressed Ameen away from the temple doors. "Come on. We've got work to do."

Chapter 14

Strangely Like Coming Home
27th of Regnsfall, 1723
The Black Barricade

Ava Claycox's green eyes went round as she took a peek inside the envelope Liana passed to her. "Captain Foley, please. This is too much! It's twice what I ask for alterations! You must take some back."

"After all the work you've done to this dress in such a short time? Absolutely not!" Liana took another glance at herself in the small vanity, adjusting to get a better view of the gown. With a heaving breath, she straightened her back, pressing her hand against the jeweled bodice. As she turned, the lines of moonstones reflected a white and gold shimmer that complimented the plum fabric. "I know you're very busy. I wanted to make this worth your time."

"It's gorgeous," Bess sighed from the desk. Beatrix had insisted on watching the lengthy process of Bess combing Liana's tresses out and gathering them up fashionably in pins. Liana had agreed so long as she stayed put on the bed. She had a similarly dreamy look as her mother, holding her cheeks in her hands as she echoed the sigh.

Liana inwardly admitted she was right. She adjusted the smooth three-quarter sleeves of silk. In lieu of jewelry, she wore a sheer white ribbon around her neck. It was Bess' suggestion. "I would have preferred a Claycox original."

Mistress Claycox dimpled, bashfully tucking a loose strand of warm ginger hair behind her ear. Liana always purchased her clothes from Claycox's shop. She would even pay extra to make her dresses more comfortable and practical, with pockets and all.

"You may make up for it by coming to the shop to design your wedding gown next week," she said with a hopeful gleam in her eyes.

"I'll make an appointment tomorrow," Liana promised. "Speaking of which, have either of you seen my fiancé?"

"I believe he was dining with Sebastian," Bess said, moving to her feet and waving at Beatrix to do the same. They closed the dining room for the evening so Liana could exit the Barricade in the ball gown without the curious eyes of the usual patrons. The rest of the crew was with Marin, preparing the ship in the event Liana needed a hasty departure. "I should probably go take my son off his hands. I'll send him up."

With the sudden absence of warm bodies from the room, she felt a chill from the open window. She shut it and tapped her chin in thought. The neckline of her gown was modest, but the shoulders tapered outwards. Liana thought the ball would likely be indoors, but she should take her black velvet cloak for the trip. She opened the wardrobe to fish it out as the door opened.

"The ball starts in less than an hour," she said distractedly. She closed the wardrobe and folded the cloak over her arm. "So, the carriage should be here soon."

She looked up to see Ameen stood absolutely still. His eyes held a heartwarming blend of shock and pride. He had never seen her this way before—with rouge on her cheeks, baubles in her ears, and an iridescent gown layered over a tightly laced corset. The last time she had worn anything like it was at Nellie's wedding, which Ameen hadn't attended.

Liana left her cloak on the desk, held out her skirt and playfully curtsied. "A little different from my usual attire."

"You are beautiful," he said with the utmost sincerity and cracked a wry smile. "And the dress doesn't do any harm to that. Though it could have come from a better source."

"Too right," she agreed, running a hand over her bodice. "This all seems so… frivolous. I still don't think this is going to help us find out what happened to my parents."

"Maybe not. But the Divine wouldn't have led us here if it wasn't for a good reason."

She crossed her arms and ran her tongue along her teeth to stem off a rebuttal. The Divine had nothing to do with it, she was sure. But snapping at Ameen wouldn't help, especially over his religious beliefs. He chuckled, knowing her body language too well.

"I don't like this, either," he admitted, looking at the floor. "But if anyone can protect the princess from this magic, it's you."

"Speaking of *magic*," she said, nearly choking on the word, "I want you to take that book down to the ship when you go. In case anything happens. Keep it locked in the cabin."

"Of course."

"The carriage is here," said Bess' voice through the door. Ameen's gaze flicked up, and she could see the dread in his eyes, despite his confidence in her. She felt it too, pooling deep and hot in her chest.

"Ameen," she sighed, reaching out her hand. He took it in both of his.

"Yes?"

"Walk with me?" She tried not to sound pleading and was mildly successful. "These shoes are a little tall."

With a lopsided smile, Ameen helped her fasten her cloak, extended his arm, and led her out of the room. When they got to the stairs, she clutched him tighter.

"Don't let me fall," she whispered, trying to keep her breath slow.

"Never."

He kissed her hard enough to take her breath away before helping her into the carriage. She watched him standing in the road pressing his Circle of the Divine to his lips until the last possible moment. Though she managed to steel herself en route to the ball, the comfort Liana had with Ameen slowly faded.

Fortunately, the driver proved to be an exceptionally polite man. After assisting her from the velvet safety of the carriage, he escorted her up the stone steps that led to the courtyard. Giving her a kindly bow, he bid her good evening and promised to return for her when she was ready. As he left, she looked to the clear black sky. She wondered where all the carriage drivers would be during the ball, but the thought dissipated when she turned to the palace's expansive courtyard.

The air hung thick with the flowery fragrances of ladies' perfumes. Liana felt out of place, standing stark in deep purple while most of the other women wore gowns of light pastel colors. A gaggle of them passed by, and Liana politely stepped aside to let them around her as she took in the sights. One of their silken dresses brushed against hers with a rush of fabric. A woman with hair the color of burnt sienna glanced back at her. As Liana smiled in apology, the woman tucked her bottom lip between white teeth and lingered, just to look at her a second longer. Her heart leapt at the fleeting moment of attraction. The music coming from the palace called the women away, and she vanished in the shimmering sea of people, like a crafty siren diving beneath the waves. The floating particles of white powder they left behind invaded her senses. She sniffed to keep her nose from dripping.

As she went along, a familiar smell hit her. Her brain jolted with memory.

"Cat piss," she said under her breath, as several laughing guests passed by her. The hedges, she remembered, smelled like cat piss, or something like it. A cloudy image formed in her mind's eye, depicting rays of sunshine seeping through green leaves, the bodily memory of small branches scratching her skin and the resounding melody of a child's laughter. Was it her own?

The crowd moved along, and someone else brushed against her, snapping her back into the present. She pressed on, hitching her skirt as she followed the stream. Wiggling her nose, she resisted the urge to sneeze and wished she had brought a handkerchief.

Whyte emerged from one of the doors that led into the palace, likely his own apartments, out onto the courtyard. The glint of his jacket caught her eye through the masses. He wore his dress uniform made from deep blue wool with silver leaf embroidery along the seams. It matched the polished medals and

111

buttons running in two neatly aligned rows along the front of his jacket. His hair was combed and tied back with a ribbon. Liana never thought she would be relieved to see him. As she pushed her way to him, he surveyed the crowd and rubbed his freshly shaved cheek. His hand paused over his lips, and his fingers twitched uneasily.

"Whyte!" she called as he started into the courtyard, away from her. When he disappeared, she mumbled a curse. He could not hear her over the buzzing conversation. She chased after him.

The foyer sprawled with pristine white marble floors. Bronze statues of Holy Guardians lined the walls—armored warriors and serenely robed wisemen. Some held spears and swords, while others carried large tomes. All watched the foyer with metallic eyes, smooth and without pupils. She paused at one she knew immediately. Petronella, the She-Warrior of the Divine. Poised with a sword and sporting full armor, she stood between Gereon the Wise and Sanctius the Fearless.

Glancing about, Liana noticed King Evanderus was missing from the row of Guardians. She wasn't surprised. Evanderus was, according to the Book of the Divine, the first king of Caerwyn and the first Romenel. Legend had it that he gathered an army to defeat frightening but ambiguously described Creatures from overtaking Vioria. Children's stories, Liana had always thought. She doubted a man named Evanderus Romenel ever actually lived.

Liana turned away from the statues. At the base of the grand staircase, she caught sight of a dark blue jacket. "Whyte!"

She finally reached him and placed a hand on his arm to get his attention. He turned around, and her cheeks burned hot as she realized she had the wrong blond man. His features were angular,

112

and he had full lips. His face held nothing exceptional—except for his eyes. They reminded her of the time she and Ivan had been traversing the market, back when they lived in Madzetal. There had been a small crowd forming around the sight of a shark hanging by its tail. She could have felt sorry for the creature if she had not been so frightened of its cold black eyes, robbed of life.

The man before her smiled thinly. "Pardon me?"

She took a step back. "I'm sorry. I thought you were someone else."

"Perhaps I can assist you," he said, his voice polite. But those eyes—the way they narrowed at her made her skin crawl. "Who are you looking for?"

"Commander Dillon Whyte."

He tilted his head. "You wouldn't be Miss Liana Foley, would you?"

She felt hot under her cloak, and she fiddled with the fastenings to loosen it. "I am."

He held up his hand to the side and snapped his fingers a couple of times to get an attendant's notice. The pretentious gesture made her nose wrinkle. The attendant, nevertheless, answered the call, demurely holding his arm out for her cloak.

"Thank you," she said to the attendant, giving him the most pleasant smile she could muster with the soldier watching her.

"It's a pleasure to finally meet the mysterious woman Dillon has been talking about," he said, giving her a nod of greeting. "I am Aliah Vitalis."

"Vitalis? You're related to the king?"

"His first cousin, to be exact."

"Whyte has told you about me?"

"Don't worry, Miss Foley." His smile widened, as though relishing in her discomfort. "He didn't divulge intimate details. I do know you are a ship captain. What a rare position for a woman to hold. You must have quite the story."

"I've been assisting Commander Whyte with... security."

"So, I was told."

"And... what *else* were you told?"

Before he could answer, Aliah's focus changed to someone approaching her from behind. Liana looked over her shoulder to see Whyte. Their eyes met, and the commander breathed a visible sigh of relief.

"Dillon, there you are!" Aliah waved in an overly cheerful manner that was less than sincere. "I was keeping the lovely Miss Foley entertained for you."

"Thank you, Aliah," Whyte replied tartly, hovering at Liana's back. "I believe I saw your father go into the ballroom. I'm sure he will be wanting to know what kept you."

"And I shall tell him that I was occupying your guest while you were galivanting the courtyard."

"So be it. We'll see you upstairs."

Aliah looked to Liana now and took her hand before she could do anything about it. He kissed it lightly, and she winced. "You intrigue me, Miss Foley. I beg that you save a dance for me."

She retracted her hand. "Please—it's Captain Foley."

"Oh. My sincerest apologies."

As he ascended the staircase, Liana noticed the predatory gaze he laid over a group of three young women chattering by the railing. She wiped her hand on her bodice with a grimace. "I think I've found our first suspect," she said to Whyte.

"Aliah? Oh, he's harmless, except for his nefarious reputation with women."

"Women fall for *that*?"

"The gullible ones, at least. I think it helps that he's the only son of the Earl of Yael," Whyte smiled at her, showing his teeth. "He is right about one thing, though. You do look lovely tonight."

"It must be the dress. We can at least say that Aliah Vitalis was wrong about your poor taste." She adjusted her sleeves. "What made you send this particular one?"

He paused, blushing as he looked her over. "The bodice," he said, with an awkward shrug. "It reminded me of armor."

She looked down and realized he was right. The moonstones lined up in such a way that mimicked a breast plate. "A warrior woman, like Petronella, am I? I'll have you know my sister was named after her."

"You… You have a sister?"

It comforted her a little that Dillon Whyte didn't know *quite* everything about her.

"Foster sister. Now, shouldn't we go inside? We're lagging with the stragglers."

Upon entering the ballroom, each attendee and their guests were announced with gusto. Before their turn, Liana leaned in to the thin-bearded servant who took their names. Whyte tried to lean in and hear what she said, but she spoke too low. She didn't care to explain herself.

"Commander Dillon Tristan Whyte escorting Captain Liana Foley."

Liana chuckled with pride as she walked beside him in the receiving line, just moments after they had been announced according to her specific instructions. The look on Whyte's face had been well worth the stares as they approached the throne.

"There are lords here that brought their mistresses and women with gowns tighter than an oyster with lockjaw," Whyte hissed, "And yet you are the most scandalous person at this ball."

"You're the one who made me come to this bloody thing," she whispered close to him. "I just want to make sure they have my name right."

Whyte mumbled something about it not being her real name.

"More real to me than the other one," she shot back. "Now stop being such a salty bugger. You're going to make me trip down these steps."

She set her sights ahead, preparing herself to meet the King of Caerwyn. Like his cousin, King Lyell had a plain face. His white-blonde hair laid in thin waves on his shoulders. He had dark, beady eyes that looked exceedingly bored. He wore a sash with the Vitalis ouroboros on the shoulder. His crown sat a bit tilted as he held his weak chin on a closed fist. But he straightened as Whyte bowed before him. Liana curtsied as low as she could.

"A commander and a captain," he observed. "Quite the pair you make. Wouldn't you agree, Princess Rhian?"

Liana's gaze shifted to the young woman sitting by the king's side. Princess Rhian Vitalis was an ivory-skinned maiden with large blue eyes and a face still barely clinging to the roundness of youth. She wore a gauzy pale pink gown with lilies stitched into the frothy material. Her hair was held up in a voluminous fashion, pinned with a fresh white and pink lily. Perfect spirals of golden hair rested on one shoulder. The princess did not look as enchanted with Liana as the king did. In fact, she looked as though she struggled to breathe. It was no wonder—her poor waist was squeezed in a bodice that looked twice as tight as Liana's. As flattering to her generous figure as it was, she looked miserable.

Liana found her gaze lingering on the princess, for more reasons than pity. Rhian Vitalis was breathtakingly beautiful. Her pale pink lips reminded her of a flower bud, with a deep curve at the top. The light of the chandeliers above reflected off her skin in an ethereal sort of way. If someone would have told Liana that the princess wasn't human, but some mythological being, she could have accepted it as truth. For the life of her, she couldn't take her eyes off that pretty face.

"Commander Whyte has informed me you have a very specific set of skills that would be well applied to the protection of the royal family."

It took a beat for Liana to realize the king spoke to her. Whyte coughed, accidentally catching Princess Rhian's attention instead of Liana's. The princess stared back at her, blinking curiously. She even gave her a small, polite smile.

Cursing herself a fool, Liana responded by shooting her gaze up at the glittering chandelier and forcing herself to speak. "Yes, Your Majesty."

"Then we must speak privately before the night is over."

Mortified, Liana felt Whyte tug her away as he respectfully excused them both. When they safely made their way past the receiving line to the tables, she pinched his arm as hard as she could. He hissed, offended.

"Have you been telling the whole bloody palace about me?" she growled. "Now the king wants to give me a job. What is the *matter* with you?"

"How else could I get you in here?" He rubbed his sleeve.

"And why *am* I here, exactly? You never did take the time to explain what you want me to do."

"I can't have eyes everywhere. I need you to stay close to the princess. You have the advantage of being a woman. It won't be as suspicious or inappropriate if you're hovering around her."

Liana spotted their assigned table, nearest to the king and princess, of course. "I hate you, Whyte."

"I know," he replied, pulling out a chair for her.

Being the closest familial relatives to the king, Aliah Vitalis and his father joined them.

"What a pleasant surprise that we meet again so soon," Aliah simpered. "This is my father, Earl Grigor Vitalis of Yael, presider of the Heartlands of Caerwyn."

The Earl of Yael was a stern-looking man with a thin line for a mouth and deep, dark bags under his eyes. As the earl sat down, his gaze settled on Liana, and she could have sworn he turned an ashy gray. She looked back at him, unflinching, though her stomach twisted. Had she been found out?

"Captain Liana Foley," she forced herself to say, looking the man straight in the eye.

Thankfully, the Earl cleared his throat, and a little color returned to his face. "Good evening, Captain... Commander Whyte."

"How are the Heartlands faring, my lord?" Whyte said courteously.

"Very well, now that the harvest season is over," said the earl. The Heartland region, which rested in the center of Caerwyn, provided much of the nation's food supply. "Are there any guests here from Stonehall tonight?"

118

"Unfortunately, no. My brother and his family were unwilling to make the trip with my mother being so ill."

"I am very sorry to hear that."

Liana remained quiet, having no knowledge of Whyte's family.

"Yes, that is unhappy news," Aliah chimed. "Is it quite serious?"

"I plan to make the trip to Stonehall soon to see her myself." Whyte glanced away. "Kristoff's last letter was... troubling."

Fortunately, she had dinner to distract her from Aliah's drawling voice. The sumptuous food was served in three large courses. After the white soup, venison, prawns, soft-boiled eggs, cheesecake, trifle, and two glasses of red wine, she felt overly satiated. Through the long affair, soothing music from a string quartet lulled her. Reluctantly, she started to feel more at ease.

"Earl Mercer Tecwyn and his children traveled here all the way from Iangard," Aliah said, subtly pointing his finger under his chin at another table. Mercer Tecwyn sat with his two children, a son and a daughter, who both looked on the cusp of adulthood. All three of the Tecwyns had flaming red hair, which branded them as family. "He left his new wife at home, it seems. Did you know she is an Islander?"

"I wonder why he didn't bring her along," she replied, as it seemed Aliah was waiting for her to answer.

"The whole marriage is quite scandalous," he said. "She is the first member of Caerwyn society to be an Islander—except for the Island Council, of course."

"Not that they have any *real* say in what goes on down there," she muttered, taking a sip of wine. Pulled in by her answer, he leaned forward. She went on. "I was raised in Madzetal. My brother was a scribe for a Councilman, a long time ago."

"Ah, then you must have an opinion of the secession of the Savarran Island colonies."

"Well, I'm certainly glad that Savarre allowed their colonies to secede instead of making a war of it," she answered honestly. Sailing in a sea of battling ships would have been bad for business. "Besides, how effective could governing a land that is an ocean away be? The citizens of Caerwyn's islands are deeply impoverished, and it's because they aren't able to govern themselves. I don't see any benefit of keeping the colonies other than—"

"Resources," the earl interrupted, looking cross, as though Liana had personally offended him. "King Lyell is not so foolish as King Renaldi. The agriculture alone is enough cause for war, not to mention the iron and jewel trade."

The earl's eyes raked over Liana's bodice at the shimmering white moonstones.

"It's been what—? Five years since the secession, and Savarre hasn't collapsed yet."

"It is a shame Lady Tecwyn did not come," Aliah continued, appearing appreciative that Liana's political opinions were ruffling his father's feathers. "You might have liked to speak with her, Captain Foley. From what I've heard, she played no small role in the secession's leadership."

"She sounds like someone I'd get along with. Are people so bothered by her origins?" She frowned. "If I was Earl Tecwyn, I wouldn't even have come at all."

"I believe he is petitioning the king to allow his son, Seamus, to marry Princess Rhian."

"Really?" Whyte suddenly became interested in the conversation. "Do you suppose the king will agree?"

Aliah nodded curtly. "Earl Tecwyn has established a solid diplomatic relationship with Rodina, despite Tsarina Katarina not being in favor of the most recent immigration accord. Perhaps she would be more willing to abide if she sees that alliance."

Whyte glanced at the princess, who was holding a still gaze at her untouched trifle. "Does the princess even know about the arrangement?"

"My son would do well to know when to restrain himself in political conversations." Earl Vitalis kept his eyes on his wine and took a sip. Aliah's jaw tensed as he looked at his father. "The king will tell the princess when the time is right."

"So, the princess' fate will be determined," Liana said as she followed Whyte's line of sight, "By an immigration law?"

The princess looked up, pinched with longing. She locked eyes with Whyte, and Liana felt something there. But, as quickly as the glance itself, they looked away from each other.

"Excuse me, I need some air." Whyte abruptly stood. Liana tried to shake her head very slightly so only he would notice. Unfortunately, it was too subtle. He turned away toward the high glass doors that led to the Royal Gardens.

"I'll go with you," she said. She was not going to let him leave her alone with these people.

Just then, the music swelled. The guests migrated to the center of the ballroom in pairs. The flurry from the tables blocked the way out.

"Whyte," she called. He didn't respond. She raised her voice a bit. "*Whyte.*"

He turned, then balked at someone behind her.

"Captain Foley." King Lyell floated down from his raised table to join the masses, his crown removed from his head.

Liana bowed her head and bent her knees. "Your Majesty."

"You would honor me with a dance."

It was not a question. As much as she wanted to tell him to bugger off, she allowed him to guide her into a dance. While they danced, Liana imagined all the ways she would kill Dillon Whyte after this night was over. The king interrupted her murderous thoughts.

"You must satisfy my curiosity, Captain Foley," he said, making no effort to hide his eagerness. "How is it that you came to captain your own private ship?"

Marin had once told her the best way to lie is to tell the truth—just not the *whole* truth. "I purchased the ship with my inheritance."

"And how is the business of private merchant sailing?"

"Lucrative, to say the least."

"How long have you and your crew sailed together?"

"I've had the same men at the core of my crew for nearly ten years," she said, unable to help the pride in her voice. "In fact, my fiancé is my quartermaster."

Surprise quirked his brow. "And your betrothed does not mind your position of power above him?"

"Should he?" She bristled but added a quick "Your Majesty" to the question for the sake of cordiality.

"I suppose if you are what he desires, then he should enjoy all of your novelties," he reasoned.

"It is a rare man who does not fear a woman in power."

He smirked. "You must have heard of my negotiations with the Tsarina of Rodina. She can be ruthless."

"I'm sure Your Majesty will find a solution."

"I must," he agreed as he turned her. "So, your men are loyal to you, even though you are a woman?"

Is he getting to a point? "Quite, Your Majesty. I trust them with my life."

"I wish I could say the same for myself."

"Oh?"

"I'm sure you understand, being a leader yourself, that you must be careful of who is in your circle."

"Of course."

"I trust Dillon Whyte," he continued. "He is a man who would do anything for his kingdom. And to say he speaks highly of you is an understatement."

"Strange. We haven't known each other long."

"You must have made an impression, then." He smiled. "He also tells me that you know how to protect yourself—and others."

"I am versed in combat, if that's what you mean, Your Majesty."

"One can never be too careful at sea."

"Truer words were never spoken," she agreed. "The sea can be a dangerous mistress."

"As well as those who sail upon it. Pirates are rampant in the waters of Caerwyn."

"Indeed."

"I am negotiating with Earl Tecwyn to orchestrate a marriage between Princess Rhian and his son. If it proves successful, I'll be sending her north."

"So, I have heard." She nodded. "What has the princess to say on the matter?"

He faltered, obviously having never thought of his sister's opinion on her own marriage. "Like any member of the royal family, she will take upon her duty with pride. I would like you to transport my sister to Iangard on your ship."

Liana's mouth fell open in ungraceful shock.

"You would be rewarded handsomely, I assure you."

"But why *my* ship, Your Majesty?" she managed to choke out.

"Because you are a woman and, in my experience, women have a tendency to keep an eye on one another. Men always have their own selfish agendas."

The song ended with a cadence, and the king lifted her hand. "If Commander Whyte can place his trust in you, then so can I."

"What is this about trust, Your Majesty?" Whyte cut in, opening his palm. The king graciously transferred her to Whyte.

"I await your answer, Captain." Then he walked away in the most august manner possible.

Liana was so stunned she hardly realized she was now dancing with Whyte.

"What did he say to you?" he murmured the question in her ear. She told him everything.

"So, he's already made his decision," he said solemnly.

"Whyte, be honest with me." She lowered her voice. "Princess Rhian. Do you have something going on with her?"

He hunched his shoulders. "I'm sorry that I didn't tell you."

"So much for trust," she muttered. "And aren't you a bit old for her?"

"How old do you think I am?" A little humor mixed with hurt came to his face. "All I want is to marry her—or at the very least, protect her from whatever is happening in this palace."

With a flurry of silken material at her feet, he twirled her, giving her a full view of the room.

"Where *is* your princess, by the way?" She glanced at the raised table, finding both chairs empty. Whyte craned his neck nearly all the way around.

"Oh, Divine," he cursed, his hazel eyes widening. He stopped dancing and instead awkwardly swayed them both. "Don't panic."

"I'm not," she said in a calm, slow voice. "You look around the ballroom and the foyer, and I'll look in the Garden. One of us is bound to run into her."

"Good plan." He nodded feverishly, and they broke apart.

Chapter 15

The Princess Thief

Once Dillon and the captain left their table, Rhian weaved her way to her uncle. Aliah looked happy to see her, likely hopeful that she could save him from being alone with his father. But Rhian was in no mood for lighthearted distractions.

"Is it true?" she said as the two men stood in her presence. "Lyell is marrying me off to Seamus Tecwyn?"

Aliah leaned back, mortified. "How did you--?"

"I have ears, Aliah. It's been rumored for weeks." Rumors were one thing, but the Tecwyn's presence at the ball turned the terrifying prospect into reality.

"It's a good match," said her uncle without emotion.

"How can you say that?"

"He is very much like you," he replied.

"Did you encourage this match, Father?" Aliah cut in.

As per usual, Grigor's attention passed over his son. "Rhian, you must not waste your potential. Together, you and—"

"I can't believe it." The room swam as tears filled her eyes. "How could you betray me like this? I thought you… You told me that I could… That I *should* rule."

Grigor leaned closer, lowering the volume of his voice. "Why do you think I gave you Alcyone's grimoire? You will carry on the legacy of our family. With the Tecwyn boy, imagine what you could accomplish—"

Rhian would hear no more. She needed to speak with Dillon and make things right with him. But when she searched the ballroom for him, she saw he was in the middle of replacing the king as the Foley woman's dance partner. She leaned in close to his ear, as though revealing a secret. Rhian sped out of the ballroom.

After obtaining her cloak from an attendant, Liana ventured into the Royal Garden. Wishing she could remember what it looked like in the daylight, she kept to the path, bordered by lit torches. The last thing she needed was to get lost. No one else was out, especially now that the dancing had begun. Given that it was cold enough outside for her to see her breath, she was sure the thin-skinned upper crust of Caerwyn society would rather not be out of doors. Though she doubted she would find the princess here, she relished taking the moment to herself.

The garden's half-wall bordered the cliffside. She peered over. The blackness of the sky melded with that of the sea, each reflecting the other. She knew her ship waited out there in case of any debacles.

A pathetic sniffle caught her attention, and a soft sob drew her closer to a grove of apple trees. Princess Rhian sat curled up in the space between the half-wall and the farthest tree. In the dim moonlight, Liana could see her dress was torn at the hem—she must have tripped over it—and she wore no cloak. The princess held herself, her head tucked in her arms. Liana could only imagine what had happened, given the gossip swirling around her that evening.

She couldn't help but wonder, if the course of history had gone differently, how similar her own life could have been to Princess Rhian's. Instead of an impoverished childhood, Liana could have been brought up in serene luxury. But would it have been worth being unable to choose her own path? Liana loved her life. She had everything she could ever want. It would do no good to think of what might have been.

Driven by a solicitous need to safeguard the princess, she unfastened her cloak and ducked down under the branches. "Here," she whispered, draping her cloak around Princess Rhian's exposed shoulders. "You must be cold."

Princess Rhian sucked in a breath and looked up sharply. She stuttered, unable to form words quite yet.

Liana settled herself down on the grass. As she used her hand to brace herself, she felt a fallen apple in the neatly trimmed lawn. She tossed it gently aside, assuming one of the groundskeepers would pick it up in the morning.

"It's so stuffy in that ballroom. It feels good to get some air." She breathed in deeply. "I love the smell of the sea."

A pause, then—

"I-I've never left the Capital," the princess said, her voice as soft as a rose petal.

"That's a shame."

"You're a ship captain, aren't you? You must have seen everything there is to see."

"Well, not everything," Liana said with a shrug. "I've never seen Yael or the Highlands. But I've been to Savarre more times than I can count, and I know the islands well. I'd like to see Rodina one day. A great friend of mine is from there, and so is my mother. The world is a big place. I'm convinced we've hardly discovered a corner of it."

"Have you ever been to Iangard?" Rhian's lips trembled.

"No, Ameen would probably freeze to death."

"Who?"

"My fiancé. He always complains when it's cold." Liana lifted her palm. Though she could not see in the dark, she could feel the hairs on her forearms stiffen as her skin turned to gooseflesh without the protection of a cloak. "If he had it his way, it would be summer all year. But I think the crisp winter air can be refreshing."

"Your fiancé…"

"Yes?"

"How… How does he feel about you being here?" Rhian tugged at the grass. "At the ball. With Commander Whyte."

"He doesn't like it. But he knows it's important for me to be here."

"And how do *you* feel about Commander Whyte?"

"Honestly? I think he's a prat."

Rhian covered her mouth and stifled a giggle. "Do you?"

"He's not exactly my usual company. But one thing I'll give him is that he cares. A lot. About *you*."

The princess fell silent, going back to picking at the grass.

"You know," Liana continued, "The commander brought me here to protect you. So maybe we should stay together for the rest of the night."

Rhian shook her head and scoffed. "Protect me from what?"

"He thinks there could be someone here who wants to hurt you."

"Hurt me?" She sniffed. "No one here cares enough to want to hurt me. All of the guests are either here for the king's favor or the food and drink. Not even Dillon noticed when I slipped out."

"He told me that he loves you. He wants to marry you."

"It's not as though it matters," Rhian sobbed, wiping newly formed tears from her eyes. She buried her face completely in the cloak, now weeping. "I have to marry Seamus Tecwyn."

"You can tell the king you won't marry someone you didn't choose," Liana said. "Tell him you want to marry Whyte."

"That's not possible," Rhian huffed, scrambling to her feet. Even as she did, she held Liana's cloak snugly around her shoulders. "He'll never allow it. He's too... powerful."

"You have your own power," Liana rose as well, looking Rhian in the eye. They stood just about the same height, but the princess' posture made her appear smaller. "You haven't realized it yet. Maybe it's because you're young, or because no one has let you to discover it, but it's there."

"I don't..."

"Don't doubt yourself. You're not the king's bargaining chip or the commander's pet. You can be your own woman."

"I wish I was like you, Captain Foley," she mumbled, her gaze drawing down. "I wish I was brave."

Liana wasn't sure what to say to that, except, "It's just something you learn. No one's brave unless they have to be."

They emerged from the shadow of the apple tree together. As they stepped back on the stone path, Rhian turned to Liana. She opened her mouth to speak, but the presence of the king himself interrupted her. Grigor Vitalis and Whyte, whose eyes softened in relief, accompanied him.

"Ah, Princess Rhian," King Lyell greeted his sister as both women curtsied to him. "I see you are becoming acquainted with Captain Foley. Very good."

"She is excellent company, Your Majesty," Rhian smiled prettily. One would not ever be able to tell she had been crying only moments earlier. Liana guessed that masking one's emotions was a necessary skill for a princess to have. Rhian spoke in a way only someone who was well-educated would, by annunciating every syllable of every word. She must have practiced her poise rigorously throughout her life.

"I'm glad that you think so," the king replied. "The journey to Iangard is a long way."

Her face twisted into a puzzled look. No matter how skilled she was, she couldn't hide her shock.

"The King has ordered Captain Foley to escort you to Iangard for your wedding," the earl stated evenly. He seemed to be better at keeping a blank face than his niece. Rhian looked to Liana, then to Whyte, whose hazel eyes were downcast.

"With all due respect, His Majesty made a request that I haven't had the opportunity to decline," Liana interrupted, speaking directly to Rhian.

This threw the king off balance. "Oh? Well, do not be too hasty with your decision, Captain. I have excellent methods of persuasion."

A shiver ran down Liana's spine. She realized why Rhian felt she couldn't refuse her brother. His tone was more than stubborn— it was *sinister*. But just as the thought crossed her mind, Princess Rhian spoke.

"There will be no need. I won't be making the journey to Iangard."

The torches shone bright enough for her to see something dangerous rising in the king's eyes. But Rhian was not afraid—not anymore.

The earl swiftly stepped between the siblings, his lengthy black cloak swinging about his boots. Finally, tension strained his voice. "Perhaps we should return to the ball and discuss this matter at another time."

"No." Rhian gathered herself up. "You will hear me now, brother. I don't care if you *are* the king of Caerwyn. I will marry the man I love whether you like it or not."

"The man you—?" King Lyell saw that Rhian's focus fixed behind him, and he turned to see Whyte with a stupid lovestruck grin upon his face. She reached for him through the opening of the velvet cloak. Whyte made a move to take her hands, but before they could touch, the King's arm launched out.

Liana became acutely aware of many things at once—the weight of the items Ava had sewn into the inside of her skirt, the urge in her gut to leap at the king to protect Rhian, and the smell of ozone enveloping her senses. It was the scent that rendered her motionless. She knew it. She *remembered* it.

The mask hiding the earl's emotion slipped to reveal pure panic as a crackling began to stir in the palm of Rhian's free hand. "Rhian, don't! You must control it!"

A blinding flash and a thunderous sound made Liana cower. When she opened her eyes, she was on her hands and knees on the stone path, low enough to be face-to-face with the prostrate king. She scrambled back.

Whyte fell upon the king's body and turned it over. His own face was nearly as bloodless as Lyell's. "You killed him!"

Rhian stood as still as one of the statues in the foyer, white fire still licking her fingertips. Then she looked down at Liana and bent towards her, as though to help her stand. With the ferocity of self-preservation, Liana tore at her skirt and unsheathed the small pistol she had hidden. Rhian screamed. Whyte made to restrain Liana, but she moved fast. She leaped up and, in one fluid motion, had the princess in a hold.

"Rhian!" Earl Vitalis called out, his voice booming.

"You don't want to do this," Whyte raised his arms in surrender. "Just let her go."

"Shut up, all of you!" Liana frantically looked about for an escape.

Drawn by the sounds of chaos outside, guards, attendants, and guests began to emerge from the ballroom. Gasps and screams of shocks echoed as they saw their king, his burned flesh still sizzling, and a weapon at the princess' throat.

Liana disappeared in a flash, hurtling through the trees, dragging the screaming princess along as a shield. Skidding to a stop at the wall, she shoved Rhian away. She wasted no time in pulling at the pocket in her skirt. When Liana struck the flare's tip against the wall, it burned a bright blue-white. It hissed as smoke gathered around her. Through it, she saw guards scrambling through the trees with rifles. *Time to go*, she decided. She hitched her skirts and lifted herself on the wall, holding the flare high above her head.

"Captain Foley."

Liana whipped around to see that Princess Rhian hadn't moved. She stood, looking at Liana as though she was a beacon in the night of a terrible storm.

"What's the matter with you? Go! Get out of here!"

Rifle shots startled them both. Rhian screamed again and threw herself into Liana. Lead blasted past them. Knocked off balance, Liana slipped and scrambled for something to hold onto. It turned out to be the princess' arm, and they both pitched into the rolling sea.

Chapter 16

Escape

"I win again."

"Holy Gereon's lily-white ass! You're cheating!" Sava stood abruptly from the barrel. He threw his dice shaker on the deck in frustration, causing hoots of laughter from the twins.

"Fortune favors me tonight," Ameen chuckled, flipping a newly won coin on his thumb. He pocketed his winnings and his dice.

"I'm not finished with you yet!"

"My father always said a good gambler quits while he's ahead," he said with mirth. He ruffled Sava's hair affectionately, mostly just to embarrass him. Sava squirmed away, pouting. "You should have walked away when you were ahead by five. You got greedy."

He dimmed the lantern they had been using for their game. Ameen had ordered a minimum amount of light for stealth. Most of the men went below anyway, where it was a little warmer, while he, Marin, Sava, Jamil, and Kahil stayed on deck.

Sava brushed his spiral curls out of his face, before tying them up in a band. "How long are we supposed to wait? The captain said these balls can last all night."

"Then we'll wait for her all night, if we have to."

"I'm bored to tears," the younger man grouched.

"Would you rather be manning the cannons in a firefight?"

"No."

"Then stop complaining."

As they bobbed beneath the cliffside, Ameen squinted up at the palace. Getting to his feet, he buttoned his coat and set his teeth to keep them from chattering. He could see the lights glimmering from the ballroom. Music played faintly in the distance.

Then he saw a shining blue light at the top of the cliff.

"The signal!" said Sava before Ameen could sound the alarm. "It's the signal!"

The crew of the *Windfall* had never dropped a dinghy so fast. Ameen hardly had the sense to take the lantern that Jamil offered before he scrambled over the side and into the little wooden boat.

"I'm going with you!" Sava called after him, his leg already dangling over. He hopped off, nearly capsizing them.

"Careful, Squiddy!" Ameen managed to keep his bearings as he grabbed an oar.

"Don't call me that!"

"Stop yer bickering and move over, laddies!" Marin lowered himself easily, despite his age and the rolled-up blanket under his arm. "I'll not have the captain drown because ya wee shites won't shut yer mouths and paddle."

The sea bubbled and churned around the cliff's base. Ameen drove his oar into a crevice to steady their boat as a wave tossed them up. Divine, it was dark—too dark to see anyone in the water.

"Captain!" Sava called, raising the lantern. He shouted louder, so his voice could carry over the hissing of water over the rocks. "Captain!"

Ameen took the lantern and sprang swiftly onto the rocks. Seafoam overtook his legs as a wave threatened his stance. Teetering, he looked up, hearing shouts of panic from above. The cliff stood as tall as the highest building in the Capital. A fall into the sea at the wrong angle could have been lethal. He called out Liana's name two, three, four times before he heard her.

"Here! I'm here!" She yelled back from the dark sea, hauling something out of the shallows. Ameen set the lantern aside and dipped down to help, wading in the icy water. Coming closer, he saw that she had rescued a young woman who had apparently fallen with her. Liana gave her a few hard taps to her deathly pale cheek and received no response.

"Is she breathing?" he asked.

Liana growled in answer, raking her soaked hair back. Without any more time to waste, she pressed the heels of her hands against the young woman's sternum in a hard rhythm. She limply rocked with each motion but was unresponsive. Liana let out a vulgar curse, before she bent to breathe into her mouth. After a few tries, the woman finally jolted up, turned over, and coughed out two lungfuls of seawater, along with the contents of her stomach. Before she could fall facedown onto the jagged rocks, Ameen caught her.

Marin approached now, climbing carefully over the rocks.

"Are ya alright, there, lass?" he asked, but Liana seemed to be in a dazed trance, touching her lips with her fingertips.

Ameen interrupted, shifting the limp body in his arms. "Tell me this isn't who I think she is."

Liana jolted and looked up sharply. "We have to go—now!"

Once they made it back to the dinghy, Sava took over for Marin, while he shimmied out of his own coat and draped it over Liana's bare shoulders.

"What the hell happened up there?" Marin lifted the collar and wiped her hair out of her face. Ameen and Sava shoved the boat off the rocks and began to row back to the *Windfall*.

"She's a w-witch," she rasped.

"Who?" Ameen asked, brow furrowing.

"Princess Rhian. She's a bloody witch."

"What are ya sayin'? This is the princess?" Marin interjected, peering over.

Liana confirmed it with a short nod. She adjusted herself and brushed against the side of the boat, letting out a pained groan. "Shit! It feels like I broke my bloody back!"

"Ye'll be alright," Marin lifted her into a more comfortable position. "Hearin' yer vulgarity is assurance of that—though I've always wondered where ya get yer filthy mouth from."

"You, obviously," Ameen interrupted as he rowed, making Marin scowl at him. He looked over to Princess Rhian, curled on the opposite end of the dinghy with the rough but dry blanket draped over her.

"Look!" Sava exclaimed. A ship approached from the direction of the harbor. Its hull and flags were royal blue with an ouroboros.

"They're after her," said Ameen to Liana.

"What do you expect us to do? Row over there and hand her off? We'll be captured, if they don't blast us to smithereens first!"

"We've only one choice then," Marin chimed in. "Run."

They managed to get the dinghy back to the *Windfall* just as the first shot rang out. The crew collectively braced themselves as a cannonball blew past them. It landed in an explosion of sea spray behind the ship—a warning shot.

"Anchors aweigh and full sail, men," Liana ordered after she sent Marin and Sava to take the princess to the sickbay. She limped towards the steps to the helm, tattered gown and all. "We have the speed to outrun them."

A chorus of "Aye, Captain" rang about as the crew dispersed. Ameen, however, went to Liana.

"You need to have Thiago look at you," he said, moving alongside her and speaking in a hushed voice.

"I am fully capable of captaining my ship. Besides, he'll be occupied with the princess."

Attempting a different tactic, he raised a brow and eyed her attire, silently communicating with his eyes. Then she hesitated, understanding him perfectly.

"I would like to get out of this wet gown, though." She cupped her hands to be heard across the deck. "Marin! Get over here and take the helm." Then she looked back at him. "Man the gun deck until I get back, and put Lucky on the rear chaser."

"Of course, Captain." He nodded before she disappeared into her cabin.

The next shot hit the corner of the stern, just as Ameen got to the gun deck. He saw Lucky dodge just in time to avoid being hit by flying splintered wood. There was a reason they called him Lucky. He was the crew's best shot—when he was sober. He also had a tendency to dive headfirst into danger and come out unscathed. Sava rushed to assist in loading the cannon as they were hit. He tripped and fell on the deck, before pulling on his thick leather gloves and scrambling to Lucky.

"They're comin' up on us fast, Almasi!" Lucky shouted back at him. "Nearly in rifle range!"

Whipping sounds from above signaled the sails unfurled. The *Windfall* rocked forward. As Lucky and Sava loaded the chaser, Ameen felt life spring into the ship as Marin steered their course. The rest of the crew raced about the gun deck, getting the other cannons ready in case of an all-out battle.

From experience, Ameen knew chases like this could last for hours—sometimes days. What was worse, they had a minimal number of men on board. If they didn't end this soon, the crew would be exhausted, and the *Windfall* could be quickly overtaken.

At that moment, Liana bounded down the steps to the gun deck. She ran her fingers through her hair, smoothing the wet strands back before tugging on her tricorn. She stopped mid-step, gripping the railing with a contorted look. At first, Ameen thought it was the pain of her bruised back, then he realized she faced the blasted hole in the stern. She looked as distressed as if the cannon had shattered her own body.

"Bastards!" she barked. "*Lucky!* Blast their mast!"

"Gladly, Captain!"

The cannon exploded with a violent shot, and the ball grazed the left side of the navy ship's main mast. For a moment, it stood standing before there was a loud crack. The mast tipped over and crashed onto the deck. Before they could celebrate, a series of rifle shots peppered the stern.

Ameen felt several hands grab his shoulders and pull him down. Lead hummed all around them, and thankfully he didn't feel the familiar heat piercing his flesh. He straightened and pulled Liana to her feet. She was unhurt, as well. A scream of agony made her duck under his arm and dash to its origin.

"Squiddy!"

Sava lay on the deck holding his right side. Already at his side, Lucky pressed down on the wound. Liana lifted Sava in her arms, cradling his head and torso. His cries had softened into childlike whimpers. Ameen wanted to go to him, but his feet wouldn't move. The world swirled around him, making his head dizzy and his stomach threaten to turn inside out. His eyes stung, but not from the smoke and gunpowder.

No, not him. He's just a boy. Just—

"Thiago! Someone get Thiago!" Liana directed one of the powder monkeys to go below. Ameen pulled himself together and joined the circle forming around Sava, who had his face buried in Liana's neck.

Lucky gently peeled up Sava's shirt, soaked with blood and plastered to his skin. A clean exit wound marred his back, and the bleeding was already slowing. That was good, Ameen thought. But the sight of the boy's raw flesh made him feel ill again.

Sava rolled his head to look at Lucky and Ameen. Their presence seemed to stir a bit of courage inside him. He had tears in his eyes, but he set his jaw hard as Thiago arrived to examine him. "Did we... get them?"

Lucky let out a nervous chuckle and sagged. "Aye, laddie. We got 'em."

Sava forced a smile.

"You're going to be alright," Ameen assured him.

"You hear that?" Liana lifted Sava a little more under his neck. "You're staying alive. That's an order."

Sava nodded as best as he could. "A-aye, Captain."

Chapter 17

Anchors Aweigh

28th of Regnsfall

Cynareth Ocean, East of Caerwyn

Liana dreamt of a storm raging around the *Windfall*. She stood at the helm, attempting to sail out of it, but she was the only one on deck. One of the ropes snapped from the strain of the sail, but she couldn't go to repair it. It was impossible, she kept thinking, as the rain beat down on her, impossible to navigate out of this alone—

"Liana."

A deep, gentle voice woke her. She straightened up and winced as pain bloomed up the right side of her back. Sleeping on a barrel and propped on a narrow space near the edge of Sava's cot had not been kind to her already sore body.

Liana looked up at Ameen, then to Sava, still fast asleep. His tawny skin had gathered a sheen of sweat. He had a damp cloth on his forehead. Ameen adjusted it so it sat straight on Sava's brow.

"Does he have a fever?" she asked, placing a hand against his cheek.

"No, it's too soon to tell if he'll have trouble. I remember the coolness helped me, though... to not think about the pain," he told her, looking down at Sava fondly.

Liana felt a tug at her heartstrings. Despite their rough start, Sava grew attached to Ameen, always doing what he could to gain his approval and following him about the deck like a shadow. Likewise, Ameen embraced the role as his mentor, and the two became inseparable.

She took Sava's hand. It laid limply in hers, though she thought she felt a finger twitch against her palm. She turned it over and patted the tops of his long fingers. He had the hands of an artist, she always thought, with skin so thin you could see every tendon move. They hardly belonged on the harsh deck of a ship. But Sava always put everything he had into his work, especially when it was a task set upon him by his captain. "He's the last person in the world who deserves this."

"We've done all we can," Ameen replied. "The rest is up to the Divine."

There was another problem. The cannonball's impact had rattled the sickbay so much that Thiago lost most of his medicinal reserves. If the wound festered, Thiago had few supplies on hand that could help him.

Liana stood and stretched, noticing only the three of them were in the surgery. When she had come down with Sava the night before, Rhian had still been unconscious in the cot beside his. But now it was empty. Panic struck her hard.

"Where is the princess?"

"Thiago took her to the galley," Ameen said.

"You let her *go*? Even after what I told you what she did? What were you thinking?"

"She didn't seem dangerous. Scared, mostly. And if she is as powerful as you say, putting her in the brig wouldn't have helped anyway."

Liana rubbed the space between her brows. Ameen allowing Rhian to walk freely about the ship felt like insubordination, though she hadn't exactly ordered the princess to be confined. To be fair, she had been busy. "She killed her own brother."

"About that…"

"What?"

"I spoke to her. She seemed… regretful. Like it was an accident."

Liana worked her jaw. It *had* been an accident. That much she was willing to admit. "Well, what about my parents?"

"Princess Rhian is too young to have had a hand in it."

"She has to know *something*."

"Ask her, then."

Liana wondered exactly how long Ameen and Rhian had spoken, before puffing out a sigh. She glanced over at Sava. He faced away, one hand resting on his chest as it rose and fell with each breath. Beneath the angle of his jaw, she could see a reassuringly steady pulsing vein.

"There are more important things to worry about," she said. "Just make sure the princess stays out of the way. Once I get some answers out of her, we're dropping her at the nearest port."

After washing up, Liana assessed the damages of the night before. She sat in her cabin and calculated what was lost. First and most importantly, they would need to restore Thiago's supplies. Sava's stability could change quickly. Members of the crew watched over him in shifts with strict instructions to bring her below when he woke. Second, they needed to repair the ship's stern. There was no telling how loose the rudder was from the hit. Not to mention, the series of bullet holes that ran across the back end of the *Windfall* could still cause a problem in the hull. Third, they needed a heading. But the very sight of a map made her head swim.

"Captain?" called an accented voice through the door.

"Come in," she said, welcoming the distraction. She ran the feathered end of her quill underneath her chin in consternation. Thiago arrived with Princess Rhian at his heels. It looked as though she had been drafted into being his new assistant. Liana narrowed her eyes at her, and the princess ducked her head down meekly.

In addition to being the ship's surgeon, Thiago would also serve as the cook when they were short on men. He had a way with seasonings. Both positions usually kept him very busy, but he seemed to like it just fine that way. He entered the cabin carrying a plate of salted beef, brown sugar beans and a hot biscuit straight from the galley.

"Lost supplies," he said sadly.

Liana took the parchment he handed to her. She glanced over the inventory with a sinking feeling.

She forced her gaze to Rhian. The princess' shoulders hunched as though she carried the weight of boulders upon them. She had clearly been outfitted by Ameen, as she recognized one of her own dresses on Rhian. The dark green fabric looked dull and overpowering against her radiant features. Still, Liana had to admit she wore the dress much better than she ever could. "You're not hurt from the fall, I take it, Your Highness?"

Rhian shuffled her feet for a moment before speaking. "No, ma'am. I'm sorry about the boy. I saw you sleeping beside his cot this morning."

Liana twirled the quill between her fingers. "Thiago, will you give me a moment to speak with the princess alone?"

"Of course, Captain," he agreed, backing out of the cabin.

"Sit down, Your Highness." Liana waved her hand in invitation to the chair opposite her. When Rhian hesitated, she added a forceful, "Please."

The princess sank down with grace and looked about the cabin. Her blue eyes went wide with curiosity. In the years Liana had been in possession of the *Windfall*, she had furnished it to her and Ameen's liking, with similar decor as their room at The Black Barricade. Rhian's line of sight rested on the painted rum bottle in a case nailed to the wall. Fortunately, it survived the battle, as fragile as it was.

"I have some questions for you," Liana said, breaking Rhian's reverie.

"I supposed you would, Captain Foley." The princess nodded, wringing her hands in her lap. Ameen was right; she did look frightened. Perhaps Liana could use that to her advantage.

"What are you, exactly? A witch?"

Rhian, to her credit, kept mostly composed. "Th-the ancients called us mystics."

"Us? There are more of you?"

"The power was passed to me. My uncle and I are the only ones I know who have it, I swear."

"Your uncle." Liana stood. "He was the one who killed King Sergus and Queen Valeriya."

"What? No. That's impossible."

146

"It's the *only* possibility."

Much to her surprise, Rhian got to her feet and snapped back at her. "My uncle would *never* use his powers for evil."

"And how do you know that?"

"What does a pirate captain care about kings and queens, anyway?" Rhian spat back.

"Huh. What makes you say we're pirates?"

The princess stiffened her upper lip. "A merchant ship wouldn't have six cannons and a cargo space converted to house at least seventy men."

Liana couldn't help but smirk. "You're clever, aren't you?"

"When I came into my powers, it was a frightening experience. I kept it hidden for a very long time. But my uncle saw the signs and helped me to control it. He taught me to be responsible. That our power should be used to help people, not hurt them."

"Is that why you killed your own brother, then? Does king-slaying run in the family?"

As Rhian winced, Liana turned away, hot with indignation. She knew she would get nothing further. But she had what she needed—the truth. Grigor Vitalis killed her parents. There was no doubt in Liana's mind. He had the same lightning magic she had seen as a child, the very same magic that Rhian possessed. Even more worrisome, Rhian was young and gave no indication that she could really control herself. Liana needed to get the princess off her ship as soon as possible, before there was another slip-up.

"I want to make things very clear to you, Your Highness. I don't trust you."

Rhian pressed her lips together but did not speak.

"I do not want you here. I did not take you as a captive. You are not a prisoner. But you are certainly not a guest. So, if I see one of your *witchy spells* cast on my ship," Liana said, wiggling her fingers with a sour look, "I will not hesitate to kill you."

It gave her some measure of satisfaction to see the blood drain from Rhian's face.

"The safety of my crew is my priority," Liana emphasized. "When we make landfall, you can head back to the Capital."

"I'm not going back there," the princess stated in that irritating way she carefully pronounced every word. At first, she'd thought it pleasantly articulate. But now, Rhian said it in a way that gave Liana the distinct feeling she thought Liana was stupid.

She crossed her arms. "Excuse me?"

"I'm never going back," the princess repeated, "Ever."

"Why not?"

"I killed my brother—the *king*. I'm a criminal, like you."

The comparison gave Liana a prickling feeling. She sneered. "No. Not like me, Princess."

A familiar rhythmic knock interrupted them.

"What is it, Marin?"

As he opened the door, he had a worried look about him. For a moment, Liana feared Sava's condition might have turned for the worst, but she recalled that Marin had been looking over the damages.

"It's as we thought," he said. "The cannonball damaged the rudder-staff."

"Shit!" Liana looked at Rhian. "Why don't you go... be useful? Just don't get in anyone's way."

"Certainly, Captain," she said with an oily smile before giving a distinctly sarcastic curtsy and taking her leave.

Marin looked like he wanted to ask about the princess, but Liana gave him a pressing look. "The rudder?"

"It's operational," Marin went on, "but we dinna know for how long." His barrel chest heaved a sigh. Something must have given away her emotions, because his gray eyes softened into wells of compassion. "What is it, lass? And dinna tell me it's the damned rudder."

"Marin," she breathed, finding herself trembling. "I know who did it. I know who killed them."

He reached out and took her hands as she sank onto her desk. "Who?"

"Grigor Vitalis." She bowed forward, unable to contain her tears. "The king's uncle. He…"

Liana thought knowing would help her. She thought it would bring her peace or closure. Instead, it widened the gaping hole in her soul that her parents had left behind. He held her, and her tears soaked his shoulder. Though she burned with shame, he did not let her turn away.

"I remember when I found you and yer brother," he said, shortly after her sobbing calmed. "Wee rascals hidin' in the hold. Stowaways. I never thought I would come to love the two of ye as my own."

Another sob sprang from her throat, and she wiped her face.

"But all the love in the world canna replace yer mother and father," he continued. "They must live on through what ye do. And I must warn ye… Dinna let this pain consume yer heart. Dinna let their legacy be tainted by vengeful actions."

"Vitalis deserves to rot!" She turned away to lean against the glass bulkhead, significantly cracked by last night's battle. The wake parted the sea before her. "He killed them, for what? To put his brother on the throne? It's unforgivable!"

"Yer right, and I dinna expect ye tah forgive the wretch," he said, his rough voice uncharacteristically soft. "But ye have responsibilities. Ye have a slew of people who care for ya. Dinna cast us aside tah feed yer anger."

"You're right." Rubbing at a stray tear, she faced him. "It's not as though I presently have the time for revenge. I need to get this ship repaired. I need to find a safe haven for the crew."

"I have an idea." He licked his lips and made his way over to the map before picking up the drafting compass. "But ya willna like it."

The ship was the safest place for Rhian. Whether she liked it or not, Captain Liana Foley was her only ally. Not even Dillon could help her now. She breathed in the salty sea air, recalling the fear in his eyes in the garden.

Did he still love her? Could he?

Well, Rhian thought sadly, *How can you love someone you're afraid of?*

Pressing Dillon out of her thoughts, she found the ship to be a harmonious place. The wind whistled in her ears as they soared across the water. Men grunted in unison as they pulled the halyards. Aloft, stretching ropes creaked. Foremast-men called from above as they heard instructions from below. Then there were the bells—rung every half hour in different patterns, to announce the time as far as she could tell.

The slick deck dipped with each jagged wave of the sea. The wind made the water choppy, and she feared she might be pitched over the side if she wasn't too careful. As it stood, she was humiliated enough. She'd had an audience of pirates to witness the fact that she had never learned how to swim.

Rhian had read books on seafaring. A vessel of this size, she supposed, wouldn't need a crew to be very large. The space was mostly meant for cargo. Pirate ships, she had read once, needed more men when pillaging and plundering so as to overwhelm the sparse merchant crews. Something told her, however, that the *Windfall* was not operating to full scale. She counted to twenty men before she'd started seeing the same faces. Of course, that didn't count who Rhian had deemed the ship's officers—the captain, the quartermaster.

The one they called Lucky appeared to be in charge of the artillery. Passing by, he barked at one of the younger crew members for a poor knot over one of the side cannons. The tattoo of an anchor on his neck bulged as he swore an oath and turned on his heel back to the upper deck. Rhian kept her distance.

One of the crew members swooped down to aid the man who had just been verbally filleted. From observation, Rhian knew he had a twin also aboard. She didn't remember their names, but the one she watched now had long hair.

"Don't worry about Lucky. He's had some bad experiences with loose cannons," he told him, giving his shoulder a shake before bending down to pick up the rope. "Here's how you do it."

A few minutes later, bells rang again, and the crew fluttered about the deck for a shift change. Rhian brushed her hair back as it whipped in her eyes. She wished she had a ribbon to tie it back. Perhaps she could find a hat below, like Captain Foley used.

Caught in the wave of men leaving and arriving to their posts, Rhian stumbled. The shoes that had been laid out for her when she had woken were a little too big for her, and she tripped on the empty toe. She caught herself, thankfully, and heard a light-hearted cackle on her right side.

"Haven't got your sea legs yet, Your Highness?" The other twin, the one with hair cropped close to his scalp, smirked at her.

"It seems not, ah..." Rhian searched her memory for the man's name. There had been a series of introductions by the Savarran surgeon and the tall Islander earlier that morning.

"Jamil, Your Highness," he said. "If no one's said it yet, welcome to the *Windfall*. That's my brother, Kahil, over there."

"Hello," she replied weakly.

"I think you're a bit in the way up here, Your Highness. It's my turn to watch over Squiddy. Care to keep me company?"

Rhian agreed, and she followed Jamil below. "Squiddy? Is that his real name?"

He laughed again. "Oh, no. His real name is Sava. Some advice, though—don't ever let him hear you call him Squiddy. Only the captain can say it to his face."

The ship groaned. Rhian pressed her hands against the sides of the narrow walkway to the sickbay as the ship seemed to turn directions. Had Captain Foley settled on a heading?

"Why Squiddy?"

"It's the captain's name for him. When he was young, he messed about, and Almasi threw him into a cart of freshly caught squid."

"Isn't he a little old for a pet name?" Rhian guessed that Sava was perhaps sixteen or seventeen years old.

"Well, he's been with the crew since he was a child."

"If he doesn't like the name, why does she call him that?"

Jamil paused. "You got a mother, Your Highness? Siblings?"

Rhian's heart sank as she thought of her family. She never knew her mother—she had died after a fever ravaged her body. Her father, King Lyulf, passed not long after. And her brother... Thankfully, Almasi had assured her that the crew didn't know details about the ball. The explanation they had been given was that the captain had rescued her from a fall into the sea.

"My parents were taken by the Divine. I'm the youngest child."

"Well, Sava doesn't have a mother either. She died when he was born, and his father either didn't know about him or didn't want him—she was Caerwyn, and he was Islander, and they weren't married. You know how that can be."

Rhian nodded. Islanders and Caerwyn folk didn't marry often. Though they were recognized as citizens of Caerwyn, or Savarre before the secession, Islanders were often thought of as outsiders or foreigners. They had their own culture, their own language, and, long ago, their own religion. It wasn't illegal to marry outside of one's nation of origin, but pressures of societal division discouraged it.

It had surprised Rhian when Captain Foley mentioned last night in the garden that she was betrothed to an Islander. She recalled the man's kind, welcoming smile when she had met him that morning. From what Rhian had seen, the captain and her crew made their own rules—had their own small community set apart from the rest of the world, built on mentorship, thievery, and a floating vessel with bells.

"Sava was raised in the orphanage with me and my brother," Jamil continued. "We looked after him, but when we got older, we had to leave and try to make it on our own."

"How did you all end up together on the same crew?"

"Sava ran away. He came looking for us. But the Capital is a big place for a little boy. He needed to eat, so he started to pickpocket. That was when he got into a bit of trouble."

"Picked the wrong pocket?" Rhian guessed.

"Or the right one, if you care to think of it that way."

They came up on the sickbay, and Rhian heard quiet voices, but they weren't speaking Caerwyn. She recognized the language as Savarran, with its fluid vernacular and trilling words. Rhian, fluent for diplomatic purposes, caught onto the conversation. When they rounded the corner, she found the captain's fiancé and the Savarran speaking.

"How many ribs are broken?"

"It's difficult to tell. The rocking of the ship is too dangerous," said the surgeon in his native tongue. "He could pierce a lung."

"Did something happen, Almasi?" Jamil interrupted.

"Sava woke," he said brusquely.

Rhian could hardly see past the three men, but she could hear Sava's labored breathing.

"The captain should know," Jamil replied. "Do you want me to—?"

"No. I'll tell her." Almasi let out a sigh that came off like a growl and slipped through the space between Rhian and Jamil. As he passed, Rhian noticed Almasi's gaze linger on the sickbay.

As he did, his necklace, a Circle of the Divine, caught her eye. She felt a strange pull to it. A whisper of magic tangled with her senses. A thrill of hope coursed through her veins. Could Almasi be like her?

"Excuse me, Your Highness." Tearing her eyes away, she forced herself to look at Almasi's face. She shuffled to the side to let him by. He didn't appear to notice her distraction, probably too lost in his worries about the boy. Giving her a polite nod, he turned away and climbed the steps to the deck.

"Dunmore Manor?" Ameen tilted his head in surprise.

"It's our only chance." Liana bent down and showed him a point on her map. "According to Marin, there is a cove with a beach, here. We can repair the ship there. Dunmore Manor is only a few miles from that point. Nellie won't turn us away."

"I'm not worried about Nellie."

Ameen had known Marin's daughter before, years ago. He recalled a pleasant half-Islander girl, a little older than Liana, with long, dark curls. But he had never met her husband. All he knew about the man was that Liana couldn't stand him. This fact was embellished by her crinkling nose.

"Rhys Dunmore can go suck an egg for all I care. Squiddy needs to get onto land, and the rudder-staff needs to be fixed. My pride won't get in the way of that."

"And if he refuses to help us?"

"The least Dunmore can do is let us borrow a wagon. We can purchase supplies in Yael."

"Yael is the heart of Caerwyn," Ameen argued. "It's also the home of the Vitalis family."

She paused, wincing at the mention of the family name. "All the better."

"What do you mean?"

"The princess confirmed my suspicions," she said. "Grigor Vitalis killed my parents."

"You're sure?"

"He has the same powers. The *same*," she emphasized, smacking a fist against her palm. "It was him. So, if we end up in Yael, maybe we can pay him a little visit…"

He sighed, shooting a pleading look for her to focus. "Liana, I'm sorry. But by now, you're wanted all over the kingdom. We shouldn't risk it."

"Then let's hope that Dunmore will find it in his heart to help us," she said. "The manor is an isolated place. I don't think word will get there for a while."

"And what about the princess?" he asked, lowering his voice. "What will we do with her?"

"Drop her as soon as we can." Liana fiddled with the drafting compass.

"Is that safe? We can't just leave her on some beach. We at least owe that to her."

"We owe her nothing." She scowled. "It's her fault we likely have the entire Royal Navy in our wake."

"I know how you must feel towards her, given the possibility that her uncle—"

"He killed my parents. I know it," she interrupted. "After we get the ship repaired and the crew settled, he's going to get what's coming to him."

He knew from experience that when Liana Foley made a statement like that, there was no doubt she would make good on it.

"So, how did Squiddy seem?"

"He's in pain," he admitted. "But once he gets steady on land, I'm sure he'll heal fast."

She nodded and bit her bottom lip.

"He's asking for you."

"What do I say to him?"

He paused for thought, knowing she shouldn't worry. One look at his captain would be enough to embolden any man under her command. "Just be there, like you were for me."

"If you say so, sailor." She opened the door to the cabin, letting in the flow of salty wind and inhaling deeply. As she made her way below deck, her hair streamed behind her, billowing like a banner of war.

Chapter 18

Duel

3rd of Deornath, 1723
Cynareth Ocean, East of Caerwyn

Captain Foley, who Rhian found to be a practical and strict woman, gave her a list of duties to be carried out each day. At first, Rhian thought it to be a fair trade. She remained insistent that she was going to stay with the crew, and she supposed that meant she would work alongside them. For the most part, the captain appointed her with many of the tasks in the galley, managing the stores and assisting in preparing the meals. She didn't mind that so much as when it came time to swab the deck. This was meant to be done after breakfast, but before preparation for lunch.

"No, no, no! I want every bit of my deck swabbed," Captain Foley yelled at Rhian when she tried to go back below to the galley before noon. "I won't have the wood split and risk an injury."

Rhian looked at the captain sourly and drew up her breeches. She hadn't worn a dress since her first day aboard. It would have made completing her chores impossible, especially at the pace the captain wanted. A couple of the aloft crew members paused their rope-climbing to peer down at them. Rhian's ears burned.

"I have swabbed it," The sound of another helpful crew member clearing his throat as he passed by reminded her of her manners. "Captain."

"Well, it's a shit job," the captain grumbled, shimmying out of her coat before snatching the mop out of Rhian's hand. "I'll just do it myself. Get down to the galley, or else the meal will be late. Go on!"

Rhian retreated tearfully. She chanced a glance back and saw that Captain Foley had, indeed, found dry spots on the deck along the ballast. With a wet flop, the captain remedied the error with speed and precision. Rhian sniffed before slinking away below.

Ameen perched on the upper deck, keeping a watchful eye on his captain. She felt far away, as though she stood across an entire ocean from him. Liana didn't notice him, too lost in her own thoughts. With the swabbing done, she stomped up the opposite set of steps to get to the upper deck. Without any sort of acknowledgement to him or Marin, who manned the helm, she swept by and peered over the stern, where the rudder had been carefully rigged. When she appeared satisfied it was still able to hold, she straightened up and held her hand over her brow, peering out onto the horizon.

Marin and Ameen exchanged quiet glances. The old sailor jerked his head back at Liana in an encouraging manner. Ameen nodded and swiftly came to her side.

"Where are you, Captain?" he murmured, leaning close. "We need you on deck."

She tilted her head and blinked at him. "I'm right here."

"Your boots are, but not your head," he told her, tapping a finger to his temple. His father used to always say that to him, whenever he caught Ameen daydreaming.

She pinched her bottom lip between her fingers. "How is the crew? How are they feeling about... everything?"

He knew what she meant. "They understand that the princess is here because we rescued her from the water. They know she's here willingly."

"And they aren't worried?"

"They trust their captain's judgement."

"Good." She nodded. "I'll have Nellie give her a horse once we get to Dunmore Manor. Then she won't be our responsibility anymore. We'll all be better off. Wouldn't you agree?"

Ameen had been purposefully silent on the matter. Surely, she wouldn't want to hear what he had to say.

Yes, Princess Rhian was a murderer, but so were they all. Unlike them, though, she had no experience in the harsh world outside the palace walls. Princess Rhian had already made it clear she couldn't go back. He knew she would be safer with the crew than she would be on her own.

But Liana's resentment ran deep. She would not see past it, no matter what he said to her. It would be a waste of breath.

"I'll agree with whatever you decide."

Liana frowned deeper. "I'm going to check on Squiddy again."

"I just did."

She stopped in her tracks and folded her arms. The toe of her boot tapped on the deck. He could feel the restless energy radiating from her body.

"I know what you need," Ameen announced as an idea struck him. She looked at him suspiciously. "Do we still have the training swords in the cabin?"

"I stuck them under the berth, I think. Why?"

"After lunch, meet me on the lower deck."

"What? But the crew…"

"We'll give them a show. They need some entertainment after everything, don't you think?"

Rhian had no idea there was a life outside more painful than the isolation of the palace. Everything hurt. Her arms and legs ached the most, especially at night. They throbbed as she laid in her hammock, sectioned off with sheets for privacy. With the sickness in the mornings, now more than ever she felt betrayed by her own body. Not to mention, she hardly slept. Every time she closed her eyes, she saw her brother's face, his empty eyes open in violent shock.

She let out a screech of terror when the hen fluttered and squawked at her. Mister Venegas chortled and moved to calm the fowl so Rhian could fetch eggs from the roost. Thankfully, she had cleaned it of droppings the night before.

"Sit," said a thick voice, breaking her of her somber thoughts. Mister Venegas tossed her an apple, which she clumsily caught, before turning to the stove. "Rest. I will take care of meal."

"No," she said, twirling the apple by the stem. "I shouldn't receive special treatment. I should work like everyone else."

"But, you—"

"If Captain Foley can work on a ship, then so can I."

"Captain Foley work on this ship for years," said Mister Venegas with his back still turned. "She has built strength and knowledge of life at sea. And you should not strain so much in your condition."

Rhian paused mid-bite and looked up at the Savarran over the crest of the apple. His spectacles glinted as he turned back to her and adjusted them on the bridge of his prominent nose. Under his gaze, she wilted.

"I have been surgeon for many years," he said in response to her guilty silence. "I know difference between seasickness and woman with child. And I have daughter and granddaughter."

Despite herself, her face crumpled, and she began to cry. Mister Venegas wiped his hands clean and calmly sat beside her. "It is miracle the child survived the fall."

Rhian wiped her nose. "Is it? Captain Foley will be furious. And I have nowhere to go."

"The father?"

The thought of Dillon forced her to blink away fresh tears. "He doesn't know."

Mister Venegas placed a gentle hand on her back. It was a little effort of comfort, but it helped.

"Captain Foley is kind woman," said the surgeon. Rhian looked at him doubtfully. He patted himself beneath his collar in a gesture of sincerity. "She let you stay."

"How can you be so sure?"

"I tell you," he said. "Years ago, my daughter, Camila became pregnant. The father abandoned her, and I had no money to raise another child. One day, the captain came to Caluz, looking for help. She say her quartermaster was dying from festered gunshot wound."

"Mister Almasi?"

"Yes. After I save him, she offer me a position on the ship as surgeon. I tell her that I could not abandon my daughter. Instead of turning me away, she offer to board us both. She pay me a salary and help Camila settle in the Capital. She even give her job."

Rhian blinked, cradling her cheek in wonder. "I can't believe that she would do that."

"Trust me. Tell her. You will not be sorry."

Rhian thanked him. He allowed her to pull herself together as he worked in the galley, and together they served out the meal. As they did, she noticed the crew chatted with excitement about something about to happen on deck.

Thinking better of asking further, she put her head down and continued her duties. She brought a plate to the sickbay for Sava, as she did every day now. Like the rest of the crew, he grew used to her presence easily. The first few times she saw the young man, he had been asleep. But when she finally spoke to him for the first time, she found him surprisingly conversational for someone who had recently been shot. Though Mister Venegas insisted that he needed rest, Sava encouraged her company.

"Better day today, Highness?" he asked upon her entrance. She shrugged her shoulders, not wanting to explain. He looked at her through half-lidded eyes with darkness around them. She supposed it wasn't a good day for him, either. He passed over the food and continued to speak. "What's the captain have you doing?"

"Swabbed the deck poorly again," she began to recount, but was interrupted by a snort.

"Swabbing the deck in this weather? She *must* hate you."

"What?"

"We swab the deck to keep the sun from splintering the wood. It's Deornath. No sun. Just clouds."

Rhian groaned. "Well, even if it's useless, I still have to do it."

He agreed. "The captain says so."

"She's just so... So..."

The sound of stomping boots thundering closer interrupted her. Lucky burst into the sickbay. "Oi, there's a fight goin' on, you hear?"

"Who?" asked Sava, straightening as best as he could.

"Almasi and the captain!" announced Lucky, giving them a roguish grin. "I'm taking bets. You want in?"

Sava's eyes brightened. "Who've ya got?"

"Almasi, of course. You'd be daft to think otherwise."

"Put me down for the captain."

"Did you not hear me?"

"Yeah. And I say put me down for five on the captain." He shifted to address Rhian. "Watch for me, would you, Highness?"

She nodded. "Only if you eat and rest."

With that agreement in place, Lucky escorted her on deck. Thankfully, the ship had anchored. The usual uneasiness she felt walking above deck lifted. With most of the crew out, it appeared more crowded than usual. "Come along, Princess. I'll get us a good view."

Despite herself, excitement sprang a skip in her step. The monotony of the last few days at sea had gotten to her. She wondered how the men could stand it for weeks on end. As Lucky elbowed his way to the bannister on the upper deck, she peered over to see the two contenders.

The captain stood near the main mast, shucking her coat. Beneath it, she wore a loose linen shirt that fell open at the collar and exposed more of her chest than modesty called for. Rhian blushed, especially when she found herself to be the only one looking. As the captain stretched and the cloth curved around her arms, Rhian could see she had defined muscles along her back. Her body was small and slight, but strong. She watched her tie her lustrous black hair in a ribbon.

Rhian couldn't help but agree with Sava. If any woman could win a fight against a man, it was Captain Foley.

Meanwhile, as the captain donned something that looked like a leather vest, Almasi patiently waited, holding two sabres. They looked similar to the ones she had witnessed the palace guards touting. When the captain had her hair in place, she opened her hand, and he tossed a blade to her. They took their places.

"Are those real?" Rhian whispered.

"Aye, yer Highness," came a voice that didn't belong to Lucky. Marin appeared on her other side. "Blunted, though. Dinna worry."

"Still sting, though," Lucky assured her. She must have looked horrified, for he continued, "They've got protection. And if you think Almasi would let one hair on the captain's head be harmed…"

A hush fell upon the deck as the captain edged towards Almasi. She made a slow, experimental strike, which he easily parried. The blades made contact a few more times. On the third, he playfully drew his sabre along the edge of hers and cocked his head in invitation. To Rhian, it paralleled tempting a snakebite. She heard a few members of the crew with closer views chuckle. Tension coiled in the captain's stance. She released a series of blows aimed at Almasi's upper body. He blocked the first one, but the blade whipped against each of his shoulders.

"Double strike!" Marin laughed victoriously, as Almasi stepped back and poked a finger through the torn cloth of his shirt.

"I thought you said they were blunted!" Rhian gasped.

"Steel is steel, Princess," Lucky snorted. "I don't see any blood. He's fine."

Marin leaned over the bannister as they took stance again. "Taught her well, I did."

"You taught the captain how to fight?" asked Rhian.

"Aye, back when she was a wee lass." He flattened his palm out as though to measure Captain Foley's height at the time. "Begged me to."

"How long have you known her?"

He grinned, standing tall with pride. "I raised her."

Curiosity drew her in, but further questioning halted when Lucky guffawed, pointing below. Captain Foley seethed as she retreated and leaned against the mast, rubbing the outside of her upper thigh, dangerously close to her posterior. Almasi already stood at the ready, knowing he would pay for that offense.

Rhian pressed on. "Are you her father?"

"No." Marin shook his head. "She and her brother were orphaned. My wife and I took 'em in, gave them a home and a name."

"Foley is *your* name?"

"Aye."

She tapped her chin. "Why not keep the one she was born with?"

"Yer an inquisitive one, aren't ya?" he said, shifting from one foot to the other.

The captain struck Almasi's leg but paid the price with a blade at the neck. After several more rounds with similar outcomes, Almasi came out ahead. Both of them gleamed with sweat. The captain stopped for a drink of water. Politely, Almasi took her offer of the canteen, but did not appear to be in as much need.

"See there?" said Lucky quietly to Rhian. "Strong as she may be, he's still got the advantage. Faster, longer reach, more stamina."

"There's still a chance." She thought of Sava, so insistent that Captain Foley would prevail. Despite the gruff treatment she received from the captain, she found herself partial to the contender of her own sex. Throughout her life, she had been defeated, silenced, and overshadowed by men. If a woman could win, just once...

A sabre flew and skittered across the deck, causing the crowd to back away.

"Almasi is two ahead now," Lucky hissed, rubbing his hands together. "If he wins this one, it's over."

Marin harrumphed. "Wind yer neck in, Lucky."

Almasi had the grace to let Captain Foley wipe her hairline before attacking again. She ducked down to parry, then swiped back, letting out a guttural cry. He swerved, and she missed. They rotated, bodies and blades in a fierce tangle. The crew parted, allowing room for the fight. Almasi held back no longer. With each advance he made, the captain stepped back. Collectively holding their breath, the crew watched as their sabres locked. She bowed backwards, straining against the side. Below her, the sea rolled against the anchored ship. In a high arc, Almasi raised his arm, the blunted tip of his blade stopping just short of her throat. Accepting defeat, Captain Foley let her weapon fall.

Lucky whistled over the cheering crowd. He tipped his hat and retreated. "Well, I'll be collecting my winnings."

"Disappointed, Yer Highness?" guessed Marin.

Rhian pursed her lips, exhaling through her nose. "I suppose. I expected her to win. She's the captain, the one in charge. Even if she is a woman, shouldn't she be able to best her own crew? How else would she have gained so much respect with the men?"

He raised his thick brows. "For someone of royal status, yer Highness, ya dinna know much about leadership."

Her mouth fell open.

"Beggin' yer pardon," he said apologetically. "But the captain doesna have the love of her crew because she can overpower them. Think of it like this: when the wind changes, ya canna beat it back. A good captain must know when and how to adjust the sails."

Though she found his words to be cryptic, Rhian accepted them. After all, the only example of leadership she had ever seen was what she had been allowed to witness in the palace. Below, she heard the captain's barking laughter. The loss hadn't diminished a bit of her pride. From a few paces away, Almasi watched her with his chin angled up in high regard. Despite Rhian's studies and all the books she read, every day she spent away from home made her realize how little she knew about the world.

The rush of battle, even if it was only for sport, had lingering effects on both the captain and the quartermaster. As the crew dispersed into their duties and the anchor lifted, they retreated to the cabin for reprieve.

A cold seawater rinse would do the trick to quell the fire in Ameen's blood. It hardly did much for Liana, however.

After removing his shirt, he absently scratched at his stomach. The dark hairs spattered along his torso rasped against his nails. That was when he caught her gaze fixated on him. The lust hadn't left her eyes since he'd had her pinned against the ship's side. Lounging stomach-down on the berth in his shirt, she still wasn't doing well to hide it.

His heart raced at the attention, accompanied by a spreading warmth. He let her watch him wash up, appreciating her admiration. Showing off a bit, he stretched, feigning sore muscles. He rubbed a hand over the scar on his shoulder, rolling his arm. She craned her head to get a better look.

When he finished, he leaned over, running a hand over the back of her bare thigh and giving it a firm squeeze. "I didn't hurt you, did I, Captain?"

She squirmed, though not from pain, and flipped over onto her back. "You left a mark, but I'll survive."

He leaned over her, pressing his hands into the berth. "Are you sure?"

"I think so," she croaked, breathless at how close he was.

He kissed her softly. "Need some time to yourself?"

She moaned her assent against his lips as he teasingly brushed against her. "Mm-hmm."

"I should stay, though…"

She narrowed her eyes at him, confused.

"If we're going to try to make a baby, of course. That takes both of us."

Pressing a bare foot against his stomach to get him up, she snorted with laughter. "Get out of here, sailor."

"I'll leave you to it, Captain," he said, dodging as she flung her tricorn at him. He exited the cabin with a fiendish smile. Deciding to stay near the door so no one would disturb her, he gazed out over the horizon to view the sunset. Just as the crew began to light the lanterns, someone joined him.

"Congratulations, Mister Almasi," said the princess as she padded to his side. "That was an excellent duel."

"Thank you."

"Is, ah… the captain busy?" she asked, fidgeting.

"Yes," he replied, doing his best to keep a straight face. "What do you need?"

"To tell her something."

"I can pass it along."

"I'd rather wait, if you don't mind," she said. Unable to give her a reason not to, Ameen remained silent. A short while passed before he glanced back at Princess Rhian. He noticed, not for the first time, that she eyed his Circle of the Divine. Spotting him looking, she blushed. "It's lovely… Your necklace."

He plucked it from his shirt. "My father gave it to me. I've worn it as long as I can remember."

"It's special to you, then?"

"Very."

"Does it have a… particular use?"

"Prayer, I suppose," he said with a shrug, thinking it a strange question. "Do you believe in the Divine, Your Highness?"

"I've… Well, I've never thought about it," she confessed. "I attend Mass, like I should, but… no one has ever asked me if I wanted to. I just did because it was my duty."

"I don't attend Mass, and I believe." He added, "I don't judge anyone for their spiritual practices. I was only curious."

They conversed for some time. He introduced her to some of the crew who passed by. She told him about her time spent with Thiago in the galley. Apparently, the chickens held a resentment for her and were fiercer than he ever thought. As she showed him a scratch on her wrist from the beasts, Liana emerged from the cabin, rejuvenated.

Running a hand through her damp hair, she looked at them with suspicion. "What is it?"

"The princess wanted to speak with you," he explained, waving his hand in invitation for Rhian to go on. She wilted under Liana's stern gaze.

"With your permission," she stammered, "I want to remain with the crew permanently."

"No," answered Liana without missing a beat.

"Please." The princess' bright blue eyes glistened in the lantern light. "I can't make it on my own."

Liana stepped closer to them, quieting her voice as a few crew members passed. "Every day you're on this ship, you put my men in danger. There's absolutely no reason for you to stay with us."

"I'm pregnant!" Rhian said, loud enough to make the nearby men turn their heads. They began to whisper, and her hands flew to her mouth.

Liana whipped around. "Get on, you gossips," she snapped, before snatching Rhian's arm and dragging her to the stern. Ameen hurried behind. Once they were clear of any listening ears, she pointed an accusatory finger at the princess. "You're lying, aren't you?"

"I'm not!" Rhian swore.

To Ameen's surprise, Liana rounded on him. "You bloody jinxed us; you know that?"

He rolled his eyes. "Obviously she was pregnant before I made that joke."

"I've known for weeks," Rhian cut in.

"Are you sure?" he asked, keeping his voice as gentle as possible.

She nodded.

"It's Whyte's?" Liana had filled him in on all the events at the ball. "Does he know?"

She shook her head.

"I think I'm going to be sick," Liana whined, doubling over the back of the stern.

Rhian's brow creased with worry.

But Ameen knew what that meant. He translated. "We'll help you," he said. "For now, you'll stay with us."

Ecstatic at this turn of events, Rhian threw herself at him. She laughed joyfully and squeezed him tight around the middle. He grunted at the impact and awkwardly patted her on the shoulder.

"Thank you," she said into his coat. "Thank you."

When she broke away, Liana pointed a finger at her again and spoke between her teeth. "You'd better believe the next time I see Dillon Whyte; I'm going to bloody murder him for this."

Chapter 19

Night Watch
7ᵗʰ of Deornath, 1723
The Cynareth Ocean

Perched in the crow's nest, Liana felt very much like the head upon the *Windfall's* mighty shoulders. Perhaps being at the helm should have given her that feeling. But when she steered, she only concentrated on what was ahead on the horizon, not within the ship's systems. At the head, though, she could see all. The nest gave her the perfect view of the deck and the rocky coastline sprawling in the distant west. The men went about their duties below, but their voices didn't reach her. Here, all was silent. Some would find the same sense of peace in their home, warm by the hearth, or looking out at a wide meadow. But Liana never liked the stillness. Movement meant life.

A high whistle sang from below, interrupting her tranquility. Peering over the side, she wasn't surprised to see Thiago calling her down from the deck. Beside him, she saw Princess Rhian's blonde ponytail flying back with the wind.

With each step down the rungs, Liana felt the strong connection she had with her vessel. After all these years of sailing, it was as though her soul had bonded with the *Windfall*'s. The dove gray sails, carried by stout timber bones, drove them forward. Wind breathed life into canvas lungs. As she descended, veins of ropes spanned out. Sinewy fibers creaked and stretched, demonstrating strength that no human muscle could possibly withstand. Liana felt it all. She and the ship were one.

"You asked for me, Captain Foley?" asked the princess when Liana came to face her.

"Yes. You and I need to have a serious conversation, Princess."

Rhian blanched.

"Captain," Thiago said, backing away. He gave Rhian a reassuring nod before going about his duties.

"Come on, then," she urged, and Rhian fell into stride behind her. "Watch your head."

"Huh?"

Before the princess's nose could collide with a pillar of lumber carried on the shoulders of two crew members, Liana threw an arm out. After exchanging a quick word about the repairs with them, she moved on. A moment later, she called back to Rhian again when they came to the steps to the upper deck.

They sidestepped past Marin and Lucky, who looked to be in a rush. After a moment's pause to look over her shoulder at them, Liana eyed the helm. Ameen had taken over. *Strange*, she thought. It was Marin's shift. She caught glances with Ameen, who gave her a quick salute. Things were taken care of for now, but she made a mental note to follow up later.

After the careful dance from the crow's nest to the captain's cabin, Liana allowed Rhian to enter first before shutting out prying ears with a firm slam of the door. She offered her a seat, which the princess took. "I'll get to the point. We're here to talk about your options."

"O-options?"

"About your *situation*." Liana looked pointedly at Rhian's midsection. "How far gone are you, exactly?"

"Ah… I'm not sure…"

"The last time you bled was… when?"

Rhian's face turned crimson.

"Listen, I'm not thrilled to be asking you this, either!" Liana snapped, waving her hands in the air. "But if you want me to help you, you're going to need to be a little more aware of your bodily functions, Princess. So, unless you want Ameen to come in here and speak with you, instead—"

"*No!*" Rhian buried her face in her hands, mortified.

"Well, then?"

"Ripnath… I remember it was in Ripnath. The beginning, I think."

Liana tapped on the table, counting for a moment. "Just over three months. Thiago told me you've been getting sick in the mornings."

"It hasn't been as bad the last few days."

"Sounds right. Usually goes away about this time."

Rhian opened her mouth and shut it, as though she had a question to ask but thought better of it.

"What?" Liana pressed, irritated by her timid demeanor.

"It just… I couldn't help but wonder if you've been… in the same *predicament*," she stuttered. "That is to say, Captain, that—"

"No. I've never been pregnant." Liana said, putting her out of her misery. "But, believe it or not, you're not the first pregnant girl I've helped."

"Mister Venegas told me what you did for him and his daughter. Is that who you're talking about?"

"I've helped many, actually."

"I didn't think that pirates usually made it a habit to get involved in such things."

"They do when they run charities."

"*Charities?*"

Liana let out a short laugh and made a vague gesture to the ship. "The *Windfall* is more than just a pirate ship, Princess. Sure, we make a profit, but we also give back."

"To who?" Rhian placed a hand on her cheek, obviously intrigued.

"People who need it. Sometimes pregnant girls. Sometimes men who lost their jobs. Women who need to feed their children. It depends."

"But why? Can't those people go to the Temple or... Or to..." Rhian drifted off, her face falling into a frown.

"The king?" Liana asked, sarcastically "The earls?"

"I suppose... there would be too many obstacles in the way of that..."

"I don't know how close you were with your brother. Probably not very, given... you know... but he wasn't exactly *at one* with the people, if you understand what I mean."

"Oh, I understand." Rhian sighed, nodding with a tight look.

"Trust me when I say that I have some experience in what you're going through. I know that this can be a... difficult time,"

Liana went on. "It can feel like you're trapped. That you don't have a lot of choices."

"That's *exactly* how it feels." Rhian nodded, wringing her hands in her lap.

"So that begs the question…" Liana took a seat across from the princess. She looked her in the eye, lowering her tone just a bit. "What do you want to do?"

"What do you mean?"

"Throwing your lot in with pirates isn't exactly an ideal future for you. Can you imagine? Raising a child while you're sailing the seas with these scalawags?" Liana tried to joke, but only succeeded in making Rhian hunch down further. "I need you to be honest with me, Princess. Do you even want this baby?"

Rhian's eyes grew wide, brimming with indecision. She lifted her shoulders, opening her hands, completely at a loss. "I-I thought I didn't. But, if you're really asking me to be honest, Captain… I think I… do."

She seemed to be waiting for Liana's judgement or a response to lead her in the right direction. But none came. She just sat and listened.

"I do," said Rhian again, with much more certainty. "I want to keep it. Or at least I want the child to live. If I can't raise it, then I want someone to do it who can do it well. I was going to use something… Something to end the pregnancy. But I'm glad I didn't."

"Why?"

"Because I thought I didn't have another choice. I thought it was the only way. I love Dillon. I would love to raise a child with him."

"Why didn't you tell him, then? I'm sure he would have jumped at the chance to rescue you," Liana asked with mirth.

"I didn't want the only reason he married me to be because of *this*." Rhian gestured around her stomach.

"I can understand that. So, if I'm hearing you right, your first choice would be to go back to Whyte and raise the baby together?"

"That's impossible, though. You were there at the garden. Dillon won't ever have me after what I *did*. He probably hates me."

"How can you be so sure?"

"Dillon is... He always does the right thing. No matter what. Me? I'm... *wrong*."

"Wrong?" Liana asked. She couldn't place why, but hearing Rhian say this about herself troubled her.

Rhian nodded, somber. "These powers. I never asked for them. They complicate things. They're too much responsibility. They don't fit in the life I want to have."

Liana took a deep breath, casting her eyes down to the maps on the table. She fiddled with the corner of one and said, "You'll come to learn that it's not about fitting yourself into some mold. It's about making your own place in this world. Asking for permission doesn't do any good. You have to carve it out. If you want to run away with Dillon Whyte, I don't think that's an impossible dream. In fact, it would be ideal—it would get you out of my hair."

A watery smile spread across Rhian's face.

"Just remember," Liana continued, smiling back, "Whyte drafted the help of a pirate. He's not all golden. That being said, if you want to go another route, then that's fine."

"It is? I thought that you were upset about me being here… and being pregnant."

"Despite what you may think, I'm not completely cold-hearted."

"I never thought that, Captain Foley," Rhian said sincerely.

"Well… thanks," Liana said. "I've had some time to mull this over. It's inconvenient, but until we can find a place for you and your baby, you can stay with us. It's your life. You should be happy about what direction it goes."

Rhian sniffed and nodded. "Thank you, Captain Foley. Truly."

As they exited the cabin, Liana spotted Marin speaking with Lucky at the bow. The latter man threw his hands up in frustration and shoved past Marin, bounding across the deck. Lucky looked up to see Liana watching. He immediately turned on his heel and went the opposite direction. The distinct glint of metal shone from his palm as he shoved something in his coat.

"Don't tell me he's pulling this shit again," Liana grumbled.

"What is it?" asked Rhian.

"Why don't you go back to the galley? I have something to take care of."

Liana followed Lucky back to the bow where Marin stood, looking cross. "Problem, gentlemen?"

"He's not fit for the night watch this evenin'," Marin explained. Lucky slumped down, crossing his arms like a guilty child. "Lookit 'im. I swear tah the Divine ya do this on purpose, Lucky."

"I'm fit for duty, Marin," Lucky slurred back, leaning backwards over the bow. "Fit as my fiddle. Iswearit. Now bugger off."

"What's that, then?" Liana pointed to Lucky's coat. He smoothed out the front of it and shrugged. "Ulliam Laughlin, I know you've got a flask in there."

"Drinkin' on duty," Marin said, shaking his head. "Imagine what Captain Bancroft would have done to ye."

"I'm not a cabin boy anymore," Lucky seethed. "And this isn't the *Siren*."

"Flogged, Lucky! Ye woulda been flogged!"

"Marin, please. You and I both know I'm not going to flog him." Liana stepped between the men. "Lucky, we can't keep having this conversation. For the Divine's sake, you're an officer. No drinking on duty."

"M'fine, Captain—"

Liana yanked Lucky by the arm, tugging him away from Marin, who took it as a cue to excuse himself. "What happened? I thought you decided to quit the drinking."

Lucky scratched at his anchor tattoo. He blinked glassy eyes and cleared his throat. "Another slip, Captain. I 'pologize."

"When?"

"The day you got engaged. At the Barricade. I slipped up," he said again. "Haven't been able to shake it since."

"Lucky." Liana moved to get directly into his line of sight. "*You* are the one who taught me that a sailor needs to be clear-headed. That it could mean the survival of his crewmates. Now, you know we're short on men. You've got a watch shift in just a few hours. Who do you expect to take it?"

"I can—"

"Not in this state, you can't. We have the Navy actively looking for us. We need to keep moving. I can't tolerate this. But given our circumstances, I can't exactly send you back to the Capital. We need you. *I* need you."

"I'm sorry, Captain. Truly."

"If it happens again, you'll be stripped of your title and the brig'll be your new home until you can get this under control," she warned. With one fluid motion, she reached into Lucky's coat pocket and snatched the flask. Sluggishly, he tried to stop her, but to no avail. She waved it in his face. "*This* is not worth the life of my crew. You get one more chance. Now get to your cot and sleep it off. You'll be woken at ten o'clock for the second half of your shift."

The sea rocked, lulling Liana like an infant in a cradle. Even the waves made soothing shushing sounds. It seemed to slumber along with the day crew—and Lucky. She strained to see the horizon in the dim lantern light. As the wind picked up from the south, Liana tucked her hair under her hat to keep it from her eyes. She would have liked to close them, to fall into oblivion. If it wasn't so cold out, she might have. They could have anchored so everyone could have a rest. But, as she told Lucky, they needed to keep moving. Stopping meant becoming a floating target.

Tomorrow, she reminded herself. *Tomorrow we'll be at Dunmore Manor.* Their destination, however, would only bring more questions, more uncertainties about where to go from there.

Something over her shoulder caught her attention. Lantern light shined brightly off golden hair, and Liana blinked. "Princess? What are you doing up so late?"

"Coffee?" she offered, holding out a cup with a sympathetic smile.

Liana sighed in relief, so grateful she could have kissed the princess. With one hand, she took the cup and sniffed. Coffee always reminded her of her childhood in the Islands, where the flowering plants grew wild and people made fortunes cultivating them on farms. Once a luxury, now merchant trade ships distributed all over Vioria and easily obtainable. As that thought passed through her mind Liana was unpleasantly reminded of the conversation about island agriculture she'd had with Grigor Vitalis at the ball. Pressing the memory aside, she grinned at Rhian. "Thanks."

"I gave Lucky a cup as well, so he can take over."

"I'm shocked you were able to wake him up," she said, before taking a sip and immediately spitting it back out into the cup. Once she recovered from nearly choking on the half-ground beans, she wheezed. "Did you make this?"

Rhian sheepishly took the coffee back. "Mister Venegas is asleep, and I thought you could use some."

"If you gave Lucky a cup from the same batch, he'll be sober in no time," Liana said, returning her attention to the helm. "It was a nice thought. You didn't have to do that."

"Well, you've been so kind to me…"

"Have I?" She looked at the princess, genuinely surprised.

"Yes," Rhian said. "You have."

The princess stayed where she stood, even after silence fell between them. Liana glanced back at her a couple of times, but it was difficult to tell what she could be thinking in the dark. "You can go to bed, if you want. I'm fine."

"Actually, could I ask you a question, Captain Foley?"

"Alright, then."

"Why did you take Lucky's place?"

"Because we need someone at the helm."

"You could have told someone else to do it."

"I don't trust many with the helm," she said, gripping the handles of the wheel. In it she could feel the strain of the tiller ropes, connected all the way to the whipstaff and the now-fragile rudder. "It's the heart of the ship."

"I see."

She continued, "We keep to a schedule so that we don't over-exhaust. Each officer has a team to carry a six-hour watch with. The shifts rotate."

"I've noticed. When the bells chime."

"Exactly. At seven o'clock this morning, Ameen's shift started. Then, at one o'clock in the afternoon, Marin took over. Lucky's shift started at seven o'clock this evening. It wouldn't be fair to ask Marin and Ameen to take on an extra watch on the same day."

"How many officers are there?"

"Not including me? Three—Ameen is the quartermaster, Marin is the navigator, and Lucky is the master gunner. They have specific roles but take on the watches as well. As the captain, I oversee everything. I try to be flexible. With so many things that could go wrong at *any* time of day… For instance, this morning I was woken because the rigging we used for the rudder started to fall apart. I helped Kahil fix it before breakfast."

"Even though you were up so early, you took the watch anyway. That's very admirable of you."

"Some might say I was too lenient on Lucky," Liana said, shaking off the compliment. "But I treat my men with respect—

go out on a limb for them, and they'll put their efforts into making this ship sail the way it needs to. It's not that I let them get away with being idiots. We all do our part. Lucky... He struggles sometimes. But he's been there for me, so I try to do the same for him."

"You've known him a long time?"

"Close to my whole life. He and Marin sailed together when they were young men. Lucky took my family in when we moved to the Capital. He didn't have much, but he helped us anyway. He was there at the beginning, when I purchased the *Windfall*. He's taught me a great deal—about sailing and other things."

"The bastard also needs a firm hand when necessary," said a voice behind them. Lucky shuffled up the steps. He bowed his head at Rhian. "Highness. Thank you for the coffee. Perked me *right* up. Captain, I hope you can forgive me for my behavior."

"Talk to me after I've had some sleep."

"Yes, ma'am," he said, flashing a smile.

"And bring me breakfast," she added, stepping away to allow him to take the helm. "Just not too early, because I'd like to sleep in."

"Of course, Captain," he said, bowing again deeply. "Will you be taking coffee with your breakfast?"

"So long as Thiago makes it." Liana glanced at Rhian. "No offense."

"None taken," she said with a giggle.

Despite herself, a grin tugged at the corners of Liana's mouth. They descended from the helm's platform and parted ways in front of the captain's cabin.

"Good night, Princess."

"Good night, Captain."

Careful not to wake Ameen, Liana tiptoed inside. His own watch would start after Lucky's ended. Despite her efforts, she realized he was awake when she slid into the berth beside him. He reached back and caught her hand, wrapping her arm around his middle. She settled in for sleep, pressing against his warm back. As soon as she did, she felt the deep rumble of laughter beneath her cheek.

"What?" she asked suspiciously.

"Nothing," he said, feigning innocence. "Sounds like the princess has grown on you, is all."

"Oh, shut up."

"I think it's good that you two are getting along."

"I said *shut up*, Almasi. Go back to sleep before I smother you with this bloody pillow."

Chapter 20

Fire

10th of Deornath, 1723

Dunmore Manor, Yael Province

With a firm turn of a key, Liana locked the trunk at the foot of the bed. She pocketed it and gave the container a little pat, as though it would help with concealing the tome. Unable to leave it securely on the ship, she thought it best to keep it with her personal belongings. With the last bit of her luggage taken from the *Windfall* and moved to the manor, it was time to start the repairs.

The officers would stay in the main house, along with Rhian, Thiago, and Sava, while the rest of the crew lodged in another building across the courtyard. The Dunmores' typically used it in the spring, when other wealthy landowners and nobility would visit or come to purchase horses. For now, it was theirs to occupy. Dunmore had told them to use it as long as they needed, but with luck the repairs on the *Windfall* wouldn't take more than a couple of weeks.

The princess had asked to watch the spectacle of the men careening the ship. She waited for Liana down in the foyer. As

Liana went downstairs to meet her, Nellie's musical laugh reverberated off the marble floor. As fashionable as ever, she sported a cobalt riding habit and matching black hat with a bow atop thick black hair. Her radiant brown skin balanced out the cool winter sunlight that seeped through the floor to ceiling windows. Nellie had always been like the sun, Liana thought. Always at the center, people were drawn to her warm nature. But from experience, Liana knew just how quick that warmth could turn to ice.

At Nellie's side stood her husband, Rhys Dunmore—a man who, in Liana's opinion, was never less than arrogant. In the few days they had been there, Rhian got along very well with the Dunmores. But Liana had no doubts that she would. They were exactly her sort. The three of them chatted amicably until Liana approached.

"Good morning, Liana," Nellie cheerfully greeted her. "Are you settling in alright?"

"Just fine, thanks. And how are you feeling?"

Nellie blinked.

"The baby hasn't made you sick or tired?"

"Oh, I'm just fine," she replied pleasantly, stroking hand against her stomach, hidden by her coat and a flattering cut of her bodice. "I've been very fortunate to have such an easy pregnancy."

Liana held back a laugh when she caught the slightly jealous look in Rhian's eyes. She could relate. More than a few times, Liana caught herself feeling envious of her perfect foster sister.

"Ceres tells us you'll be flipping the ship upside down?" Nellie went on.

To avoid any questions as to why a princess would be seeking refuge with pirates, Liana had suggested she use another name while they were at the manor.

"Careening, Mistress Dunmore," said Rhian before Liana could speak. "It's when the crew takes out everything in the hold and pulls the ship on her side. That way they can easily see what's wrong with the rudder. Isn't that right, Captain Foley?"

"That's right," Liana said, smiling despite herself. "You've been listening."

"Quite the apprentice you have there, Liana," Dunmore praised.

Liana's lips pressed into a thin line. She wouldn't take it *that* far. But Rhian beamed with pride, and she didn't feel right cutting her down. She still wore Liana's borrowed breeches, despite Nellie having offered several times to provide her with a dress. With the linen shirt neatly tucked into the waist, Rhian excitedly shoved her hands into a worn gray overcoat.

"Might your sister and I join you?" Dunmore interrupted as Liana and Rhian began their exit. "I'm sure you'd also like to see my own ship."

"Do you mean the sloop on that dock in the cove?" she asked. She would have hardly called that little thing a *ship*. Even calling it a sloop was generous. But whatever Dunmore needed to stoke his ego was no skin off her nose. "Sure. Come along, then."

Without waiting for an answer, Liana strode outside, the sound of the princess' light footsteps trailing just behind her. She was learning to keep up.

The estate sat high on a hill overlooking the sea with a hefty thousand acres, boasting several agricultural and residential buildings. Due to its isolation, Dunmore Manor was nearly self-sustainable. They even had a family crypt, which Rhys explained housed the remains of five generations of Dunmores. Liana found that rather bone-chilling. She couldn't understand how Nellie could live there. Liana needed freedom. She could never have committed to a life at the manor. Then again, Nellie had never had the same yearning to travel as she always had.

Liana shielded her eyes from the bright morning light. They walked down a cobblestone lane past the stables and the guest quarters. Looking almost too decorative for use, the buildings stood in an expansive grassy courtyard, its burgundy bricks covered in green vines that would bloom yellow flowers in the spring.

She led the way down the trail to the cove, only glancing back as they descended down a particularly steep path.

"Careful now," she said, a little nervous for both Rhian and Nellie to go down. After all, they both were in delicate conditions. Turning around, she held out her hand to Rhian, who was two steps behind her, and helped her down to the beach. It was fortunate that she did, because as soon as the princess took it, she slipped on a loose shelf of sand. As it crumbled beneath her feet, Rhian careened forward, but Liana caught her. Spooked by the near fall, Rhian giggled nervously and clung to Liana's arm the rest of the way down.

When they came to the bottom, Liana surveyed the *Windfall*, lying angled on its side. The crew took a rest after the fierce undertaking. It had taken most of the day to empty the ship of all cargo, including the cannons. Everything that wasn't attached to the *Windfall* now stood in a neat row along the beach. The men had already begun inspecting the rudder. Ameen and Lucky stood near the stern, gathering rope. She chewed her thumbnail as she watched from afar.

"There she is!" exclaimed Dunmore when he and Nellie finally caught up. Liana peered over her shoulder to find he wasn't talking about the *Windfall*. He sauntered down the beach toward the dock where a single-mast sailboat was tied off.

"Mine's *bigger*," she said. She didn't realize she spoke loud enough to hear until a titter caught her attention off to her left. Rhian covered her mouth, face flushed with effort of holding in her laughter. Thrilled that someone appreciated the joke, Liana shot her a sly wink.

"Be nice," said Nellie, clucking her tongue. Apparently, she heard as well. "He's very... *proud*."

"There the two of ya are!" called Marin, jogging over from the shoreline. He swept Nellie up in an embrace. Then he placed an arm around Liana's shoulders. "I canna tell ya how it feels to see my two girls together again."

"It's so good to have you all here, Da." Nellie kissed him on the cheek and flashed Liana a dazzling smile.

"How does the *Windfall* look, Marin?" Liana asked.

"Well, we've heaved her down. They're takin' a look now."

"How did you manage that?" Rhian asked, with wonder-filled eyes on the ship.

"At high tide we brought the anchor ashore and secured the top halyard to that tree there." He pointed across the beach.

"And the hull?" said Liana. "I suppose we might as well have the men scrape—"

"Looks to be a dangerous undertaking." Dunmore came strolling back to them, after seeing no one followed him to the docked sloop. "Can you be sure that the ropes will hold?"

"The ropes are fine," she drawled back without even looking at her brother-in-law. "They're well-oiled to stretch, and my men know how to tie a good knot."

"Ah, yes. I'm sure they do."

"It's all very well-planned, Rhys," Marin said. Liana crossed her arms and squinted out at the ship. It bothered her that Marin felt the need to defend her and the crew. "And it's not as if we havena done this before. Liana, do ya recall—?"

An explosion rattled the beach as a fist of fire punched through the *Windfall*'s hull from the inside. Smoke had barely bloomed into the sky when Liana took off like a shot. Hoarse howling sounded off from the crew as they called out two names: "Lucky! Almasi!"

Diving into thick smoke, Liana joined the calls. Somewhere far off, she heard Jamil's voice—she was sure it was him, for Kahil would never be so level-headed—directing the efforts to extinguish the fire. The wild search came to an abrupt end when she rounded the stern to find Lucky treading water. He held his head, pleading for someone to check on Almasi. Liana's eyes followed Lucky's pointed finger to her quartermaster, sitting up in the shallows and covered in ash.

"Ameen!" She dropped down to meet him, hardly feeling the frigid water soak through her clothes. Holding him around the jaw, she forced him to look at her. He hissed at the sudden movement and blinked hard, tenderly rubbing his ears. His brown coat had been charred black.

"Threw himself in front of the fire to save me," said Lucky, sloshing to her side.

"Are you hurt?"

"No." Ameen began to come to his senses. Seeing her distress, he tugged her down closer so her forehead pressed against his. He rubbed his hands over hers to soothe her. "I'm fine. Liana, I'm fine."

With Lucky's help, she got Ameen to stand. Thanks to Jamil and the rest of the crew's efforts, the fire quickly got under control.

Hours later, she waded in front of the blasted hull. Marin stood at her side.

"Thiago is takin' a look at Ameen," he told her. "It's mostly his hearing, from the explosion, but Thiago said he should be right in a couple of days. Lucky wouldn't go to the house. He insisted on helpin' to put out the fire."

"But what *happened*?"

He turned back and called Jamil over, who brought something wrapped in canvas. It revealed a lantern, shattered and melted beyond repair. "Three powder kegs were left aboard, Captain," he told her. "And this."

"Powder kegs?" she repeated, as realization washed over her. "*Lucky!*"

Marin and Jamil must have also immediately made the connection, because they kept their eyes solemnly fixed on the tide. Liana scanned the beach, stomping through the parting throng of men to search for an anchor tattoo. "Lucky!"

He showed himself, with his hat in his hands and shame in his stance. "Captain."

"Explain to me how the gun deck wasn't cleared."

"An oversight, Captain…"

"An oversight, was it? You were responsible for that inventory. Your oversight has put back our repairs by weeks, at best!"

"I have no excuse. For neither the inventory nor the lantern."

"The lantern?" she said, feeling as though she'd been gutted. "The lantern was yours?"

Gripping his hat so tightly his knuckles turned white, he nodded. "Aye, Captain."

She took a staggering step back, very much aware that the crew watched them. Still, she didn't bother to keep her voice quiet. "You were drinking, weren't you?"

"I forgot about the last load and left my lantern on the gun deck. When we heaved her over, the lantern must have..."

That forgetfulness nearly cost her the ship and the man she loved. But it was her own fault. She had let Lucky off too easily.

"Jamil," she called. Lucky looked up sharply as Jamil padded over. Liana looked Lucky in the eye as she spoke her next words. "Your bravery and alertness played no small part in containing the fire. You took control under dire circumstances and led the crew. You are exactly what I need in an officer. I'm promoting you to master gunner."

Jamil shifted in the sand. He was clearly shocked, but rather than question his captain, he inclined his head, avoiding Lucky's eyes. "Thank you, Captain. It's an honor."

"Have Kahil take the lead on the repairs. I want a report on the damages and an execution plan by tomorrow at noon. Is that feasible?"

"Yes, ma'am. I won't let you down."

"I should hope not. As for *you*," Liana now addressed Lucky. He stood frozen to the spot, mortified and red as a beetroot beneath his black- and silver-streaked hair. His roguishly handsome face had gone gaunt. The crew surrounded them now, their hostile sentiments toward him painted clearly, cutting through the silence as they waited for the captain's judgement. "You will be confined for the remainder of our stay at the manor. When the ship is repaired, you'll remain in the brig. As soon as we are able to safely make landfall, you'll be dismissed."

Lucky didn't say a word. His eyes, brimming with regret, begged for forgiveness. But she was drained. She had nothing left to give. With betrayal heavy in her heart, she motioned for two of the crew to escort Lucky. He hung his head, his hair dripping with sweat and seawater, but went away quietly.

As she looked after them, she spotted Rhian amongst the crew. Taken aback by her presence, Liana waited until Lucky had gone and the crew had dispersed before approaching her.

"What are you still doing here? It's not safe for you to be here, with all the smoke and whatnot," she said, gesturing to the sky.

"I stayed back after Mister and Mistress Dunmore left," Rhian replied. "I wanted to make sure you were all right."

I'm not, Liana wanted to say. Her ship was in a much worse state now. Ameen had nearly been blasted to pieces. Lucky had made an absolute fool of her. Bitterness filled her soul, splitting her open and leaving her raw. "Don't you worry your pretty little head about me. I'll walk you back to the manor," she said instead.

After they crested the hill in silence, Rhian spoke. "That must have been very difficult for you, Captain Foley."

"Of course, it was," Liana snapped, stomping toward the courtyard. "It's difficult, being captain. They all look at me, expecting me to know what to do. And if I make the wrong decision… Do you know how hard I had to work for their trust, to make them believe that even though I'm a woman and I'm younger than half of them that I could be a competent captain? Earning their respect was a feat in itself, but *keeping* it… Do you know what it's like to be surrounded by men, constantly questioning yourself, wondering if you really have what it takes to lead them?"

"Actually," Rhian said softly, "I do."

Liana paused before the courtyard. She lifted her hat and ran her fingers through her hair, embarrassed by her bitter ranting.

"You care so much about them," the princess went on. "It shows. They know it."

"I cared too much about Lucky," Liana said. "I was too kind. He took advantage of me, and now the rest of the crew will pay for it. They won't be able to go home, until… Well, who knows when? What if they never make it home? It's all my fault."

Liana carried on, hurrying several steps in front of the princess. Rhian followed until Liana managed to break away in the foyer. She bolted up the stairs, leaving the princess behind.

Chapter 21

Fox Tales

11ᵗʰ of Deornath, 1723

Even though Captain Foley had been clear she wanted to be alone, Rhian was still disappointed when she didn't see her at dinner the next evening.

"She's in a mood," Marin replied when Rhian asked after her. "The fire set us back much farther than anticipated."

"How long will it take to fix?"

"Several weeks, possibly months. That's not quick enough for the captain. She would like tah patch it with what we can find on the grounds," he said with a sigh and a shake of his head, like a father exasperated with the foolhardiness of his child. "But Ameen and I agree that we must take the time to repair the rudder and the hull properly."

Rhian opened her mouth to ask if Mister Almasi was feeling better.

"Of course, you must," Dunmore readily agreed. His eyes met his wife's. "We don't mind the company, do we?"

"But dear, we can't *force* them to stay," Nellie looked to Rhian, who blinked. She expected Nellie to want them to leave least of all. She seemed very happy to be in the presence of her father and foster sister.

Marin added, "Liana argued that we could finish the repairs in a port city. But we may well lose the ship on the way."

"And Lucky?" asked Rhian.

"Ah, dinna worry. He's comfortable."

"That's right," said Dunmore. "We have him staying in the old overseer's house. Small thing by the treeline."

"Is anyone… guarding him?"

"Well, he doesna have anywhere tah go, lass." Marin picked at his fowl. "Even if he chanced walkin' about the grounds, the crew is still furious with him."

"Our staff has to bring him meals because everyone in the crew refuses," Nellie said sadly. "It's such a shame. I remember when Lucky lived with us when we came from Madzetal."

"More like we lived with him," Marin corrected. "No surprise that Liana is takin' this so hard."

"Perhaps you should try speaking with her, dear," Dunmore suggested to Nellie, who balked.

"Oh… I don't know. Liana and I…" she began, taking a moment of thought for the right choice of words. "It's been a long time since we've been close."

"Well, certainly all that is past," he said, lifting his wineglass. "That whole business with that *girl*. What was her name again?"

"Asha, darling."

"Who is Asha?" asked Rhian.

Nellie smirked behind her own glass. "Let's just say she was very *close* with Liana."

"O-oh."

"Petronella," Marin interrupted, in the strictest tone Rhian had ever heard from him. "Please. Have a thought for your sister's privacy."

"I'm sorry, Da." Nellie gave a thin apology. She exchanged looks with her husband as though they shared a private joke.

Rhian didn't find anything about the conversation funny. She wished she hadn't naively asked about Asha. In no way did Rhian think it would lead to knowing such personal information about the captain. A wriggling need to apologize to her, despite her absence, wormed its way in her conscience.

In court, she'd heard of such relationships, between two men, two women, or sometimes multiple sexual partners of varying genders. As sheltered as Rhian was, she'd gathered the topic was forbidden to speak of openly. Perhaps, she thought, if she'd been raised with a loving and supportive parent like Marin, instead of stiff palace staff, Rhian would have been able to explore how she fit into the world of such romances. Dillon had been the first person to ever show interest in Rhian outside of her title. They'd shared a passionate affair, sneaking moments together in private while remaining agonizingly distant in public.

Rhian found men, with their strong bodies and bold mannerisms, attractive. But if Dillon had been a woman, she paused to wonder if their romance would have played out the same, except, of course, without the resulting pregnancy. Rhian had always admired her own sex, especially in comparison to their male counterparts. Even a ruffian like Captain Foley held a certain poise that could not go unnoticed. She dressed in trousers and leather tricorns, but something feminine showed through all of that.

Marin's voice drew Rhian from her thoughts of the captain, and she focused on the current conversation about Dunmore's hunting exploits.

"I canna believe that ya nearly killed the poor creature!"

"It was a fox," Dunmore replied blandly. "We hunt them all the time."

"Blasphemy!"

"Sailors are very superstitious, Rhys," Nellie explained. "And the fox is the great love of the swallow."

"A beautiful thing, he was," Dunmore lamented. "He would have been a gorgeous pelt."

"What do foxes and swallows have to do with sailing?" Rhian tilted her head curiously.

"Swallows are sacred to sailors. They carry drowned souls back tah land."

"Well now you *must* tell the story, Da," Nellie insisted.

"I suppose it would be great practice for the child." Marin winked at his daughter, who let out a short laugh that, to Rhian, sounded a little forced.

"Long ago, when man was first beginnin' tah sail," Marin began, settling back in his chair, his empty plate before him, "The Eagle was the King of the Sky."

"I thought the story was about a fox," Dunmore interrupted, already bored.

"It is, but the Eagle is the one who begins the story. One day, he was observin' from his perch on the cliffs. He saw the Swallow flyin' from the south for the summer. Now, as ye know, the Swallow is a small bird—agile and quick. The Eagle admired her shimmerin' blue feathers and how she could twist and turn and perform acrobatics and the like over the sea.

"Once he had it in his mind to make the Swallow his Queen, the Eagle came down to claim her. But when the Swallow saw the Eagle comin', with his sharp talons and powerful wings, she feared that she had angered the King of the Sky with her whimsy. So, she flew as fast as she could toward the forest.

"She could never outfly the Eagle, so she flitted about the trees, tryin' tah lose him. Finally, she had no choice but to dive down into a hole beneath the roots of a rowan tree. That was when she came beak to nose with the furry creature that lived in the den—the Fox!

"Now, at first, the Fox was angry for the intrusion—he had been living a solitary life after the King of the Forest, the Bear, had exiled him for his trickery. That is quite the story as well..."

"Da," Nellie said gently.

"Yes, o'course, one tale at a time," Marin said apologetically. "So, when the Swallow told him that she had angered a King as well, the Fox figured that now banishment may not be so lonely. He allowed the Swallow to share his tree with him. She made a nest in the center of the branches. And so, they spent the rest of the summer together in the meadow of the rowan tree. Both had playful spirits, so they got on very well. By the time autumn came, they had fallen in love.

"As the wind became colder, the Fox's fur grew thicker, but the Swallow's feathers couldna keep her warm. It was time for her to migrate south. The Fox begged her to stay with him, told her he would keep her within his tail all winter if he had tah—he could not bear to be alone again. But they knew that if she stayed the cold would kill her. He had tah let her go.

"After promisin' her return in the spring, the Swallow left the rowan's meadow. But, durin' the migration, the Eagle had learned of the Swallow's love for the Fox. He swore that upon returnin' tah the north, he would kill him for makin' a fool of yet another King.

"When spring came, the Fox looked tah the sky, awaitin' his love—but instead he was confronted with the Eagle's talons!" Marin leaned forward, pressing his hands on the table. "It was a *fierce* chase, and many creatures of the land and sky gathered in the rowan's meadow tah watch.

"When the Fox was cornered after stumblin' over the roots of the rowan, he accepted his fate and waited for the Eagle to end his life. But, in that moment, the Swallow came to his rescue! She intercepted the Eagle's attack with her aerial talents and spread her wings tah shield the Fox.

"The Eagle tried tah stop himself, but before he could, he already had the Swallow's body clutched in his talons. So ashamed at what he had done, the Eagle rested the Swallow down beneath the rowan and took flight tah the mountains."

"And the Fox?" Rhian found her own voice soft with sadness.

"He curled his tail around the Swallow and mourned. He cried, pleadin' for her tah live again.

"The spirit of the rowan, who had witnessed the bloomin' love between the Fox and the Swallow, heard him and answered his plea. It gave him the power tah heal.

"The Fox, so lost in his grief, hardly realized that the red tip of his tail was turnin' white, while the Swallow's white belly became red. The creatures who witnessed also saw the berries of the rowan change to match the Swallow's new feathers.

"And so, the Swallow lived. Though she still must migrate every spring, she returns to the same nest in the rowan tree tah be with her love. That is why sailors never harm foxes, for fear of betrayin' the Swallow, who guides drowned sailors' souls to their rest, just as she always finds respite every summer in the meadow of the rowan tree."

Nellie sighed dreamily. Her gray eyes, the color of clouds before a storm, matched her father's. "I love that story."

Marin looked to his daughter, his own gaze hazy with tenderness. Rhian thought that perhaps Nellie looked like her mother and that Marin was seeing a ghost of her, joined with them at the table in her smile.

"Have you ever heard that story?" Rhian asked Sava the next day when she came to bring him breakfast. Even at the manor, she continued her duties helping Thiago tend to him.

"Many times," he replied, scarfing down some toast. His appetite had returned in full force. He could even take walks about the manor on good days. "Marin likes to tell it to the children at the Barricade."

"Romantic, isn't it?"

"Yeah," he agreed after swallowing his last bite.

Rhian sighed and for a moment pictured a young Liana Foley, enraptured as her foster father told a bedtime story of the love between two woodland creatures. It made her wonder what the captain had been like as a child. Rebellious, no doubt.

He shot her a teasing look. "Thinking about your love, Highness?"

"Perhaps," she mumbled, blushing as Dillon's handsome face replaced the image of Captain Foley.

"You want to go back to him?"

She sighed, taking his plate. "Of course I do. But there are so many risks." She couldn't explain her fears to Sava. He had no idea about her powers. Still, he seemed to understand at least one of her hesitations.

"Right. Impossible, with the ship in such a state."

"I can't have this child alone, Sava," she said. "Dillon is my only chance at building the family I want to have. But I have no way to get to him."

"If you speak with the captain, I'm sure she could figure something out."

"She has enough on her mind as it is. First, she was worried about you, now Lucky and the ship... I'm sure she hardly has a moment for me."

"Didn't you say she offered to help you get back to him?"

"Yes, but it's too much. She's already done enough for me. I think I need to figure this out on my own."

Chapter 22

Guidance

21ˢᵗ of Deornath, 1723

The princess routinely slipped out of the manor in the early hours of the morning. On the third morning of witnessing this behavior, Ameen decided it was time to follow her.

Observing her from the crest of a hill north of the manor, he had a good view. He resisted the urge to go and help her as she clambered down to the beach in her borrowed breeches. Liana's old coat shielded her from the icy ocean breeze. Once she made it to the shoreline, she paced for a moment, as though steeling herself. Then she faced the nearby cliff wall, raised her hands, and shot a single bolt of lightning from her palms. The rock split, making an unsightly gash in the cliff formation. It joined at least twenty more like it, each smaller than the last.

He staggered back so quickly he nearly tripped over his feet. Forcing himself to breathe, he caught the scent of unnatural ozone, nearly hidden beneath the briny sea. Grasping the trunk of the nearest tree, he managed to balance himself. Now he understood Liana's fear. He found himself holding his Circle. The sight of magic shook him to his core.

He peered out and approached again to see Rhian shaking her hands, steeling herself for another spell. Again, the princess unleashed her power, this time causing a circular hole. She gripped her fist and laughed, twirling once in celebration. At the end of the turn, she looked up and saw Ameen at the crest.

She took a frightened stance, but he raised a peaceful hand. "It's alright," he called. "I'm coming down."

Rhian paced the beach again as she waited for him. When he did, he stopped a safe distance away, lifting his palm again.

"You're going to tell the captain, aren't you?" she said, holding herself.

"You know that I will," he answered, glancing over at the marks on the bluff. "But first, I want to talk."

She followed his line of sight. "I was practicing."

"I can see that," he answered, taking a few steps toward her targets. He touched the smallest mark, her last one, no bigger than his fist. "You're trying to control yourself... Limit your strike."

"Yes..."

"Why? Why risk it when you know how the captain feels about your power?"

The princess wrung her hands. "I don't want to kill anyone else. If I don't practice, then I won't ever learn how to stay in control."

After a moment's pause, he said, "I'll walk you back to the manor."

"To see the captain?"

"She's busy at the ship. But I think Sava could use some company. Come on. It's freezing out here."

Liana removed her coat. Her gloves came off with them, and she approached the sofa to hang her hat at the fireside. She turned to the window, feeling helpless. The world outside looked ugly, wet, and bare. A few patches of ice laid strewn on the courtyard, below the naked, twisted trees.

"I thought winter would be more beautiful here," she sighed, averting her eyes from the sight.

Ameen lifted his gaze to her and moved his arm, inviting her to join him before the fire. She sank down and curled into his side. He muttered something in Islander when her nose touched the hollow of his throat.

"In Caerwyn, please?"

"When are you going to learn Islander? For the Divine's sake, you were raised there."

"After we're married—now what did you say?"

"You're colder than a dead man's broken toe," he said, and she smiled into his neck at the oddly translated phrase. He gathered her hands and rubbed them between his palms, warming her gelid skin. "You're later than usual."

"I spoke to Dunmore and Marin," she explained.

"Dunmore hasn't taken issue with us staying, has he?"

"Not at all," she replied glumly. "In fact, he'd like to have a gathering for us all for Mid-Winter."

"You don't sound happy about that."

"I'm not." She closed her eyes, listening to the steady thrum of his heartbeat. "The men should be with their families for Mid-Winter, but instead they're stranded here."

"Staying is the right choice," he assured her. "They know that. It keeps us safe, and it gives Sava more time to heal."

As he continued to massage her hands, Liana sulked, thinking of Thiago missing his daughter and granddaughter for the holiday.

Ameen plucked up her finger, devoid of pearls, with a disapproving look. "You've stopped wearing your ring."

"Don't worry. I put it in the drawer."

"You don't want to lose it?"

"No, I don't want to subject the manor to the wrath of Petronella Foley Dunmore when she realizes that I inherited her mother's wedding ring." She took her hand back. "I think that would surely ruin any Mid-Winter festivities."

Ameen's arm wedged its way between her back and the sofa's cushions, adjusting her so he could hold her closer.

"I know you're disappointed that we can't leave. But there is a chance we could be here when the baby is born," he said hopefully. "How long does Nellie have?"

She paused for thought. "I'm not sure. In the letter Marin received in the Capital, she wrote that she was a few months along. The letter would have taken another several weeks to arrive, the way the mail carriers can be. So, by now... she is six, seven months along?"

His deep voice went a notch higher. "Really?"

"Why?"

"She looks... Ah... Never mind."

Liana lifted up. "Say it."

"I'd rather not."

"Spit it out, Almasi."

"She looks..." he cleared his throat, "Slender?"

"Well, she has always preferred her corsets to be tighter than I have."

"I meant for a woman who is pregnant."

"How observant of you."

"So, you haven't noticed that her pregnancy isn't showing?" he challenged.

She had, but didn't feel it was her place to say it aloud. Ameen must have felt differently in the sanctity of their room.

"Knowing Nellie, she has altered her wardrobe to make herself... What was the word you used? *Slender*."

"No need to be jealous."

"Just be careful lest you forget which Foley woman is which," she advised.

"It's your brother-in-law who needs reminding."

"Dunmore?" She had made a point to remain placid and aloof around him to appease Nellie. Something about Rhys Dunmore was absolutely vexing to Liana. "I've hardly been around the man since we've been here."

"That has not stopped him from asking after you," he said, letting a mildly annoyed frown slip across his lips. "I swear to the Divine, if he asks me one more question about you..."

"That's... odd," she remarked. "What sorts of questions?"

"About your childhood—before Marin took you in."

"You don't think Nellie told him, did you? She's always been such a gossip."

"Forget Dunmore. We'll have all winter to deal with him."

"All winter..." She groaned. "I wish there was something we could do. How is the Barricade going to manage without us?"

"It doesn't need the income from the *Windfall* to be a simple tavern, Liana. Perhaps that's all it needs to be, for now. Bess is just as resourceful as you are. She'll keep it going."

"But people need us. They depend on us."

"For years, you've given to the people at the expense of risking your life. You left behind a community which owes you everything. They can take on some of the burden for a while. Take this time for yourself."

"For myself?" The phrase sounded as odd to her as if he had spoken in Islander again.

"Yes," he insisted. "Think of this as that holiday away from sea we talked about."

His fingers moved from her jaw to the base of her skull, massaging her scalp. She immediately relaxed, neck going limp as he replaced its strength with his own. "Mmm, that feels nice."

He went on for several minutes before speaking again. "Liana, there's something I need to tell you…"

Of course, he was buttering her up for something.

"What?" she said, opening one eye.

"This morning I saw the princess practicing her magic."

His hands slipped away as she twisted around to look at him. "What?"

"She's trying to control it."

"By using it?" she snapped, aghast that he was taking the princess' side. She sprang to her feet. "She could kill someone, *again*."

"If she keeps holding herself back, she will. She'll let loose at the worst moment. What Rhian needs is guidance, not restrictions."

"And who is supposed to guide her? You? Me? We don't know what we're dealing with. Even if she was open to us helping her, how could we rein her in? What if she betrays us?"

He looked up at her. "Have you considered the fact that she's more afraid of us than we are of her?"

"Yes," she snapped. "I'm counting on that to keep us safe."

"Fear breeds anger, Liana. If we don't get her to trust us, then she *will* betray us."

She turned away, rubbing at her eyes in frustration. He came behind her and held her against his chest. She squeezed his forearms tight, dragging her teeth along her bottom lip.

"I think that you should give her the spell book," he said.

She pulled away. "Now, that's too far. Absolutely not."

"It's obvious it was her that Whyte saw in the library. The book belongs to her."

Liana buried her face in her hands. "Why'd you have to say it out loud?" She had conveniently suppressed that notion. It made being around the princess easier. Despite herself, she'd started to enjoy Rhian's company. To even think about the connection between their families... It made her fear what the princess could be capable of.

As though reading her thoughts, Ameen said, "You can't hold her responsible for what happened to your parents."

She let her hands fall and looked up at him. "What if I can't let it go?"

"You have to. It wasn't her fault. And, Liana, she needs us."

"Show me."

A bolt struck the fist-sized hole in the rock, precisely at its center. Liana flinched, despite the warning scent of magic in the seabreeze. She squinted against the wind and tucked a strand of hair behind her ear. The markings on the bluff, just as Ameen said, were progressively smaller and more precise. He stood behind her, next to Rhian, who lowered her palms and slouched against the cold.

"I'm sorry that I didn't tell you," the princess said again. Liana turned around and waved an arm to quiet her.

"I'm not interested in apologies, Rhian," she said sternly. It was only after Rhian looked her in the eyes that Liana realized she'd slipped and used her name instead of her title. She pressed on. "I want safety. You'll continue to practice here every morning under my or Ameen's supervision until we are able to set sail again or until you have the baby. Is that clear?"

"Yes, of course. Thank you, Captain... Thank you."

Liana pointed a stern finger at her. "Don't thank me yet. And don't ever lie to me again, do you understand? You're not that good at it, so I *will* find out."

"Yes, ma'am," she said, tucking her chin. "Of course. I'm just so happy. I've never had this much freedom."

"Really?" Liana looked at her, baffled.

"Yes," said Rhian. "I've never been able to practically apply my powers. All the knowledge I have is from books. In fact, *everything* I know about the world has come from books."

She continued, looking between Liana and Ameen. "My parents weren't very involved in my upbringing, and… I was kept in the palace for much of my life. The two of you are the first people to help me with my magic… Well, besides my uncle."

"You're welcome, I suppose," Liana said, trying to make it seem like her chills were because of the winter air. She sniffed and caught Ameen carefully watching her reaction. "Just try not to bring down the cliff, alright? I don't want to explain to Dunmore how we made a cave behind his manor."

Chapter 23

Revelations
27th of Deornath, 1723

"I won't make a move," Ameen resolved, holding his hand closer. Liana could see the cogs and wheels of his mind turning as he determined his strategy. Rhian sat with them, blue eyes wide with intrigue. "Your turn."

Crooks and Cavalry was Ameen's favorite game. It was played with two separate decks of cards—one blue and one red. Each player would choose which side they wanted. Ameen always chose red—Crooks. His amber eyes narrowed as he drew a card. On the other side of the table, Sava pondered his next move. He nervously fanned his blue-backed hand before drawing a card, examining it, and setting it down on the table.

"I'll add another Horseman," he announced. "And attack your Bandit with my Dragoon."

"Taking a risk, I see." Ameen looked mildly impressed. They picked up the dice and rolled.

"Ha!" Sava raised a triumphant fist. "Six beats four!"

Ameen coolly flipped the card over and set it aside. He drew again and smiled. The younger man's face dropped when Ameen revealed all four cards in his hand. He placed each one, with portraits of hooded figures, over all of Sava's cards. The game was over.

"You were saving all of your Assassins!? You sneaky bastard! I almost had you!"

"What is going on here?"

The four of them turned to see Marin and Dunmore enter the green salon. Rhys looked perturbed by the outburst.

"Crooks and Cavalry?" He peered over Ameen's shoulder. "I haven't played this since I was a child."

"Ameen just took out all of the Cavalry," Liana explained proudly.

"Laddie, face it. You'll never beat Ameen. *Never*." Marin looked to Sava with a sympathetic shake of his head.

"I was hoping that he would go easy on me since I'm injured," Sava pouted, tossing his hand onto the table.

"May I play next?" piped up Rhian, surprising them all.

Liana cleared her throat. "Ceres, may I speak with you privately first?"

"Oh." She flushed red. "Of course."

They met in the hall around the corner. Liana leaned against the wall, noting Rhian's fidgeting. "Breathe, Highness." she said gently, remembering what Ameen had said about fear. "You're not in trouble."

She nodded.

"I just wanted to ask how long you have now," Liana said, gesturing to Rhian's middle.

"About four months."

"Have you thought of what you want to do?"

The fidgeting began again.

"Go on."

"I think you were right before, about me going back to Dillon," Rhian admitted. "I don't mean to make things more difficult for you…"

Liana waved her hand dismissively. "Ameen wouldn't let me hear the end of it if I dumped you and your kid anywhere you don't feel safe. It may not happen as soon as you'd like, but we'll figure it out. We'll make it happen one way or another. I promise."

"Captain Foley?"

They both started at the voice coming from the stairs. A shy young maid—one of Nellie's favorites among their hired help—beckoned Liana.

"What is it?" Liana felt a deep pit of worry open up in her stomach at the maid's pale face. "Is Mistress Dunmore alright?"

"She has requested to speak to you in the boudoir."

"Should I get Mister Dunmore?" Rhian sensed the urgency of the maid as well. "Is something wrong with the baby?"

"Please don't." the maid looked even more distraught at that suggestion. "Mister Dunmore shouldn't be troubled. Nothing to concern him or yourself with—with all due respect, of course."

"I'll come down soon," Liana told Rhian, and they parted ways. The maid led her up the staircase and to the boudoir.

She softly knocked on the door, and a shaky voice from the other side called, "Rhys?"

At the pitiful sound, the hole in Liana's gut grew wider.

"No, Mistress," the maid said gently. "He's in the salon."

"Nellie, I'm here. Open the door," Liana demanded.

She did, looking at them with round watery eyes. Even by looking at Nellie's attire, anyone who knew her would quickly realize that something was wrong. She was still in her nightgown despite the late hour, covered by a silken robe with painted roses along the hem. Her undone curls floated like a black nimbus cloud around her shoulders. She hadn't even powdered her face, and the map of freckles over her cheeks—which Liana had previously thought she had long outgrown from childhood—were now visible.

Liana stepped inside the boudoir behind the maid. As Nellie allowed her in, Liana saw she held the neck of her robe high. It wasn't enough to hide the bruises blooming across her throat. Liana's heart dropped down to her feet. "Divine, Nellie."

Anger bubbled up from the pit in her stomach. Nellie flinched as Liana leaned closer to look. "Did Rhys do this to you?"

Nellie's beautiful features crumpled, and she looked away.

"Tell me the truth," she demanded, harsher than she meant to. She balled her fists at her sides, body tense and ready to spring, as though Dunmore himself would appear at any moment. "I've got a whole crew of men here who would throttle him for you at my word. They would be more than happy to beat any man who would do this to his pregnant wife."

"Please, Liana. I need a sister—not an angry pirate." Nellie collapsed on the lounger by the window, forlorn. Liana had always felt small next to Nellie, who had a good bit of height over her. But now she looked delicate and broken.

"What happened, then?" She forced her voice to soften. Nellie continued to avert her eyes. Liana began to wonder why the hell she had been asked to come in the first place, if she wasn't going to speak up. "At least tell me if the baby is alright."

"You want the truth?" Nellie said, shaking her head. "There is no baby."

Rhian sat between Ameen and Sava in the chair the captain had left behind, wishing Captain Foley had invited her along. She listened to Ameen politely reviewing the rules of Crooks and Cavalry for Dunmore. She felt that she should say something to the man about his wife—but she wasn't sure what. There was no evidence that something was wrong. Simply a feeling.

"That is all well and fine." Dunmore waved his hand dismissively. "But I never play a game unless I place a bet. There must be a gain. Otherwise, there is no thrill for me."

"I'd be happy just to win," Sava chimed in glumly. He glanced over to Ameen, who smirked back at him. Marin chuckled at the exchange.

"Surely, you've won at least once." Dunmore examined the blue Cavalry deck. "It's a children's game."

Ameen scoffed, and the other men turned to look at him. Rhian bit her lip to keep from laughing. Instead, she politely coughed.

"Care to show us your infamous skills, Almasi?" Dunmore asked lightheartedly. "I hear you're a gambling man."

"It's like you said." Ameen shrugged. "There must be something to gain."

"Have you no interest in money?"

"What need do I have for it? I'm under your gracious hospitality."

"Ah, of course." Dunmore seemed quite pleased by his reply. His chest grew outward with satisfaction. The man's entire appearance was made up of proud straight lines, from his coat tails to his square jaw and strong nose. Even his russet hair was tied in an unbending tail down his back.

"Speaking of hospitality, I think I've had my fill of games for the night," Dunmore continued. "Almasi, let's have a drink, shall we? I have a decanter of some fine whisky in my trophy room."

Ameen paused, as though he was searching for an excuse not to accept. When he couldn't find one, he said, "I could use a drink."

"How could you lie about something like this, Nellie?" Liana paced the boudoir, hands shaking with fury. "Have you any sense in your head at all? Do you have any idea what this is going to do to your father? He'll be devastated!"

Nellie sobbed shortly before replying in a breathy voice, "I didn't know what else to do." She clutched a handkerchief, eyes glistening like the dark waters of the sea, her face streaked with tear tracks. The maid demurely stood by the window, hands folded over her apron, nearly invisible.

"This is so *typical* of you."

Nellie threw the handkerchief down. "You have no idea what I have been living through while you and my father have been having a merry time traversing the seas! How else was I supposed to get you here?"

"Me? You lied to get *me* to come here?"

"And the pregnancy wasn't even why you did," Nellie spat bitterly. "Liana Foley, always weaseling herself out of trouble. She couldn't care less how it affects her family."

The words stung. Would Nellie ever let go? Would she ever forgive her for what had happened with Asha? Liana clenched her jaw, glaring down at Nellie as she continued.

"I figured my father would force you here under the right circumstances. But instead, your excuse is a broken... broken ship end!"

"Rudder," Liana muttered, crossing her arms. She looked Nellie over; even in her anger, she still looked deflated. Her eyes returned to the bruises on her neck. "You wanted me to come because of Rhys?"

"Not just you—anyone! I even wrote Ivan!"

"You've been in contact with Ivan? How long had *this* been going on? Why didn't you tell me?"

"You haven't been here!" Nellie snapped. "And of course, I have. But it doesn't matter. He was just as much help as you—so busy with... Well, I'm not exactly sure, it changes so often, every year or so. You know how he is—"

Liana decided to circle back to Ivan later. "All you needed to do was tell us what was happening. Why go to such trouble to create this pregnancy?"

"Rhys reads all my letters before I send them off," she replied sullenly. "I've hardly left the manor since we've been married. And even when we go on trips to Yael, I'm either at his side or told to keep to the townhouse. It's been like living in a prison, Liana."

Liana's voice dropped low. "You want to leave him?"

Nellie nodded, chin quivering. "But it's impossible now. We can't leave. None of us can."

"Horseshit," Liana cursed, making Nellie flinch. "I'm not afraid of Rhys Dunmore. He's one man. What could he possibly do with all of us here?"

Dunmore's trophy room was likely once a library—one of the walls had a floor-to-ceiling bookshelf. Various antlers and stuffed heads of woodland beasts decorated the rest. As he sat in a leather chair, Ameen saw on either side of the double doors were stands of long twisted... bones? Tusks from some sea creature that Ameen had seen a sketch of once—a peaceful, smooth, blubbery thing that kept to the ice-capped waters north of Rodina. He looked down at his feet and felt a twinge of guilt. They had been stepping on what he had thought was a rug. A full bear skin stared at his boots with unseeing glass eyes.

"Impressive collection, isn't it?" Dunmore lifted the decanter. "I can't take credit for every single one. The foreign trophies are purchased. I'm collecting from all over Vioria. But the antlers are mine—the mountain cat as well."

Ameen looked to where Dunmore gestured, and by the window, he saw a full-bodied feline, stiff and stuffed in a hunting pose. He looked above the mantle to see that the rug was not the only bear trophy Dunmore owned. The centerpiece above the fireplace—which a servant must have lit—was a bear's skull, clean and white, along with two flexed taxidermy claws.

"And the bears?"

"They were my father's." Dunmore handed Ameen a stout crystalline glass. "I have an affinity for bears, even though I have never had the opportunity to face one myself."

Ameen sipped, unsure how to respond. He felt disturbed being surrounded by pieces of animal carcasses, some of them even looking straight at him. Dunmore didn't seem to notice his discomfort.

"The old stories of Caerwyn say that the bear rules over the forest as a king. Wouldn't that be a wonder—to triumph over a king? To win the battle and claim his kingdom as your own?"

Dunmore looked down at Ameen expectantly, who was again unnerved. He seemed to be trying to get at something. Could he know about what had happened at the royal palace? Had Nellie, as Liana feared, told Dunmore about her birth? Ameen thumbed over his Circle of the Divine anxiously. "I suppose it would."

"That is a lovely trinket," Dunmore commented, suddenly intrigued. "May I?"

Unable to find an excuse to refuse, Ameen unclasped the Circle and carefully handed it over. He added, "I've had it for as long as I can remember. It was my father's."

Dunmore didn't reply right away. Ameen thought it strange how closely he examined the necklace. "An heirloom, then?"

"I doubt it's worth enough to be called that."

Dunmore looked up and smiled. "It's special to you. That makes it worth something. You were close with your father, weren't you? The way you speak of him... I'm sure he is very proud of who you have become."

"Doubtful." Ameen's father had always been a lawful man. After his death, Ameen often thought about what he would have to say about the choices Ameen made, the crimes he had committed.

Dunmore chuckled, swirling his own glass. "I like you, Almasi. So humble and dignified. I appreciate your ambition.

Have you always wanted to be a sailor, or is there something more that you wish for?"

"Not particularly. I sail because it's what I know. My father changed professions after my mother left us," Ameen said. "He became a sailor, and so did I."

"You have come quite a way—and soon to marry well!" Dunmore raised his glass. Ameen returned the gesture, and they drank. As soon as he found his glass empty, Dunmore refilled it.

"There's something about women, especially our women. They seem to share this... ability, like fire. They can make people gather, give them warmth and comfort. But they can burn you just as well if you're not careful, if you don't... contain it."

He took another drink, leaning over the mantle. Ameen frowned, wondering if perhaps the Dunmore's marriage was not as idyllic as it appeared. He had the distinct impression he just discovered a devastating crack in an otherwise perfect marble sculpture.

"You must be looking forward to becoming a father," Ameen said, attempting a more joyous subject.

Dunmore turned back with a wide, toothy smile. "Of course. We have been wanting to complete our family for years. But I'm curious about you. When can we expect an Almasi heir?"

"Interesting choice of words— 'heir.'"

Dunmore watched Ameen from behind his glass.

"I don't have anything for a child to inherit," Ameen clarified. "The ship, perhaps, but it's Liana's, not mine."

"But you will, of course." He seemed absolutely certain of it.

Ameen shrugged.

"All a man has when he dies is his legacy—and his legacy is passed on by his sons."

"Right," he said, shifting in his seat. "If it's all the same to you, Mister Dunmore, I'd rather not speak of something so personal."

"Fair enough. And please, call me Rhys. As for the real reason why I brought you here…" Dunmore walked over to the bookshelf and pressed his hand against the side. With a small bit of force, he slid it over, and behind it laid a glass case with four pistols, a shotgun, and a rifle. "As soon as I laid my eyes on that beautiful pistol you have," he said, waving at Ameen's belt, "I wanted to show you my collection. I thought you would appreciate it."

Ameen stood. If he did not feel uncomfortable before, then he certainly did now. He was rather curious about what else lay hidden in Dunmore Manor. "You have your own armory, Rhys. What's it all for?"

"Do you like it?" he asked. "Go on. Choose one. I'll gift it to you."

"It's alright, really."

"I insist." Dunmore inclined his head. "We're family. We'll be brothers-in-law. But I'm hoping for a more… advantageous relationship in the future."

Ameen furrowed his brow. He'd had enough. "If there is something you want from me, Rhys, then all you need to do is ask."

Dunmore started to laugh. "Oh my. You prefer to cut to the quick, then? What a king you will make."

"I told him this morning that I wasn't pregnant," Nellie said, her voice hoarse now. "I even wrapped it in a weak lie that I lost the baby months ago but was afraid to tell him." She gestured to her neck. "And this is what he did."

"That bastard is going to pay, Nellie. I promise." Liana already had some creative ideas, and she was sure that Ameen would have his own input once he knew about this.

"I don't want him hurt. I just want to leave," she insisted. She stood up and sighed, looking to the maid. "Fiona, would you excuse us?"

The maid curtsied and left. As she did, Nellie turned back to Liana. "There is something else."

"What is it *now*?"

"Rhys wants to keep you here for his own purposes."

"What could he want from us? He's been so... well, *generous* since we've arrived. He knows we don't have anything to give in return."

"He received a letter from his old friend—a man named Aliah Vitalis."

Liana's blood ran cold as she recalled those black, deadened eyes.

"We know that Ceres is really Princess Rhian. We know what you did to the king." Nellie looked down at her silken sleeves.

"It wasn't me!" Liana said louder than intended. She dropped her voice. "I swear to the Divine, Nellie, I can explain."

Liana told Nellie everything—about Whyte's letter, the ball, the murder, the firefight out of the Capital.

"The princess killed the king?"

"It was an accident. She's not as dangerous as it may seem. She's on the run with us."

"So, you… didn't go to the ball to assassinate King Lyell?"

"No, Nellie. Of course not. All I wanted was to know more about what happened to my parents. That's all. I swear. It's all a bloody mess now, but I never intended for any of this to happen."

Nellie relaxed, laying a hand over her brow. "Oh, thank the Guardians. I told Rhys that you weren't after the throne. I knew…"

"Rhys knows about me?" Liana's eyes grew wide.

Nellie suddenly shrank, realizing she had slipped. "He's my husband. Of course, I told him."

"Nellie! It was not your secret to tell!"

"I'm sorry," she said, barely over a whisper. "I told him a long time ago… I-I didn't think it would matter."

Liana kicked a lounge chair. It slid halfway across the room. "Blast it! He's going to turn me in. You've damned me, Nellie! You've damned us all!"

"He's not going to turn you in," Nellie assured her. "He wants to make a deal. No matter what I say, he thinks you are trying to overthrow the Vitalis' reign—that you're building an army from the ground up."

"With a broken ship and a handful of pirates? *Really?*"

"He thinks you kidnapped the princess for leverage and even convinced her to join your cause."

"He must think I'm exceedingly ambitious."

"Not you," Nellie said dully. "You think my husband would believe a woman could lead a revolution? No. He thinks Ameen is the mastermind behind it all—that he is marrying you to get an opportunity to become the next king."

"That idiot thinks Ameen wants to be king?"

Nellie swept herself up from the cushioned seat and strode up to Liana with a harrowed look on her face. "Rhys has been rubbing elbows with the Vitalis family his entire life. He knows things about them—secrets. He plans on confronting Ameen with Aliah's letter. He wants to support your claim to the throne. He's hoping it will be enough to get him more land and titles once— Liana, wait! Where are you going?"

Liana tore the door to the boudoir open. "Stay here, Nellie! Things are about to get bloody ugly downstairs."

Chapter 24

Maelstrom

Liana burst through the doors of the green salon to find Rhian, Sava, and Marin in genial conversation. "Where is Ameen?"

"Dunmore took him to the trophy room for a drink," said Sava in a rapid jumble, startled by her entrance.

"Are you well enough to be able to get to the crew's quarters?" When he nodded, she went on. "I need you to gather the men. Rhys Dunmore has made the biggest mistake of his life. I need them ready."

"Aye, Captain!" He rushed to get his coat and hurried out.

Marin came to her side. "What in the hell are ya talkin' about, lass—what has Rhys done?"

"I think it's best if you see to Nellie, Marin," Liana said in a gentler tone. "Make sure she stays upstairs. She can explain everything."

"Divine," he replied gruffly. "Alright then, I'll see to it she stays out of this mess."

"Rhian?"

The princess stood to attention. "What can I do?"

"Stay on me. I may need your… talents."

"You're asking me to use my magic?"

"Dunmore is out to blackmail us. We need to confine him in any way possible. He knows who you are… and who I am."

"What do you mean, he knows who *you* are?" asked Rhian, following Liana to the hallway.

"There's no time to explain," she answered. "Dunmore may say things about me. Things I never wanted anyone to know. He's manipulative. He's going to try to get into your head."

"Captain Foley."

She paused on the stairs, looking down at the princess.

"I trust you."

"Thanks…"

"Would Dunmore turn us in?"

"Not if his legs are too broken to run."

She opened the door to the trophy room. What she found shocked her hard enough to stop her short, and Rhian fumbled into her shoulder. Ameen and Rhys were examining a pistol. Rhys held it out for Ameen to see but kept a firm hold of the handle. They stood in front of an open wall beside a bookshelf with display cases of firearms.

"Ah, Caerwyn's prodigal daughters return!" Rhys greeted them jubilantly.

Liana wasted no time. "What's your game, Dunmore?"

He laughed and playfully elbowed Ameen in the side. "I am beginning to see now why you're marrying her. You are so much alike. You'll rule Caerwyn together splendidly."

Rhian stiffened at Liana's side, but she kept silent.

Ameen bowed his head for a brief moment and cleared his throat, an indication that he was about to start acting. "I don't mean to spring this on you. But Rhys has just informed me that he would like to join our cause."

"And why should we involve him in our affairs?" she asked, gaze gliding over to Dunmore. Out of the corner of her eye she could see Rhian stared at the guns. It was best to play along for now—with Rhys' instability and the wall of weapons, who knew what he was capable of.

"I am already involved," he said. "My good friend Aliah Vitalis has informed me you were witnessed murdering the king and kidnapping his cousin, Princess Rhian."

His eyes rested on Rhian. "But clearly she came with you willingly. Quite the surprise. Tell me, Princess, how are you adjusting to a life of piracy? Is it everything you ever hoped for? Have you found a kindred spirit with your counterpart?"

Before Rhian could speak, Liana snarled, "Shut your mouth, Dunmore! You don't know anything about me or her."

"And what does she know of you? Does she know who you are?"

"I know she saved me," Rhian spoke up. "She saved me when she didn't have to. That's all I need to know to trust her. Now, let's return to the point. What did my cousin tell you?"

From a drawer below the decanter, Rhys procured the parchment and handed it to Liana. She read the letter, skimming over Aliah's neat penmanship. One part caught her eye.

I do wish to inform you, as your friend, I recalled after the tragic incident that 'Foley' was your wife's maiden name. My father advised against writing you, instantly thinking you a betrayer of the Crown, but I could not believe in such folly. I felt that you must know what sort of people your wife may be involved with.

"Divine," she breathed, her eyes pricking with tears as she read on. "They raided the Barricade."

"What?" Ameen came to her side. Rhian held her hands over her lips, stepping back.

"It's g-gone," Liana choked out, shoving the letter into his hands. "They burned it down. They *killed* people—our people. Bess... Camila... the children..."

"We don't know everything," Ameen said, scanning the letter. But his usually sure voice shook with uncertainty. "They might have gotten out."

"'Might' isn't good enough for me, Ameen!" she shouted. It took everything for her to hold herself together. She turned away, unable to face anyone in the room for fear that her resolve would break.

"They know our connection," Rhys continued solemnly. "The manor may be the next target."

Liana whirled around. "Stop the act. You don't care about any of them. All this is to you is an opportunity for you to exploit us."

"Liana." He came closer and looked down his nose at her with false affection. "I've known your identity for almost ten years now. Surely, if I had ill intentions towards you, I would have informed King Lyell of your location long ago."

"You were waiting for me to be vulnerable—trapped and at your disposal. Just like you waited until you married Nellie to reveal your true nature to her. I know your kind."

"You're just as hysterical as your sister, it seems." His thin lips curled.

"Who wouldn't be hysterical, having to suffer at your hand?"

Liana hadn't forgotten that Rhys still held a pistol. She saw the slightest hint of muscle movement in that arm. Before he could even aim, a bolt of lightning struck Dunmore in the shoulder. He staggered back, holding the small wound, and dropped the pistol. Rhian lowered her hands, still laden with white magic.

Liana took her chance and struck Dunmore in the face with her bare knuckles. "You won't ever lay a hand on my sister again. Do you hear me?"

Dunmore scrambled out of the trophy room and landed flat against the wall. Ameen came up shortly behind him and caught him with a hard blow to the gut. Dunmore made a high-pitched wheezing sound and sank to the floor, gagging.

"Get up, you wretch!" Ameen held Dunmore by the scruff of his neck and dragged him to his feet.

Even if Dunmore wanted to reply, he physically couldn't. Instead, he groaned as Ameen pulled him by his collar through the house like a dog. They turned the corner, and Liana and Rhian followed quickly behind.

Ameen finally stopped when he reached the foyer. He kicked Dunmore in the small of his back and forced him down onto the smooth wooden planks of the floor. When Dunmore looked up, he faced the boots of as many rallied pirates that could fit in the foyer.

Jamil stood at the front, looming over Dunmore with a malicious smile. "What shall we do with him, Captain?"

"Please," Dunmore sniveled. "Take whatever you want from the house. But have mercy! Let me go!" He flipped over to grovel at Liana's feet. "There are things I can tell you," he gasped, pointing at Rhian, who remained at Liana's side, "About the Vitalis family..."

"I've had enough of your *generosity.*" Liana turned away. Jamil grabbed one of Dunmore's arms, and Kahil took the other. She addressed them. "Take him outside—"

"Don't you want to know what really happened to your parents? What they did to them?"

"What's he talking about?" Rhian stared at her in deep contemplation. Realization spread across her face as she put all the pieces together. "Your parents..."

"That's right, clever girl. You know who she is."

Liana kicked Dunmore in the back of the knee as he tried to stand. "You've had your piece. Now, be quiet!"

"Captain?" pressed Jamil, looking like he was itching to punish. So was she.

"Rhys Dunmore abused his wife, Marin's daughter. He forced her to endure his brutish behavior for ten years. I'd say he's earned himself some lashes. Take him outside!" she ordered, fury flooding her veins. "To the stables!"

"Wait!" Rhian called after them as the men dragged Dunmore out. Liana tried to ignore her, but she headed her off. "Is it true? Are you really Sergus Romenel's daughter? You're Ilyana Romenel?"

"Done well for myself, haven't I?" Liana retorted venomously. "At least for a girl who was orphaned by and large thanks to your uncle."

She left Rhian standing in the foyer. Just behind the men, she crossed the courtyard and arrived at the stables as they bound Dunmore to a post by his hands. Ameen stood off to the side, observing with an indiscernible expression.

"I need a whip," she said. "A crop… Something."

He said quietly to her, "We don't use corporal punishment."

"He bloody deserves it. He deserves all the pain in the world and then some. I want to be the one to give it to him."

Ameen turned and gripped her arm, stopping her mid-step. "What will it prove? Just lock him up."

"It'll prove that men like him—men like Grigor Vitalis, these *fucking* sadists—don't get to do what they do and not feel pain for it."

"So, it's your own method of justice then?"

"No one else will do it, why not me?" She yanked her arm, but he held fast.

"I can't watch you do this, Liana."

"Then *don't*. Go hide in the house with the princess. I don't need you out here if you'll only hold me back!"

He let her slip out of his grasp. She didn't even look back to see if he stayed. Instead, she whistled and called for a whip from the stables. Once she had it in her hand, she gripped it firmly, pacing behind Dunmore's back. The men had removed his coat. He whined like a wounded dog, and she hadn't even struck him yet.

"Don't like being hit, do you? Well, I doubt your wife likes it, either."

The first crack of the whip sent a pulse of deliverance to her rage. It did anything but quell it, and before she knew it, she had given him another lash, then another. Everything around her faded. All she saw, all she knew was her fury. Her throat hurt, and she realized that she was screaming in her rampage. Before the fifth lash, a gruff voice stopped her.

"*Liana!*"

All eyes drew up, and silence fell. The only sounds were Dunmore's quaking whimpers and Marin's footsteps. He passed through the gate and shouted, "Yer a lucky man, Dunmore!"

Liana swiped a loose lock of hair from her face but kept the whip in a vice grip.

"My daughter has appealed to my better nature and asked that ya not be harmed," he announced, approaching Liana. "Do ye suppose we can meet that request?"

"Marin," she said. "You know what he's done to her. It's unforgivable."

"I'm not sayin' it is. I'm sayin' that yer sister has begged he be spared from any harm. Can ye agree to this or not?"

She looked around at her crew, a stillness settling over them as they listened for her answer. *Undermined again*, she thought bitterly and threw down the whip.

"As much as he deserves it," she said, between her teeth, "I'll agree. But we can't let him go. He knows too much."

Marin gazed down at his son-in-law. His eyes crinkled in thought.

"M-Marin... th-thank you..."

"Quiet, ya fiend!" Marin shouted in a harsh tone that Liana had never heard from him before. "Stop yer weepin'."

Dunmore cowered but said not another word. His linen shirt shredded apart where the whip had struck him. He bled, but only a little—not enough to satisfy Liana. Some of the servants came out from hiding in their quarters and the manor to watch. Liana had never realized how many people were in Dunmore's employ.

"Ye'll give my daughter a divorce."

"Yes, sir—"

"I'm not finished!" Marin bellowed, his voice reverberating through the yard. "After we've gone, none of us will ever see your face again. Ye'll leave the house to Nellie. Everything on the grounds. Every mare and stallion, every blade of grass, every crystal on the chandelier is hers to do with as she pleases."

Dunmore feverishly nodded, clearly afraid to speak another word.

"Keep him in his precious trophy room," Liana told Jamil. "It'll do for now. But make sure you sweep for weapons. He has one hidden case—I'm sure there are more throughout the house. I want at least two men at the door at all hours. I also want men on patrol about the grounds. In light of new information, there is a chance that we may be ambushed. Am I clear?"

"Yes, ma'am."

The men dispersed while Lucky and Kahil led Dunmore back to the trophy room. As he passed, he gave Liana a look of silent contempt. She returned it in full.

Once she and Marin were alone, he looked at her with a deep exhaustion and concern. "Are ya alright?"

She swallowed. "F-fine. I'm fine."

"No, ye're not."

"Who came for you? Was it Ameen?"

"Fortunate I did come, or ya would've made Rhys Dunmore a stain on the grass."

"Was it Ameen?"

"No, it was me," came Rhian's voice from the fence. "I told your sister, and she asked him to stop you."

"This was a family matter," Liana growled, stomping to her. "It was none of your business."

"I couldn't let you abuse him."

"He *abused* my sister!"

"Liana." Marin sighed. "What did I tell ya about revenge? It's—"

"Don't patronize me, Marin! I am not a child, and you are not my father!"

He recoiled, wincing. She immediately regretted her words. But he swerved around her before she could even think to apologize. "I know that as well as ye do, o'course. Now, ya may want tah go see to yer fiancé. He was much perturbed when I saw him last."

"Fine," she muttered.

Rhian stood alone after he had gone, blinking tearfully.

"There is so much evil in this world, Rhian," Liana said to her. "You have no idea. Don't be a coward."

She marched back to the manor. Inside, she found Ameen packing. The sight was like a punch to the gut, leaving her just as winded. He didn't look up, even upon her entrance. "Are you going somewhere?"

"I'll sleep with the crew tonight. I need… time to myself."

"Ameen, what the hell—why are you doing this?"

"I couldn't stomach what I saw from you today," he said shortly, throwing a shirt in his bag. Another punch.

"So… so what, Dunmore's comfort means more to you than being with me?" she choked out. "We're pirates. We don't rely on justice from the kingdom. We take. We give—"

"We seek our own justice?" he muttered. "Is that it?"

"Ameen, please! Look at me. Is Dunmore worth this?"

"What do you want me to say?"

"Say what you want to say," she hissed between her teeth. "Say it, as long as it's what you feel. Do you want me anymore or not?"

"I told you, I need time—"

"Well, I need an answer!"

"It's not just Dunmore, Liana. It's you," he said, tossing the pack aside, as though that was the very thing that frustrated him the most. "You've changed, or you're not the person I thought you were. Ever since you told me your real name. You—you talk about the past. You take out your frustrations on Rhian. But it's obvious what you really want."

"And what's that?" she spat.

"Blood."

"I do," she admitted. "What else will make things right? How else will Dunmore pay for hurting Nellie? How else will Grigor Vitalis know the pain he caused me and my brother?"

He came around the bed and reached out for her. "You need to let it go. Nothing is going to change—"

"Don't!" she shouted, drawing back. "Don't tell me that! You don't think I've tried? I can't!"

She recalled the rush she felt at drawing Dunmore's blood. For a moment, the anger, the fear, the pain all were replaced with deliverance. Nothing else gave her that feeling of liberation. Nothing else lifted the crushing weight of her trauma.

"This is who I am. If you don't want it, then fine! You've already made your choice."

The finality of her words sent a shockwave through both of them.

She fled the room but stopped short at the stairs. Out the window; she saw a cardinal perched, its brilliant red plumage catching her eye. It cocked its head to the side as she paused to look at it, then took flight into the trees. She found herself envious.

Below, she heard Marin and Jamil in deep discussion over who should take the first patrol shifts. She could also hear Rhian, helpfully offering to do whatever she could. Rather than face them and the rest of the crew, Liana went to the only place she could think of.

"It smells like roses," Liana murmured, sniffing the sleeve of her borrowed nightgown.

"Of course," Nellie whispered in the dark, her voice laced with exhaustion. She sounded as though she had not slept in years. "Roses were Mama's favorite."

Liana gave a contented sigh at the memory of Leda. She curled under the duvet beside Nellie. They had already talked for hours, and it was getting late. Her swollen eyes stung with salt.

"I remember when Da first brought you home," Nellie said, still hushed. "Even though I was young too, I remember thinking how small you were."

"A runt," Liana scoffed, adjusting her head on the pillow to look toward her. Nellie giggled.

"Always getting into trouble," she continued sleepily. "Always fibbing to get yourself out of it."

"Not much has changed."

"You grew up. We both did."

Liana remembered too. She had been afraid of the dark, especially when the island storms came. The sound of thunder had haunted her. On those nights, she had been glad to share a bed with Nellie. She felt safer with her there.

Silence passed between them, until Liana heard Nellie's soft breathing lapse into a gentle snore. She wondered how long it had been since she'd had a good night's sleep. How could anyone rest peacefully beside a man like Rhys Dunmore? But no more, Liana promised silently. She would take care of Nellie, just as she had looked after Liana when they were children. With that thought, Liana drifted into sleep.

It was unclear how much time had passed before a chill in the air woke her. She rose groggily, careful not to wake Nellie, and noticed the window was open. She stumbled across the room. She didn't remember it being open.

Liana reached out to close it, when an unseen force swooped out of the shadows and collided into her. The breath was forced from her lungs as she was thrown to the ground. Someone mounted over her and closed a fist around her throat.

Dunmore! Even in the dark, she could make out his form— feel the crazed retribution in the cold fingers that curled tighter around her windpipe. He hissed and squeezed tighter when she clawed at his face. She bucked and twisted, kicking her legs, desperate to breathe.

"Get off her, you bastard!" A shrill cry rang out from above, followed by a shattering crash as a hand mirror collided with the back of Dunmore's head. The weight fell away, and Liana's hands flew to her freed throat.

"Nellie!" she wheezed hoarsely as Dunmore wrestled Nellie to the floor. Liana leapt onto his back, wrapping an arm under his chin. Too easily, he shook her off, and she fell back hard on the floor. The barrel of a pistol glinted in the moonlight.

The door flew open, and Marin burst in. At the same moment the gun fired, Nellie cried out again. The bullet struck Marin in the center of his chest—a hunter's aim. He fell.

"Da! *No!*"

"*Marin!*" Liana butchered her throat with screams of horror.

Dunmore fled, clambering out the window. More shots rang outside in the distance.

The men came and began to gather around them. She looked up and saw Rhian, mouth open in speechless shock. Ameen shoved his way through and knelt down to the floor.

"Ameen! Do something!" she cried over Marin's agonized groans. He looked at her, the light from his gray eyes dimming as he tried to speak. But he couldn't. Instead, he clutched his wound, mouth forming soundless words. "Where's Thiago? We have to save him!"

"G-get him up!" Nellie gasped out, motioning to her bed. A couple of the crew, including Ameen, lifted Marin and took him out of the hallway. Thiago shoved his way through with his kit over his arm. Liana scrambled to her feet and tried to follow, but Nellie blocked her way. "I think you've done enough!"

She slammed the door in Liana's face.

Chapter 25

Thy Name Was Writ in Water,
But Thy Deeds in Stone

"Please, Captain... you must try to drink some."

Liana had the strangest feeling, like she was looking at Sava from an unfocused spyglass. He lifted her weak hands, coaxing her to grasp the cup of tea. Once he seemed sure that she would hold it on her own, he wrapped a wool blanket over her shoulders. Flaring fingerprints bloomed across her throat.

A gentle knock at the door made Sava hop up to answer. "Liana?" Ameen peeked inside carefully.

Despite their strife, she tried to greet him. "Ameen, how is Ma—"

The effort threw her into a fit of coughing. Now that the fire in her blood had quelled, her throat had started to ache and swell. When she came out of it, Ameen crouched inches from her face, raising her hair to see her neck.

"That bastard," he breathed.

But she would have none of his pity. She swatted him away, her palm colliding with his wrist with a hard *smack!* She spilled her tea on the blanket, and the cup shattered on the floor.

"Don't! Just tell me about Marin."

As Ameen rubbed his tender skin, Thiago came through the open door, drawn by her coughing, and asked Ameen something in Savarran. They conversed, and Liana picked up the pieces of the broken cup. She placed them on the little bedside table and dropped the blanket onto the chair.

She felt like a beast had dragged its claws inside her esophagus. The ever-observant Thiago saw this. "I get more tea, Captain," he said, excusing himself.

"I'll come too," Sava quickly offered.

Ameen called after him, but he had already gone. He clicked his tongue in annoyance and looked back at Liana uncomfortably. She scowled, turning away towards the window. Nothing could be seen in the black of night except for her own reflection.

"Can I see Marin yet? Is Nellie finished being a brat?"

His heaving, shaky breath made her look back. "Marin passed."

The world seemed to fall out from under her, tilted like a trick mirror. She struggled to breathe, as if her very life force had been taken from her. Stepping away from Ameen and pressing back against the window, she numbly shook her head. "No. No, no, no. You're lying."

"I wish I was. Thiago did everything he could. I'm so sorry." His eyes were bright and moist. He bit his lip, and his Adam's apple bobbed.

He tried to go to her, but she held up her hands, before covering her face. "Tell me what happened. *How* did this happen?"

"It seems that Dunmore Manor has more secrets than we thought," he said. "Another false wall."

"Divine. We should have known." Her voice cracked, and she smoothed back her matted hair.

"We couldn't have known, Liana. I'm sorry."

She hunched forward, rocking with her arms crossed. A sob broke through, and she looked up at Ameen, speaking her need for comfort with her eyes. He answered the call, wrapping her in his warm arms as she cried. Sometime after she could breathe again, she adjusted her head against his chest. She noticed something missing. "Your father's Circle. You took it off."

Ameen reached for his chest, brows furrowing.

They both jumped as Nellie opened the door so hard it cracked against the wall. She pointed at Liana. Her tear-stained face flushed with anguish. "*You!* I want you out of my house, now!"

Ameen stepped between them.

"Nellie, please," he said calmly. "This is a difficult time for both of you—"

"I just put my father in a crypt! And it's all your fault!" Nellie ignored him completely. Her sleeves were rolled to her elbows, the nightgown smeared with copper stains.

"If I recall, it was your husband who killed him," Liana said, her voice sounding like it was being dragged over rocks. "He nearly killed me, too. You should have let me finish him off when I had the chance."

"If you had not gotten my father involved in all of your trouble, then he would still be alive!"

"Marin believed in the *Windfall* as much as I did. We helped people—"

"I'm not just talking about the piracy, Liana! It's everything! From the moment he brought you home, you have done nothing but destroy our family!"

"Nellie—!" Ameen tried to interrupt again, but she wouldn't hear him.

"You were always causing mischief! *Always!* You never learned! It was because of you that we had to leave the Islands. I had to leave the place where my mother is buried! All because you wouldn't listen to me and leave Asha Ganem alone! But no! It was all fun and games to you, wasn't it? Until you murdered someone!"

Ameen shouted in order to be heard. "Marin loved both of you! If he was here, he would be the first to say that his death isn't anyone's fault but Dunmore's!"

"You don't get to tell me what he would have said!" Nellie snarled at him. "He was *my* father. Not yours—and most certainly not *hers!*"

Liana seethed. Her nostrils flared, and she marched over to the bedside drawers, digging around the top one. "Then why do I have this?"

She slammed the ring on the surface of the table, but Nellie snatched it up.

"This is my mother's! Where did you get this?"

"*Your* father," said Liana.

Without warning, Nellie lunged at Liana, who backed up so quickly she stumbled onto the bed. Before Nellie could spring, Ameen caught her.

"Don't touch me!" she screamed at him, free hand clawing for Liana. "They were my parents! Not yours! You had no right!"

"That's enough!" Ameen swiftly encircled his arm around Nellie's waist and hoisted her over his shoulder.

"You had no right!"

Liana laid on the bed, sprawled out spread-eagle for a long time after Ameen dragged Nellie out. She stared at the ceiling, dazed, lost in her grief. It could have been a few minutes or an hour. Time didn't matter anymore. Everything was slipping away—the *Windfall*, the Barricade, Ameen, Marin... Nothing seemed salvageable.

Then she remembered a promise she had made only hours earlier. She sat up sharply. *Maybe,* Liana thought, *I can do something right.*

She scrounged up her clothes and began to pack. When she was nearly done, she hesitated on the last item. After unlocking the trunk, she set the spell book on the nightstand. Leaving it behind wasn't an option. It was too dangerous. But returning it to Rhian could be potentially worse. Liana didn't think she could stand another betrayal. Making up her mind, she shoved the book as deep in her bag as it would go. She took a moment to readjust the belt that held her coat around her waist.

In the hallway, Liana looked over her left shoulder, then her right. No one stirred—and why would they? Though she hadn't slept a wink, everyone else in the house should be fast asleep at this hour. In the quiet, she'd had time to think, and she knew the choice she was making now was the right one.

Just for a moment, she dithered about, wondering whether or not to wake Ameen to let him know she would be leaving. But if anyone could convince her to stay, it was him. Though it broke her heart to do it, she moved on, adjusting her bag on her shoulder.

Liana knocked sharply on another door and heard the sound of a body rolling over in bed, then silence. Again, she knocked, harder this time.

Rhian, in her nightgown and robe, opened the door and winced when Liana lifted her lantern up. She shielded her face from the light. As she took a step back, her bare heel scraped lightly against the floor. "What—?"

Liana gave her a light tug back into her room. "Shh!"

"What are you—What time is it?" she asked huskily, nearly tripping over herself.

"Get dressed."

Rhian looked at her, rubbing her eyes. "What are you doing here?"

Liana set the lantern down beside the basin. "You're not a coward," she said.

"Huh?" The princess rubbed a hand over her cheek, looking a bit more awake.

"I shouldn't have said that, and I'm sorry for it." She pulled her tricorn down over her brows and turned her head away. "It took courage to stand up to me. You're not a coward."

"Captain Foley, shouldn't you be asleep?" Rhian asked her, approaching her like she was a timid creature who would bolt at the wrong movement. "You don't... You don't look well."

"I'm well enough," she said, blinking hard. Her eyes still burned from tears shed earlier. "Gather your things together. We're leaving."

"We—As in you and I? Where?"

"I can't stay here, and I promised to find you a safe place to have your baby."

"Now?"

"Now."

Rhian went quiet, crossed the room, and sat down on the side of the bed. The sheets were twisted and thrown to the side, as though she had slept restlessly. She pinched the bridge of her nose.

"I could go alone," Liana went on. "But I wanted to give you the opportunity to come."

"Why leave? Why not stay?"

"Nellie doesn't..." Her voice faltered. "She doesn't want me here anymore. It's best that I go somewhere for a while."

"Does... anyone know about this?"

Liana knew she meant Ameen. "No."

Rhian tucked a strand of golden hair behind her ear. "I-I appreciate your efforts, but the burial will be in a few hours. You need to say goodbye... to Marin."

"I spent my entire life with Marin. There's nothing left to say. You don't have much time before the baby comes. I owe it to you to follow through on my promise."

"What if Dillon refuses to help me? What if we're caught? I'll be charged with Lyell's murder," Rhian said, running a hand over the curve of her stomach.

"From your cousin's letter to Dunmore, it sounds like it's being pinned on me. Maybe you'll be able to get away with it. You'll have that life you wanted with Whyte."

"You can't know that for sure. You know what could happen if everyone realizes the truth."

"You'd be imprisoned, at best. Executed, at worst."

"What about you?"

"Me?"

"If you're being blamed for the crime I committed, those things would happen to you. You could be…" Rhian trailed off. "I can't let you take that risk for me."

"I don't want to see that happen to either of us. But let's be honest," said Liana. "No matter what, if I'm arrested, I'd be sent to the gallows. I accepted that a long time ago. Even before I became a pirate, I was wanted. It's how I've lived my entire life. Call me a lost cause, but you have a chance to find your happiness. The only question you have to answer is, what do you want, Rhian?"

She looked back up at Liana squarely. "I don't think anyone has ever asked me that before you, Captain Foley."

"So, what'll it be? I want to leave before sunrise."

"Give me some time to pack."

"I'll help. We should get going, though. There's someone else I need to see before we go."

The old overseer's cottage, though only a short distance from the house, felt like a journey away. It stood past the entrance to the crypt, a stone arch with bronze doors leading below a mossy hill. Liana felt a pull towards it.

"That's where they laid Marin until morning. Do you want to go inside?" Rhian asked her, seeing her hesitate when they came past the crypt.

She could go in to say goodbye. The arch rose high above her, as though welcoming her to the eerie in-between. But something inside her resisted the call. It wasn't fear, but a strong desire to withstand the temptation. Dread should have plagued her upon looking at the threshold of death, but instead she felt longing.

"No," she said, tearing herself away. She trudged on with heavy feet. When they came to the decrepit fence that surrounded the cottage, she set her bag down. "I'll only be a moment."

Rhian leaned against one of the sturdier posts, hugging her coat around her. "Take your time."

Liana kicked a rock as she meandered down the trail to the cottage. A plume of smoke rose from the chimney. Lucky could be awake, but it was also possible that the small home got so cold he had to keep the fire going all night. It must have been the former, because as soon as she came to the door, it opened.

"Captain," said a hollow voice. Liana took one look at Lucky and thought, *He knows*. He appeared smaller, weighed down by the same torturous grief that Liana felt. He hadn't slept either. Behind him, the candles inside the small living space still burned, but low. "I'm so sorry."

"Who told you?"

"Almasi was here hours ago," he explained. "He told me everything."

"Oh. How did he seem?"

"He's just... hurt, is all," he said, catching a glimpse of Rhian waiting at the fence with the bags. "Are you leaving, Captain?"

"I am."

"But why? Where will you go?"

"Back to the Capital. I made a promise. I need to keep it," she said. "I came to tell you that... Lucky, after everything that happened... The fire, and all... I forgive you."

Lucky pressed a hand to his heart. "It does me such good to hear you say that, Captain. Thank you."

"With Marin gone," she continued, "The crew is going to need you."

"I suppose it'll be a chance to get back in their good graces," he said with a humorless laugh. "You know, I remember when your father was king."

"Ah, so Ameen told you that, too," she croaked, embarrassed.

"I was there when Marin found you, you know, on the *Siren*. Just a young man, barely more than a boy," he said, taking her hands. "I had no idea who you were or of what you'd become. But you changed my life and that of many others. You be careful, Captain. Dunmore got away—he has no reason not to tell the world your secret."

"I'll be fine. I always am."

"Won't you stay to say goodbye to Marin?"

She abruptly shook her head. "No. No, I can't. He's lying in that *place*. It's not him anymore. I can't."

"I understand."

"The last thing I said to him…" she said woefully. "Lucky, I was awful."

"Marin was my best friend." He pressed her hands together in his. "No matter what you said to him, he knew what he meant to you. His deeds—raising you and your brother, being the father that you needed—they're written in stone. They'll never be forgotten."

She threw her arms around him, and he held her hard, nearly lifting her off her feet. A bit of the lonely weight she felt subsided.

They remained in that embrace, taking the last moments they could to grieve together for the loss of a great man.

"Princess." Lucky suddenly let Liana go and greeted Rhian as she approached the cottage.

"The sun is rising," Rhian pointed out. Indeed, it was, spreading light over the horizon. But that's not what caught Liana's attention. Behind Rhian stood the twins.

"Thought you had us out here to stop anyone coming in, Captain," joked Kahil, "Not anyone going out."

"I suppose there isn't anything we can say to stop you," added Jamil. He eyed Lucky, who shook his head in agreement.

"Nothing at all, Jamil. You'll repair the ship with whatever materials you can find," Liana said. She took a step back so she could address them all. "And you'll vote a new captain to see you through this until I return."

Lucky rolled his eyes. "You know very well that the only man we'd vote to be captain in your place would never do it."

"Then you must make him, for all of your sakes," she said. "You lot need someone to order you about."

Kahil chuckled. "Aye, Captain, right as always."

"Captain, is there anything you want me to tell Almasi?" asked Jamil gently.

Guilt knifed at Liana's heart. "Tell him that I'm sorry."

"Will do, Captain."

"I'll write once I get somewhere safe," she said. "If you can repair the *Windfall* before I get back, leave without me."

"But—" Kahil began.

"I won't have you wait for the Navy to come and capture you. We'll find each other."

"Captain," called Lucky as they turned to leave. When she looked back, he hesitated for a moment but pressed on. "Do you suppose Bess made it out of the Barricade, before...?"

Liana forced herself to nod. She spoke slowly to keep her voice even, as she thought of her Rodinian friend. "Yes... Yes, I think so."

"Right. I'm sure she did."

"Once I get to the Capital, I'll find her and anyone else who got away."

"Good. Well, get on, then," Lucky said, shaking his shoulders. "Goodbye, for now. Be safe until we see you again, Captain."

Liana had thought she would be relieved to put some distance between herself and Dunmore Manor. But as she and Rhian walked down to the beach, she found herself caught in a feeling of deep dread. Standing on the dock, she took one last look at the *Windfall*, empty, hollow, and in mid-repair.

"I don't think I'll ever get used to it," Rhian said at her side.

"What's that?"

"The running."

"Welcome to being a lost princess."

Rhian smiled grimly. "I couldn't be in better company."

Liana thought it best not to linger. She gathered her courage, blanketing it around her like a shield against her grief. "Well," she said, helping Rhian board Dunmore's sloop, "One good thing about a smaller vessel is that it'll only take the two of us to sail."

Taking a bit of pride in pirating a boat from one of the men she hated most in the world, she weighed anchor. They sailed southeast toward the rising sun. The moon hung heavy in the sky, looming over the manor.

PART THREE

The Divine's Favored have no fear of Death.

He has cast a Circle of Protection on this World. It is inscribed on the horizon—between sky and sea.

Unto this World we are born and returned to the Heavens, as is the Traveling Sun.

Under His Blessing, we shall always return to carry out the Divine's holy will.

Those who have fallen from His Favor are not trusted to return and will remain eternally inert in the bowels of Hell.

—

Scroll of Gereon the Wise,
The Book of the Divine

Chapter 26

Tradepost Landing
2nd of Cambath, 1724
Tradepost Landing

Tradepost Landing, a lovely seaside town, sat upon the rugged coastline. After sleeping in the sloop for several days, it was nice to be in a real bed and have a real meal. They dined in a crowded taproom, inconspicuously seated toward the back, eating in amicable silence as rain poured down on the windows. It was a miracle Rhian and Captain Foley had made it before the storm. Throughout their journey over the last several days, their light conversation was refreshing, given everything that had happened at the manor.

"Cap—er, Liana...?"

She smirked at Rhian's accidental slip. "Liana's fine," she assured her, placing her spoon back into an empty bowl. "Don't really have a title anymore, do I?"

"When we get to the Capital, what do you suppose we'll do then?"

"Well…" Liana drummed her fingers on the table, one leg folded in, while the other extended out to the left. Rhian tried to think of a time when she had ever seen Liana sit properly. She recalled when her old, crabby governess would shout at her for her persistent slouch. "I still have some contacts there. We'll hide out with them, then try to get in touch with Whyte."

"Then there's the difficult part," Rhian whined.

Liana shook her head. "No. That man would do anything for you."

"Do you think so?"

"He was willing to blackmail a pirate in order to keep you safe."

"Blackmail?"

Liana spoke softly. "Whyte knew about me. He promised not to tell anyone who I was if I agreed to help him look after you."

"Oh." Rhian couldn't help but be surprised. Perhaps Dillon kept just as much from her as she had from him. "I'd say you've done your part, then."

Liana rested back, laughing. "I should hope so."

A short while later, their table was visited by the innkeeper, a full-figured woman with a loose flaxen braid that fell over her shoulder. She carried over a bottle of wine and set it down in the center of the table.

"Oh, hello," said Liana with a bashful smile.

The woman held out her hand in a forward manner. "Aelin Carey. I own this inn. I overheard you telling the barkeep that you also own an establishment like this."

"Used to," Liana replied huskily. Then quickly made up an explanation, "Fire."

"I'm terribly sorry. Was it recent?"

"I actually just received the news last week."

"Then please consider this bottle as a token of my regrets," she said, sliding it closer to Liana. She motioned for one of the dash-girls to bring them glasses. "Do you mind if I join you?"

Rhian expected Liana to refuse, seeing as how they were trying to keep a low profile, but instead she made room at the table. "Not at all."

"What brings you to Tradepost Landing, Miss...?"

"Leah Sutton," Liana said with ease. She launched into an explanation that involved returning to the Capital to collect insurance on her tavern.

"Are you partners?" Miss Carey asked.

"Partners?" asked Rhian.

"Of a business nature?"

"We're c-cousins."

The woman looked between them. "Really? You look nothing alike."

"Ceres and I are *distant* cousins," Liana clarified, looking at Rhian pointedly.

"And how are you traveling?"

"I'm a sailor, Miss Carey," she said with the utmost pride.

"That explains your attire," the innkeeper noted, looking them up and down. Rhian flattened the legs of her breeches.

Liana wrinkled her hawk-shaped nose. "It would be a bit difficult to sail a sloop in a dress."

"Oh, I meant no offense," she said, placing a hand on Liana's arm. Rhian could have sworn Liana blushed. In that moment, pressure rose in Rhian's chest. An ugly feeling began to fester. All she wanted was for the innkeeper to leave them alone. But she had no right to speak those feelings aloud.

"Actually," Miss Carey continued, "I think it suits you. I can always appreciate a pragmatic woman like myself."

Liana smiled and pulled her hair out from behind her neck. Rhian felt absolutely invisible. She hated it. She'd felt that way all her life. But never with Liana—not until now.

"I think I'm going to go to bed," Rhian said, a little more forceful than she meant. But she couldn't just sit there prettily while they pretended she didn't matter, like she wasn't even there. The other two women stared at her in response. Without giving them a chance to speak, Rhian pushed in her empty bowl and swept away from the table.

An hour passed as Rhian absorbed herself in a book she had borrowed from the manor. Managing to bring five of them, she had already read through three by the time they arrived in Tradepost Landing. But now she just stared at the cover, deep in thought.

The baby performed a lively dance within her womb, which was equally entertaining and uncomfortable. Convinced there was now a foot lodged in her ribs, Rhian let out a breath and shifted her position. Lying on her side, she wondered what fate would have in store for the child. Would they be a boy? A girl? She secretly hoped for a boy—life would be easier for them, if they were.

But that was already decided, Rhian knew. It would only be revealed with the birth. But would they make it to Dillon before then? Would Dillon want them, or...

Liana entered quietly, opening the door slowly to avoid a persistent creak in the old hinges. But when she peeked in and saw Rhian sitting on the single bed, candles lit and all, she stepped in fully. "Thought you'd be asleep."

"Enjoy your bottle?" Rhian asked, setting the book aside and unwilling to look at Liana's face.

"I did, actually," said Liana. "Miss Carey is good company."

"I'm *sure*."

Liana scoffed at Rhian's abrasive tone. "What's your problem?"

"Nothing," she lied and lifted the covers of the bed before burrowing herself in the sheets. Liana leaned over, hands on her hips, and Rhian squeezed her eyes shut.

"Why are you so cranky? Is it because of the baby?"

"I'm *not*." Rhian glared at her with one eye momentarily before closing it again. A moment passed before something soft suddenly struck the back of her head. She shot up, seeing Liana holding one of the pillows.

"Out with it, Princess."

"Stop calling me that!" Rhian snapped. "If you're not a captain anymore, then I'm certainly not a princess."

Liana brandished the pillow, and Rhian flinched. "Come on, then."

"Don't you dare hit me with that—"

The pillow smashed into her shoulder. Rhian jumped up and swung the other one on the bed at Liana. It lamely hit her in the stomach, causing both of them to dissolve into laughter.

After a moment, Liana flopped down on the bed. "So, what's with the attitude?"

Rhian looked down, hugging her pillow close. In the meantime, Liana removed her boots and breeches without a thought for her presence. Rhian wondered if the woman had a bit of modesty in her or if she'd simply had too much wine to care.

She snuck a glance as Liana kicked up her lean, powerful legs and cozied herself under the duvet.

"I'm listening," she said, closing her eyes and making herself comfortable at Rhian's side. "Hurry up before I fall asleep."

"Nellie told me about Asha."

Liana's eyes flew open. "Oh."

"I'm sorry," Rhian said frantically. "I wasn't prying. She just brought up the name, and I asked—I'm so sorry."

Instead of being furious like Rhian had suspected, Liana just sighed. "That woman is the biggest gossip I've ever met in my bloody life."

"You're not upset?"

Liana shrugged, opening her palms helplessly against the pillow behind her head. "Nellie is Nellie. Just don't ever tell her anything you want kept between the two of you."

"Good to know."

"What exactly did she tell you about Asha?"

"She implied you were romantically involved with each other," Rhian mumbled shyly.

"You'd think I should be the one to be embarrassed," Liana teased, nudging her.

She covered her cheeks, mortified. Her mouth felt dry. "You're going to laugh."

"Try me."

"I think I'm like you," she said, barely above a whisper. "I think I could be with a man or a woman."

"That's nothing to be ashamed of," Liana assured her, flipping over onto her stomach. "You can't control who you're attracted to. It just happens. The best you can do is be alright with it. And anyone who isn't alright with it can eat shit."

Rhian giggled.

"Doesn't really explain why you were upset."

"I thought that... you and Miss Carey..."

"Ah, you thought I'd forgotten about Ameen," Liana breathed. That wasn't the reason, but Rhian didn't correct her. "I'm sure he would be quite touched you're so protective of him."

As Rhian slipped into the bed beside Liana, she said softly, "Ameen is a good man."

"He is." Liana clutched her pillow, plucking stray downy feathers from the edges. Rhian could tell Liana missed him terribly. "You know, I've only had two loves in my life. Just because I find *some* women attractive doesn't mean I'm promiscuous. I love Ameen. Our relationship is... unstable at the moment, but I would never betray him like that."

Rhian asked, "Will you tell me about Asha?"

"If I tell you this story, will you promise to stop assuming I lust after every attractive woman we meet?"

"I didn't—Ah, just tell me!"

"Asha was," Liana began, her smile transforming from teasing to wistful, "Everything to me *and* everything I wasn't. Confident, elegant, well-spoken. She was a councilman's daughter. Well-educated. But she was also very brave. She spoke out for the people and tried to convince the council to secede from Caerwyn's rule."

"That *is* brave."

"We kept our relationship a secret. But one night, we convinced Nellie to come with us to a gathering—a party on the beach for the young and wealthy on the island. I didn't belong there, but Asha made me feel like I did."

"She didn't know about your birth?"

"No. I thought it would only complicate things. We had our fun. But when we walked home that night, some men attacked us over some political statements Asha's father made at the council. We were walking along a cliffside by the water when they came at us. I pushed one of them off, and we ran. I killed him. Asha's parents helped us all book passage to the Capital, where we could start a new life. They covered up my crime. Nellie has never forgiven me for that. It was my fault she was forced to leave her home."

"I'm sorry, that's not fair."

"My first murder."

"If *that* made you a murderer," said Rhian, "Then what am I?"

Liana's brows drew together, and she shifted her position again. They both laid on their sides, facing each other. "Rhian, it's not the same."

"I killed Lyell because I was *angry*. So angry I couldn't control myself. You killed that man to protect the girl you loved. You're a good person."

Liana looked at her doubtfully. "You saw what I did to Dunmore… What I tried to do. How can you believe I'm a good person after that?"

"You stopped. You listened to Marin. That was your choice. Just like you chose to help me. You have a defender's spirit. You try to be a hero."

Liana snorted. "*Try.*"

Rhian thought about Liana's story—a small, tragic piece of a life of displacement. Liana Foley certainly wasn't a woman without fault. She disregarded the law and had plenty of blood on her hands. She was rugged and scrappy but held such raw strength. Dillon used to tell her about his childhood home, a castle built on the magnificent cliffs of Stonehall. Beaten back and eroded by storms and tide, the geography had been shaped by the sea to carve out the perfect home for seabirds. Rhian thought that, like for the gulls that inhabited those cliffs, Liana served as a shelter for those who were so lucky to cross into her good graces.

Throughout her life, Rhian felt so faded and out of place, like the moon, pale in the sunlit sky. After being with Liana, learning from her and her crew, Rhian felt bolder; tonight, she stood bright against the starless dark.

"I used to think that the law was everything," said Rhian, "the decider of what was right and wrong. You and your men break the law, but they're good people. And you—you have a good heart."

The muscles in Liana's throat visibly constricted, and her dark eyes became glassy. "You're a good person too. And you're going to be a good mother. That I know for sure."

"Thank you." In a moment of abrupt bravery, Rhian pulled her close. Squeezing Liana tight, she caught a whiff of salt and sea, a permanent scent that was firmly her.

Liana's lean body was rigid at first. After a few long seconds, she relaxed into the embrace. She breathed in deeply, making Rhian wonder if she was taking in the smell of her hair too. The lengthy sigh that she released confirmed Rhian's suspicions and made her smile as wide as her face could hold. Liana leaned back to look at her and placed a rough but warm hand on Rhian's cheek. It was a distinctly affectionate gesture that ignited a fire in Rhian.

"For what it's worth," said Liana, "any woman would be lucky to have you."

The look she gave Rhian sent her heart into a frenzy. A distinctly lustful haze blanketed over Liana's eyes, dark with intoxication.

"Do you think so?" Rhian whispered.

Slowly, Liana nodded, looking directly at Rhian's mouth. Her own shapely lips parted and she cocked an eyebrow, bordering on suggestion. "I certainly know that I would be."

Rhian's eyes slid closed and she leaned into Liana's palm. *Kiss me, kiss me, kiss me.* She prayed to the Divine that before she opened them, Liana would do it. Damn the world outside that room. Damn the law. Damn politics and duty. Damn Ameen Almasi for taking possession of the most perfect woman in Vioria. Damn him for crushing her spirit in her hour of need. Damn him for treating Liana as if she didn't deserve someone who would take her for all she was, all her beauty and pain.

A tremor ran through Liana's fingertips. Rhian allowed herself to look just in time to see the moment of indecision hanging in suspense. Of course Liana would hesitate. Of course she would stop herself from kissing Rhian, from sweeping the sheets over their bodies and making love to her. Because Liana was the most loyal person alive. She would never do anything to harm someone she loved. She would give and give until she had nothing left. But never would she take what she needed.

"Well," Liana said, before swallowing audibly. "Let's get some sleep, then. Long day of sailing tomorrow." She slipped away and rolled onto her other side, leaving Rhian cold. "Goodnight."

"Goodnight," said Rhian. She trembled as she sat up to blow out the last candle.

The room plunged into darkness. For an immeasurable amount of time, she stared at the ceiling. She tried to steady her breath as her eyes filled with tears. The last thing she wanted was for Liana to know she was crying. Luckily, she had fallen asleep so quickly that she never heard Rhian's sniffling.

She felt ridiculous. There she was, halfway back to the father of her child, and yet she wanted nothing more than to stay with the woman beside her. Liana had said she shouldn't feel ashamed of who she was attracted to. But who she loved—that was another matter entirely.

The realization took her breath away. Then, she wiped her eyes and buried it deep.

Rhian's world wasn't like the *Windfall*. It wasn't built on dreams or bravery or love. In her world, she was trapped. There was no freedom. There was no endless horizon. No wind to carry her sails. She didn't have the power to mold it the way she wanted. She couldn't stand at her own helm to steer her course. All Rhian could do was savor Liana Foley in all her splendor before she would have to step back into the gilded cage.

Liana found Dunmore's sloop to be easy enough to sail alone. After all, there was only one mast, a mainsail, and a headsail. It was nothing Liana couldn't handle on her own. But Rhian insisted on helping. Teaching Rhian to sail gave Liana more gratification than she would have liked to admit. As Rhian manned the helm, Liana watched her, pretending to relax against a pile of rigging rope. She peeked out from beneath the brim of her tricorn.

"This isn't too difficult," Rhian called out over the wind. Her mouth spread into a wide smile that showed all her teeth. Even with her cheeks slightly chapped and her hair streaming in a tangled tail behind her, she looked so happy.

Just as Liana thought about taking a late afternoon nap, a wall of cold seawater crashed over the deck, completely dousing her. She scrambled to her feet, gasping for the breath she'd lost in the icy collision. "Rhian!"

"Sorry!"

"I t-told you..." she spluttered, swiping off her hat. Her teeth chattered as the winter wind whistled over the small deck. "Cut across the waves, *n-not* into them!"

"I'm sorry!" Rhian squeaked again. She looked like she wanted to rush over to help. But like Liana had taught her, she kept her hands firmly on the helm.

"Try not to r-run us aground while I get out of these c-clothes," Liana managed to say, tugging at the now-sopping scarf around her neck. After setting her hat aside, she wriggled down to the cramped space below deck where they had set up makeshift cots. Once she had gotten into dry clothes, she climbed back up again.

Something in Rhian's demeanor had changed drastically when she got above deck. Her grip on the helm's handles hadn't lifted, but her arms trembled. Fear painted her face.

"What's the matter?" Liana immediately asked.

"Something's wrong," she answered, her voice tight with pain.

"The baby?"

Rhian nodded and blinked several times in rapid succession. Still, she never let go of the wheel. Swiftly, Liana threw the anchor over and helped Rhian sit on the deck, where she had just been resting herself. She tried to remember how far along Rhian was. Five months? Much too early for the baby to come now.

"Oh, Rhian…" she said gravely, as she spotted a dark stain forming in her breeches between her thighs. "You're bleeding."

"I know," Rhian whimpered.

Liana gripped her arms firmly. "Listen to me. You're going to be fine. These things happen."

Yes, they did, and very often, Liana knew it could put the mother's life in danger. Even if the baby had died, Rhian would still need to birth it. She couldn't do that on the deck of a sloop. And if there was a chance that both lives could be saved…

"We have to go back to Tradepost Landing."

After getting Rhian comfortably settled below, Liana took back the helm and redirected their course. Though it was difficult to sail windward on such a small vessel, she knew it was possible. But by the time she had singlehandedly turned the sloop about, the southward wind blew stronger. An hour ago, this would have been a blessing, and they would have pressed on to the Capital at the highest speed possible. But now…

Still, Liana couldn't give up. She angled the keel against the wind, with steady, practiced hands. With her eyes narrowed to the north, she pinched the wind and zigzagged along the waves. But time passed, and as the sun began to set, Liana feared they wouldn't make it back to the Landing before dark.

That was when she saw a vessel approach in the distance. It came behind them from the south. Liana snatched up her spyglass. White sails approached like clouds over the horizon, with Caerwyn's banner floating at its highest mast. With a feeling of deep dread, she lowered the spyglass.

She knew what she had to do.

After waiting for the Navy brig to come closer, she reached for her belt and removed the pistol at her side. She steeled herself and gulped, before aiming straight up and pulling the trigger. The shot split the sky. Within moments, the brig changed its course, heading right for the sloop.

Rhian emerged from below, drawn by the sound. She had cleaned up and cloaked herself in a blanket. "What was that?"

"I signaled for help," Liana said, numbly replacing the pistol to its holster.

Rhian smoothed her hair back, squinting out. Then her hand dropped. "That's the Navy! Liana, what were you thinking? They're going to arrest us!"

"No," Liana shook her head. "Not you."

"What is *that* supposed to mean?"

"I know you're terrible at lying," she continued, replacing her hat on her head. "So, you're going to have to add a little more contempt to that tone if you want them to believe I kidnapped you."

"*What?*"

"There you go, that's better." Liana forced a smile, moving to go below. "But don't strain yourself. The baby is in enough danger as it is—"

Rhian gripped her arm to stop her. "You can't do this! They'll hang you!"

"They'll have to catch me first." Liana shook her off. "Watch the deck," she ordered, before rustling around below. She gathered Rhian's clothes and books to pack them. Only after a moment's thought, she scooped up her own things and carried them above.

"How's the pain?" she asked, hoisting the bags and dropping them at Rhian's feet.

"It's fine. Nearly gone now." Rhian sniffed, biting her lip. She looked fit to collapse, as she clutched the helm. Her previously rosy cheeks had gone deathly white.

"Liar." Liana reached into her bag, rummaging around. "Now, stop your blubbering and listen to me. We don't have much time." She procured the spell book and handed it to Rhian. "Here."

Her jaw dropped. "This is mine!"

"I know."

"Why do you have it?"

"Whyte gave it to me," Liana said, standing to face Rhian. "He asked me to help him find the owner. He thought it would be some evil sorcerer, but instead, it was you."

"If you knew it was mine, why didn't you give it back?" She pressed her hand on the cover, cradling the book.

"Because I was scared." Liana's voice trembled despite her best efforts.

"Scared? You could have asked me! These spells are meant to help people. They're for healing. Besides, I don't even know how to read them. No one does!"

"All I've known of magic was that it ruined my life. But then I met you, Rhian."

She started to cry again, silently letting tears slip down to her chin as she clutched the grimy tome. Her eyes flicked over to the Navy brig. They were close now.

"I'm sorry," Liana said, removing her hat once more and holding it to her heart.

Rhian's mouth moved, and she said something so quiet that Liana couldn't hear it in the gusty wind. Then she said it again. "It's alright, Liana. I forgive you."

"Can you just promise me one thing?" Liana asked. "Promise you'll only use your magic for good. Like you said... To help people. Can you do that?"

"Yes." Rhian rubbed her reddened nose and gave her a watery smile. "I promise."

Liana helped Rhian shove the grimoire into her bag before securing it on Rhian's shoulder. Then Liana unsheathed her sword. "Still trust me?"

"Always, Captain Foley," Rhian whispered, even as Liana came behind her and held the blade to her throat.

As the brig pulled alongside, Liana drew up, making herself as large as she could, like a threatened blowfish against a predator. She strapped on her fiercest facade—the one she used when boarding a targeted ship. With her free hand, she pinched her mouth to whistle.

"Come about and take your sweet princess, men!" she barked. "Best hurry and fetch your captain, before I accidentally slit her pretty throat!"

Navy sailors gathered along the broadside, aiming rifles at the sloop.

"I..." Rhian started, but Liana was afraid she would say something stupid.

"Shut it, girl, or your last words are going to be spilled all over this deck!"

After what seemed like an eternity, the captain of the brig, a stern square-jawed man looking to be near retirement peered over the side. He glowered down at Liana with complete abhorrence. "What's this, then? A ransom?"

"If you'd like," Liana called back.

"Rather bold of you, miss," sneered the captain, the compliment laden with disgust. "To take on the Navy with that dinghy. Or perhaps, the word is *desperate*."

"Since fleeing the palace, I've come into some bad luck. The princess is more trouble than she's worth, and I'll be giving her back now—for the right price."

"And how do we know she *is* Princess Rhian?"

Liana fisted Rhian's collar, giving her a shake. "Go on, tell them!"

"My name is Princess Rhian Ceres Vitalis! I was taken from the palace at my ball, and I need help!" Rhian tipped up her chin, drawing herself up and speaking in the most regal manner. She opened her blanket to display her abdomen. "I'm losing my baby!"

The captain lost face for just a moment, shocked.

"You're going to scrounge up whatever you can give me," Liana told him. "Then you can have the princess and perhaps save the child."

"At ease, men," the captain ordered, and they lowered their weapons. "But keep your wits about you. The woman is clearly mad."

They dropped a dinghy in the waters between them. Per Liana's instructions, only two men came to retrieve Rhian. One carefully took her hand and helped her into the small boat. The other begrudgingly gave Liana a sack of coins. On instinct, she looked inside at the hefty sum.

Rhian's sharp cry of warning made her head snap back up. Liana staggered, narrowly missing the downward stroke of a blade.

She knocked her head into the mast, but she quickly came back to her senses.

"Get her!"

She clashed swords with one of the sailors. Before she knew it, she was fighting off both. As she slunk back towards the bow, one sailor headed her off and shoved her into the side. She nearly fell overboard, but her ribs cracked against the sturdy wood. Wheezing, she shakily held herself up.

Half-blind with pain, she lunged out with her cutlass but was easily blocked. A fist crashed straight into her nose. The painful shock of it made her drop her weapon. Blood flowed from her nostrils. She collapsed to her knees, holding her face. Through her blurred vision, she could see a pistol aimed between her streaming eyes.

"*No!*" Rhian's earsplitting scream echoed from the dinghy, making him hesitate. Liana couldn't see her, but she silently hoped that Rhian's outburst hadn't blown their false scenario.

"Not in front of the princess. She's been through enough," one sailor said to the other. "Besides, a quick death's too good for this one Pirates are only good for the rope."

Liana spat blood on the deck. Accepting her fate, she allowed them to drag her to the dinghy. Her face strained tight and hot— her nose was definitely broken.

She could hear Rhian close by even as they boarded the Navy ship.

"What are you going to do with her?"

"This woman," the captain announced, "Is a pirate, abductor, and the murderer of our king. I suggest you all remember this day and what you witnessed. Don't you worry, Your Highness. She'll get what she deserves."

Liana blinked hard to see Rhian looking back at her as she was escorted below by the surgeon.

"Grannon!" the quartermaster called out. "Throw her in the brig!"

As the hefty sailor named Grannon shoved Liana down below deck, she overheard a group of sailors speaking to one another.

"How much of a reward do you suppose we'll get?"

"Who's asking for ransom now?" Liana blurted cheekily. Her comment earned her a full-forced wallop to the gut that brought her to her knees. She coughed, struggling to breathe as the air was forced out of her lungs.

"Quiet, woman!" growled Grannon.

Aching terribly, she hunched into herself, and the thought crossed her mind that she may vomit. As her muscles and organs ceased their spasms, she clenched her teeth, bearing them at Grannon as he came at her again.

He tried to grab her. She probably should have let him, but the instinct to flee took over. Throwing herself back against the bulkhead, she kicked her legs wildly and hooked her boot under his chin. Shouts of surprise tinged with sympathy for Grannon's now-broken jaw echoed from the nearby sailors. Then Grannon's meaty fist curved around to the side of her head, and it was all over.

Chapter 27

Memory
4ᵗʰ of Cambath, 1724
Dunmore Manor

Damn, he hated this weather. It had stopped sleeting, finally, but the air was still cold in the aftermath of the storm. Ameen rubbed the back of his aching neck, doing his best to oversee the repairs on the hull. Most of their time had been spent deconstructing older buildings throughout the grounds, searching for worthy lumber. Unfortunately, scrounging up enough materials without traveling to town proved to be their most difficult challenge. Then the storm came from the south, delaying them again.

"Captain?"

Behind him, Sava and Lucky approached, carrying a cargo box filled with weapons left over from Rhys Dunmore's treasure trove of firearms.

At first, he had flatly refused the vote. But after days of persistent pestering from the crew, he had accepted, only after convincing himself that the title wouldn't last long. The days passed, and he began to settle into the role. All he could do was take comfort in his faith that the Divine had a plan. He prayed every day, like always. He prayed for guidance to lead this wayward crew. He prayed for the swift repair of the ship. But most of all, he prayed for Liana. The thought of her weighed heavily on his mind at all hours.

"Look at this beauty!" Sava exclaimed, taking up a hunting rifle.

Lucky nodded with approval as Ameen went to see. The former master gunner had spent the last two weeks running grunt work, doing his best to make up for his transgressions. Ameen had to admit that Lucky showed a great deal of humility. As the new captain, he had done his best to set an example for the crew. He allowed Lucky to earn his place again. Often, Ameen wondered if he had made the right decision, if he undermined Liana by showing compassion for Lucky. But Lucky's integral role in the crew couldn't be ignored. Besides his role as master gunner, he had been a sailor for thirty years. Not to mention, he knew every nook and cranny of the *Windfall*. The ship was his home, just as much as it was for every other man in the crew. He had a stake in making it whole again.

"Captain, are you well?" he asked with quiet concern. "Getting much sleep?"

Ameen rubbed at his eye, as though it would erase the dark circles beneath them. "Don't worry yourself, Lucky."

"That one is mine," called Nellie's voice from across the beach.

Once she got closer—close enough to look upon his face, she stopped short and said, "Are you ill, Ameen?"

"I'm fine," he replied crossly. The pity in her gray eyes reflected what he had seen in everyone else over the past few weeks. It was too much to bear, and he'd had enough of it.

"You know how to shoot, Mistress Dunmore?" Sava interrupted, handing Nellie the rifle.

"Yes, my father taught me," she said. "And please, call me Nellie."

"Yes, ma'am." Sava glanced sideways at Ameen, who gave him a nod of reassurance. It was a far cry from the ill-mannered pickpocket he'd once known.

"Lucky, help Sava load the crate," Ameen said, feeling as though he had been out in the cold for too long. Even the touch of the crisp wind on his face was too much.

Jamil came then, with his twin following behind. "Captain, I have good news. It appears all the material will hold for the hull. And Jamil has just informed me the repairs on the rudder are complete."

"Good, that's good," he said with a nod of approval. "When will the *Windfall* be ready to sail again?"

"Tomorrow."

"We'll need to take her about the coast before I feel comfortable letting her go out to open sea."

"Rightly so, Captain."

"After that, we have Mistress Dunmore's permission to load the ship with everything valuable from the manor." Ameen looked back at Nellie, who gave him a tight smile.

"And do we have a heading?"

"No. Not yet."

"Aye, Captain. I understand."

Ameen extended his hand, and Jamil took it. "You've done a tremendous job here. Both of you," he said, looking to Kahil as well.

"Thank you." While he appeared grateful for the praise, Jamil's brows knitted together in concern. "Captain, if you'd like to have the afternoon to rest, I can take care of the rest of the day's operations."

"What makes you say that, Jamil?" Ameen released his hand.

"You're… feeling rather warm."

Perhaps he was ill, after all. After a moment's deliberation, he decided to accept Jamil's offer. With everything going on, the last thing this crew needed was to have their captain down for more than a day.

As the twins saluted him, Ameen crossed the beach, determined to get out of the sunny chill. He made his way up the hill, stretching his legs to release the tight knots. It felt rather like growing pains he had experienced as a child, in a time when he had suddenly shot up in height. Divine, he hoped he was not about to grow any taller. As it was, he towered over most of the crew.

Casting his eyes down, Ameen headed inside the main house. Thiago was there, sterilizing and taking account of the medical supplies he had gathered from the servants' stores. Nellie had let the help go shortly after Mid-Winter with a hefty severance pay. Everyone had taken their own share of keeping up the manor. It was the least they could do for Nellie—and for Marin. Thiago, of course, had volunteered to lead the kitchen duties. It distracted him from constantly wondering what happened to Camila and Lucia after the raid at the Barricade.

Thiago's spectacles gleamed in the firelight of the green salon as he inspected a small jar of clear liquid. As Ameen approached, Thiago addressed him in Savarran. "Already they are asking what is for dinner. It's only just past breakfast. You'd think these men were starving."

"Hmph."

Thiago placed the jar gently with the rest and took a look at Ameen.

"You're ill," he concluded without even so much as a blink.

"It's this damn weather."

"Yes, the weather," Thiago said with some skepticism and looked at Ameen over his round spectacles. "I do hope our fair captain was in a sheltered place for the storm."

"I'm sure." He kept his face as still as he could. "She can take care of herself."

Ameen was devastated to find her gone the morning of Marin's burial. But when he had looked across the way at Nellie as they buried her father, he began to wonder if he should have really blamed Liana for leaving. He understood why. But what he couldn't shake was that she had gone without a single word to him. Nothing.

Yes, they'd fought. But after everything that had happened, after he'd held her as she grieved for Marin, Ameen thought they would come to forgive each other in the morning. He'd never been more wrong in his life.

It had taken him some time to begin to look forward—to prepare himself and the crew for a future without Liana. Thiago, for one, had a family back in the Capital to think about. Ameen thought perhaps he was making up for it by projecting his grandfatherly duties on him. "When was the last time you ate, my boy?"

Ameen wet his lips, trying to remember. To his surprise, he tasted salt. How could he be sweating when it was so cold? "I don't know."

Nellie came in, carrying an icy breeze from outside with her. She held the hunting rifle in her arms, headed straight for the salon.

"I'll be in my room," Ameen told Thiago in Savarran. Without greeting Nellie, he went on his way.

After his abrupt exit, he glanced back and saw Nellie followed. What did she want? Despite his best intentions, he couldn't shake the ugly feeling of blame whenever he looked at her.

"Is there something you need?" he asked, stopping in the hallway.

"I-I just…" she began. "I wanted to ask you where we're going, after all this. Since you're the captain now…"

"As I'm sure you heard me tell Jamil, our repairs on the ship are nearly complete. After that—Well, I'd like to get the crew back home safely."

"So, you don't intend to… go after her?" she asked him carefully.

Everyone was so cautious around him, as though the very whisper of Liana's name would make him crumble. It had felt like that for the first few days—but it wasn't the first time he had been abandoned. He would live.

"I *intend* to take care of the crew. I'm not going to drag them all over the coasts of Vioria looking for her if they want to go home to their families."

"But if they did want to find her, would you—"

"She left with no explanation—of course I would want—"
he began, then stopped short. He pinched the bridge of his nose
to alleviate the building tension in his head. "To be honest with
you, Nellie, how I feel toward Liana is not your concern."

"I feel terrible, Ameen. I really do."

"Liana made her choice. I'm sure she thought it was for the
best."

"I know. If there was any way we could get her back, I…"
She trailed off.

"Me too." He allowed a slip of emotion, but quickly diverted
the conversation to the rifle. "I hope you know what you're doing
with that."

Nellie glanced over the weapon, flared her nostrils, and took
in a deep breath. "I know exactly what I'm going to do with it,"
she replied with morbid finality.

"Just… be careful with it, alright?" he managed, feeling quite
awkward now. It was as though the words came out too slowly,
but it could have been his imagination—or the sudden wave of
exhaustion that had come over him.

Nellie gave him one last look with a familiar sense of
determination. "You know, you really do look bloody awful. Get
some rest, would you? These men need you."

As she walked away, Ameen found himself thoroughly
convinced, for the very first time, that Nellie and Liana were raised
in the same household.

Sometime after dark, a timid knock woke him. He had
returned to staying in the room he had shared with Liana after she
left. It was either that or share a guest room with three to four
other men.

"Dinner, Almasi!"

"Captain," the quieter, nearly identical voice corrected.

"Right," the first one stammered. "*Captain.*"

Ameen groaned, keeping his eyes shut tight. Sleeping hadn't helped. His bones continued to ache down to the marrow.

"Has he gone back to shutting himself in, I wonder?" Kahil asked. Jamil shushed him.

Ameen lacked the strength to retort, and the twins' voices faded away. With each beat of his heart, the pain pulsed in his head, throbbing down to his very fingertips. He pulled the bedclothes over himself and found his reprieve in sleep.

Hours later, he woke again, parched.

Once, when he was young and lived in the little island borough with his parents, he had eaten sand. It certainly hadn't been intentional. He had been let loose from his chores early that day, with the promise he would go and try to make friends with the other children playing at the beach. An older boy had pulled the soft, coiled hair of a girl his age—hard enough to make her cry. Ameen had tackled the boy to the ground. The next thing he knew, his face was shoved in the sand. His father had laughed at him when he had come home with his mouth coated with the fine, gritty substance.

His mouth was *that* dry.

Strange that he'd forgotten about that day, until that very moment.

Trembling weakly, he crawled to the edge of the bed toward the pitcher and basin. But when he tried to lift the pitcher—he was so damned thirsty he was going to drink it straight—his wrist gave out and it spilled everywhere. The porcelain pitcher broke to pieces. Ameen blinked dumbly at it. What was wrong with him?

He peeled off his shirt and laid it over the mess, before gathering the broken pieces in it. The effort was too much, however, and he sank to his hands and knees. Nausea hit him hard, and he covered his mouth with his fist.

No. Divine. Please don't let him be sick. Not going to be sick.

Not going to be sick.

The door creaked. "Captain?" A different voice now. Sava.

Ameen's stomach lurched, and he gagged. He hadn't eaten in a few days, luckily.

"I've got you?"

Sava's arms hooked under his to pull him back to the bed. Sava stopped short upon seeing the sweat-soaked sheets and retrieved a dry quilt from the sofa. He settled it around Ameen's shoulders.

"She used to read to me..." Ameen rasped, with no awareness that Sava hadn't a clue what he was talking about. He sobbed with abandon. Treasured memories long forgotten came rushing back to him. So overwhelmed, he gasped for breath.

"Who...?"

"She was going to teach me—" he kept on, looking at Sava, but not really. He was trying to go back, trying to remember her face. "She didn't want to leave."

"The captain—? I mean..." Sava said. "I mean," Captain Foley?

"No... no..." Ameen blinked a few times, tears sliding down his face. He clasped Sava's shoulders tightly, thrilled by realization. "My mother..."

Sava pried them off. "Bloody hell, you're burning up!"

He held them open and looked down, suddenly realizing his palms were growing hot, like he was holding them to a flame. In fact, it was as though a fire had been lit in his very veins. In the dark of the room a red-orange molten glow pulsed in his wrists, through his hands, to the tips of his fingers.

Ameen looked up so sharply it made him lightheaded. "What's happening to me?" He grunted as his stomach twisted again, more painfully now.

"Don't move," said Sava, adjusting the quilt so it covered Ameen's hands. "I'm going to get Thiago, alright?"

He had forgotten that Sava still stayed in the house, sharing a room with Thiago—who slept like the dead, save for his snoring. But if Sava had heard him through that, then it would not be long before—

"What's going on?" Nellie. She was suddenly in front of him, stepping over the mess of soaked porcelain.

"S-sorry..." he said, trying to smile apologetically at her, but he could hardly move his slackening face, and the sound of his own voice seemed to be fading...

Please, Father. I have to know. I have to know why she left us.

He sat on the cot in the cabin he shared with his father. The cot was so low that his knees were nearly at his chest. He had sprouted up that summer, too quickly for him to know what to do with his gangly limbs.

It became too difficult. It was for the best. That is all I can say.

It wasn't enough. Why could he not trust him with the truth? He was grown, now. A man.

That's all you can say?

He drew up, furious with the same old answers. It was the first time he'd realized he had finally reached up to his father's imposing height. They glared at each other. Amber bored harshly into dark maroon.

Then, Anise started to speak again. But there was no sound. His black-and silver-bearded mouth moved with words unheard. and Ameen realized the cabin was filling with seawater.

He remembered the night of the storm. The water had been so cold. So, crushing.

He should have died.

For a long time after that storm, he wanted to die.

In the surreal vision of the cabin, the water reached his mouth and covered his head. His throat filled with water. Anise kept looking at him as though nothing had happened.

Cold.

So cold.

So—

A cry reached his ears as he was doused. Completely disoriented, he thrashed his arms and legs, finding himself thrown in something hard and cold. Water sloshed as he scrambled to escape. He spluttered as it came down dripping from his face.

"Keep him down!"

"We're trying!"

As he was pressed back into the water, he clutched the side of whatever he was in. It was slick, hard, and cold. He grasped to find an anchor, touched an arm, and clung to it tight. A much smaller hand squeezed his as he shivered, folding in on himself. His teeth chattered so hard his jaw hurt.

"Must we do this? It looks like absolute torture," Nellie said, sounding near tears. She was the one holding onto him.

"The fever could kill him," Thiago's thick voice told her sternly. "This will help. Just a bit longer."

He closed his eyes again, pressing into Nellie's hand, which had moved to hold the base of his skull. His muscles had gone rigid.

"I'm telling you—it wasn't a fever rash! It was something... something else!" Sava argued with Thiago.

Nellie interrupted. "That's enough, it's too cold—he's starting to seize up! Get him out!"

He attempted to move again and managed to lift his leg out of the tub. That was when he realized his clothes had been removed. He tilted his head to Nellie, swatting her away with one hand, covering himself with the other. "Get... out."

Nellie took a long step back, stung.

Sava snorted and tried to mend her hurt feelings. "I don't think he wants you looking at his bits, Mistress Dunmore."

"Well, if he's able to be modest, then I'm sure he'll survive," she said, and he was able to hear the mirth in her voice. "I'll get the fire on, then."

Soon he was warm and clothed again. They laid him on the sofa near the fireplace. He stared at the flames as his eyelids grew heavier. He heard Nellie leave with Thiago close behind.

"I'll stay with him," Sava said.

Ameen found himself mesmerized by the bright ribbons of light dancing over the log. They sparked and snarled over the wood. The acrid scent of smoke soothed the lingering ache in his head. If he'd had the strength, he might have gotten closer, for he was beckoned, enticed, entranced...

The sunlight woke Ameen. He blinked carefully, finding his fever and aches to be gone. The fire had turned to slow embers. When he sat up, his feet touched something soft. A long body curled up on the floor beside the sofa, with tufts of black spirals sticking out from beneath a duvet.

The corners of his mouth pulled up, despite his pride beginning to gnaw at him. He had known Sava since he was a boy. Now, here he was, sleeping at his side like a worried parent. He recalled the young man wrapping him in the heavy quilt with a look of extreme concern, even fright.

That reminded him—

He opened his palms and inspected them. All looked normal and well. Just the same broad, square hands. He turned them over a few times. The middle finger of his left hand was still crooked from smashing it between the mast and a cargo box when he was fourteen. Same knuckles, a darker brown than the rest of his hands. Raised veins, from years of straining the bones. The pads of his fingers and mound of his thumbs were still worn and rough.

Not even a bit of glowing, though.

Sava stirred at the sounds of excited voices outside. Ameen stood and stepped over him with caution, quite surprised at his own strength after last night's ordeal. He peered through the gossamer curtains.

A wagon drawn by a single horse stopped just outside. Lucky rushed out of the guest quarters to greet the man driving. They embraced like lost family members. More people stood up in the back of the wagon. Two women, three children. Suddenly, one of the women jumped into Lucky's arms and he lifted her, laughing joyously.

Ameen knew her immediately—Bess.

More shouting. Thiago came next, nearly collapsing into the arms of his daughter, Camila. He peppered his granddaughter with kisses. The three of them sank to the ground in sheer relief.

As the driver looked on at the reunions, he spoke with Lucky, arms over each other's shoulders. Then, with a running start, Nellie flew out of the house and threw herself into the man's arms.

"Glad you survived the night," said a drowsy voice behind Ameen. Sava had gotten to his feet and stumbled to the window. "Who's out there?"

Ameen looked out again, drawing the curtain back further. He suddenly smiled in recognition as he watched the man approach the house, Nellie at his side. "I'd know that pompous stride anywhere."

Sava looked at him curiously.

"That's Ivan Foley."

Chapter 28

The Prince

Ameen dressed with a speed he would've thought impossible the night before. He left Sava, who still rubbed the sleep out of his eyes, upstairs and bounded down the stairs, where he spotted Bess, Camila, Thiago, and the children. They greeted him ecstatically. Beatrix, Sebastian, and Lucia ran to him first at full speed. He squeezed the three young ones tight, kneeling down to gather them all up in his arms.

"I can't believe you're here," he said to Bess and Camila once the children finally let him go.

"Neither can we," said Camila. Her Savarran accent still held fast to her voice, but it wasn't as thick as her father's.

"We'd heard the Barricade was gone, and we thought…"

"Ivan saved us," Bess said, tenderly patting his arm. "We're just fine."

"The Barricade is gone, though," Camila admitted. "They came in the night, a few days after the ball. We've been coming this way ever since."

"Ameen," Bess said. "It was Commander Whyte. He told them where to find us."

Ameen furrowed his brows, wishing he could say he was surprised. "Are you sure?"

Camila nodded mournfully. "He was there that night."

Seeing the dark fury growing in Ameen's eyes, Bess interrupted. "What matters is that we made it safe, and we are all together again."

He sighed and shook his head. "Not all of us."

"I can explain," Thiago said to the two women. He looked to Ameen. "Mistress Dunmore ask after you."

"I'll go see her," he said and moved aside so the two families could march up the stairs to settle in.

Ivan Foley bore a striking resemblance to his sister. They had the same deep brown eyes, raven black hair, hawk-shaped nose, and thick expressive eyebrows. Their mouths curved into the same lopsided smile when feeling amused or bashful. Though ten years Liana's senior, Ivan's natural charisma would often lead people to believe he was still in his twenties. He walked with the gait of an aristocrat; a man born to be king.

"Where the hell did you come from?" asked Ameen, announcing his presence as he entered the green salon.

Ivan twisted around, barking a laugh. It was deeper but sounded very much like the melody of Liana's. He stood.

"Ameen Almasi!" He left Nellie's side and crossed the room to exchange handshakes. Clapping Ameen on the arm, he continued, "It's so good to see you. How long has it been?"

"Ten years," said Ameen breathlessly. "Almost ten years."

"I've heard you and my sister have been busy since then." Ivan looked around Ameen, as though Liana would come walking in after him. "Where is she, by the way? And Marin?"

Ameen and Nellie exchanged looks.

"What?" Ivan caught the glance. "What's Liana gotten up to this time?"

"Ivan…" Nellie took her foster brother by the hand and gently tugged him down to the sofa. Ameen, though he felt the urge to run away, sank down into a chair across from them. "Da has… He's passed away."

Ivan dropped her hand, letting it fall limply. In that moment, he looked very much his age. "He's dead?"

Nellie sat back with tearful eyes. Ameen decided to step in.

"Dunmore betrayed us," he said softly.

"What about Liana?" Ivan asked, his words colliding together rapidly. "She's not…? Nothing's happened to her, has it?"

"She left," said Ameen. "Just before Mid-Winter, she left and headed back to the Capital."

"Ah!" Ivan exclaimed, standing with his fists balled. "That little—That's where I just came from! I've been looking for her for weeks! What was she thinking?!"

"You came from the Capital?" interrupted Nellie. "I thought you lived in Riven."

"Riven? That's where you've been this whole time?" Ameen stood as well, outraged that Ivan had been so close to the Capital and yet never made an effort to contact Liana.

Ivan clapped his hands together. "Can we *please* focus?"

"No. We'll be asking the questions here." Ameen said. He knew Ivan well and wouldn't fall for his distractions. "All of a sudden, you show up after a decade of complete silence with a cart of women and children from the Barricade, which last we heard had been burned down. Start from the beginning. When were you in the Capital and why?"

"I went looking for my sister, obviously. After the word spread that she killed the king and kidnapped Princess Rhian—"

"She didn't—" Ameen began.

"Do you want to hear my side of the story or not?" scoffed Ivan, leaning back on his heel. Ameen rolled his eyes and waved him on. "I know Liana. I never once thought she *actually* did it. She's never wanted anything to do with the throne or anyone who sits on it. I went to The Black Barricade trying to find answers as to what really happened. That was when I met Bess and Camila.

"The first night into my stay, the place was raided. Soldiers came and tore everything apart. Bess and Camila were working that night. I got them and the children out. I thought *maybe* Marin would think to come here."

"He did," said Ameen. He told Ivan everything that had happened since Dillon Whyte sent the cryptic letter to the Barricade. When he got to the ball and the murder of King Lyell, Ivan didn't look terribly surprised to hear about the lightning magic. However, he allowed Ameen to speak. He continued on to Dunmore's betrayal and the events thereafter that caused Liana to leave.

When he was done, Ivan took a moment to let everything sink in. He sat back, rubbing his hands over his knees. "They're headed straight into a bloody snake pit. She doesn't stand a chance."

"Liana seemed to feel very strongly that Whyte would take Princess Rhian back, that he could clear her name or find her a safe place," said Nellie.

"No. I mean *Liana* doesn't stand a chance," Ivan said gravely. "As soon as Dunmore made it to someone with ears, he probably let our secret out. If Grigor Vitalis knows the last two Romenels are alive, he will stop at nothing to see us dead."

"So, he really was the one who killed your parents?" asked Nellie.

"Yes," Ivan said, voice dripping with hatred. "Bloody hell, I hate talking about this... I'm going to need a bath first." He looked to Nellie. "Where... did you bury your father?"

"Behind the manor," she said tiredly. "We laid him to rest beneath a tree on an overlook."

"Could we meet there?" asked Ivan. "I'd like get my thoughts together, then go pay my respects. After that, I'll tell you everything. Both of you."

A smooth, round stone marked the grave of Marin Foley. It bore no etchings. Nellie thought it would be safer. She feared her husband would return and desecrate the site. Unable to bear the thought of her father's remains being disturbed, she had asked for a simple marker that faced south, so Marin would always be looking to the place where her mother rested. Above the stone, a naked tree stretched out, thin and spidery.

Sava sat before the grave with his knees drawn up and his arms folded over them. He hid his face in the crook of his arm and pretended not to notice when Ameen came to sit beside him. For an uncomfortable amount of time, they were silent. Ameen thought if Sava wanted him to leave, he would have said so, and resolved to lean back on his hands under the pleasantly tepid light that peeked through the branches.

Finally, Sava said something into his shirt. Ameen blinked. "What?"

The young man turned his head so his mouth was free to speak. "You should be resting."

"I'm meeting Ivan and Nellie here," Ameen explained, shrugging off the subject of his health. He felt fine.

"Did you... Did you see what I saw last night? Your hands..." Sava trailed off, flexing his fingers, unsure how to finish the sentence.

"So, I wasn't imagining it." Ameen sighed, feeling a little relieved.

"Did it hurt?"

"No...I just felt... hot," he faltered, still quite unsure how to explain it. Sava seemed to understand.

"You were burning up, and your breathing sounded off—like you were struggling with it."

Ameen listened, brow creased.

"I got scared," he confessed. "I didn't want to lose you too." He heaved a sigh as he looked down at the grass. "My mum, you know, died when I was born. Marin's gone now. Captain Foley left. And you..." He took another shaky breath, looking to the sky.

Before Sava could say any more, Ameen took pity on him and placed an arm around his shoulder. He shook Sava slightly, easing the tension and making him laugh a little.

"We're family," Ameen said helpfully. "All of us."

"Why'd she have to go, then?"

Please, Father. I have to know. I have to know why.

Ameen shifted his glance away. "I think... she felt she had done too much damage. She thought it would make us better off. Even if we'd been there to stop her...You can't force that woman to do anything, once she has her mind made up. She has to figure it out on her own."

"And... you're alright with that?"

Ameen shrugged. "I have to be. I need time, and so does she. That's what I tried to tell her. But she—she shut me out anyway."

"We'll see her again."

"I know we will."

A while after Sava went to the house, Ameen spotted Ivan and Nellie climbing up the hill. He waited as the former prince walked past them and knelt on still-soft soil. Nellie stood at his side. They shared a quiet, respectful moment, a temporary respite from the turmoil.

"I can't believe he's gone," Ivan murmured. He pressed his gloved fingers to his lips and placed them on the stone. It was about the size of an adult cat, curled up for a long nap. Ivan rose and looked at Ameen and Nellie, a darkness in his deep brown eyes. Ameen caught an eerie flash of Liana in his face. "I'm going to rip Rhys Dunmore apart."

They regarded Ivan with a sense of shared sentiment. He wiped his eyes and addressed Ameen. "I'm ready."

"What exactly are we facing here, Ivan?" Ameen prompted gently when he didn't immediately begin. Ivan ruffled a hand through his shoulder-length hair and took a deep breath.

"As you both know, our parents were King Sergus and Queen Valeriya Romenel. Our mother was born from an aristocratic family in Rodina, the Koshkins. In her youth, she was one of Tsarina Katarina's favorite companions, apparently. The Tsarina thought she would be a good match for the young king of Caerwyn, to solidify the fragile stability between the two nations.

"I was born not long after. But there's a reason why there's ten years difference between Liana and me," he continued. "They failed to produce another child. And you know what they say—an heir and a spare...

"I remember Mother would be ill every so often—shut up in her apartments in the palace for days at a time. I suppose, looking back, it's obvious she had been miscarrying. As this went on, rumors began to spread about Grigor Vitalis' new wife. Her name was Lady Alcyone. People thought she was a witch."

"And was she?" Ameen asked.

"I suppose so," Ivan said sullenly. "I remember Mother said the rumors started because she was a commoner—a commoner practiced in the healing arts. One day, Lady Alcyone came to the palace. Less than a year later, Liana was born."

Nellie shivered. "A witch cast some sort of... fertility spell on your mother?" She wiggled her fingers.

"I don't know." Ivan sighed. "But that didn't do anything to deter the rumors."

"So, then what?" Ameen urged.

"So, then, there she was—a baby girl. Our father saw her birth as an opportunity to carry on the tradition of solidifying political ties. He made a pact between the Romenels and the Whytes."

Ameen felt like he was suspended in the air. The blood drained from his face. His arms, which he had crossed over his chest, fell heavily to the sides. "Did you say Whyte?" he asked.

"Yes. The very same Dillon Whyte who contacted you," said Ivan, looking mightily regretful. "I might have reached out to the Whytes, back when we first came back to Caerwyn. I thought... they could help us. Bayard was close with our father. He wrote back and proposed we uphold the betrothal to get our way back into Caerwyn society."

"Does Liana know about this?" Ameen raised his voice enough to earn a half-step back from Ivan. He took a breath to settle himself down.

"Why do you think we haven't spoken in ten years?"

"But about Whyte? Did she know you wanted her to marry Dillon Whyte?"

"No, it didn't get that far! I doubt he knew anything about it either. I received a reply from Bayard, and he died not long after." Ivan swore, raising his hands in surrender. He looked at Nellie as though pleading for help.

"It's a long story," Nellie placed a calming hand on Ameen's shoulder. He shrugged it off.

"When I proposed the arranged marriage to her, we argued, and she stole from me to buy that ship of hers. So, I left," said Ivan stiffly. "I know I've done wrong. We both have."

Ameen didn't reply. This was all so difficult to swallow. Liana, royalty, arranged marriages, magic—it all swirled in his mind. After a silence, Ivan cleared his throat and continued his story.

"Lord and Lady Vitalis had a son, as well. Our father could have chosen to ally himself with the family that allegedly brought about Liana's birth. But I suppose that would have been too suspicious. After all, magic is nonexistent to the common man. But those of us who know better see it for what it is—a crime against nature."

Ameen couldn't help rubbing his hands together. "So, what you're saying is that a battle for the throne began because Liana was betrothed to the wrong boy?"

Ivan shook his head. "Not exactly, no. Our father became deathly ill when Liana was about a year or two old. Again, we were visited by Lady Alcyone. But this time, her husband had stayed behind in Yael with their son. She came alone. Father began to recover, and she left shortly after. Another coincidence."

"Doubtful," Nellie commented.

"What's worse is that Lady Alcyone never made it back to Yael. She and her carriage party were found murdered on the road, about a day's ride out from the Capital. Authorities said it was bandits, but..."

"Why would anyone assume it was your parents?" Ameen asked. "What motive would they have when the Vitalis' supposedly helped them *twice*?"

"No one knows exactly what happened for certain," Ivan said gravely. "No one alive, at least. What I do know is that Grigor Vitalis killed our parents, because I saw him there that night, with my own eyes.

"The Vitalises are a family almost as ancient as the Romenels. The magic must have passed through several generations. I can't imagine the damage they have caused throughout history. Who knows how many families like them are out there?"

Again, Ameen's attention went to his own hands. Was he, perhaps, the same as Rhian? Could he have inherited something similar?

"Grigor Vitalis blamed our parents for the death of his wife. After he killed our parents, Liana and I ran away." Ivan looked down at the grave somberly. "That was when Marin found us."

Ameen knew the rest. He turned away, taking a moment to collect his thoughts.

"Liana spent this whole time thinking it was the princess who needed to be protected," said Ivan in a low voice. "If I know anything about Grigor Vitalis, he'll make sure Rhian returns safely, but Liana will pay the price. Between him, Dillon Whyte, and Rhys Dunmore, Liana won't stand a chance the moment she steps into the Capital."

"We have to go after her," Nellie said, looking to Ameen. "She'll be killed!"

"We will," answered Ameen. The gut-twisting image of a rope around Liana's neck left him nauseated. Pressing a hand against the rowan tree, Ameen made a silent prayer. "But first, I need to gather the crew."

An hour later, just after noon, the lot of them stood on the beach before the *Windfall*. He wanted every one of the men to hear the truth. He told them Ivan's story and did not leave anything out. In fact, he emphasized the role magic had played in the downfall of Sergus Romenel. They needed to know what kind of danger they were up against. Ivan was there to embellish.

"Captain Foley," Ameen said once he finished, "She was always a fair woman. She would never want any man aboard the *Windfall* who didn't believe in her cause. So, I will leave it to each one of you to make your own choice."

He looked out at thirty pairs of eyes that stared at him, many still wide in shock at the tale they had just heard.

"But I've decided I will retrieve our captain, so long as we have the men to sail."

Murmurs of agreement tumbled over the crowd.

"Any man who wants to leave may take a horse with supplies and be on their way," he said, nodding to Nellie, who gave a nod of assent.

Not one man came forward, not even in private. That night, Ameen slept restlessly, with swirling thoughts of royalty and sorcery rattling his brain. The next morning, he woke early to see to the *Windfall's* repairs. Sava, Lucky, Jamil, and Kahil already waited for him outside, with the entirety of the crew at their backs.

Together, they went to the cove to finish their work.

Chapter 29

Prisoner

9th of Cambath, 1723

Cynareth Ocean, near the Capital of Caerwyn

"The baby is safe."

Liana woke in the corner of the brig, curled amongst a pile of rigging rope, damp and cold.

"Huh?" She squinted through the darkness to see a narrow face. She rubbed her eyes, lifting herself up from the floor of the brig.

"I'm sorry, ma'am… I thought you were awake."

The young sailor held her morning corner of bread. For the past several days, Liana had lived on that and water. By now, she was so desperate for the small ration, it tasted even better than Bess' stew.

"What did you say about the baby?" she asked, taking the scratched-up iron tray.

"The princess didn't lose her baby," he said. "I saw her last evening. She thought it was important for you to know."

Liana sank back against the bars, doing her best not to show her relief. "Good on her."

The youth crouched down to her eye level.

"Are you thirsty, ma'am? The bread is even drier today," he said with some regret.

Liana nodded before she took a good look at the young man. With the memory of Sava heavy in her heart, she thought this boy was about the same age. Instead of black spirals, though, his deep auburn hair stuck out bone straight. Freckles speckled his sun-browned nose and cheeks.

"You were trying to save the baby, weren't you?" he said as he handed her a canteen.

"What makes you think that?"

"The princess isn't good at lying."

Liana smirked. "No. She's not. Are you going to tell your captain?"

"Wouldn't it save you?"

"Doubtful. But it might condemn the princess for a number of reasons. So best to keep it to yourself."

"As you wish, ma'am." He let her drink and took back the canteen. She spotted an etching on the canteen that said *Meagher*. Every time she had taken a drink, he had given it from his own personal water supply—a precious resource on any ship.

"What's your name, kid?" she asked, gripping the bar as he left.

"Private Tomas Meagher," he said. "You might hear the other men call me Trout. I'm a fisherman's son. I hate that name—Trout."

"Be grateful it isn't Squiddy," she said with a little smile.

"What?"

"Never mind."

They arrived in the Capital the next day. Liana could feel it when the ship came into the harbor. She waited, supposing they would wait to retrieve her until Rhian had gotten a safe distance away from her captor. Finally, after hours went by, four men, including Tomas and the captain, came for her. The captain and a man who appeared to be a scribe kept their distance from Liana, as though she was a rabid animal. Tomas placed a pair of shackles on her wrists before leading her out of the brig.

"The earl has ordered the servants to prepare a cell in the old dungeon—away from the other prisoners," the scribe said to the captain.

Liana held her shackled hands up to her chest, interrupting. "How kind. Just for me?"

They rightfully ignored her as the scribe led her, Tomas, and the rest to the dinghy that would bring them into the Capital proper. In the distant sky, storm clouds rolled in. It was going to rain tonight.

Walking the docks, Liana felt much like she was being paraded as a prize of war. It was evening, nearly sunset, and many citizens still walked out and about. They ogled at the company as they made their way to the road. She bowed her head forward, afraid she would see someone she knew. It was very likely. The docks had been her domain. In fact, if she peered far enough down the road, she would be able to see The Black Barricade—

Liana froze. Though she knew in her heart and mind that the Barricade was no more, nothing could have prepared her for what she saw. She looked at the remains of the corner tavern with an unblinking stare. Perhaps it might have been easier to see nothing but ashes. It appeared, though, that the fire had been doused before it could spread to the other buildings. Someone spoke a few gruff words to her, but all she could focus on was the boarded windows, just barely hiding black charred marks from a fire. The place had once been so full of love and life; now it looked like an empty shell, a corpse. She squinted up at the topmost window just below the attic, where she used to look out at the harbor and the palace spires.

The soldier shoved her into a barred cart before she could linger. Whispers of shock and awe surrounded her as sailors and shoppers gathered. Retreating to the corner, she hid her face in her knees, praying for the humiliating ride to end soon.

"Any effects?" The scribe gathered up his papers, preparing to drive the cart.

Tomas placed her sheathed cutlass and hat on the seat beside the soldier. "That's all. The rest is on the sloop we towed in the harbor." He retreated toward the back of the cart and spoke out of the side of his mouth. "Try not to say anything stupid. Could get you hurt again."

"I'll try my best," she replied so only he could hear. She decided to take a chance. "If you see the princess, can you tell her... tell her I'm alright?"

"Let's hope I'm better at lying than she is," he muttered dryly.

"Thank you." She tried to put a great deal of meaning behind the simple phrase of gratitude. Truthfully, she appreciated his kindness. She imagined it would have been easier for him to be cold to her.

A half-hour later, she arrived at the prison. Though bound, she rubbed a hand along her neck at the sight of the gallows in the prison square as she was led to her cell. She hoped it would be quick. A sharp snap of bone, then it would be over.

"Food is brought at six o'clock in the morning, noon, and six o'clock in the evening," the scribe droned, and she tore her eyes away from the sight of her imminent doom. They pressed on through the old, crumbling section of the prison and down a set of stone steps, through the deepest reaches of the dungeon to the very last cell. "Water will be replenished as well."

"Lovely." She frowned, peering inside. It looked as though *most* of the cobwebs had been cleared. Darkness blanketed the barren place, barely kept away by a single hanging lantern.

"And where do I...?" She looked around and noticed a wooden bucket in the corner. Her nose crinkled. "Ah, never mind. I found it."

The scribe took his leave unceremoniously. Liana sighed deeply when she was finally alone, a cloud of vapor escaping her lips. It was bloody cold down here. In the opposite corner of the bucket sat a filled pewter pitcher. She took a moment to rub water over her face and her chapped lips before taking a drink. Above her, metal clinked together, and she looked to see a pair of shackles suspended from the ceiling. Shuddering, she settled herself down on the bench, longing for her cozy berth in the captain's cabin of the *Windfall*.

She closed her eyes and imagined her crew, working in their shifts until the bells rang to signal the trade-off. She pictured Ameen, his hand over Sava's shoulder as he watched him tie his first sailor's knot. Her last thought was of Marin, stepping lightly to the upper deck, celebrating their heavy jewel haul. It was enough to help lull her to sleep and dream of better times, sailing the sea.

Rhian wandered the room like a haunting specter. She ran the tip of her index finger along the spines of her books as she went. Passing a mirror, she caught a glimpse of herself. Nothing in the apartments had been moved or changed since she left, but Rhian found herself transformed, both inside and out.

The first thing she had done upon returning to the castle was bathe. She found it helpful to focus on that. After the bath, then she would...

What?

What was she to do now?

A maid announced her presence with a soft knock and a gentle *ahem*. "Your Highness. Commander Whyte would like permission to enter."

"Yes. Yes, of course." Rhian smoothed out her day dress and turned on her heel, pretending to be occupied with the fire. The blaze twisted above burning black embers of ruby and amber. Ash crusted on the logs, falling to bits into its velvety resting place. When Dillon entered, he brought a draft with him, making the flames momentarily disappear. In a quick moment, they resumed their slow burn.

"Rhian..."

Dressed in his uniform, the silver stitching appeared to be the only part of him that she found bright. His broad shoulders sagged. When she looked at him, she felt like she looked at a stranger. But she supposed he likely felt the same, from the way his gaze fell on her bodice.

"It's yours," she blurted, announcing the obvious.

Dillon crossed the room slowly, possibly fearing she would turn him away. He reached out, and before he could change his mind, she clasped his wrist. Pressing his palm against her midsection, she willed the baby to move. After prodding a few spots, a foot ran along the inside of her womb, making Dillon's face lift with a smile of wonder. His happiness flowed through her. She found herself laughing tearfully at the impossibility of this perfect moment.

Her giggles evaporated, suppressed by a kiss. Their connection electrified, and no longer were they unfamiliar. The man she fell in love with broke through the tired stranger. Tossing her arms over his shoulders, euphoria overwhelmed her. He pulled back to look at her lovingly and say, "Marry me, Rhian."

She could have melted, right there in his arms. "Yes."

He held her cheek, kissing her again, longer this time. His mouth lingered, reveling in her lips, her presence, her body. It was just like every passionate night they had spent together in these apartments. Breathless with desire, she threaded his fingers through his hair, nails dragging upwards on his scalp, pulling loose a few locks of honey-colored hair from his ribbon.

"Divine, I thought I would never see you again," he said. "And now you're finally home."

"It was Liana. She saved me," she said, drawing back a step to look at his face. "She saved us."

His brows drew together. "Saved you?"

"Yes! She lied."

"What are you saying?"

"I wasn't her captive, Dillon. She's been protecting me this whole time. Just like you asked her to."

His hands left her. He tucked the wayward strands of hair behind his ear. "You're saying you went with her willingly."

"Well, yes."

"I saw her drag you over the wall."

"I *fell*. We fell. Her crew rescued us," she explained. "I had just killed my own brother, Dillon. The Navy came after us. What else was I supposed to do?"

He sank down on the chaise. "If I'd have known that, I would never have…" His gravelly voice faded, and she came to his side.

"Dillon." She clutched his hand. "What's happened since I've been gone?"

"It doesn't matter. What matters is that you're home."

"Don't do that," she snapped. "Don't brush me aside. I won't accept that anymore. I deserve to know."

He rubbed a hand down his face. "After you disappeared, your uncle became acting regent."

"He's here still?"

"Yes. Aliah and I pursued any avenue we could to find you," he said. "You have to understand… How desperate I was…"

"Tell me," she whispered, coaxing him.

"There's something you need to know about Liana. She's hidden her true identity…"

"I know who she is," she said, taking him by surprise. "But what does that have to do with what you've…" Then, she paused. "Dillon, you didn't…"

"I told Aliah and your uncle everything. I told them who she was and where I found her."

"Her tavern. All her people…" Rhian stood and backed away from him. "You betrayed her."

He got to his feet as well. "I blamed myself for what happened, for getting Liana involved. I thought she betrayed *me*."

"People died, Dillon! Was it worth it?!"

"No one died! Some were arrested, but others got away," he swore. "There was a man leading the women and children out. I looked him in the eye. I diverted the soldiers' attention so they could get away."

"They wouldn't have been running if you hadn't sold them out." She narrowed her eyes at him. "Liana kept her promise to you. She protected me. She saved me and your child by pretending to be my captor. She sacrificed herself for us. And this is how you repay her?"

"Please, believe me. If I had known, I would have taken her secret to the grave."

"I suppose we'll never know, will we?" She maneuvered around him and rounded the corner to the white armoire with gold handles. Dillon followed her, continuing to beg.

"Forgive me, Rhian. I only did what I thought was best. I just wanted to bring you home."

"That won't save Liana." She snatched her cloak, turning to leave, but he blocked her.

"What are you doing?"

"I'm going to the prison."

His eyes bulged. "What? You can't just break a criminal out of prison."

"She didn't do anything wrong!"

"She's done wrong her whole life," he retorted. "What? Will you join her at the gallows, then?" Rhian stopped short, but before she could say anything, he went on. "Liana has made her choices. Even before all this, she's committed enough crimes for a dozen hangings. I'm not going to sit by and let you get yourself killed for her when her fate has already been decided."

"She took care of me, Dillon," she said tearfully. "I can't let her die."

"If you're asking me to choose between you or her," he said. "I'm going to choose you, every single time. Not only are you the love of my life, but you are the mother of my child and the queen of Caerwyn."

The last bit of what he said echoed hollowly in her brain. She placed a hand on her breast, looking at him blankly. "Queen?"

"Pending a coronation, of course," he muttered. "But, yes. Your uncle has been keeping your place on the throne, but now that you've returned, it's yours."

She sighed shakily, shuffling back to sink on the bed. He followed her movements, bending a knee before her. "I know. This is all overwhelming, especially after everything you've been through. Nothing needs to happen tonight."

As he slid his arms around her, she rested her chin on his shoulder. "Dillon, I need you—I need you to be on my side."

"Always," he whispered, holding her as thunder rolled in the distance. "No matter what it takes. I'll always support you, as my wife and as my queen."

Chapter 30

The Serpent's Fangs
10ᵗʰ of Cambath, 1723
Midnight
Capital Prison

Something shook Liana hard enough to roll her off the bench. A bright light blinded her, and she blinked hard to regain vision. When she did, Aliah Vitalis' cold eyes stared down at her. *Shit.*

"I'm assuming you're not here to bring me breakfast," she snarled.

"Get up," he commanded. "My father wishes to speak to you."

"Your father can rot!"

That earned her a hard palm across the face. Her nose exploded with renewed pain, and she bowed forward to prevent another blow to the already sensitive cartilage. She started to bleed again, slow and thick. She dabbed it away with her sleeve, biting back a whimper.

"Aliah, step aside." Liana tilted her head up, squinting her sensitive eyes to Earl Grigor Vitalis. His voice vibrated with such absolute authority that it nearly drowned out the sound of rain.

Leather boots and the hem of a cloak swept in front of her. The ground shook with his steps. His black gloved hand reached out, and she flinched. Instead of striking her, however, he lifted the dark tangle of hair out of her face.

"Incredible how you look just like her," he said in a quiet rasp. She watched him warily and scrutinized his face. He looked haunted behind the heavy bags beneath his slanted eyes. The lines above his brows deepened as he turned her face to examine her profile. "The same nose. The same eyes. The same corrupt, self-serving soul."

Liana wanted to lash out, or at the very least slink away into a dark corner of the cell, in defiance. But she was tired of fighting—so tired. He continued to stare at her until she broke the silence. "What do you want from me?"

Aliah rummaged into his pocket and threw something down onto the ground. There was enough light from the small lantern for her to see it.

"You know what this is, don't you?"

"A Circle of the Divine," she drawled. "Obviously."

"Look closer."

She picked it up and squinted at it in the dull light. Her thumb rubbed against the surface, smoothing over the familiar three-lined inscription. Her exhaustion fell away, giving in to terror. "Where did you get this? Dunmore? He's in the Capital?"

Aliah smiled thinly. "Tell us everything you know about Ameen Almasi."

Her heart hammered in her throat. It stuck there, making it difficult to breathe.

"You leave him out of this!" she said, with more potency than she thought herself capable of at that moment.

She kept her eyes on Earl Vitalis as he began to pace the cell, willing him silently, desperately to forget this strange obsession he had with Ameen.

"I don't know what Dunmore said to you, but Ameen Almasi and I are no longer involved with each other."

"Perhaps she is ignorant, Father."

"We can't take chances, Aliah. We need to know what we're dealing with," the earl told him firmly. He began to slowly remove his gloves. "Almasi could be more dangerous than we assume."

Utterly confused, Liana glanced between them. The earl made a quick nod to his son. She wriggled about as Aliah yanked her up. He swung her against the wall, hard enough to take her breath.

"This is a powerful rune," the earl said in his surly voice. "Did Almasi enchant it himself?"

"You're insane," she snarled.

"He wore it every day, didn't he?" He drew closer, his cloak whispering over the stone floor. "For what? For protection? For stealth?"

She managed to get to her feet and stood in the corner as tall as she could. A moment of silence went by, and he let out a resigned sigh.

"Your mother was much cleverer than you are," he said. "She surrendered easily. Her compliance was rewarded with a quick death."

Blinded by rage, Liana screamed, took the pitcher, and threw it at the earl. It collided with his shoulder, spilling what remained of the water over his cloak. She threw a punch. He caught her arm.

It began as a searing burn at her wrist that charred her flesh. The current of his power made a conduit of her body. Each of her nerve endings lit aflame, every muscle seized up taut. She couldn't move. She couldn't breathe. She couldn't even open her mouth to scream.

When it stopped, she could only manage some soft sounds of distress through the aftershocks. The Circle slipped from her fingers. Aliah was quick to snatch it up. The earl let her fall, and she collapsed. The smell of natural rain and magic choked her. Her ears rang, the sound of thunder echoing from far away.

As the earl stepped back, his son strutted forward, speaking in a patronizing tone. "Are we ready to speak now?"

"Is this how you killed Queen Valeriya, too?" she croaked.

"That Rodinian bitch murdered my mother!" Aliah bent forward and shouted into her face, a vein pulsing in his temple from the effort. "She deserved nothing less!"

Aliah could have been telling her the truth. But something inside her resisted, making her buck and kick her legs out. He was already close, so she made good impact against his ribs. As Aliah made a move to swing back, Grigor caught him by the collar. "Aliah, I am beginning to think you were right. She is quite ignorant."

"She deserves to know what sort of filth she's bred from," Aliah agreed, gingerly placing a hand on his side, where she had kicked him.

"Don't I? Tell me then," she managed to rasp.

"I'll consider it—if *you* tell me about Almasi," the earl said. "And confess to the murder of King Lyell."

"I won't let you have him." She sealed her quivering lips. The pain had only solidified her stance. She would never allow Ameen to fall into the Vitalis' clutches. She would never let him know this kind of torture. They would have to kill her first.

"Very well, then."

Liana choked out a cry of pain when Aliah dragged her across the floor by her burned arm. He secured her wrists in the hanging shackles. She swallowed back a revolted whimper as he leaned so close she could feel his hot breath on her cheek. His cold hands lingered on her, trailing lightly down to her throat, almost in the way a lover's would. He grasped her jaw and forced her to look into his empty eyes. It gave her a dreadful feeling, like she was peering into a void that promised her death.

"Last chance," he hissed in her ear.

She spat in his face, and his fist smashed into hers. Her chains rattled as she was propelled backwards, spinning by her wrists. With the second blow to her broken nose, blood freely spilled over her front and dripped to the floor.

Aliah disappeared behind a wall with a look of delightful determination as he wiped the saliva off his chin. A cranking sound of mechanisms from above echoed in the cell, and she was pulled upwards, the toes of her boots barely touching the ground. As the earl drew closer, she fixed her focus on the fallen pitcher. The empty vessel lay forgotten in the corner of the cold stone floor. She sobbed like a child as the smell of ozone filled the air.

Rhian looked up into the smooth pupils of Petronella the Warrior. They were nothing alike, she had decided long ago. Petronella was brave, Rhian was meek. While Rhian was happy to keep to her books and studies, she could never imagine Petronella anywhere indoors. The woman of legend was known for slaying monstrous creatures and supporting Evanderus' ascension to the throne of Caerwyn. Perhaps she wasn't even real. But the stories said she had led a life of adventure. Rhian had just had an adventure of her own, nothing like she ever thought possible. She stood in the marble foyer, taking a moment to steel herself. Dillon approached behind her, just a step away from the hem of her champagne-colored dress.

"You can do this," he said softly, as though reading her thoughts.

Rhian turned and forced a smile, unsure whether to believe him. She remembered what Liana had once told her. *No one's brave unless they have to be.*

Together, they walked through the series of drawing rooms where she would meet her uncle. It would be the first time seeing him since her return. When she came upon the salon, she found Aliah seated with his father. Despite the seriousness of the congregation, Rhian felt a thrill at the sight of him.

"Aliah!" she exclaimed as he stood to greet her. He swept her in a tight hug.

"Dearest Rhian," he sighed, giving her a light kiss on the cheek before releasing her. "I'm so glad you're safe."

"As am I," said her uncle, standing. Aliah stepped aside, giving his father the room to grasp Rhian's hands. "What you've been through, Rhian… Well, I can't imagine."

"I'm fine, Uncle," she said. "Truly. I must thank you for all you've done in my absence."

He inclined his head. "It is my duty, as it will be yours. You must need some time to settle in and become reacquainted with life at the palace, I'm sure. I will remain in the role as long as you need."

"That won't be necessary. I would like to spend some time today discussing my transition into my duties as queen."

Grigor frowned in surprise, or it could have been skepticism. "And what, pray tell, did you have in mind? Surely you would want to wait until after you're married to have a coronation. We will need to find a Commander of your Guard..."

Rhian glanced back at Dillon, who gave her an encouraging smile. Together, they all sat in the drawing room as she answered, "That won't be necessary. Dillon will continue his duties as commander, even as my consort."

Aliah snorted ungracefully. "Consort, Dillon?"

"We've decided that Rhian will hold the sovereignty of Caerwyn alone," said Dillon coolly, "A position which she is surely capable of."

"I see," said Grigor slowly. "And when do you plan on executing these changes?"

"Immediately. I see no reason why we must wait until the coronation. You have a province to preside over, Uncle, and I fear you've been gone for too long."

"Aliah can handle any pressing matters. Best for him to start taking on some responsibility while I'm still alive to correct his mistakes," he answered, as though the very man wasn't in the room. "I feel it's best that I stay here to support you."

"Speaking of support," she said. "I need yours in order to determine the fate of a certain prisoner."

Shifting in his seat, Aliah made a scraping sound with the leg of his chair. "The pirate?" he said with disgust.

Rhian turned to him. "We all know she's more than that. She's the daughter of Sergus Romenel, a descendant of Evanderus."

"And what would you do with her?" asked Grigor, leaning back to cross his legs.

"She didn't take me on her ship by force, and everyone in this room knows she didn't kill Lyell."

Grigor licked his lips, nodding as he slipped a hand into his jacket. "Then why do I have this?" He tugged out a parchment and handed it over. When she opened it, she couldn't believe her eyes. At the bottom of a statement of confession to regicide, written in scrawled penmanship, was the signature *Ilyana Romenel.* Her real name.

"She signed this willingly?" Rhian asked, looking over the top of the paper at her uncle.

"This is your saving grace," he continued, avoiding her question. "With this confession, no one will ever question what happened to Lyell at the ball. It's a copy. Keep it if you'd like. The prison has one as well. Because she signed the confession, no trial is necessary."

"Necessary for what?"

"I think you know," said Aliah pointedly.

"The hanging is scheduled for noon," Grigor added, folding his fingers together and resting his hands in his lap calmly—too calmly.

Dillon stood to read the clock on the mantle. "It's already past eleven."

"It would just be easiest to let it happen, Rhian," Grigor continued. "You need this behind you, if you want to be a good queen... a good mother. Imagine what you'll accomplish."

She looked down at the confession, her heart breaking as she smoothed out the signature with her fingers. There wasn't much time left. There was only so much she could do. "You're right, Uncle. You're right about everything."

"It's tragic," he lamented. "But necessary to protect yourself."

"I may need some time, like you said... A few days, at least. I'm not feeling well."

Rhian looked over her shoulder, and immediately Dillon was there, taking her by the hand. Lines of concern lengthened his eyes. "Do you need to lie down?"

"I think so."

Weakly, she bid her uncle and cousin goodbye and allowed Dillon to lead her away. They made it through the drawing rooms and into the foyer before Rhian sharply changed directions, dragging him by the arm.

"What are you doing?" he hissed. "I thought you were—"

"I lied," she shot back, throwing the doors to the courtyard open. A carriage awaited them with a familiar figure pacing nearby.

"Private Meagher!" she called, and the young auburn-haired man came to a complete stop and bowed.

"Your Highness. How may I be of service?"

"Where did you come from?" Dillon stood agape. "Who are you?"

"Private Tomas Meagher of the *Contender,* sir," he said, saluting Dillon. "The ship that rescued the princess."

"I had a servant retrieve him before you woke," she said before turning back to the private. "We need to get to the prison. They're going to hang Liana at midday. I need all the muscle I can get in case there's resistance. Can I count on you, Private?"

Meagher visibly gulped, and his face turned so pale that his freckles stood stark against his skin. "We're breaking her out?"

"Don't think of it as a breakout. Think of it as a rescue, or a swift delivery of justice," Rhian encouraged. Private Meagher nodded and opened the carriage.

Chapter 31

The Righteous

Liana trudged up the scaffold, nearly losing her footing on the second to last step. A pair of rough hands kept her going, that and the promise of sweet release the noose held. She saw it up ahead, perfectly tied to slip over any sized head and squeeze the life out of any neck.

Divine, she hurt. She hurt everywhere. Every movement brought renewed pain, a sickening reminder of what she had endured. She must have looked grotesque. Not one man in the square could look her in the face. Congealed blood still stained her clothes. She could only imagine what her skin looked like beneath, split apart and raw across her body. Unable to properly move her left wrist, she was sure it was broken or dislocated from the shackles. Taking account of these injuries wouldn't do any good. Soon, it would be over.

When the rope slipped over her head, a storm gathered inside her. Panic. The blunt realization that this was the end of the line. She probably should have been thinking of someone she loved, someone she would miss. But her mind craved emptiness, thoughtlessness, blackness. The edges of her vision went, even as she tried to savor the taste of her last moments of life.

Some official bellowed on about something, likely rehearsed for all the condemned, but Liana couldn't hear him. He sounded warbled, as if he spoke underwater. She wished he would shut up and get it over with, or she wouldn't have the strength to stay standing through the whole ordeal.

A mechanical click signaled her cue to take her final breath. She looked out to the sky above the square, her gaze drawn upwards by a crack of lightning. A bright bolt crossed her vision, headed straight toward—no, *above* her. The rope snapped, breaking apart before it could go taut. She met the hard, dry mud beneath the scaffold. The impact drew a ghastly sound from her throat.

Dillon Whyte rushed over, dragged her out from beneath the scaffold, and flipped her onto her back before tearing the noose off her. Her ears picked up her own name through the shouts of outrage and wonder.

It was Rhian's voice. Hearing it gave her the same relief a drowning sailor felt when they were able to breathe again. Soft hands held her face. Rhian's fingers glided over her lips, checking to see if Liana was breathing. Liana weakly caught her fingers with her good hand. She felt the rush of emotion she should have on the scaffold. "Glad to see your pretty face, Princess."

Rhian let out a sob of relief that turned into a gasp of horror when she saw her wrist. As she gently unbuttoned and rolled up Liana's sleeve, the material fell apart in gritty flakes, revealing the skin beneath burned in a spidery patter.

"Oh, Divine! Divine, Liana, what happened to you?" Rhian asked, sputtering out her words. "Is this why you signed that damned paper?"

Liana blinked slowly and shook her head. "No…"

"Then *why*?"

"You're a terrible liar," she said with a weak smile. "You already know why."

"Who did this?"

Liana looked into Rhian's bright, determined eyes. "You already know who."

"How dare you!" Rhian slammed her palm onto the table. "How dare you commit such an atrocity behind my back!"

To his credit, her uncle sat quietly, taking in her reprimands without a single word before she finished. He looked at his hands, one folded over the other on the table. She sat down opposite him, ready now to hear his explanation.

"What do you have to say for yourself?"

His piercing blue eyes flicked up to look at her. "All of my actions have been perfectly legal."

"Legal and moral are two very different concepts, Uncle," she said tartly. "I would think you are wise enough to know the difference."

"Is it not moral to care for the wellbeing of your pregnant niece?" he said. "Ilyana Romenel—Captain Foley, whatever name she goes by now—is a threat to this nation and to your reign."

"So, you kept this from me to spare my nerves?" she spat. "If I'm to become the queen of Caerwyn, it's my duty to decide what is a threat in my own domain. You had no right to deceive me. I will never condone torture under my reign."

It was difficult for her to tell if the remorse in her uncle's expression was genuine, but she wanted to believe it was. He gently unfolded his hands and revealed a Circle of the Divine beneath them.

"Rhys Dunmore took this from her righthand man. You recall an Ameen Almasi?"

"You... Dunmore is here?"

"Rhian. Do you know who Ameen Almasi is?"

She looked at the Circle, and a vision of the tall, Islander with amber eyes came to her mind. "Yes."

"Hold out your hand. Flare your power."

She removed her gloves and extended her palm. Sparks emitted from her fingertips with a soft crackling sound. She held her breath as he dropped the Circle into her hand. Immediately, the sparks snuffed out. "It's a rune?"

"Yes. A power inhibitor," he said.

Rhian curled her fingers around the Circle, careful not to get caught up in the excitement. Her uncle had shown her runes before, always etched into ancient artifacts and weapons. But this... this meant there were others like them in the present day. They were not the last of their kind.

"She has to know more about this than she says," he carried on. "She denied it, of course—"

"During your *interrogation*?" she snapped. He had the grace to silence himself. She inhaled deeply. "If we are to one day reveal our powers to the world, then we mustn't give people a reason to fear us. That's what we want, isn't it? To show them the good we can do?"

"I'm sorry," he said quietly. "But I cannot forgive the atrocities her ancestors committed against our kind—against our family."

"Is it true, then?" she asked tensely. "Did you murder the Romenels?"

He swallowed and replied with more emotion than he had ever revealed to her before. "They killed my wife."

"Did you obtain proof? Was there a trial?" She didn't wait for an answer, because it didn't matter. "Why should a daughter pay for her parents' supposed crimes? If I've learned anything from my time away from the palace, it's that you can't take justice into your own hands. You can't lead on self-righteousness. You lead for your people, not for your own selfish desires."

"Selfish desires?" Grigor's calm exterior finally broke. A spray of spittle visibly left his mouth as he spoke. "Valeriya Romenel killed Aliah's mother."

"Revenge is selfish, Uncle," she replied evenly. "And you should take care who you speak to in that tone. As an earl of Caerwyn, your fealty is to your queen."

He flinched and contained himself, sinking down in his chair. "My apologies, Your Highness."

"The prisoner will remain in my custody." She decided to bring the reprimands to a close. "Until the coronation, I will rule as the crown princess. There is no reason for you to stay. Your time as regent is over. Return to Yael and carry out your duty as the earl of the province. Whatever happens to her will fall to me. Is that understood?"

"Yes, of course."

"You are dismissed."

After a tense moment, he stood and stiffly bowed. His gloved hands stayed balled up at his sides. "Kindness is weakness, Princess Rhian. Don't fall into that trap. Those for whom you would stick your neck out could just as soon stab you in the back. I made that mistake, and I would hate to see you do the same. You have so much potential."

He walked past her seat, and she felt the air shift with his stride. But Rhian wasn't afraid of him, not like Aliah. She remained still as he stormed out, closing the Circle in her hand.

A few seconds later, Dillon entered the room, likely having waited in the hall for her uncle to exit. He sat at her side. "She's resting. I thought you'd like to know."

"Thank you."

"Private Meagher assured me that the men in the square didn't see your magic," Dillon said just a bit quieter. "You aimed high enough, and everyone was focused on Liana. They're certain it was a faulty rope."

"Good," she said with a sigh of relief.

"What will we do with her now?"

"I have a plan—a much more humane one than my uncle's."

"I'm sorry, Rhian."

"I always wondered," she said, closing her eyes, exhausted. "Always wondered why Aliah feared his father so much. Now I see it."

"You don't think Aliah was involved in the torture, do you?"

"He would *never.*"

"I don't know. He would do just about anything to get his father's approval."

"Liana hasn't told you what happened?" she said, raising a brow.

He shook his head. "She refuses to speak of it. Maybe she'll talk to you."

"Maybe." She leaned forward and kissed him softly. "Thank you for everything."

"Always."

Together they left the drawing room, arm in arm.

Chapter 32

Heads and Tails
16th of Cambath, 1724
The Royal Palace

"The queen requests your audience at eight o'clock this evening," said the maid.

"Did you say 'queen?'" Liana grimaced as she picked up her cards. She'd been teaching Private Meagher how to play Crooks and Cavalry. Her arms and torso burned something fierce. The marks would scar, the surgeon had told her regretfully, in fractal patterns across her body. They resembled ferns, in Liana's opinion, and perhaps weren't as ugly as the surgeon likely thought. Her left wrist was dislocated and recently reset. Luckily, it wasn't serious—only an injury sustained from being suspended by chains. It was bound with thick bandages to prevent accidental use, but Liana still forgot.

"Yes, ma'am. Queen Rhian had a small coronation ceremony yesterday."

"Oh. Where does she want to meet?"

The maid lifted a fair brow. "Why, here of course, ma'am. She doesn't expect you to come to her, given your condition."

"Right," Liana replied, before pinching her bottom lip nervously.

The queen arrived mere seconds after the tall clock in the corner chimed eight times. Tomas announced her cordially as Liana waited for her at the square table by the fire. When Rhian entered, Liana's gut twisted with irony. Months ago, they had met in such a way, in the captain's cabin of the *Windfall*. It was then that Liana had to decide what to do with her stowaway. Now, the tables had turned, and she had the feeling this meeting would decide her own fate.

She shakily stood and bowed, holding one hand on the table to keep herself steady. "Your Majesty."

"Please, don't exert yourself," Rhian implored, taking a few quick steps forward. Liana sat back down without much trouble.

As usual, Rhian was a vision of beauty. But now, she wore a crown and her gown's blue and gold bodice extended over her swollen abdomen. As Rhian joined her at the table, she herself seemed to have a bit of strain in her face. She sat down with one hand pressed to her side.

"So long as you don't either," Liana quipped. She supposed, a moment too late, that pointing out the queen's condition was probably rude of her.

Rhian smiled. "I'm sorry for not coming sooner. I've been quite busy, and I wanted to give you some time to recover. How are you feeling?"

Liana glanced down at her arm, covered by a linen shirt. She groped for something to say. "I've been better."

Rhian hid glassy eyes behind lowered lids. Her hands shook as she covered her crumpling face. She looked like she had been barely holding herself together. "Liana, I'm so sorry."

"It's alright," Liana said, scooting her chair to lean toward her. She placed a hand on hers. In return, Rhian squeezed it back. "You have nothing to apologize for."

"I do," Rhian continued, strangled. "When I was in your custody you *never* showed me such treatment. Your men were so kind to me, even before they knew I was pregnant. I'm not asking for your forgiveness. But as queen, I must take responsibility for the actions of the earls of Caerwyn, especially when they were taken by my own uncle. I want you to know I will never let anything like this happen again."

"I don't doubt it."

"I just... Will you tell me what happened in the prison?"

Liana's hand slipped away and drew back into her lap. "I'm sorry," she replied quietly. "I can't talk about it. It's hard to even think about. I can't."

Rhian's rosebud lips quivered as she begged with her eyes. "Please? You can tell me."

Liana remained silent, shaking her head. She couldn't give Rhian the burden knowing what her family had done to her. She would blame herself. Even more, she never wanted Rhian to have an inkling of how helpless and weak she had been in that cell.

"Could you just tell me why you signed the confession? You *knew* it would condemn you to death. Why did you do it?"

"You already know," Liana laughed breathily.

"I need to hear you say it."

She swallowed. "Because I care about you, Rhian. I couldn't let your life be wasted when mine was right there for the taking."

"How could you ever think my life was worth more than yours?"

"I've done… a lot of bad—most often when I thought I was doing what was right," Liana said. "I knew I deserved to die. I just wanted to do it for something—for *someone* I believed in. You're going to be an excellent queen, better than any Romenel could have been. Certainly, better than my parents."

"Not every Romenel," Rhian said, wiping her eyes. "You taught me everything I know about how to lead."

Liana forced a laugh, unsure what to say to that. "Well, that may do you more harm than good. You'll be fine so long as you use that big brain of yours. I know as well as everyone else that you're more than just a pretty face."

Rhian laughed too, blushing. When the moment passed, she opened up a small pocket in her silk jacket, reached inside, and retrieved a small object. "Here. I think it's right that you should have this."

She opened her palm to reveal Ameen's Circle. Liana felt tears prick her eyes as Rhian handed it over to her. She took it and cradled it close.

"This Circle is enchanted. It was meant to hide his power."

"Power?"

"Ameen… He's like me. I'm absolutely sure of it."

"That's not possible."

"People like us," Rhian said, "Must live a life of secrecy. The world isn't ready to know we exist yet."

"This Circle belonged to his father," Liana argued. "If Ameen knew about this, then he would have told me. I know it."

Rhian nodded somberly. "You're probably right. I don't think he knows what he's capable of."

"Your uncle wanted to know about him. That's why he—" Liana cut herself off, taking in a shaky breath.

"I already spoke to my uncle. He won't be of concern to you anymore." Rhian heaved a sigh. "I think now we need to discuss what happens from here."

"I understand," Liana said, fidgeting with her bandage.

"Because of your treatment in the prison," Rhian began, "I have the grounds to grant you protection. Your only punishment would be exile from Caerwyn and its territories. You'll be escorted outside of the borders, and you will be freed. But if you return…"

"Then I'll find myself back to the gallows." Liana paused. "That's… quite an offer." It seemed to solve everything—except, "There's still the matter of Dunmore Manor."

Rhian stiffened. "Unfortunately, as much of a cad as Rhys Dunmore is, he is entitled to his land legally. It will be restored to him. But as for your sister…"

"Yes?"

"She'll have the opportunity to report the abuse she suffered, and I'll implore my uncle's court to grant them a quick divorce."

"What about the crew?"

"Do you think they would surrender the manor without a fight?"

"I'll make sure they do," Liana insisted. "If you could, permit me to go to Dunmore Manor and retrieve them. If they aren't there, I'll let it go. I'll leave Caerwyn and never come back."

The queen took a moment to consider this proposal. She tapped her chin and looked at Liana squarely, then smiled. "Agreed," she said. "Are you ready to get back to your ship, Captain Foley?"

"Oh," Liana sighed. "You have no idea."

"Your Majesty; Commander." Private Meagher greeted Rhian and Dillon as they entered the room. "We were just about to be off."

"Better late than bloody never," said a voice from behind the private. He stepped aside to reveal Liana standing there, with her arms crossed and a dark brow raised. Rhian was relieved to see the color had returned to her face. The only sign she had been harmed was the bandage wrapped over her right hand. A gray overcoat covered the rest of her. Even the bruises on the bridge of her nose and across her cheeks had faded. She peered behind Rhian to give Dillon a wry smile. "I thought I was finished with you, Whyte. I hear that congratulations are in order. Prince Dillon—the biggest promotion of all!"

"Not quite yet," he said meekly. "We'll be married next week."

Rhian giggled at his modesty.

"Right." Liana nodded. "Well, Whyte, you're going to marry the girl you wanted all along. All is well. You got everything you wanted."

"And you'll be freed," he said. "You'll be reunited with your crew."

"That's right," she said with genuine gratitude. "Thanks to you and Queen Rhian."

"Just Rhian, to you," Rhian interjected with a smile.

Liana shrugged.

"You and Rhian are quite alike, I've realized," Dillon said with a tilt of his head so he could look at both women. "Two sides of the same coin."

"I suppose if that's true," said Liana, "I must be tails, then."

"I just wanted to say that," he went on, rubbing his hands together, "I wish the best for you and your crew."

Rhian cleared her throat, prompting him to go on.

"And I wanted to thank you for keeping your promise," he continued. "For keeping Rhian safe."

"I wish I could say it was my pleasure," she said dryly. She winked at Rhian. "But we had some good moments. Take care of that kid, Whyte. Fathers are important, you know."

"On my honor." He smiled. "Goodbye, Liana Foley."

"Goodbye, Dillon Whyte—you salty bugger."

On her way out, Liana paused at Rhian. Despite wearing trousers, she jauntily gave her a little curtsy. She pointed to Rhian's stomach. "May I? I've got a few words for her."

"Her?" She laughed. "What makes you so sure she's a girl?"

Liana shrugged. "Just am." She got down on one knee and placed a hand on Rhian's bodice, causing her heart to flutter. "Hello, in there. Make sure your mother stays safe, alright? She's one of the best people I know. I'd hate to have to come back here and rescue her again." Standing up, she looked back up at Rhian fondly.

"You'd stick your neck out for me again, after everything?"

"Absolutely." Liana grinned. She bit her bottom lip, as though she wanted to say more, but held back. Rhian responded by bringing Liana in for a hug, which she returned in full.

"I'm happy for you, Rhian," she said softly, close to her ear. "Please, just be careful.".

"I will be."

"And don't forget about me either. Promise you'll think of me every so often between queenly duties."

Before Liana could pull away, Rhian couldn't help but press a soft kiss on her cheek. "I could never forget you, Liana Foley."

Liana let out a husky, bashful laugh and tenderly touched where Rhian's lips had been. "Goodbye, Rhian."

"Goodbye."

And with that, Private Meagher opened the door, and the captain was gone. Rhian let her gaze linger at the empty threshold. Dillon placed a comforting hand on her back. "She'll be just fine. You don't need to worry about her. She's the sort of woman who could survive anything."

Rhian cast her eyes to the floor so he couldn't see her longing. "I know."

Liana closed her eyes as the gentle caress of the breeze lifted her hair. It had been too long since she'd seen the ocean. She felt its rhythmic ease as the waves rolled under the dock.

But it was a false comfort. Beneath it, a storm brewed, as mighty as the sea itself.

As they approached the *Contender*, Liana looked up to see Aliah Vitalis greeting them on deck as they boarded. Fear replaced the tranquil peace she had felt only a moment before.

"Private Meagher," Aliah simpered. "You've done well. A successful transport. Please, allow me to personally escort the prisoner to the brig while you settle in."

"The queen has commanded that I be responsible for the prisoner until she is escorted outside of Caerwyn, sir." Tomas stood his ground, much to Liana's relief. "I should see where she'll be held."

"Then I'll show you both to the brig," Aliah replied.

Memories of Aliah in that cell still haunted her—the delight in her pain, the lines of depravity the lantern made on his face as he watched her suffer. She was jolted out of her thoughts as the creaking door to the brig opened. Without daring to speak a word, Liana stepped inside and turned to face Tomas and Aliah.

"I'll take the key, sir," said Tomas stiffly, patting his belt where the keys to her shackles hung. "I should have them."

"Very well." Aliah reached for the key, stuck in the lock. "You should see here, Private. If you don't pull it out just so—"

Tomas leaned forward to look. Aliah reached under his cloak and procured a dirk from his belt.

"Look out!" Liana shouted, but Aliah's arm had already swung down to stab Tomas in the back. She grasped Tomas' coat and yanked him into the brig. The blade missed him, but only barely. They stumbled, falling off balance onto the wooden floor. By the time Tomas leaped up, Aliah had closed the brig and locked them both in.

"The queen will hear of your betrayal!" Tomas shouted as Aliah began to walk away. The latter paused and turned to look over his shoulder.

"The queen will hear of yours," said a cruel voice from a dark corner away from the cell. "Of how you sided with the pirates in the battle for Dunmore Manor." Rhys Dunmore himself emerged from the shadows with a look of pure gratification. "You'll be dead by then, of course."

"Dunmore!" Liana shouted, before he came close to the bars. She stepped back, unable to stand being near the vile man. "You know my crew would surrender the manor at my command!"

"And what justice would there be in that?" he hissed before joining Aliah at the other end.

"Don't you *dare* speak of justice to me!"

"Do you know what sort of justice I think you deserve, Liana Foley?" he continued, ignoring her. "I think you should hang for all your crew to see—the ones who survive, of course. It would be quite the spectacle. And I do look forward to seeing my wife again."

"Don't do this, Dunmore!" Liana called, her voice breaking. But he turned away and disappeared with Aliah above. "Dunmore!"

Tomas slammed his fist against the bars and leaned back against them. He sighed, before unclipping his key from his belt and freeing her from her shackles. They dropped with a metallic thud.

"I-I've still got my pistol," he said. "And my dirk."

"Idiots," she muttered. "Hide them. We'll use them once we have a chance."

"I'm so sorry, Captain Foley. Perhaps... Perhaps your crew has already gone?"

"Divine, I hope you're right." Liana flopped down to the floor and held Ameen's Circle, which hung around her neck, tightly in her hand.

Chapter 33

Crooks and Cavalry
1st of Sulnath, 1724

"Ameen? What are you doing?"

He emerged from the galley, face painted with a guilty smile. Nellie and Thiago thought they had come upon one of the crew members impatiently rummaging for something to eat. They found their captain, instead.

"I forgot to come down from watch for lunch," he confessed, one hand on his grumbling stomach. He had skipped breakfast too, but kept that to himself. Admittedly, he had much more difficulty balancing all his duties than Liana ever had.

The galley smelled distinctly of brine and hot oil. It was acrid, though not entirely unpleasant. Lucky had announced he wanted fresh fish for dinner, to which Bess had irritably replied, "Well, go and catch some, then!"

Lucky had taken several of the off-duty men and done just that. Ameen allowed them to anchor for half a day. They were triumphant at the end of it, with enough haddock for all. Sava had waved his catch before Bess, shouting with glee at his trophy. She had given him a somewhat forced smile to hide her revulsion at the flapping gills. The older men of the crew, along with Ivan, remained fishing from the deck, hoping they could catch more.

With the ship finally repaired and afloat, the search for Liana had begun. Without any way to tell whether or not she had made it to the Capital, they stopped in every port they could, riding the south wind. With each one, they sold off some of the goods from the manor. Soon, they would have enough to send home some of the men with families back in the Capital.

"I'm starved." Ameen sat down on a chair by the oven.

"Dinner will be soon," said Thiago. "Have apple, while they're still fresh."

Thiago tossed the fruit to Ameen, which he swiftly caught. He devoured it; Nellie rolled her eyes. She looked like she was about to say something before Ivan burst into the galley.

"Ameen!" he gasped. "Lucky's spotted a ship—Navy—headed straight for us!"

It was a good thing Ameen had already finished his apple, because he probably would have choked on it. Rather than fall victim to panic, he stood.

"You're sure they won't just pass us?" Ameen frowned. Usually, other vessels would sail by without trouble, especially if unprovoked.

Ivan nodded and glanced to Nellie. "Jamil looked through the spyglass and saw Dunmore on the deck."

"He knows the ship," Nellie said, tugging at Ameen's arm. "He's probably told them to attack!"

"Ivan, go find Camila, Bess, and the children. Take them to the captain's cabin." Ivan didn't answer. He had a dazed look about him, so Ameen added, "Go!"

Ivan shook out of it and rushed out of the galley with Thiago at his heels.

"Nellie, go with them," Ameen told her when she still hadn't moved.

"Rhys is coming," she said, her eyes fixed somewhere over his left shoulder.

"I know."

"Will it come to a battle?"

Ameen nodded solemnly. "It's likely."

"I'll fight. I'll fight him."

"You want to kill him," he stated. There was no question about it. He had seen the look in her eyes when she held that hunting rifle.

"It doesn't ever sit well with you," he warned. "None of us— the crew, I mean—make it a habit to kill, just because we feel like it. We kill to protect ourselves, the people we love."

She listened quietly. The silence in the galley sent a chill through them both, despite the heat of the stove.

"The first time, I hardly thought about what I was doing. Thinking back on it, that was the most frightening part. I was shot, right after it happened, so I didn't have much time to dwell."

"Do you regret it?"

"I've had a long time to rationalize it," he answered. "But like I said—it never sits well with you. If I hadn't done it, something terrible would have happened. I can't tell you what you should do. It's your choice whether to fight or not."

She looked discouraged, having possibly hoped he would bolster her confidence.

"I'll kill him for you," he offered. "So, there's no blood on your hands."

She looked tempted, but she slowly shook her head. "I can't ask you to do that for me."

"You didn't." Ameen stepped to the door and opened it, allowing her through first. "I'd do it for you, at your word. But, if not... I'll do what I can to give you a clear shot."

"Something's happening," Liana said, hushed, as she listened intently.

"How can you tell?" whispered Tomas.

"I've been sailing for half my life," she replied, finding a good grip on the handle of the dirk behind her back. "I can feel it. We're slowing down. Be ready and stay calm."

He nodded and crossed his arms, holding himself against the cold. A late afternoon fog had settled over the ship. Soon, two soldiers came down to retrieve them.

"Your presence is requested on deck," one said curtly.

"Where are we?" asked Liana.

There came no answer as the soldier with the key fiddled with the lock—stuck, apparently. She steadied herself, waiting to strike.

A faint succession of blasts from afar made her prick up her ears. She was the only one who heard the cacophony. "Get d—" she was able to manage before a cannonball blasted through the hull.

Moments later, Liana was drenched, her ears ringing so loud she could barely hear Tomas shouting at her. His hair dripped at the ends. The familiar smell of hot gunpowder burned her nostrils as he helped her stand.

"Are you alright?" Tomas asked as Liana jammed her finger in her ear and wriggled it about to help her hear again. "What was that?"

She worked her jaw a bit before answering. "Either pirates or a foreign ship."

"Your pirates?"

"I hate to hope," she said, loud enough to hear herself speak. "But I've only met one man who could split apart a Navy hull on the first try."

She sloshed about the flooded cell. The blasts left gaping holes in the hull. Cold seawater bubbled up from below. "The soldiers?"

"One is dead," said Tomas morosely. He pointed to a motionless figure floating the steps. "The other ran off. We're sinking."

"Looks that way, but it'll take some time," she said distractedly. She was now focused on the lock. The soldier had left the key inside. With a bit of force, she unjammed it, and they were free. "Come on, we have to get out of here."

Another blast came before she could rush up the steps. She staggered back into Tomas. When the sea spray and shrapnel had cleared, the steps had been destroyed. She screamed in frustration as the water began to fill faster. It was up to their knees now.

"*Lucky*, you sharpshooting bastard!" She whirled around to look at Tomas, who appeared to be at a loss. "Lift me up."

The idea was short-lived. Something blocked the hatch from the other side, and though she could reach it, she couldn't gather enough strength to break it open. A lurching movement forced Tomas to drop her with a splash, leaving her sopping, sore, and stunned.

"Damn it!" Liana scrambled to her feet, grasping her arm, the burns stinging from sea-soaked bandages. She groped for an idea, any idea that would prevent them from drowning. She fixated on the hole at the bottom from the cannonball. "Tomas, can you swim?"

"Of course," he said, standing beside her and following her line of sight. He caught on and began to shimmy off his coat. "Under a ship, though—Well, I can't say I've done it before."

She waded over to the soldier's body and searched for weapons, finding another dirk and a sword. "Your gun is useless wet. Take this and hold your breath!"

With no time to waste, Liana sank down, holding all the air she could in her lungs, and plummeted into the cold abyss. She couldn't afford to wait for Tomas, and she didn't have to. He glided up beside her, clearly a better swimmer than he let on. Water swirled strong around her limbs, a vortex sucking them back into the sinking ship. Wood creaked, deep groaning like the dying cries of a doomed giant. Tomas came out ahead of her from beneath the ship. Scattered light from the sun gave the world a transience, never still, always moving. She kicked hard, propelling herself up to the surface. Breaking through, she opened her mouth wide, gasping for air.

"We made it!" he exclaimed victoriously.

"Now, we just need to get *out* of the water." She blinked the salt out of her eyes. Behind her, the Navy ship sat dangerously low. Perhaps it wouldn't appear that way to the untrained eye, but when compared to the fully functional that came up alongside...

"There! Is that your ship?"

She paddled over to Tomas, giving her a better view of the other ship. The *Windfall* approached, repaired in all her glory, masts piercing the sky like spears.

"It's them!" she gasped. She waved an arm, trying to keep afloat while calling out. The percussion of waves, crashing against one another, drowned out her voice. Shooting a look back at Tomas, she said, "Come on. We've got a ship to catch!"

"They're taking on water, sir!" Kahil shouted. He rushed up to the helm to repeat himself, interrupting the ongoing squabble between siblings.

"I'm not going to hide in the cabin with the children!" Nellie huffed, gripping her rifle tighter. She sported a riding jacket and breeches in preparation for the battle. "The *captain* wants me on deck!"

"Ameen, you're allowing her to stay out?" Ivan shoved past Nellie to shout at him.

"She can take care of herself," Ameen replied before turning to Kahil. "Tell the men to disengage. They won't be after us if they know what's good for them."

"Come along, Mistress Dunmore," said Sava. "We'll find you a good position."

After shooting Ivan a smug look of triumph, Nellie followed Sava to the main deck, rifle in hand. Ivan started to go as well, but he stopped when they heard a shout.

"*Almasi!*"

Despite himself, he turned to look at the sinking ship. It was a frantic scene, soldiers running every which way like a colony of ants that had been discovered under a rock. They were fleeing—desperately dropping dinghies in attempts to escape to the distant coast. But one figure stood still amongst the chaos.

Ivan stepped forward. "Dunmore! Go back to your manor and rot, you filth!"

The figure leaned over to call back. "Ah! A family reunion! I'll have you know your sister is aboard!"

A cold feeling settled in Ameen's gut.

"He's lying!" cried Nellie from near the bow. She had her rifle aimed right for him. "The bastard is lying!"

"Hello, *darling!*" Even through Dunmore's shouting, his voice held cruel amusement. "You can still save her, if she hasn't drowned yet!"

A high-pitched whistle came from the stern of the navy rig. The frenzy lulled as the soldiers looked to its origin. Even the *Windfall's* crew fell into silent disbelief. Ameen leaned against the helm, squinting out with a hand over his brow. There, on the upper deck of the Navy brig, stark against the setting sun, stood Captain Liana Foley, sleek with seawater.

"Prepare to board!" Ameen commanded, his heart soaring at the sight of her. With an echo of battle cries and hoots of joy, the *Windfall* came alongside as close as he could get to her. Ameen joined the fray, roused by a thrill of pride in his captain. He tried to keep an eye on Liana, but the soldiers—those not scrambling to abandon ship—descended on her. He and Ivan boarded at the same time.

"Look, at the steps!" Ivan cried, batting away an attack with a swing of his sword. He, like his sister, had always preferred close combat to firearms. Ameen whipped around, and there she was, defending herself from a barrage of attacks from the lower deck. A young sailor fought at her side.

"Liana!" Ivan sprinted past Ameen, barreling toward his sister at full speed. She saw him, and Ameen thought he caught the words "What the hell" crossing her lips before an attack drew her back into the battle. Ivan protected her back while she tossed aside two dirks and procured a sword from one of his fallen comrades. She came back up with a fierce cry and killed another.

"Aha! Good form, little sister! Just like I taught you!" cheered Ivan.

"You're such a liar!" she retorted, tossing back her dripping wet hair.

"What?!"

"Marin taught me!"

"That's not how I remember it!"

"One lesson does *not* constitute as—"

"Tighten that stance, Liana, you're making me look bad!"

Ameen leapt over to the bottom step and shoved back a sailor about to strike at Ivan's neck. Standing over the attacker, who scrambled away, Ameen stepped between the pair of siblings. "Will you two shut up and get back to the *Windfall?* You can argue later!"

Liana turned to see who spoke, and her eyes shone with pure happiness above the most wonderful of smiles.

A gunshot interrupted the reunion. Ivan stumbled and fell, bellowing in agony and groping at his left leg. Ameen dropped to his side in an instant, helping him to cover the wound just above his knee. Liana stopped short of joining his efforts, then she suddenly vaulted over the bannister. A ringing clang of swords crossing came from above. She made it just in time to cover Ameen's back and was now engaged in combat with a blond soldier with a vengeful look in his cold black eyes.

No one else attacked; the clever sailors had already made it to the dinghies. The slower ones scrambled with the pulleys with ferocity. Jamil and Lucky led the efforts of beating back a few of the stragglers, but all in all, they had won.

"It's over, Vitalis!" Liana shouted. "Your men are abandoning ship! Get on with them before you lose your life!"

"Not until I have yours!" His eyes stretched wide like those of a predatory animal, lost in the frenzy of the hunt. He struck down, but she blocked, barely managing to hold the stance.

"Go!" she yelled to Ameen, tossing her head back to the ship. "Take him and go!"

"No—!" Ivan managed to huff. Never one to disobey his captain, especially under the most dire circumstances, Ameen threw Ivan's arm over his shoulder.

He was about to drag Ivan away before he caught a glimpse of a rifle pointed in their direction. Dunmore was at the other end of it, aiming straight for them. Another rifle's fire exploded. The shot propelled Dunmore backwards, flinging him overboard into the embrace of the sea. Ameen looked back at the *Windfall*, where Nellie held her position.

"Ha!" Liana shouted triumphantly, shoving Vitalis away. Holding him back must have taken most of her strength, because she sagged. A few of the crew came to help Ivan, including Sava.

"Get back to the ship!" Ameen told them once they had him. He sprinted to help Liana. Vitalis, crazed and unrelenting, continued to engage her. He had beaten her back to the end of the bow. Her stance was even looser than before.

Vitalis latched a hand onto Liana's sword arm—Ameen saw bandages wrapped beneath her sleeve. She yelped and twisted in his grasp before he drove his sword straight through her middle. Her mouth fell open with a stifled cry.

A fearsome rage burned in Ameen; unlike any he had ever felt before in his life. He launched himself at Vitalis as Liana sank down to the deck. So lost in his victory, Vitalis didn't see Ameen coming. He withdrew his pistol and, before a comprehensive thought crossed his mind, he pulled the trigger. The bullet blew straight into Vitalis' back. He made a terrible garbled sound that sounded surprised and crumpled with a heavy thud.

Liana hunkered down on her hands and knees, agonized cries shaking her body. She coughed, but it sounded more like gagging as she spat out blood. Her damp hair cobwebbed over her face like the image of a shattered mirror. He smoothed it back tenderly, revealing a smear of red in the corner of her mouth. "Look at me... Look at me, Liana!"

Her eyelids fluttered, sending tears down her cheeks. Lifting her bloodied and trembling hands, she showed him the gushing wound. She shook her head. "I'm..."

"No! Stay with me, damn it!" he pleaded, gathering her up. Weakly moaning, she clung to him, leaving scarlet handprints on his shirt.

The last one off the doomed vessel, he boarded the *Windfall* with Liana in his arms. He shouted a strangled order for someone to take the helm and pull off. Everything sounded so far away beneath the roaring in his ears. Even his own voice sounded muffled as he called for Thiago. The men split away, making a path for him. Sava was the only one brave enough to trail after him.

"Captain! Captain!"

Ameen wasn't sure who he was calling for—if it was her or him—but he didn't care. His drive to save Liana blinded him to all else. He burst into the sickbay, where Thiago worked to make a tourniquet for the unconscious Ivan's leg. He looked up, horrified at their arrival.

"Thiago!" Ameen called as he rested Liana on the opposite cot. Nellie, already there with Ivan, came to Liana's side, weeping.

"Liana, you'll be alright," she gasped through tears. Liana gritted her teeth at Nellie in an attempt at a reassuring smile. "*Both* of you are going to be alright."

Thiago approached, sweating and exhausted, but worked diligently to keep Liana alive. Ameen could only watch, helpless, as the spark in her eyes began to dim. She held onto something hanging from her neck. Seeing him look, she opened her hand to reveal his Circle of the Divine.

"Where... How did you...?"

"Here... you daft sailor..."

He let out a quick, breathy laugh, finding his vision blurred. "It's Captain now, actually."

"Good... That's good..." She grimaced again, in that same near-smiling way. He felt an overwhelming urge to kiss her, despite the bloodstained teeth. Instead, he wiped his eyes and bent down to his knees to sidle up beside her. He clasped her hand as it held the Circle.

Her eyes drooped heavily as she tried to focus on him. "Should've stayed..."

"Yes, you should have."

"Sorry..."

Liana always liked hearing him pray aloud, even if she didn't believe in the Divine herself. Something about his voice soothed her, she had said once—especially when he spoke in melodic Islander. The verses of devotion added to that effect. So, he prayed desperately for her life, even as he felt it slipping away. She listened with strained, shuddering breaths and closed her eyes.

A painful silence pierced through them all when another breath didn't come. Grief weighed down upon him as Thiago stilled. He kept praying, silently now, no longer able to speak. His voice caught somewhere in the back of his throat, behind the sobs that threatened to overtake him. He folded her slackened hands in his, and the vision of a rope came to his mind—a tether that held her to the living world and to him. If only he could grab it, take it, pull her back. He held Liana's body, lifting it just above the cot, willing her heart's beat to match his own.

And then it did.

Liana's ribs expanded as her lungs filled. She drew a single deep, creaky breath and jerked, flailing as though catching herself from a sudden fall. Ameen threw his eyes open and lost his own balance. He slipped, and they both tumbled onto the floor. Nellie dropped, throwing herself at the gasping Liana. Sava joined them.

She was alive.

She was going to live.

With that confirmation, Ameen fell limp and gasping beside her, drained of all his strength.

"Your hands…"

Ameen looked up at Thiago, who had just given him a glance after stabilizing Liana back on the cot, then raised his palms to see. They glowed like firelight. He closed his fists, visualizing in his mind's eye tying that tether with the tightest knot he could.

Chapter 34

Call to Sea
2nd of Sulnath, 1724
Cynareth Ocean

Stories tell of forlorn sea creatures that live in the reefs of the Island colonies, with the bodies of beautiful women and the tails of fish. Sirens, they were called—the spirits of grieving maidens who had lost their beloved sailors to the sea. To many mariners, they were as real as the winds that carried their ships.

Ameen had seen many artistic depictions of them in his life, beckoning ships and sailors to rocky shores and reefs with their songs, to their drowning and destruction. Once, in the dock market in Quiculpa, he had seen a charcoal image of a black-haired siren, resting on a slab of rock, her tail curving into the waves as she watched a ship in the distance.

Liana sat similarly, sinking her knees sideways as she lifted the bloodstained shirt over her head. He helped her to rinse her hair in a bucket of seawater. It stuck to her neck and shoulders. Its color was that of the sea at midnight, striking almost white where the sun hit it through the glass bulkhead. Her hair wasn't as long nor her body as soft as the image of the Savarran siren. Ameen had never been one to become absorbed in art, but he appreciated the hard work it took to create something so beautiful.

That was what he saw in Liana—the hardened muscles in her back, the slope of her bicep, the bruises and scars of wounds she had endured. He saw her strength. He saw a lifetime of trials and triumphs. He saw all the work it took for her to survive up to this very moment. But he supposed he'd had a hand in that. Unfamiliar fern-like marks now appeared on her arms and across her body. After he had removed the bandages, he could see them.

Liana must have heard the change in his breathing, because she looked back at him. "I, uh… I didn't want anyone else to see…"

"What happened, Liana?" he asked with a sickening twist in his gut.

"I don't really want to talk about it."

He respected her wishes and continued his ministrations, dabbing away at the dried blood along her back. She shivered at his touch, her skin turning to gooseflesh.

"Cold," she awkwardly explained. She smiled, though he noticed her lips twitched nervously. "Not that I'm ungrateful, but… Would you care to explain this?"

She lifted herself up to show her wound, a deep reddened line that marred her skin, just below her ribs. Washed of blood, it was clearer to see. It looked to be nearly healed.

He leaned back on the stool and rubbed a hand down the back of his neck. "I can't."

"Well, you must have some idea." She paused for a moment as he wrung out the cloth. "They were saying things."

"Who?"

"Grigor Vitalis and his son. I don't know what Dunmore told them. But he had this idea that you're like him and Rhian."

He looked down at his hands, flexing his fingers as he recalled the way they had glowed.

"Rhian thought so too," Liana continued, looking over at the glass bulkhead, where the sea stretched out along the horizon. "He wanted me to tell them everything about you. But I wouldn't."

She rolled her shoulders as though she was shrugging off the predicament of choosing what Bess would cook at the Barricade that week. He looked at her back, marred by white and pink scars.

"They hurt you because of me," he said.

Her deep brown eyes hardened like the earth itself as she shot a look back at him. "No, they were after *you* because of *me*."

Liana leaned forward and bent her knees to stand. When she had first woken up, she could hardly walk. Now, some hours later, she could take a few weak steps in a way that reminded Ameen of a newborn fawn. She still needed help. He tried to help, but she held up a hand. She got to her feet on her own, though it looked to be a difficult task. Despite her damp skin, she tore a shirt over her head.

"I won't have you or anyone else I love die. And I will be damned," she said with great ferocity, "If that *monster* lays a finger on you because of me. I won't have it; do you hear me?"

"What are you saying? That you want to leave again?"

"I don't really have a choice—"

"I can't believe this." He stared at her. "You leave me, your crew, your ship. Weeks later, I find you, just having escaped from the brig of a Navy ship. I pull you from the brink of death, and the first thing you want to do is leave again!?"

He was yelling by the end of it, but he couldn't hold back. She had broken his heart and was staring at the pieces like they were nothing.

"No," she said softly. Her wide eyes betrayed the raw reaction to his anger. "You don't understand. I have to leave. Showing my face in Caerwyn would be... Well, I can't. I had the chance to leave the kingdom, but I came back for you—for the crew. I couldn't leave you behind. And I want to stay with the Windfall, if you'll have me."

The distance between them, though it was only a few steps, seemed so far, like a perilous wooden bridge over a deep gorge. How had they gotten so far away from each other? Would he be willing to risk the fall to reach her? Or was it best, perhaps, to turn the other way and move on, to walk on solid ground?

"You should stay," he said. "It'll be hard. So much has happened. I know that nothing can be the same as it was. When you left, it was—I wasn't sure how we would go on. How I would go on. It almost broke me."

Saying it aloud to her—he could hardly stand to do it. Her mouth clamped shut, forming a mortified line beneath her strong nose. But she looked right at him, and it took all of his willpower to hold her gaze. And though the breach between them was vast, he felt their bond across the old, rotted steps of the imagined bridge. She was bare to him, and in her eyes was a love as boundless as the sea. It called to him. It was so tempting to dive in, but how could he ever trust her again?

"There's only one other person in this world," he said, "Who hurt me in the same way—my mother. I... think that I couldn't let you go, like my father let her go. I've been holding on too tightly."

He reached into the pocket of his coat, which was draped over the berth, and gave her back the Circle. Its brass luster had vanished, almost as though something had been taken away from it. She accepted it without question.

"If you promise to keep this, I'll promise that we'll stay close. Our time apart has made me realize that I've leaned on you far too much, for far too long. I didn't realize that I could be strong without you. I'm sorry. I should have..."

"It's alright," she interrupted him, placing the chain over her head nevertheless. "We've always been great friends. We always will be. This is no goodbye, not in the least. We'll stay together, but as we were before, two pirates who shared a dream. I accept your terms... Captain."

She said the title awkwardly. Ameen wanted to laugh and tell her that the captaincy was hers for the taking whenever she pleased. But he didn't want to place too much responsibility back on her too quickly—only when she was ready.

But only Captain Liana Foley could cross over the horizon of death and return in full force. Ameen knew better than anyone how unstoppable the bloody-minded woman was. It would only be a matter of time before he would be relieved of duty. He wouldn't have it any other way.

He hugged her gently, marking the fragile beginning of their reconciliation. She sank into him, and the world seemed to regain just a bit of its brightness. With that simple gesture came hope.

After helping her into a pair of breeches and her boots, they went above to greet the crew. Bess came rushing out first, shoving aside even the burliest men in the crew. Liana looked like she could burst, like she didn't know whether to cry or laugh.

Glistening tears filled her eyes. She stumbled out of Ameen's reach.

"Bess! I can't believe you're here," she cried. "I can't believe it!"

"Liana, the Barricade—"

"I know. I'm just glad you're safe. I was so worried."

After the wave of pirates who had come to greet her as they returned to the ship had settled down, the throng parted to reveal a frightened auburn-haired youth. It seemed they had picked up another stray.

"Tomas!"

The young sailor sat on a barrel, pale with shock and lack of sleep. He no longer wore his uniform, but borrowed clothes. Smiling in relief upon her arrival, he began to stand. Sava hovered behind him, and when he rose, Sava pushed him back down by his shoulder.

"I was kind to her, I swear it," Tomas told him.

"He was," Liana agreed and looked down at him. "I'm so glad to see you alright."

"You as well, ma'am." He smiled, but still looked nervous. "I-I never expected I would end up here… on *your* ship."

"And where will you go?" she asked.

"It doesn't appear that I have anywhere else to go," he answered. "If it's all the same, I'd like to join your crew. I don't think I'd mind becoming a pirate."

Liana turned to Ameen, who simply said, "What say you, Captain?"

Saying her title breathed a new life into her. She even appeared taller, as she took a steeling breath. Looking about the crew, Ameen wasn't surprised to see that no one challenged the swift change in positions.

"Well, I doubt we'll do any plundering in the near future, but we'll probably be up to something nefarious in due time," Liana reasoned. Sava smiled and gave a bouncing nod and shrug in agreement.

"I don't think I can go back now," Tomas said. "After everything, they'll call me a traitor."

"There you have it," she said, reaching out to shake his hand.

Tomas stood, sagging in relief. "Thank you."

Ameen had Sava make sure that Tomas had some food to get him along. He heard Kahil grumble about having another mouth to feed. It was a fleeting half-joke of a complaint.

"Oh quiet, you," Liana shot a retort. "Or would you rather we let *you* go hungry to compensate?"

"No, Captain, I would not," he said behind a beaming smile.

A rumbling wave of laughter fell over the crew.

"That took about half as much time as we expected," said Sava, offering his arm to Liana. "Allow me to escort you to see your brother, Captain?"

After helping her sit on the opposite cot to Ivan, Sava left to give her privacy. She was sure it was actually a ploy to get her to rest. Even though she had only been awake for a few hours, she was admittedly exhausted. Nevertheless, the moment she was alone, she treaded over to her brother, peering down as she knelt by his side.

Ivan lay just where Sava once had, but he looked even worse. His skin paled into an ashy gray, contrasting his black stubble.

"Hey…" she said, near a whisper. "Idiot. Wake up."

He didn't, and Liana hoped he was in a deep, restful sleep and not fighting for his life. She chanced a look at his leg, but couldn't see much under the blanket, except for a peek of thick bandage wrappings.

The Romenel siblings sure could get themselves into a mess, she thought. It was a good thing there were so many willing to pull them out of it. But even with all the help that could be given, would both brother and sister survive this ordeal? If Marin was alive, he probably would have been standing here with her, puffing his pipe with consternation. Maybe he would have been scolding her for leaving the crew or wrapping her in one of his warm, tight embraces, telling her she was safe now.

Nellie appeared in the doorway.

"Liana! What do you think you're doing?"

"Good morning," she smiled guiltily.

"That's *all* you have to say?"

"Um… Is it morning, because I'm really not sure—" Liana managed to push herself into a standing position, but not for long. Before she could fall, Nellie rushed to catch her.

"What am I going to do with the two of you?" she groaned. Liana had to admit she felt much better once Nellie got her back into her cot. Like a mother to her child, Nellie pulled a scraggly, old blanket over her and tucked it into her sides.

"How is Ivan?"

"Thiago is sure he'll live," she told her. "But he's worried about his leg. He thinks that it'll need to be amputated."

"Divine."

Nellie pressed her lips together grimly.

"He won't like that."

"I don't want to be the one to tell him."

"Hell, neither do I!"

"We'll just... see what happens when he wakes up."

Liana was about to ask further but spotted something sticking out of the pocket of Nellie's apron. "What's that?"

She pressed her lips together and revealed a bottle of rum.

"Did you get that from Lucky?" Liana smirked.

"No. Look closer."

She did; it was a blend Marin always preferred. Nellie was never a drinker, and Liana wondered if she had kept the bottle around the manor for him.

"A bit early, isn't it?" Liana croaked, laughing a bit.

"Given the night we had?"

"Too right. Can I have some?"

"Don't tell Thiago." Nellie took a gulp, grimaced, and coughed. Not a drinker, after all. She quickly gave it back. "You know what? Just have the bottle. It's yours."

"Thanks," Liana said, sitting up. But after one sip, she decided it was too early after all—and Marin liked to drink the hard stuff.

"I'm so happy we found you," Nellie went on.

"Are you?" she asked, lifting a brow. Nellie bit her lip, and Liana immediately regretted the dig.

"I didn't mean what I said. I was angry and so... devastated."

"So was I."

"You didn't deserve that."

"It's alright, Nellie," Liana said with a nod. "I'm sure I've said worse things to you when we were little."

"Like the time you said you hoped I got eaten by a sea monster?"

"I was seven." Liana rolled her eyes. "But, yes, like that."

"We've always been like real sisters," she said. "Always fighting… I know I'm closer to Ivan. We were already very similar, and I suppose I never tried to understand the way you saw the world. Maybe the Divine meant for Da to connect with you in a different way than me so he could guide you."

"I'm sorry, Nellie. I'm sorry I wasn't there for you when you needed me. I wish it hadn't taken…" Liana weakly made an airy gesture. "All of this for us to be together."

Nellie shook her head, her face crumpling with grief. "I'm the one who should be sorry. I should have let you in… when Da was—" She covered her face, unwilling to relive the terrible loss. "I can't believe he's g-gone."

"I know," Liana breathed. "I keep thinking he's going to come around the corner, or I'll smell the smoke from his pipe. It doesn't seem right to sail this ship without him aboard."

"He asked for you," Nellie confessed. "You should have been with him when he died. But I was so—so jealous. I had no reason to be. I shouldn't have been angry about the ring, either." She leaned forward and took out a silver chain from beneath her collar. "Mama's locket. Da gave it to me on the morning of my wedding."

"I remember that day," said Liana wistfully. "You made me wear the most terrible dress. So, you got the locket, and I got the ring, hmm?"

"We're the daughters of Marin and Leda Foley. They wanted to make sure we wouldn't forget it."

"It means a lot to hear you say that. Really," she said through her thickening throat.

"You know," Nellie said, wiping her cheek and delicately sniffing, "Ivan and I have been writing to each other ever since I got married. I kept him up on things after we had our falling out. I don't know if it helped or hurt..."

"I plan on making amends, once he pulls through this," promised Liana, peering over at her sleeping brother. "We'll be alright—the three of us. Don't you worry."

Chapter 35

A Push of the Wind
13th of Sulnath, 1724
Cynareth Ocean

Liana laid back on the berth, taking a moment to herself. The ship rocked and made the ceiling of the captain's cabin appear hazy and dreamlike. Shadows cast from the lanternlight played against the bulkhead, forming shapes. She blinked hard, but they remained. When one came together before her eyes in a humanoid figure, she thought she surely was going mad.

Ameen entered. His presence chased the shadow, or whatever it was, away. Like the rising sun against the dark, the closer Ameen got, the more the shadow thinned and lengthened, then altogether disappeared.

He peered down at her. "Are you alright? If I knew any better, I'd say you look seasick."

"I'm fine," she said, scrambling to her feet. "I'm fine."

"Are you sure?"

"It's Ivan I'm worried about."

He gave her a warm, reassuring smile. "Thiago insists the amputation went well. If he's half as strong as his sisters, then I'm sure he'll pull through."

"You're right."

"Are you ready?" he asked. "They're waiting."

"Send them in," she answered, smoothing the wrinkles out of her shirt. He handed her one of her old, weathered tricorns. The one she usually wore had been lost after her capture.

Ameen opened the door and beckoned. Nellie and Bess filed in.

"We've already spent too much time dithering about," Liana said to the three of them. "We need a heading."

"We could go back to the Islands," suggested Nellie. "Find our old home. Settle back there."

"I can't show my face in Madzetal ever again. Besides, we'd still legally be in Caerwyn. Even if we tried to go to one of the other islands on the other side of the Imperial Divide, we'd have to stop for supplies."

"You said Rhian was reasonable," she countered. "She was going to set you free. Perhaps she could grant you one last day in port to sort everything out."

"I doubt she'll feel the same now." Liana shook her head. "After what happened to her cousin."

Ameen lifted his chin, obviously not feeling a bit of guilt for killing Aliah Vitalis.

"We can't trust the Vitalises—not even Rhian anymore. Word will get to her soon about the battle. She'll think we betrayed her. Her uncle will make sure of that," she continued. "He's too powerful. You have no idea."

"If we went to Savarre," said Ameen, "We'd have to sail past the Capital, or abandon the *Windfall* and cross the entire span of Caerwyn."

Bess stood poised properly with her hands over her apron. "We need to get out of Caerwyn waters. The closest kingdom is Rodina."

"I won't do that to you, Bess," Liana said firmly. "I know what's waiting there for you, and I won't let you face it on my account."

"But—"

Liana raised her hand. "I won't hear any more about it."

"We can't go south, and we can't go too far north. It seems we only have one option, then," Ameen said grimly. "Stonehall."

"You're mad," Liana accused, narrowing her eyes at him.

"No, no, no... He has a point," Nellie said. "Ivan said Earl Bayard Whyte was willing to honor that marriage pact just ten years ago—"

"Oh, please don't bring that up," Liana sneered. She'd had no idea that Dillon Whyte had been the one Ivan wanted her to marry all those years ago. It was a damned good thing she'd refused it. If she hadn't pilfered Ivan's savings out of spite and bought the *Windfall,* who knew where she would be?

"It's not a terrible idea. They might be willing to help us..." Ameen trailed off, deep in thought.

"You're right. It's the best chance we have," she said reluctantly. "We can at least ask for sanctuary while we figure out what to do next."

The next few hours were spent in preparation for casting off northbound. Slipping back into her role as the captain was easier than Liana had thought. There was no flak from the men about it, either.

The *Windfall* rocked sleepily in the cove, waiting to be woken. Liana crossed the deck, neck craning up to assess the spire-like masts and the webs of ropes and pulleys above. Below, the water churned a murky blue-gray, holding as many mysteries within its depths as their future.

Lucia, Beatrix, and Sebastian leaned over the bow, anxiously anticipating their departure. They were allowed on deck, so long as they stayed out from under the crew's feet. Nellie and Camila stayed with them while Bess was below, helping Thiago tend to Ivan.

Walking past the children, Liana spotted Sava showing Tomas the ropes—literally. It made her glad to see they were already getting along. She had a feeling that Squiddy and Trout would work well together.

The masts groaned, yawning awake as though from a deep slumber, as wind filled the sails. She had half a mind to join the children at the bow to taste the salty sea spray on her lips or climb up to the crow's nest to soar with the birds. After all, this was her ship. She could do whatever she pleased.

Liana was home, and everyone was there with her. Well, almost.

She swallowed back her grief, thick as tar in her throat. Marin had taken a piece of the Windfall's spirit with him to the other side. Nothing would be the same without him. Though she had told Nellie that she had forgiven her, Liana's heart ached as she was reminded that she never got to say goodbye to the man who had saved her, who had raised her to be everything she was now.

But Marin wasn't the only one missing. Liana looked up at the helm, still half-expecting to see Rhian there, studiously observing, with the wind caught in her golden hair. Instead Ameen was there alone, steering them out to the open sea.

"At your word, Captain." Lucky had sidled up to her without her noticing. He gave her a sideways smile. She returned it, drawing her shoulders up.

"Make her fly, Lucky."

He whistled. Moments later, the Windfall picked up speed as she sailed out of the cove. With skilled feet, Liana traveled across the slippery deck toward the helm. Just as she began to ascend to the upper deck, shouts and gasps of wonder rose from the bow.

An echelon of birds soared past them. As twilight advanced, they silhouetted black against the orange sky. They danced above the sea, diving down in a swirling formation to catch surface-dwelling water bugs. Liana leaned over the side to see. "What are those, I wonder?"

"Cliff swallows, come for spring, most likely," Lucky answered. "A fine sign for sailing!"

"So early?" she said with a degree of surprise. Lucky merely shrugged and went off about his duties.

Liana supposed nature ran on its own time, predictable as the change in seasons and yet at the same time completely incalculable. One could not foresee when a shift in the wind would come or when a wave would crest and fall. But the birds knew. The trees knew. The sea knew.

With that thought, she continued her way up the steps to take the helm from Ameen. He watched the echelon as well, hands gripped firmly the wheel. His amber eyes filled with the same childlike awe she heard at the bow.

"Captain," he acknowledged when he saw her. He stepped aside without another word so she could take the helm herself. The position gave her a brilliant view of the ship, sea, and sky. He stepped away, leaving her alone at the heart of the ship.

Standing there, Liana couldn't help but remember the night that Rhian had come to her, to bring her coffee and to ask questions. She hoped that as a queen, Rhian would grow. She hoped that Rhian would keep that thirst for knowledge of things that others are less willing to understand. As a mother, that would be invaluable.

Liana hoped that she would see Rhian again, just once. She wanted to tell her that she had tried her hardest to keep her word. She wanted to beg her forgiveness for breaking it, but she'd had no other choice. The death of Aliah Vitalis would be blamed on Liana. She was wise enough to know that. But she prayed that Rhian would also be wise enough to see that it wasn't Liana's fault. In the moments before sunset, Liana let her thoughts linger on the queen, who had slipped into her world and rescued her in her darkest moment. She thought of her quartermaster, who had come into her life and lifted her, fueled her dream of commanding the boldest crew in the sea. She thought of that crew, so hearty, brave and boisterous, running as reliably as gears in a clock on the deck below. Inevitably, she would fall. But time and time again, the ones she loved would catch her and carry her upon their steady wings. Like the swallows, she would never fly alone.

Epilogue

Mother
20th of Lengnath, 1724
Castle Iangard

Sleep was as elusive to Lady Tecwyn as spring's warmth in this stone castle. Even with the fire going, nothing could make Iangard as warm as she liked. It wasn't only the temperature that kept her awake, but her husband's snoring. He wasn't as young as he used to be, and the long journey from the Capital had taken its toll on him. He had caught a chill and, as he slept, sounded like a whistle as he breathed through his nose. It stayed with him since his return after Mid-Winter.

Rolling her amber eyes, she resigned to wake fully, throwing the thick duvet off her body. She shoved her arms into her burgundy dressing gown. Before she headed to her favorite cozy chair in the sprawling bedchamber, she placed a gentle kiss on Mercer's cinnamon and silver brow.

The fire was dying. With a flick of her wrist, her palm shimmered, and the flames came back to life. With a mere stretch of her finger, she ignited the candle in the corner. It cast a light on the book she had been enjoying before she had gone to bed.

Mercer had joked the previous night she was getting too old to read such folly, that these heroic tales were meant to entertain children. That had earned him a nasty look, and he had meekly padded to her side, bidding her to come to bed with him. As hard as she worked, she found a good adventure story to be the best release. And she certainly deserved to enjoy her hobbies. There had been so much on her mind lately.

So lost in the story, she only looked up when dawn's light crept into the bedchamber. With a regretful sigh, she glanced at the tall clock in the corner. She would have to close the book soon, but only after the riveting scene whereupon the bloodied and battleworn hero gathers the damsel up and—

A loud whistle and nasally snuffle from the bed, barely muffled by drawn curtains, interrupted the paragraph she was on. With her own soft snort of laughter, she stood to wake her husband.

"You're late," Lady Tecwyn said crossly as Seamus scampered into the library. She snapped her book closed. Luckily, knowing her stepson's lack of punctuality, she had brought it with her.

Moira, his sister, trailed several steps behind him. She loved to watch them work, and Lady Tecwyn allowed it, provided she wasn't a distraction.

"It was her fault." Seamus narrowed his striking green eyes at Moira, who crossed her arms.

Her red curls bounced as she leaned back on her heel. She held a couple pieces of parchment in her delicate hands. "I was only wanting to show him this."

Lady Tecwyn took the paper and examined the topmost page, a wanted criminal notice. Looking menacingly back up at her was the inked depiction of a black-haired Caerwyn woman, her mouth curled in a grimace.

By Royal Proclamation,
Ilyana Romenel
Otherwise known to the Public as
Liana Foley
Wanted by Her Royal Majesty Queen Rhian Ceres Vitalis for—
Indecency, Assault, Inciting the Public, Theft of Property, Piracy, Murder, Insurgency, Violation of Exile, and Horrid Regicide.

"So, this is Ilyana Romenel?" She gave an impressed nod. "What do they mean by indecency, I wonder?"

"Everything else that won't fit on one parchment," said Seamus dryly. He was not quite as enchanted as his sister with the swirling rumors of the swashbuckling exiled princess.

"They say she dresses and fights like a man," said Moira, with glimmering wonder in her eyes. "But when we saw her at the ball, she was in the most beautiful gown. She was absolutely gorgeous."

"Moira, dear, I think you're in love," Lady Tecwyn grinned. Seamus snorted.

Moira flushed bright red but laughed. "Oh, no, here is who *I* fancy!" She slipped off the top parchment, revealing a second notice. "Isn't he handsome?"

"Divine, Moira, he's a pirate. Could your taste be any worse?"

"Oh, be quiet—let's not speak of *your* taste!"

It was Seamus' turn to blush now. He opened his mouth to retort, but Lady Tecwyn interrupted him with a raised hand. She tore her eyes from the paper and looked to her stepchildren.

"We'll continue our lessons tomorrow," she said, doing her best to keep her voice even.

Seamus whined childishly in disappointment, despite his near twenty years of age. "But why?"

She took a breath and looked at him squarely. "Other than your tardiness, something has come to my attention that I must attend to. I'm sure your tutor is due to begin your lessons in Rodinian soon."

"Even though I'm already fluent..." Seamus grumbled, but looked stricken when she locked eyes with him. "I'll be on time tomorrow, I promise."

"Nahveena, my love, please take a breath. Are you absolutely sure it's him?"

She released a powerful rush of air from between her lips and slowly brought down her arms, palms down. It had been a long time since it happened, but when she was young, she would use this technique to calm herself before her magic would accidentally unleash.

"Yes, of course, I'm sure," she said. "Can't you see it?"

Mercer glanced back down at the notice. "I do." He cleared his throat of phlegm, nodding his head, then looked back to her. He still didn't look well, despite having insisted he was recovering. "He has your eyes. The shape, at least. This artist was quite good."

"And his name, Mercer—" her voice cracked, and she clenched her fists at her breast. "That is my son's name."

"Ameen Almasi," he read aloud. "Known associate of the Romenels. Wanted for theft of property, assault, piracy, insurgency, and murder."

"How did this—His father swore to keep him safe, to keep him on a good path," she stuttered. "And now he's fallen in with pirates?"

"Not just any pirates at that," Mercer handed her back the notice and crossed the study. It was hers, decorated and stocked to her liking. The walls were lined with rare and ancient tomes, jars of useful herbs, even a shelf of bones in various shapes and lengths, including a set of lizard skulls, each progressively larger than the last. "But the children of King Sergus."

She touched the corner of the parchment to her chin, frowning as she watched him meander over to the orrery—a brass model contraption with gemstone spheres that replicated the sun, Earth, and moon's trajectory. He tended to fiddle when he was nervous and couldn't help but press his finger upon the opal that represented the Earth.

"Mercer, please," she snapped.

He instantly straightened, the sudden movement pushing the Earth as well as the moon. They began their orbit, the milky moonstone making small circles about the blue-green opal. The opal made a slower, longer turn around the amber sun at the center. The true sun filtered through the window, making the orrery glimmer as it ran its course.

"Sorry," he said sheepishly. She continued on as though nothing had happened, despite the ticking of the turning orrery.

"I need to find him."

"After all this time? Nahveena, you haven't had any contact with him in... how long?"

"Not since he was a boy," she said, taking in the image, gently touching the inked impression with her fingertip. Yes, he had her slanted, pensive eyes, but otherwise, he looked just like his father. "Twenty-five years."

She looked up at her husband. He stood, lost in his own memory.

"Mercer?"

The column of his throat flexed as he swallowed. "If he's with the Romenel children—now that they have come out of hiding—then I'm sure he'll come to us sooner than we might think."

Here's a sneak peek at the sequel to *Windfall*

Between Wind and Water

The Dangers of Good Wine

A clock tower made of harled stone greeted them, along with the echo of music and excited voices. Across the tower stood the minarets of the largest Temple of the Divine in the city. Ameen's heart lifted at the sound of the drumbeats. A rainbow of colorful costumes rushed around them. Joyful festival goers paraded through the square. Feathers and sparkling sequins were everywhere. He found it marvelous, given how gray the city usually was, with the sky, sea, buildings and streets all melding together into one uniform color.

"And what exactly is your real name, Lucky?" Nora asked.

Ameen laughed, adjusting the blue mask on his face. "Please tell her."

"When he says it, it sounds like he has something caught in his throat," added Sava.

Lucky shot them both what Ameen assumed was a deadly look from beneath his mask, before turning his attention back to Nora. "Ulliam Laughlin."

"Bold of you to laugh at a name," Ameen said, out the side of his mouth. "Squiddy."

At Ameen's side, Liana barked a laugh as Sava gave him a lighthearted shove. The exchange ended with Sava conceding and crossing his arms over his chest with a huff.

Tomas shrugged sympathetically. "I still say Trout is worse. Squiddy is…endearing."

"But why 'Lucky'?" Nora continued her inquiries, as Sava turned his blushing face away.

"Well, I was a bit reckless as a boy," he said with a grin. "My mam would always tell me, 'You're lucky you did not drown!' or 'You're lucky you did not break a bone!' My young brother started to think that my name was Lucky, she said it so often! So, it stuck with me."

Bess, Nellie, Ivan and the children had gone ahead to meet up with the Venegas family, while the rest of them dressed for the occasion. Liana stood on her toes to search them out. He peered down at her and noticed the shimmering white scars on her skin, peeking out from beneath the collar of her red dress. Without drawing too much attention, he helpfully slid the cloth over and adjusted it for her. Blinking, she realized what he'd done. For a tense moment, he thought that he had crossed the line. Relief washed over him as she smiled, gratefully.

"It's a bit big," she said, gesturing to herself and the dress she'd borrowed from Nellie.

"I like that color on you," he said. He knew that Liana preferred to wear muted tones, especially greens and browns. She'd told him once that she didn't like to wear red, because it made her feel like a walking target. Even so, she smiled sheepishly at the compliment and pushed her mask up. It was made of red and white feathers, with a black tipped nose.

Before she could open her mouth to reply, a masked attendant swept between them, wordlessly offering the last two cups on his tray. They were everywhere, spreading wine from Vineyard Grove about the Festival. They conceded and before they knew it, the attendant vanished, likely to refill his stock.

"Cheers!" Liana said, raising her glass. What little sun there was glinted off the pearls on her ring. She still wore it on her right hand, after they had broken off their engagement. It was a family heirloom, after all.

Their glasses touched and they drank. He watched her over the rim, pleased to see her momentarily forget their troubles.

That moment was interrupted. With a mischievous look beneath his multicolored beaded mask, with a texture that resembled scales, Sava swiftly took Liana by the hand. Paper fin-like appendages flapping as he moved, he started to drag her deeper into the square, where the musicians played.

"Oh, Squiddy—No!" She dug her heels into the cobblestone, as Sava relieved her of her glass and shoved it into Ameen's hand.

"Come on, now. Don't be shy!" called Lucky, coming to help Sava along.

"I hate all of you!" Liana said, specifically eyeing Ameen, who had his hands full with their cups. He shrugged helplessly as she was pulled away to the dancers.

Looking on, Ameen spotted Bess and Ivan sitting together on the lip of the fountain. Beatrix, Sebastian and Lucia, Thaigo's granddaughter, gorged on festival food, while Thiago and his daughter, Camila, danced. They cheered as Liana reluctantly joined. It couldn't have been all that bad. She threw her head back, with laughter on her lips, as Sava turned her in a circle.

"She looks happy," said a feminine voice in Savarran behind him.

Ameen turned. Jacintha, the waitress from The Meetinghouse, had come in costume as well. Her mask of black feathers came down to a point above her mouth.

"How did you know I spoke Savarran?"

"I could just tell. The rhythm of your words. It's your first language, isn't it?"

"Second, actually. I spoke Islander and Savarran growing up."

"And Caerwyn is your third?"

"I also learned Rodinian from a friend," he added, gesturing over to Bess, who sipped wine by the fountain.

"That is impressive," Jacintha said. "You know every spoken language in Vioria. Does it simply come easy to you, or is there a purpose for your studies?"

It was more of the former, but he felt that answer to be too pretentious. "I thought it would be useful. I can speak with anyone, no matter what part of the world they're from."

She shook her head in wonder, then became distracted.

"Oh, look over there! You can see the Earl's balcony from here," she observed, pointing to the northernmost part of the square. He could make out a small group of people overlooking the Festival from the Temple of the Divine. "Let's take a closer look, shall we?"

Quickly, she took the empty wine glasses from his hands and set them on a passing attendant's tray. Before Ameen could say a word, she began to weave through the crowd. He followed behind, not wanting to be rude.

"Ah, yes. You can see the Earl and his wife from here."

The balcony wasn't terribly high, perhaps only a story or two. Even nobility had come costumed, though in much a much finer fashion than the average citizen. Earl Whyte was younger than Ameen had expected. He had the same honey-colored hair as his little brother, but a stockier frame. Something about him reminded him of Ivan—youthful and carefree in demeanor, but with the terrible burden of inheritance upon his shoulders.

Since coming to Stonehall, Ameen had been made aware that Lady Whyte hailed from Savarre. Still, he was surprised to see her in traditional Savarran dress, a flowing white gown with embroidered flowers and a mask to match. She stood taller than her husband and had an elegantly graceful posture. An infant slept in her arms, nearly unseen as it was wrapped in a linen blanket. On either side of her were two dark-haired children, an elder boy and a younger girl.

"Who is the woman next to Earl Whyte?" Ameen had to ask. Her hands spread out over the balcony's stone railing, looking over the crowd. She wore a gown of deep blues and greens and a mask with a fan of peacock feathers along the side.

"That's Lady Tecwyn. Haven't you heard about her?"

He had a vague memory of Liana speaking the name 'Tecwyn.' That's right—she'd seen Earl Tecwyn and his children at Rhian's ball. But she hadn't mentioned anything about his wife, at all. "No."

"A very mysterious woman, to be sure," she said, with something like admiration. "She's Earl Tecwyn's second wife. An integral part of the revolution in the Savarran islands, so no Caerwyn nobility trust her. Is that not where you're from? The Savarran side of the old Imperial Divide?"

He nodded. "It is, actually."

"She has made great friends with Lady Whyte. And the people of Iangard adore her."

"How do you know all of this?" he asked.

Jacintha winked at him. "I work in a tavern. I know things. Now, enough gossip! Shall we have a dance?"

"I—ah, Nellie?"

Jacintha followed his line-of-sight to the woman in gold rushing towards them. Panicked behind her mask, Nellie looked at Ameen with tears in her eyes.

"What's the matter?"

She bounded up to him, grasped his arms and hissed, lowly. "I saw him."

"What? Saw who?"

"Rhys! He's here!"

Ameen instantly went from shocked, panicked to confused. He addressed Jacintha first. "I'm sorry—just a moment." He angled Nellie to the side and spoke to her closely and quietly. "Nellie, Rhys Dunmore is dead."

"But—"

"We were both there when you shot him. He's dead."

"You have to believe me. He was carrying a tray, wearing a mask... He looked right at me!"

"You can't be sure if he was wearing a mask," he said, evenly.

"I know my husband," she told him. "I know his look and—and that smile. Ameen, something's going to happen. I know—I know that look. Please, we have to get everyone together. We could all go back to Fisher's Wynd."

Glancing to Jacintha, he gave her an apologetic look. "I'm sorry. I have to take her home."

"Is there anything I can do?" she asked, stricken. He was sure that they'd spoken low enough so she hadn't heard them, but the way she looked at him, it was clear she'd caught onto Nellie's panic.

"We'll manage."

Nellie gave Jacintha a tight smile, her arms crossed over her willowy from. "We should find Liana. I saw her..." Then, in a flash, Nellie took off, cutting through the dance floor.

He went after her, bumping into the dancers as they moved into his path. The musicians still played, and he couldn't see what was happening ahead. But he heard Nellie's alarmed shouting.

"Liana! Liana!"

Ice formed in his belly and the colors of costumes blurred around him. The world tilted on its side. His heart beat rapidly, threatening to burst through his ribs. He shoved harder, no longer caring about stepping on anyone.

Liana had fallen. She leaned against Nellie, clutching her stomach, sweating enough that her hairline was slick. With her teeth clenched and bared, she looked up at Ameen, desperately. He dropped his knees at her side.

"What happened?" he demanded to know.

"Sh-she just... fainted and..." Sava began. He held Liana's fallen mask in his hands.

Nellie asked, "Did she drink anything?"

"Damnit!" answered Ameen before Sava spoke. Unwilling to leave Liana's side, he searched the crowd with his eyes. Nothing stuck out in the sea of faces, closing in on them. Whispers floated around them. They knew who she was.

A whimper of pain brought him back down to Liana. Her eyes raised to the sky, wide and glassy. She convulsed. Her lips, usually a warm rosy pink, fell pale. A tinge of purple spread from the corners of her mouth.

He had to do something. He'd saved her once and he could do it again.

"Ameen!" Bess helped Ivan push through the crowd, as he batted away a couple of onlookers with his cane.

"Get out of the way! That's my sister!"

"Soldiers are coming. The three of you need to leave—now!" she said, loud enough to be heard over the panic.

"Let them come," said Ivan. "Get out of here, I'll stay with her."

"And I'm not leaving either of you." Ameen lifted Liana from Nellie's arms. If he was going to try something, now was the time. With only a fleeting thought to the people surrounding them, he cupped Liana's face and placed all of his concentration into the palm of his hand. He felt a subtle sense of draining, as her cheek masked the glowing of his hand. But whatever was happening to her sapped his meager effort.

Above him, Ivan shooed Lucky, Bess and Nellie away, ordering them home. If it wouldn't have sacrificed his balance, he might have started to beat back the crowd. But he didn't have to. Blue-coated men filed their way through. They created a circle, pressing them back to make room for the Earl. Using his cane, Ivan drew up to face him.

"Kristoff Whyte."

"Prince Ivan. It's been a long time."

Months of the Year in Vioria

Cambath - Month of the Peak
Sulnath- Month of Mud
Lengnath - Month of Longer Days
Eastnath - Month of Revival
Oestnath - Month of Birth
Brydlfest - Month to Wed
Candelath - Month of the Sun
Cynefest - Month of Kings
Ripnath - Month of Harvest
Baelfest - Month of Remembrance
Regnsfall - Month of Rain
Deornath - Month of Darkness

About the Author

Shawna Barnett was born and raised in San Diego, California. is an author, mother and Californian living in Nashville, Tennessee. After graduating with a degree in Politics and Literature, she worked in victim advocacy with survivors of domestic and sexual violence. Later, she worked in the behavioral health and healthcare field. Her experiences and strong beliefs that everyone deserves to be safe and respected seep into her swashbuckling tales. When not writing books and working full time, she spends time with her daughter. Her first novel is WINDFALL.

You can find Seabird, the prequel to Windfall, on Kindle and Nook.

CPSIA information can be obtained
at www.ICGtesting.com
Printed in the USA
LVHW011456221021
701206LV00007B/595

9 781735 323930